P9-BBV-933

DATE DUE

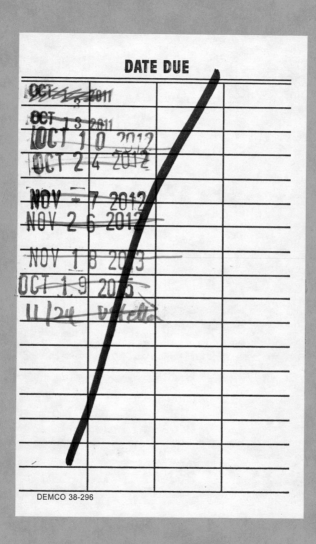

OCT ~~13 2011~~		
OCT 13 2011		
OCT 1 0 2012		
OCT 2 4 2012		
NOV 7 2012		
NOV 2 6 2012		
NOV 1 8 2013		
OCT 1 9 2015		
11/24		

DEMCO 38-296

JANE

JANE

April Lindner

poppy

LITTLE, BROWN AND COMPANY
New York   Boston

Poppy

Hachette Book Group
237 Park Avenue, New York, NY 10017
For more of your favorite books, visit our website at www.pickapoppy.com.

Poppy is an imprint of Little, Brown and Company.
The Poppy name and logo are trademarks of Hachette Book Group, Inc.

First Edition: October 2010

Library of Congress Cataloging-in-Publication Data
Lindner, April.
    Jane / by April Lindner. — 1st ed.
        p. cm.
    "Poppy."
    Summary: In this contemporary retelling of "Jane Eyre," an orphaned nanny becomes entranced with her magnetic and brooding employer, a rock star with a torturous secret from his past.
    ISBN 978-0-316-08420-8
    [1. Love — Fiction.   2. Nannies — Fiction.   3. Secrets — Fiction.   4. Orphans — Fiction.]   I. Brontë, Charlotte, 1816–1855. Jane Eyre.   II. Title.
    PZ7.L6591Jan 2010
    [Fic] — dc22   2010006365

10   9   8   7   6   5   4   3   2   1

RRD-C

Printed in the United States of America

To my sister, Melody Lindner,
whose friendship and support I count on more than I can say,
and whose presence in my life makes the good days
better and the bad ones bearable.

And to my mother, Grace Lindner,
who shared with me her love of language
and books, especially *Jane Eyre*:

"The words she taught me are the shapes I see:
because she spoke the sun, it came to be."
— Rhina P. Espaillat

Also, in loving memory of my father, Edward Lindner:

"I see my daddy walking through them factory gates in the rain."
— Bruce Springsteen

JANE

CHAPTER 1

The chairs in the lobby of Discriminating Nannies, Inc., were less comfortable than they looked. I sat stiffly in the one nearest the exit, where, feeling like an impostor in my gray herringbone suit from Goodwill, I could watch the competition come and go. I'd had some trouble walking up the steps from the subway in my low pumps and narrow skirt. The new shoes chafed my heels, and I had to keep reminding myself to take small steps so as not to rip the skirt's satin lining. I dressed carefully that morning, pulling my hair away from my face with a large silver barrette, determined to look the part of a nanny — or how I imagined a nanny should look — tidy, responsible, wise.

But I had gotten it wrong. The other applicants seemed to be college girls like me. One had situated herself in the middle of the taupe sofa and was calmly reading *InStyle* magazine; she wore faded jeans and a cardigan, her red hair tousled. Another, in a full skirt and flat shoes I coveted, listened to her iPod, swaying almost imperceptibly in time to the music. But maybe they weren't feeling as desperate as I was, acid churning in my stomach, pulse fluttering in my throat.

In my lap rested a leather portfolio containing my woefully brief résumé, my nanny-training certificate, a copy of my transcript, and nothing else. The portfolio had been a Christmas gift from my parents just a few short months ago. It was one of the last gifts they had given me before the accident. But as I waited, I couldn't let myself dwell on how my mother had handed me the box wrapped in gold paper and, her eyes not meeting mine, how she had apologized for not knowing what sort of present I would like. I felt a pang of remorse; her tone implied the failing was mine. I'd heard it before: I was too reserved, too opaque; my interests weren't normal for a girl my age. Still, my mother had let me give her a thank-you kiss on the cheek. She appeared relieved when I told her the portfolio was just what I would need when I finished school and went out into the world looking for a job. Of course, neither of us realized then how soon that need would arise.

"Jane Moore?"

I looked up. A thin woman with an asymmetrical black bob stood in the doorway. I jumped to my feet. *Too eager*, I chided myself. *Try not to look so desperate.* The woman quickly sized me up. I could see it in her sharp eyes and closed-mouth smile: I was dressed like a parody of a nanny, too fussily, all wrong. She introduced herself as Julie Draper, shook my hand, turned briskly, and strode through the door and down a long hallway. I hurried after her.

2

The narrow office held too many chairs to choose from; was this a test? I took the one closest to her desk, careful to cross my legs at the ankles and not to slouch. I handed my certificate and my résumé — proofread ten times and letter perfect — across her enormous mahogany desk. Through purple-rimmed reading glasses, she scanned it in silence. Just when I thought I had better say something, anything, she looked up.

"You would be a more attractive candidate if you had a degree. Why are you dropping out?"

"Financial need." Though I had expected this question and rehearsed my reply, my voice caught in my throat. On the subway ride downtown, I had considered telling the whole story — how my parents had died four months ago, black ice, my father's Saab flipping over a guardrail. How they hadn't had much in the way of life insurance, and the stocks they left me in their will had turned out to be almost worthless. How the house had been left to my brother, and how the minute he sold it he disappeared, leaving no forwarding address, no phone number. How the spring semester that was coming to a close would have to be my last. How I'd been too depressed to plan for my future until it dawned on me that the dorms were about to close and I'd be homeless in less than a week. How the only place I had left to go would be my sister's condo in Manhattan, and how very displeased she would be to see me on her doorstep — almost as displeased as I would be to find myself there. But I couldn't trust my voice not to quaver, so I stayed silent.

Julie Draper looked at me awhile, as if waiting for more. Then she glanced back down at her desk. "Your grades are strong," she said.

I nodded. "If you need more information, faculty reports for each of my classes are stapled to the back of my résumé." My voice sounded clipped and efficient and false.

She rifled through the pages. "I see most of your classes were in art and French literature." I waited for her to point out how hugely impractical my choices had been, but she surprised me. "That kind of training could be very attractive in a nanny. Many of our clients want caregivers who can offer cultural enrichment to their charges. A knowledge of French could be very appealing." A pause. "And you've taken a couple of courses in child development. That's a plus."

"I've been babysitting since I was twelve. And I took care of one-year-old twins last summer." Too bad I'd had to spend all my savings on textbooks and art supplies for the spring semester. "My references will tell you how reliable I am and how much their children like me. I'm strict but kind." I paused to inhale; apparently I'd been forgetting to breathe.

Something changed in her voice. "Tell me: how do you feel about music?"

"I took violin lessons in middle school," I answered. "I don't really remember how to play."

She waved one hand as if I'd written my answer on a blackboard and she was wiping it away. "Popular music. How do you feel about it?"

The question struck me as odd. "Well," I said, stalling a moment. "I don't mind it, but I don't listen to it much." Would this be a strike against me? "I tend to like classical music. Baroque. Romantic. But not the modern atonal kind."

"And celebrities?" She leaned in over the desk. "Do you read gossip magazines? *People? Us, Star,* the *National Enquirer?* Do you watch *Entertainment Tonight?*"

The hoped-for answer to this question began to dawn on me. Fortunately, it was the truth. "I don't care much about celebrities."

"How do you react when you see them on the street?"

"I don't know," I said. I might as well be honest. "I've never seen one on the street." I sat up a little straighter. "I believe I would leave them alone."

She pursed her lips and narrowed her eyes. A moment passed. Then she smiled for the first time, a wide smile that revealed slightly overlapping bottom teeth. "You just might be perfect."

The morning after the interview, my cell phone rang. I was walking back to the dorm from the bookstore where I'd turned in my textbooks for a not-very-satisfactory amount of cash. I paused on the pathway and let the other students flow around me. On the line was Julie Draper, sounding slightly breathless, much younger, and less formidable than she had in person. "Jane, I'm so glad to catch you. I have great news, a position to offer you."

My heart thumped so loudly I worried she might be able to hear it through the phone. "That's wonderful," was all I dared say.

"More wonderful than you know," she told me. "This is a plum position. By all rights it should go to a more experienced child-care provider, but until you came along, I hadn't been able to find a candidate I could trust to have the right"—her voice trailed off—"the right attitude."

I cast around for my job-interview voice, the one that had apparently served me so well yesterday. Though she couldn't see me, I threw back my shoulders and raised my chin. "I look forward to hearing more. Where will I be working?"

Julie Draper laughed in a surprisingly musical tone. "This will sound bizarre, but I can't give you any more details over the phone. How soon can you be at my office?"

When I arrived at Discriminating Nannies, the first thing Julie Draper did was offer me coffee in a slightly chipped mug. Then she swore me to secrecy.

"You can't tell anyone the details of this position," she warned. "Not your friends, not your family."

"I promise." It would be an easy vow to keep. Who would I tell? My best friend from Sarah Lawrence had transferred to a school in her home state, Iowa; on top of classes, she'd been working extra shifts to save up for a semester abroad in Italy, and we hadn't spoken in months. And after the accident I hadn't had the heart for socializing. I knew I would drag down any party I went to, so I spent most of my time in the studio, priming canvas after canvas, trying to settle on something to paint. Every idea I came up with — the stand of trees outside the wide window, an abandoned bird's nest I'd found on a walk, my own pale face in the mirror — made me tired, my arms too heavy to lift even a paintbrush. More nights than one, I'd slept on the sagging, paint-flecked studio couch, unable to face the five-minute walk back to the dorm. My parents had never quite understood me, and Mom had never made any secret of the fact that my conception had been a less-than-welcome surprise. You might think those things would make me slightly less miserable about losing my parents, but in some ways it made the loss even worse. Not only had they never shown me the kind of attention and appreciation they'd given my brother and sister, now it was official: they never would.

"Your future employer is, well, let's just say, he's of interest to the media." Was that a dimple in Julie Draper's cheek? "A celebrity. It's crucial that you not do anything to call attention to him. Anything that goes on in his house, no matter how big or small, must not be discussed with outsiders." The dimple disappeared. "There will be a confidentiality agreement to sign. You are free to run it by a lawyer."

A lawyer? A confidentiality agreement? It did me little good to wonder what exactly I was getting myself into; at this point, I was already in it up to my ankles. "That won't be necessary," I said, trying to sound calm. "I'm happy to sign."

"To be absolutely honest, you were chosen because I have an instinct about you," Julie told me. "You seem trustworthy."

I nodded as solemnly as I could. But then I couldn't help myself; I blurted out, "But what sort of person is my employer?"

"Jane," she said, dimple returning, "surely you've heard of Nico Rathburn?"

She didn't say "surely *even you* have heard of Nico Rathburn," but the "even you" was in her voice. And it was true, even I had heard of Nico Rathburn. I probably knew all the words to his hit song "Wrong Way Down a One-Way Street." It was one of those songs you heard everywhere you went — at the mall, in the grocery store, blaring from the radios in other people's cars. I could still recall Rathburn's cool dark stare in a poster tacked up on the wall above my brother's bed, his denim-clad form posed in front of a brick wall, a flame-red electric guitar brandished in his hands. Mark had gone to one of his concerts. I was little then, maybe in elementary school, certainly too young to stay home alone, so my mom dragged me along on the ride into the city, Mark and his best friend chortling in the backseat, playing with the Bic lighters they would ignite to demand an encore. I remember being afraid they would set the upholstery on fire. And I'd been brought along on the ride to pick them up from the Spectrum too. I remember the strange and pungent smell that clung to the oversized black concert T-shirts they wore over their usual clothes, and the lights of the city, a thrilling expanse of electricity and skyscrapers glimpsed from the highway overpass that hastened us back to the suburbs.

But even if Mark hadn't been a fan, I would have heard of Nico Rathburn. For as long as I could remember, he'd been one of those celebrities whose name conjured up instant associations, most of them having more to do with his dramatic personal life than his music. I vaguely recalled something about his being busted for possession of cocaine, something else about a car crash and a string of high-profile girlfriends. Then there was the on-again, off-again marriage to a model whose name I couldn't remember. Hadn't they both been junkies? Suddenly chilled, I rubbed my arms for warmth. How badly did I need this job? I thought of my dwindling savings account, of the few belongings I hadn't carted to Goodwill that were crammed into a couple of suitcases on the floor of my dorm room.

"Sure, he's been out of the papers for a few years," Julie continued, "and you'd think he wasn't such a hot commodity anymore. But the tabloids are like sharks, always circling, hungry for blood. He needs his employees to be absolutely discreet."

8

"Um," I stammered. "He has children?"

"A girl, five years old, named Madeline. It was in the news, but you don't remember, I suppose." Julie's voice turned impatient, despite the fact that she hired me precisely because I wouldn't care about such things, much less remember them. "Madeline's mother was a pop star in France; she cut a solo album on a U.S. record label a few years back. That was the high point of her career. Maybe you've heard of her? Celine?"

The name was familiar. "What happened to her? The mother, I mean. Does she have shared custody?"

"The details shouldn't concern you." Julie was back to the brusque, professional version of herself. "Not that they wouldn't be hard to find if you went looking for them. But I'd advise you not to buy into every overblown story you read in the tabloids. That business with his wife, with Celine, the drug use.... He's been sober for a while now. That's all you really need to know."

"Oh," I said. "I'm glad to hear it." My voice didn't have much conviction in it.

"Listen, Jane." She looked pointedly in my eyes. "Nico Rathburn is a devoted father. That bad-boy stuff is old news. Besides" — she paused for emphasis — "the pay is excellent. You'll be living in a mansion in Connecticut. And you'll get...you'll get *proximity* to one of the gods of rock-and-roll music. You do know how many nannies would kill for this position, right?" She rifled through a folder and drew out a document on legal-size paper. "You're a lucky, lucky girl."

CHAPTER 2

Despite Julie's advice, I spent my last evening on campus in the library computer lab, reading everything I could find about Nico Rathburn. It wasn't so much that I cared about the story of his love life, criminal record, and meteoric rise to stardom; if anything, the details made my stomach twist in knots. But I believe in being prepared.

The lab was air-conditioned to an Antarctic chill, and I thought longingly of the lone sweater still hanging in my closet. Classes were over, and apart from me the lab was empty. Every now and then I'd hear laughter and shouts as groups of students passed the window on their way to some celebration of the semester's end.

It didn't take me long to find an astonishing amount of information about my new employer, little of it reassuring. Rathburn's early press was mostly positive, fawningly so. The Rathburn Band had weathered middling success for a while, playing clubs up and down the East Coast until their third album bowled the critics over and became a breakaway hit. I could remember that album blaring from behind the locked door of Mark's room every afternoon for months. One song in particular, "Wrong Way Down a One-Way Street," played irritatingly in my brain as I read record reviews and Wikipedia articles, my eyes glazing over. Nicholas Rathburn's Wichita boyhood had been unremarkable. An indifferent student, he disappointed his parents by running off to Brooklyn and starting up a band instead of going to Kansas State. Rathburn and his bandmates had shot abruptly from obscurity to fame — a *Rolling Stone* cover, multiple platinum records, international tours.

At a fan site I discovered photos of Nico Rathburn at the peak of his celebrity, in leather pants and mirrored sunglasses, dragging a blonde, miniskirted model past the paparazzi. There were many variations on that theme; the sunglasses remained the same, but the blonde girlfriends were interchangeable. At his official website, I found tons of in-concert photos, Rathburn grimacing in concentration as he played guitar or throttling the mike as he sang, head thrown back. Then there were the stagey professional shots — his dark hair fluffed up, his smoke-gray eyes fixed on the camera as though he were looking past it to the person who would be viewing the photo years later.

In his twenties, he cultivated a quieter look, exchanging the skin-tight leather pants and muscle shirts for black denim and plaid flannel. Despite his new low-key persona, he dated debutantes and actresses, and owned a penthouse apartment in Lower

Manhattan, a villa on the Ligurian coast, and a mansion in the Hollywood hills. Many of the stories were about his wedding to Bibi Oliviera, a model who had just made her first appearance in *Vogue*. Unlike his other girlfriends, she was dark haired with sun-kissed skin, a big, engaging smile, and leaf-green eyes. They'd met in her native Brazil when she starred as the love interest in one of his music videos. On their first weekend together they'd gone out and gotten matching tattoos — a coiled green serpent with a heart clenched in its bared fangs on his left forearm, and its twin on her right one. A few days later, they flew to New York City and got married at city hall.

From the wedding onward, the news stories piled up, too many for me to read. I skimmed several. There were drug busts, minor car crashes, violent public fights and recriminations. In one strange episode, a male neighbor discovered Bibi shivering in her underwear, mascara dripping down her face, apparently disoriented, cowering on his front porch. "Nico locked me out," she had told the policeman called to the scene. "It wasn't really him — the devil was looking out at me from his eyes. I would have slit his throat if I'd had a knife." Blurry photos documented this story; I lingered over them awhile. But for the snake tattoo, this version of Bibi looked nothing like her earlier, glamorous self. Skinny as a famine victim, black hair matted, she slouched between a pair of cops, her wide green eyes broadcasting panic. Someone had thought to throw a blanket over her shoulders at least; just looking at her made me feel cold and anxious. Still, I forced myself to read on. Bibi's break-down had led to a stint in celebrity rehab. Released after a few months, she seemed to be on track to recovery. She'd gone back to work and was even featured on the cover of *Femme*, but there didn't seem to be much news about her after that.

A loud bang just outside the computer lab window startled me back into the present. It was only fireworks; more of them crackled and fizzed out on the lawn to laughter and cheering. Still, the noise had set my heart pounding, and a strong surge of foreboding seized me. In what kind of universe did people wander through their neighborhoods in lacy black panties, too stoned to care what other people thought of them, squandering their tremendous good fortune on cocaine and heroin? No universe I cared to live in. Still, I needed to understand what I was getting myself into. I took a few deep breaths, steadied my hands, and kept clicking.

Not long after Bibi's release, the couple had separated. Nico Rathburn's next album, a downbeat collection of songs about disillusionment and romantic dysfunction, was reviewed favorably — "Grown-up songs for sophisticated listeners," the *New York Times* had called it — but didn't get much airplay. Maybe the songs were too somber, or people were simply ready for the next big thing. He fired his band, telling the press he was ready to shift gears. I couldn't find many articles from the months right after that, but then Rathburn began dating a French pop star so famous in her native country that she was known simply as Celine. The sheer volume of magazine articles gushing about the happy couple made my eyes start to glaze over. Fortunately, there wasn't much more of the Nico Rathburn saga to get through. After their very public breakup, he sued her for custody of their daughter, Madeline. He won, bought an estate in Connecticut, and went into seclusion.

A recent *People* profile brought the story up to date. Rathburn had reunited the band to record another album — his "big comeback," the article called it. His story was a bit sad, really, or so it seemed to me. All that success hadn't kept him from having to woo the public all over again.

The computer lab closed at midnight. I made my way across campus, sticking to the well-lit paths, and slipped into the dorm and past the downstairs lounge, where I could hear laughter and music. I felt exhausted and sorry I had stayed up so late poring over celebrity gossip like an obsessed fan. I had to catch an early train in the morning. But after I brushed my teeth, pulled on my nightgown, and climbed into bed, my eyes refused to shut. I stared at the thin bands of street light playing around the edges of my window shade and tried to silence the voices in my head.

Of all the jobs I could have been chosen for, this one seemed a peculiarly bad fit. Unlike most people, I wasn't drawn to glamour and excitement; quite the opposite. I just wanted regular work and a steady paycheck. I'd seen what striving after fame and admiration could do to a person. My older sister, Jenna, had acted as a child. She was featured in a few local commercials and had some roles in community theater. After college she went off to New York City to pursue what she loftily referred to as *"my career,"* but after some disappointments — a lot of rejection and then a sizable role in a TV pilot that didn't get picked up — she had gotten engaged to an investment banker and moved into his condo in Tribeca. Jenna and I hadn't spoken since our parents' funeral, but at the lunch afterward, she kept leaving the restaurant to smoke, winced almost imperceptibly whenever her fiancé spoke, and mentioned — twice — that she was just biding her time until the right opportunity came along. Jenna would have jumped at the chance I was being given to live in a mansion among the rich and famous. She'd be making plans to seduce and marry one of the rock star's wealthy friends, if not the man himself. If she could see me now, panicking in the dark, she'd roll her eyes and call me anal-retentive and prissy.

The pay is good, I consoled myself. In fact, the amount Julie Draper had quoted me was much better than I'd hoped for. I'd be able to live very cheaply and save almost all of my earnings. If I could just last a year, I might even be able to go back to school, although probably not to Sarah Lawrence. Still, I would be able to earn my degree. My time in the alternate universe of coke-snorting rock stars and their strung-out wives and girlfriends would be brief.

In the meantime, I'd get by, doing exactly what I'd solemnly promised Julie Draper I would do before I signed a pile of legal documents relinquishing the right to sue her agency or Nico Rathburn if anything should go wrong: I would behave with absolute professionalism no matter what debauchery went on around me. I would stay as anonymous as possible, do my job, and blend in with the furniture. That should be easy. I'd never been the kind of person people notice.

The ride to Penn Station was packed with commuters; I got more than a few glares from men and women stuck behind me as I struggled to hoist my suitcases into the overhead rack. The outbound train to Connecticut was emptier; I chose a window seat so

16

I could get a good look at the countryside where I would be living. Unlike my classmates, many of whom had spent semesters abroad and backpacked across Europe in the summer, I had never traveled much. My sister's many auditions and occasional acting jobs had kept us close to our home just outside Philadelphia most summers, and my parents had never cared for traveling anyway. "We have everything we need right here," my father would say. "We're two hours from New York, two hours from Baltimore, two hours from the mountains, two hours from the shore. We're right in the middle of everything." We never went to any of those places, though.

Of course, there were school field trips to the zoo and to the natural history museum and out to Amish country. And my sister's auditions often brought us into Center City Philadelphia after school. My mother would drive us in her Volvo, her hands tightly gripping the steering wheel. Once at our destination she would herd us nervously through the parking lot, so quickly that I never got a chance to look around. In the elevator, Jenna would fret about the wrinkles in her dress from sitting so long in the car, while Mom would check Jenna's makeup and smooth down any flyaways in her curly auburn hair.

After Jenna and Mom were called into the office, I would read in the waiting room, losing myself in that day's book. Jenna's appointments usually took a few minutes or half an hour, but whenever she came out was too soon. Sometimes she would be snippy, dissatisfied with her dress or hair. "I'll never get jobs if I don't have the right clothes," she'd complain. Other times, she'd be happy. "I nailed it, Mom, didn't I? Don't you think they liked me?"

she'd say, and our mother would spend the whole ride home reassuring Jenna of her beauty, poise, and talent.

"Jenna got the looks and the personality," I once heard Mom whisper to Dad over a six o'clock cocktail; she must have thought I was in the back room watching cartoons instead of behind the couch, playing spy. "Nature doesn't play fair."

"Jane's good-looking enough," Dad had responded in a voice meant to be consoling. "She's shy, but she'll come out of her shell. She'll learn to compensate."

"You think so?" The ice clinked and sizzled in Mom's glass. "She's so intense and serious. Not a very appealing personality. You really think she'll grow out of it?"

I can't remember my father's reply or whether or not they caught me eavesdropping, but I do remember looking up *compensate* in the dictionary and being disappointed by the definition. I had hoped it would mean something like "blossom" or "grow up to surprise us with her poise and beauty." I remember wishing on first stars and stray eyelashes for my wispy brown hair to grow thick and shiny so that Mom might decide I was pretty after all.

While the train halted in the tunnel for a signal, I checked my reflection in the dark glass. In high school, I had taught myself to do my hair so that it was at least neat — straight, parted down the middle, held in place by a French braid. Like Jenna, I was thin; how often had my suitemates marveled at my ability to eat heartily without gaining weight? Unlike Jenna, I'd never grown much in the way of breasts. She got the long legs too and stood a whole head above me. My nose was straight, my teeth okay, my mouth decently shaped but a bit thin in the lips. I'd inherited my father's green eyes, not the long-lashed, ice-blue ones nature had given my mother and sister. In my white oxford blouse, I looked perfectly average, the opposite of flashy.

At the sight of my reflection in the train window, I felt a familiar deflation. I didn't expend a lot of effort on my looks; I liked to think I had better things to do with my time than shop for lip gloss and clothes. In fact, I didn't think about my appearance much, usually. Still, what girl doesn't want to be pretty? At the movies, I'd identify with the inevitably gorgeous heroine and walk out believing myself a member of her species — willowy, glossy haired, graceful. Then, hurrying home, I'd catch my reflection in a shopwindow and be brought abruptly back to reality.

The train chugged to a start, daylight mercifully erasing my image. The morning had turned out crisp and nearly cloudless, a good day for a fresh start. I tried to settle back in my seat, to relax and collect myself. *Calm, cool, capable,* I silently repeated to myself. *That's what I'm going to be. Calm, cool, capable.*

The ride passed too quickly. Before I felt remotely ready, the train was pulling into Old Saybrook station. I hurried to lug my bags out before the doors shut. As the agency had told me, a driver stood waiting, holding up a small cardboard sign with my name on it. Tall and leather-skinned with a full head of white hair, he nodded briskly when I walked up.

"I'm Jane Moore," I said unnecessarily, holding out my hand, but he had already bent to gather up my bags.

"Nice to meet you, Miss Moore." Had anyone ever called me that before?

"Oh, please, call me Jane." He gestured for me to walk ahead of him, though of course I had no idea where we were going.

At the curb stood a black Range Rover; he opened the back door and motioned me in. "I'm Benjamin."

Though I would have preferred to sit in front with him, I complied. He started up the car, and we made small talk about the landscape and the weather for a while. There were so many questions I wanted to ask: Was my new employer temperamental? Had he really sobered up? And what about Madeline, his daughter? Was she spoiled to death or overlooked by her career-driven father? Or both? Or neither? Was the house furnished in leopard skin? Would there be wild parties? But all of my inquiries would have sounded rude. Besides, I would have my answers soon enough. We rode most of the way in silence.

I suppose I shouldn't have been surprised when we reached a tall green-painted iron fence next to a guardhouse; the gate swung open as we drove slowly up, and a man in uniform leaned out, waving us in. The mansion loomed at the top of a hill, ornate and Tudor-style, with a massive turret and an imposing arch leading to the front entryway. Around it spread the widest, greenest lawn I had ever seen, and down the hill, a pair of swans bobbed on a small sparkling pond. Benjamin led me to the front door.

"I'll see to it your bags are put in your room," he said, and disappeared before I could thank him.

I inhaled as deeply as I could and rang the doorbell. A woman answered it — trim, high cheekboned, fortyish, in a simple royal blue dress. A pair of gold-rimmed glasses hung around her neck. "You must be Jane." She shook my hand. "Welcome to Thornfield cilycia pope

A GOOD BOOK IS THE PRECIOUS LIFE-BLOOD OF A MASTER SPIRIT, EMBALMED AND TREASURED UP ON PURPOSE TO A LIFE BEYOND LIFE

MILTON

Park. I'm Lucia Porth; I manage the estate. You must be tired." I detected a slight German accent.

"Not really." I stepped into the foyer and glanced around quickly — marble floors, cathedral ceilings, a wrought-iron chandelier like something out of *Masterpiece Theatre*. "But thank you. For your concern, I mean."

Lucia chuckled. "Of course. Let's get you set up in your room, and then I'll give you a tour. How does that sound?" I followed her past a living room that had an enormous fireplace and polished wood floors, then around a bend. The rooms we walked by were furnished in a surprisingly sedate style — leather sofas, heavy wooden tables, Oriental rugs, walls in varying shades of cream and tobacco — all very dark and masculine, with none of the funky zebra stripes and electric reds and purples I had been expecting. As we hurried along, I caught tantalizing glimpses of art — mostly abstract paintings in glowing jewel-like tones — hung almost offhandedly, over fireplaces and in hallway nooks.

"Was that a real Rothko?" I asked Lucia as we zoomed past a formal dining room, its long mahogany table accommodating a startling number of chairs.

She laughed. "Well, yes. Of course." She led me up a flight of ruby-red carpeted stairs.

The bedroom at which we finally stopped was large and empty but for a four-post bed, a writing desk, a dresser, and a deep velvet armchair. My suitcases stood against the wall; Benjamin must have taken a shortcut. "Not very homey," Lucia said, opening the shutters to reveal a view of the pool house below. "You can fix it up however you like." She showed me a bathroom that would be mine to use and invited me to freshen up and come downstairs to have lunch with her.

"How will I find you?"

"Press that button." She pointed to a panel on the wall above the desk. "It's an intercom. Don't worry; I haven't lost a nanny yet."

Though I'd kept to myself much of the time, I had gotten used to dorm life and sharing a suite and a bathroom with three other girls. In my tiny shoebox of a room, I had been surrounded by other people's stereos, slamming doors, quarrels, late-night conversations, boyfriends sneaked in after hours. At Thornfield Park, I'd be living at the end of a long hallway, with no companionable sounds to ease my loneliness. I unpacked a few days' worth of blouses and skirts and hung them up so they could uncrease. They looked paltry in the oversized, otherwise empty closet.

I splashed water on my face, brushed my teeth, and grimaced in the mirror. *Quit worrying*, I thought to myself. *You're living in a mansion. Really, how bad can it be?*

Lunch consisted of a salad and crusty French bread. We ate in a sun-drenched breakfast room just off the kitchen. Of the rooms I'd seen that morning, it was the cheeriest, with crisp white curtains and a view of a sparkling swimming pool; between it and the house spread a lush expanse of grass on which a gaggle of Canada geese was encamped. "You can really eat for such a skinny thing," Lucia told me. She'd barely finished half of the salad on her own plate. "Sorry. I didn't mean to get personal. I guess you're used to dorm food."

I nodded, my mind on all that I still didn't know about my new

life. "It's so quiet here. I don't know what I expected, but..."
I poured myself some more mineral water.

"For now, it's just you, me, Benjamin, the grounds crew, and the housekeepers," Lucia said. "Maddy has a playdate; she'll be back this evening. Usually there's a cook, but he's on vacation. And Nico has a personal assistant who travels with him."

"He's away?" Relief washed over me.

"Off promoting his new album." She cut a slice of bread and set it down on the edge of her plate. "Doing the *Tonight Show* and radio programs. I don't know yet when he'll be back. His manager keeps adding dates to his schedule."

It occurred to me that Lucia might answer my questions. "What's it like? Working for...Nico?" I tried the name out; it sounded presumptuous coming from me. "Mr. Rathburn, I mean. What's he like?"

Lucia smiled cryptically. "Not what you would expect."

Not used to getting his own way? Not self-centered? Not given to temper tantrums, orgies, trashing hotel rooms, driving sports cars into swimming pools? "I don't know what I expect." I fibbed.

"He's more serious than you would think. Normal, like anyone else. He puts his pants on one leg at a time, believe me." She smiled again. "But still, more serious than I expected when I first got here. He doesn't like to be interrupted when he's composing. He can be short-tempered. His work takes up a lot of his energy, especially lately. He doesn't have time for foolishness. Not these days. And he can't tolerate disloyalty. If one of his employees says so much as one word to the press..." Her voice trailed off. "I wouldn't want to get him angry like that."

A whole new Mr. Rathburn began to take form in my imagination — less hedonistic, more driven but no less formidable. "Is he angry often?" I asked.

Lucia speared a cherry tomato on the end of her fork, then appeared to inspect it closely. "I don't mean to make him sound like an ogre," she said. "He's just...what's the word? Exacting. He has certain expectations. But he's generous; he pays us well, and he's not unkind. I've had lots worse jobs, believe me." I was able to get her talking about her own past. She regaled me with stories of the many petty and capricious bosses she'd had, the indignities she'd suffered as a salesgirl, a waitress, and a hotel chambermaid. "So after all that, Nico isn't so hard to work for. Even with all the craziness that goes with the territory — fans somehow getting his number and calling in the middle of the night, the band tromping through here for rehearsals, all the hangers-on. You know what I mean."

Though of course I didn't know.

"It's rarely dull," she concluded.

I nodded. "And what about Maddy?" I asked. "What's she like?"

"Maddy?" Lucia clucked her tongue. "She's been through so much in her five years. That mother of hers." She made a sour face. "Dragging a baby, a toddler, to nightclubs and afterparties, like a toy poodle in a pocketbook. When we got her, the child was sleeping all day and staying up all night. Like a vampire!"

"How long has she lived here?"

"Going on a year. She's on a regular schedule now, thankfully. But that's not the worst of it. When Maddy got a little older and less easy to control, her mother would leave her alone night after night to fend for herself. Can you imagine that? A child that young left by herself?"

"That's terrible," I said. "Poor thing."

"When Nico brought her here, it was all we could do to get her to trust any of us. She wouldn't say a word for the longest time, wouldn't let any of us touch her, except Nico of course, but he's away so much."

"But now she feels more at home here?" I asked.

Lucia bent to adjust the dishwasher's controls. "Bridget — her last nanny — drew her out of her shell and helped her to learn English. Now she speaks it all the time. Can you imagine being four years old and coming to live with a father you barely know in a place where nobody speaks your language? It took months, but Bridget helped Maddy become, I don't know, more like a normal child. She's an affectionate, funny kid. She can talk your ear off."

"She must miss Bridget." Maddy would have to get used to me, a whole new person in her life. I suspected the transition wouldn't be easy.

"Maddy cried every night for a week," Lucia said. "She still asks about her. I've been minding her as best I can, but there's so much to take care of around here. I've only been able to watch Maddy with half an eye. I'm so glad you're here now."

I nodded. It sounded as though Maddy was in real need of consistency and love. It would be my job to give her those things. She would need to feel like the center of someone's world, even if that someone was hired help. I knew what it felt like to be on the periphery, to feel unsafe and uncertain. But then a question occurred to me. "Why did Bridget leave?"

Something changed in Lucia's voice. "Personal reasons." She wiped her hands on a dishcloth. "Now I'll show you the rest of the house."

CHAPTER 3

Lucia walked me through the house, pointing out objects of interest — a room with a Steinway and a row of guitars where Nico Rathburn did his songwriting; a workout room full of weight machines; a hallway decorated with about forty gold and platinum records; Madeline's room, done up in every imaginable shade of pink. When the tour ended, I still doubted I'd be able to find my way from one end of the building to the other. Though the decor looked expensive, the place was less flashy than I'd expected and full of cozy spots, including, to my surprise, a well-stocked library with shelves so high a ladder was needed to reach them. *What kind of books would a rock star read?* I wondered.

"Nico won't mind if you borrow his books, as long as you return them," Lucia said, as if reading my mind.

"Am I allowed to use any of these rooms?"

She turned to shut the library door behind us. "For the most part. Except for the third floor. It's completely off-limits to most of the staff." She led me back toward her office, a comfortable den with a desk and a sofa, where we sat down.

I nodded. "What's on the third floor?"

"I suppose…well, nothing. It's just there." A crease appeared between Lucia's brows. "It's dangerous. The floorboards are old and rotting. You could fall through." This struck me as strange. Why wouldn't a multimillionaire have his floorboards repaired? But something in Lucia's voice told me not to inquire further. I promised to avoid the third floor.

Lucia then proceeded to lay out my duties, hour by hour. I took notes, writing as quickly as I could for fear of missing a crucial detail. Maddy's days sounded like a blur of preschool, ballet lessons, and trips to the aquarium or zoo — a schedule that would be exhausting for any grown-up, and all the more so for a small child. I was reviewing my notes when the doorbell rang. I followed Lucia to the front door, and a little girl swept in, her T-shirt, jeans, backpack, and sneakers all in pink. "Come and meet someone," Lucia urged her, taking her by the hand. "Did you have fun at Cassandra's house?"

"We made play-dough out of flour and water and food coloring," the girl said. "See, my fingers are purple."

Lucia maneuvered Maddy in front of me, and I crouched down to be at eye level with her. "This is Miss Jane," Lucia said in a kindly voice. "She's going to live with us and help Daddy take care of you."

Maddy's blond pigtails stood high on her head; her T-shirt read, in letters made of glitter, PRINCESS. "Hello," she said, looking down at the carpet.

"Hello," I said back. "I'm happy to meet you. Those are the purplest fingers I've ever seen."

Maddy's shoulders rose to meet her ears. "Can I go to my room now?"

"You'll be having dinner soon," Lucia said. "Macaroni and cheese."

Maddy nodded absently, her gaze still fixed on the floor.

"You can go play now," Lucia told her. "Miss Jane will go with you. You can show her your figurine collection."

"I don't want to," Maddy said.

"Show her your stuffed animals, then. Or your fish."

Maddy ran off toward her room. I followed at a distance, down the hall and up the stairs, and knocked on the door she slammed shut behind her.

"It's Miss Jane," I said through the door. "You don't have to show me your things or even talk to me, but it would be nice if you let me in."

The door opened a crack. "I like Miss Bridget. I don't like you." But she stepped aside to let me in.

"You don't know me very well yet. Maybe you'll like me when you know me better." I sat down in a pink, child-sized armchair. "You don't need to talk to me if you don't want to."

I watched as she pulled a box of Disney figurines out from under her bed and began arranging them on the carpet. "You go here," she said to Pluto, putting him beside the Little Mermaid. She hummed softly as she sorted the figures out.

Ten minutes went by before she said another word to me. "Are you going to take me places?" She kept her eyes on her playthings. "To FAO Schwarz?"

"If you want me to," I answered. "We don't have to."

"Miss Bridget was going to take me to FAO Schwarz." Maddy looked up at me. Her eyes were deep-set and brown, fringed with long lashes. "She promised."

"I never make promises I can't keep."

She crawled nearer to me, a figurine in both hands. She held one up an inch from my nose. "This is Beauty from *Beauty and the Beast.*"

"I recognize her," I said. "Is she your favorite?"

"I like all the princesses." She crawled back to her collection. "My mom is prettier than you."

"That's okay," I said. It was true; I'd seen pictures. "Pretty isn't everything."

Maddy raised an eyebrow, a neat trick for a five-year-old. "Miss Bridget's prettier too," she told me. "I heard Miss Lucia talking on the phone. She said Miss Bridget was fired because she went up to the third floor, but I think she was scared. Of Miss Brenda."

"I don't know Miss Brenda."

"She lives on the third floor. I think she's scary too." She set Goofy down next to Eeyore. "Miss Brenda doesn't play with me ever."

"Maybe she's busy."

Maddy nodded. "I could paint your fingernails" — she held out a hand — "like mine, see?"

"Pink? I'd like that. But not before dinner."

Maddy warmed to me slowly over the course of our first few weeks together, as our days started to pick up a rhythm. Getting her up and dressed in the morning was always a struggle. "Why can't I stay home and watch TV?" she asked from the luxurious depths of her bed that first morning. "When I'm at school, I miss my toys. I have better toys here."

"You'll be back with your toys this afternoon. Now get up, and I'll let you pick out your clothes."

"I want to wear my pajamas all day."

"Well, maybe on a Saturday. Not on a Tuesday."

"Why can't I?" When I didn't reply, Maddy made a face. "My throat hurts. I think I have a fever."

I pressed my palm to her forehead. "You're as cool as a cucumber."

"Why do I have to go to school? If Daddy was here, he'd let me stay home. Daddy lets me do whatever I want."

"Daddy's not here, though. He left me in charge. And you need to go to school. Now get up." I clapped my hands smartly. "Quick, like a bunny." The bunny thing had worked on other kids I'd sat for, but Maddy was a tough customer, apparently used to getting her own way in just about everything; it took work to get her dressed, fed, and out the door that morning. But each day she got up and dressed a little faster.

31

I didn't much like dropping her off at the Waldorf School, either. It seemed to me the mothers and other nannies looked me up and down, curious about the newest addition to the household of the town's most famous resident. Their narrowed eyes told me they didn't find me half glamorous enough, and though the mothers would chat happily with each other, not a single one of them ever said as much as hello to me those first weeks. But I was relieved not to have to make small talk. Besides, once I'd said good-bye to Maddy, I was free for the morning. In Mr. Rathburn's red Mini Cooper — the least luxurious car in his fleet — I would drive to Long Island Sound. I would skip stones in the cold steel-gray water, and paint watercolor after watercolor, trying to capture the changing moods of water and light.

By the end of our second week, Maddy took to chattering for the whole car ride home, telling me about whatever she and her friend Cassandra had done together that morning. At home, she and I would eat lunch in companionable silence, all her chatter gone. Then, while Maddy spent quiet time in her room, I would lie down in mine, headphones on, acquainting myself with the music of Nico Rathburn. This particular project hadn't been my idea. When I happened to mention to Lucia that the only Nico Rathburn album I'd ever heard was his third one, she had reacted with undisguised shock.

"You can't be serious." She'd disappeared and returned with a CD player in one hand and a stack of CDs in the other. "You need to listen to every single one of these."

I felt myself blush. "I'm sorry to be so unprepared," I said.

"Unprepared?" She let out a peal of laughter. "I'm sorry, I don't mean to laugh. Knowing Nico's music isn't part of your job description. There isn't going to be a quiz." She thrust the CDs into my arms. "You need to listen to these albums for *you*." Her eyes took on a faraway look. "Nico's music will change your life."

So while Maddy rested, I listened to Nico Rathburn's first album, then his second. Headphones on, I read the liner notes and looked at the pictures: the Rathburn Band lined up against a brick wall, all looking surly, and the man himself on a city street, hands deep in his pockets, posed before a security-grated storefront. At first, I wasn't impressed with the music, much less transformed by it. I'd never liked rock music much; the vocals often struck me as abrasive, more yelling than singing, and more about attitude than talent. The first album was made up of simple three-chord pop songs, with an occasional romantic ballad thrown in. The second was more musically and lyrically complex. I remembered from my research that a critic had called the second album "Dylanesque in its wild inventiveness," but to my ear the lyrics were undisciplined, full of free association and cryptic personal statements.

It took me a few days to make it to Nico Rathburn's third album, the one that had catapulted him to fame. Before I pushed Play, I studied the cover: the upper half of Nico Rathburn's famous face, a lock of hair falling across his forehead, his dark gaze daring the viewer to look away. Though I'd heard Lucia praise Nico's generosity and decency, this photograph broadcast arrogance. Still, I expected to like this album better than the first two because I'd heard it wafting from my brother's bedroom so many times. But when the first track began, I felt the muscles in my face tense. I didn't have to read the lyrics; it turned out that I knew them by heart.

Mark had loved this album, had played one song in particular — the megahit "Wrong Way Down a One-Way Street" — over and over. Our rooms were side by side; some nights I hadn't been able to sleep because his music was so loud. If I had knocked on his door and asked him to turn it down, he would have ignored me, or worse. I was the youngest; Mark had been six when I was born, and Jenna five. They knew how to pick at me until I fell apart, crying till I was as limp as a rag doll. Even worse, when Mark was in one of his terrible moods, he would hit me. He didn't need a reason. And if I ran to my mother to ask for protection, she would say, "I've never known such a crybaby." My father could be counted on to protect me, but he worked long hours and Saturdays; it felt like he was almost never home.

One time, when Mark had teased me to tears, I'd made the mistake of telling my dad about it when he got home from work. That night, my father took a belt to Mark. I was seven; Mark was thirteen and not much shorter than Dad. I could hear him yelping from his bedroom. He emerged from his spanking red-faced and surly, looking more embarrassed than hurt. He'd waited a day and a half until both Mom and Dad were out of the house to take his revenge. I was in my room, minding my own business, when he knocked on the door.

"Janey-Pain, I've got something to show you. A secret passage."

I should have known better than to go with him. But I was happy that he wanted to show me something special, that he had thought of me at all. I followed him up to the attic. It had been a while since anyone had gone up there, and a thick layer of dust coated the cardboard boxes that held our old toys and family photo albums. Behind the rocking horse, Mark dropped to his knees.

"Look." He pointed to a door that came to my waist. "What do you think is in there?" He unlatched the door and pulled it open.

"What is it?" I crouched down beside him. "Is that a closet?"

"Something even better. It's a tunnel. There's a door on the other side."

"Where does the other door open?" I asked. "Mom and Dad's room?"

"I don't know," he said. "Maybe. Or some other room we've never even seen." He stuck his head through the door, then popped back out into the attic with me. "Go ahead. Check it out."

I liked the kindly tone of his voice and wanted to do as he said, but I was scared of the dark and afraid of spiders. "You go first."

"Are you *scared?*" Mark asked, scorn creeping into his voice. "I show you something this cool, and you're too big a baby to explore?"

"I'm not afraid," I told him. "I'm not a baby."

"Then go ahead." He scrambled to the side so I could get by him. "Go on."

And I did. I crawled in as far as my waist. The space was dark, with only a square of light from the open door. "I don't see the other side," I told him.

"Keep going. You'll see it."

Feeling my way along the floor with my hands, I crept a few inches forward, then a few inches more, until my feet had passed the threshold. Then the door slammed shut behind me, and I heard the latch being fastened.

"Mark!" I pleaded. "Please don't. Please!"

I listened for a moment. "Mark?" I expected him to laugh on the other side of the door, or to blackmail me for some of my left-over Halloween candy or the contents of my porcelain piggy bank. Or maybe he just wanted to hear me beg. "Mark, *please* let me out. Please?" But there was no sound, no footsteps, no creaking floorboards. I waited and waited, but Mark was gone.

I curled up in a ball, making myself as small as possible. When I moved, cobwebs brushed my arms. I lay there whimpering until my eyes grew used to the dark. Then I crawled forward, foot by foot, until I reached the wall. I felt along it, all the way from side to side, from floor to ceiling, looking for a secret exit that wasn't there. Then I crawled back and banged on the entrance, screaming for help. Maybe a neighbor would hear me? It would be hours until Mom and Dad got home. How could I stand it in there for so long? I screamed and screamed until my throat felt torn.

A long time passed. I fell asleep — maybe I passed out with fright — but I woke with a start, feeling something crawl across my face. A spider? A mouse? I screamed some more. Was it day, night? Had my parents come home? Would they look for me and be surprised not to find me in my room? Would they ask Mark where I was, and would he tell them?

Then I had the most terrifying thought of all, one that seemed truer and truer the more I contemplated it: nobody would even notice I was gone.

"Miss Jane? Come get me. Miss Jane?" Maddy's crackly voice over the intercom summoned me from my memories. Had I fallen asleep? It took a few moments to recall where I was. I jumped up and pressed the intercom button.

"I'll be right there. Hold on." I straightened my clothes and rubbed sleep out of my eyes with hands that were undeniably shaky. *Calm down*, I told myself. *Don't be silly. You're safe.* My parents hadn't realized I was missing until the next morning, when Mom came into my room to wake me for school. They had run around the house calling my name until I heard their muffled voices and screamed back in return. When they found me, they were angry at me for scaring them. I opened my mouth to tell them about Mark's part in the episode but took one look at the expression on his face and swallowed my words.

"We thought you'd gone to bed early," Mom told me, brushing cobwebs out of my hair. "How were we supposed to know you weren't in your room?"

Why didn't you come in to kiss me good night? I wondered, but knew better than to ask. Instead I threw my arms around her waist and hugged her hard, refusing to let go until she pried me loose and sent me off to get dressed for school.

Get over it. You're an adult now. Maddy needs you. I started toward her room but, still sleepy and disoriented, turned a corner and found myself in a darkened wing I didn't recognize. Maddy's room was down the hall from mine; I had gone right past it and taken an unnecessary turn. I hesitated. It was then that I heard a laugh, so indistinct at first I thought I had imagined it. I froze, then heard the laugh again, louder this time.

"Maddy?" I called, though the laugh hadn't sounded like hers.

37

Then I heard it again, still louder. It seemed to be coming from somewhere above me. Rough and mocking—it wasn't a pleasant sound. Instinct told me to walk away from it, to go back in the direction from which I had come. I rounded the corner and almost bumped into Lucia.

"Slow down," she chided. "You almost knocked me over."

"Sorry. Maddy called me on the intercom, and I got a little lost and…" My voice trailed off. "Did you hear someone laughing?"

"Laughing?" Lucia asked, hands on her hips. "No, I don't think so."

"It was pretty loud. It seemed to be coming from the third floor."

"Must have been Brenda," Lucia said briskly. "Her room is up there." A few times since my arrival at Thornfield Park I had passed a broad-shouldered, mannish woman, older than the rest of the housekeeping staff. That must have been Brenda. But hadn't I been told the third floor was unsafe and off-limits?

Anticipating my question, Lucia said, "I know, I said it wasn't safe up there. Brenda's room is the only structurally sound bit—the turret's a death trap."

"I'd better get to Maddy." I excused myself.

By the time I reached her room, she was calling out my name. When I opened the door, she ran to me. "I was calling you," she said. "Why did you take so long?"

"I got a little lost. I came as fast as I could." I put my arms around her and held her, and she didn't pull away. "I'm sorry, Maddy, I really, truly am."

38

CHAPTER 4

Five weeks passed without incident, and it had begun to feel as though Nico Rathburn might never show up. My days with Maddy and Lucia had fallen into a peaceful rhythm, but instead of being relieved by the calm, I found myself feeling restless. On one of my days off, cold rain kept me in my room until late afternoon, when the sun finally broke through. I pulled on my rain boots, grabbed my raincoat and my tackle box full of art supplies, and hurried out the door. It felt so good to be outside that for once I didn't stop at the high iron fence surrounding Thornfield Park. The guard on duty was a young, open-faced man with long blond hair. He waved me through the gate, smiling, and looked for a moment as though he wanted to speak to me. I considered stopping to introduce myself, but the very thought brought a flush to my cheeks. I looked down at my feet, letting my hair fall forward to curtain my face, and kept hurrying along.

"Smile at the other children," I remember my mother telling me at the little playground near our house. "Don't cling to me. Go over to the monkey bars and say hello."

I followed her instructions and walked over to the monkey bars. I even tried to say hello to the laughing girls hanging upside down from the topmost bars, but they were so happy and familiar with each other, their long hair sweeping from side to side like banners, that I felt the words die in my mouth. I stood frozen a long time until, still laughing and chattering, the girls unfurled down to the ground and ran off to the swings.

My mother's anxiety about my social skills grew more acute the older I got. "By the time she was your age, Jenna had three boys fighting over her," she would say. "Why don't you ever go on dates?" Usually I would brush the question off and retreat to my room, but once I made the mistake of answering.

"I'm not as pretty as Jenna," I said, as though it needed saying.

"If you smiled you'd be more approachable." She put a hand on my arm. "Isn't there a boy you like?"

There was: Michael, a popular boy with creamy skin, roses in his cheeks, and dark brown eyes, a basketball player. I'd liked him since fourth grade. Unlike the other popular boys, he wasn't unkind to girls like me. Once in junior high when the bell rang, I left my pencil case on my desk, and he ran after me, shouting my name.

"You forgot this." He pressed the case into my hands. "It's nice. You wouldn't want to lose it." He was gone before I could thank him. But he knew my name. And he had cared enough to run after me. The next time I saw him, I wanted to speak to him but hadn't dared to.

"Well?" asked my mother. "There's no boy you like?"

I couldn't bring myself to utter his name, to break the magic spell of secrecy and expose my crush to the ordinary light of day. "Not really."

My mother withdrew her hand. "You're a cold fish," she said.

Tears rose to my eyes. I knew there was no use pleading my case, and before I could think of anything more to say, she turned and walked away. "I'm not," I whispered to the empty room.

I knew, even if the world did not, that I wasn't cold. But maybe my mother had been right about one thing: maybe I should have smiled at the cute gatekeeper; maybe I would on the way back in. For now, though, it was too late. I kept walking.

The driveway fed into a two-lane road at the bottom of the hill. Lucia had mentioned horse farms a mile or so east, so I headed in that direction. The shoulder was narrow, the road winding. I picked my way along the marshy grass, trying to stay out of the street. Traffic on this road was infrequent, but the cars that did drive by tended to be going above the speed limit, or at least that's how it felt as they whooshed past close enough to rustle my hair.

The road was slick. Petals from a stand of dogwood trees had been driven down by the torrential rain and made a pretty pattern on the black asphalt. I had been walking for about ten minutes and had just reached a sharp turn in the road when a sleek black sports coupe — quieter than the other cars had been — approached me from around the bend. I jumped back in surprise and before I had time to think heard the squeal of tires behind me and the wrenching

41

sound of metal on metal. The car had slid on the wet pavement and skidded into the guardrail on the opposite side of the road. It screeched to a stop, its front compartment filling with pillowy white air bags.

I gasped and found myself running up to the car, where a man in a navy blue jacket and mirrored sunglasses was picking his way out from under a deflated air bag.

"Are you okay?" I asked him. "Are you okay?"

"What the fuck were you doing in the road?" he yelled at me, his voice thunderous as he removed his sunglasses. "It's dangerous...the road is wet. I could have hit you, for chrissake. I could have *killed* you."

This struck me as unjust. "I wasn't in the road," I told him, working to keep my voice calm. "I was on the shoulder. And *you* were speeding." I hated being sworn at and being wrongfully accused; one reminded me of Mark, the other of my parents.

The man looked at me strangely. He rubbed his chin, then ran a hand through his dark hair. "My car's going to be in the shop for a week," he said sullenly, as if conceding a point he'd rather not have admitted to.

"Are you all right?" I asked him again. "Should you go to the hospital?"

"The hospital?" He looked at me blankly. "What for?"

"If you bumped your head. Or strained your neck. You seem disoriented."

Then he startled me by throwing back his head and laughing. "Disoriented? I'm oriented all right. The air bag knocked the wind

42

out of me, that's all. But my dog could have gone through the windshield."

An enormous, panting black Labrador retriever stood on the backseat, his nose poking over the partially rolled-down window. "Is he hurt?" I asked.

"He's shaken up. You're lucky he's indestructible." Then his voice grew gruff again. "Where could you be walking to all the way out here in the middle of nowhere? I suppose you're one of those *fitness walkers*." He emphasized the last two words with something like scorn.

"I am *not*," I said, as if he'd accused me of being a criminal or a con artist. What business was it of his why I was out walking? "Maybe you should check your car and see if it will start."

He stared at me a moment, then stalked back to his car. I watched as he expertly pushed aside the deflated driver's side air bag and turned the key; I guessed this wasn't the first time he'd performed that maneuver. The ignition caught. He rolled down the window and called to me. "It's apparently indestructible too."

"And you're really going to be okay? You shouldn't drive if you feel light-headed."

He smiled condescendingly. "Thanks, nurse. I'll be fine. I don't have far to go."

"Okay then." I wasn't about to let him spoil my walk. "Good-bye."

I'd only taken a few steps when I heard him calling after me. "Wait!"

I turned back.

"I can't let you keep wandering on this road that way. I didn't kill you, but somebody else might." He squinted and shielded his eyes. "Look, the sun's getting lower. Do you know how hard it is to drive with the sun in your eyes? A driver can barely see the road this time of day, much less pedestrians lurking around corners."

I stood there, not knowing what to say.

"I'll take you wherever you're going."

"Thank you but no." I took a step away from him. There was no way I was going to get into a strange man's car. "I'm only going to walk a bit farther, then I'll go home. I live less than a mile from here."

"You do? There aren't any houses around here."

I spoke without thinking. "Yes, there are. Well, one — at Thornfield Park." I immediately regretted my words; if I didn't trust him enough to ride in his car, why on earth had I told him where I lived? But then I remembered the high fence and the guardhouse and felt a wave of relief wash over me.

"Thornfield Park?" He looked at me quizzically. "You live at Thornfield Park?"

Of course, I thought. He's like the Waldorf mothers, wondering what someone like me is doing living in a celebrity's mansion. For a moment, I wished I were dressed the part, in thigh-high boots and a silver lamé dress, or whatever it was a rock goddess would wear. Then I imagined myself struggling up the hill in three-inch heels. "That's right," I said, "I'm the nanny."

"The nanny." His mouth twitched in that wry, one-sided smile I'd seen earlier. "Of course you are."

"So I'll be perfectly fine," I told him, not liking to be smiled at in that mocking way. "You don't need to worry." And I spun again and walked off, as fast and as purposefully as I could.

"For God's sake, stay out of the road!" he shouted after me, but I kept on walking, determined to salvage the rest of my afternoon. After about a mile or so, I found a field with a long view of a horse farm in the distance and a stump perfect for sitting on. I spread my coat across it and set about trying to paint. But my hands were unsteady; I had been more shaken up by the accident and subsequent encounter than I realized. My mind raced too; I had difficulty concentrating on the pad in front of me. After a few false starts, I packed up my paints. The sun was getting lower in the sky, the air unusually chilly for June. I pulled on my coat and headed for Thornfield Park.

Lucia met me at the door, as if she'd been on the lookout for me. "Is everything all right?" I asked her.

She motioned me to hurry in. "Nico's back," she told me, sotto voce. "Usually he lets us know when he's coming home. This time…total surprise!" She looked and sounded flustered. "Usually I have days to make sure the house is in order. The cook isn't even here."

Can't he make himself a sandwich? I wanted to ask. "It'll be all right," I told her, but she looked at me strangely. "Right. I don't know the first thing about him — but until now you've made him sound like a pretty understanding boss."

"I know it's your day off, and I'll really owe you one, but can you please take care of Maddy so I can track down the cook?"

"Of course, no problem. Where is she?"

"In her bedroom. If you could dress her in clean clothes, the nicest ones you can find…" Lucia's voice trailed off, and she darted toward her office.

"Consider it done," I called after her.

I found Maddy almost as worked up as Lucia, jumping on her bed and shrieking with laughter.

"Miss Maddy, you'll hurt yourself like that," I scolded her. "Put your feet on the floor right now."

"Daddy's here," she told me, getting in one last bounce for good measure. "He always brings me presents."

I made a quick assessment of the closet's contents. "And you want to look your best for Daddy, don't you? Let's see. What color should we choose: pale pink, poodle pink, pig pink, or hot pink?"

"Hot pink!" she squealed.

I handed her a flouncy skirt and a polka-dotted T-shirt. "Here, let me help you get that over your pigtails."

Once dressed, Maddy paced the room in circles. "When am I going to see Daddy?"

"Soon." I tried pressing the intercom to contact Lucia. Should we wait until Maddy was called for, I wanted to ask, or should we just come out? But Lucia seemed to be elsewhere. We waited a few minutes, and I tried again. Nothing.

This is crazy, I thought. *He's her father. She shouldn't have to wait here like a servant until he summons her.*

I grabbed Maddy's hand. "You ready, kid?"

She held my hand almost all the way downstairs and then tugged free. "Daddy? Daddy?" She broke into a run into the living

46

room, where a fire roared in a fireplace big enough to roast a wild boar on a spit.

"Is that my girl?" The voice came from the high-backed arm-chair closest to the fire. From behind, I could see the silhouette of a man — my employer — start to rise, but Maddy tackled him and he sat back down, laughing. Of course his voice was familiar; I'd been listening to his music for a month...no, most of my life.

"You're here!" Maddy shrieked.

I stood in the doorway, hands clasped before me, wondering whether I should stay or go. I was still wearing the grubby clothes I'd hiked in — a pine green T-shirt and a pair of jeans. I'd just about decided to slip back to my room when Maddy's voice rang out again. "Daddy, guess what? I have a new nanny. Her name's Miss Jane."

"Is that right? Is she good to you? Do you like her?"

"I like her better than Miss Bridget," Maddy told him.

"And where is Miss Jane now?" he asked, peeking around the corner of the chair. Behind him, I heard the jangle of dog tags and saw a long shape stretched out on the rug before the fire.

I took a step forward and froze. It was the man who had swerved to miss me and sideswiped the guardrail. He looked more natural than on his album covers and was younger-looking than I'd expected, but, still, he was unmistakably Nico Rathburn. How had I not recognized his face? In the many photos I'd seen of him, he had always seemed so removed from the world I lived in that now it was hard to believe he was standing a few feet away and looking right back at me.

Lucia chose that moment to sweep into the room. She glanced

at me, quickly registering disapproval of my sweaty and disheveled state before passing me by to address our employer. "I see you've met the new nanny," she said brightly, then slipped back out the door.

"Not exactly," Mr. Rathburn said, looking right into my eyes, "not officially."

I stepped up to him and extended my hand. He held it a moment and then gave it a brisk shake. "Welcome to Thornfield Park."

I wondered again how I had failed to recognize him on the side of the road. True, his dark hair was shorter now than on his album covers. The clothes he was wearing earlier camouflaged his wiry physique and made him look more like a businessman than the front man of a band. And he'd sounded educated, not like I'd imagined Nico Rathburn would sound. But now that he'd taken off that stockbroker's jacket, I could see the familiar serpent tattoo on his left forearm. He wore a silver hoop in each ear — how had I missed that? — and what looked like a shark's tooth hung from a leather cord around his neck. His smoke-gray eyes bored into me, taking my measure. I tried to think of something sensible to say and could not.

"What did you bring me, Daddy?" Maddy's voice rang out.

Mr. Rathburn turned back around in his chair. "There's a box in my suitcase. Why don't you go take a look? It's in my bedroom."

Maddy jumped down from his lap and took off running. A second later, she was back in the doorway. "Did you bring a present for Miss Jane?"

"For Miss Jane?" he repeated, laughing. "Miss Jane, did you expect a present?"

"Of course not," I replied.

"Why don't you come in and sit down," Mr. Rathburn said, "so I don't have to keep twisting around in my chair to look at you?"

The room contained a number of armchairs. I chose one in a corner.

"Not there," he said. "Come and sit by the fire so I don't have to shout across the room. Despite how it must have seemed to you this afternoon, I won't bite your head off." I shifted to the chair beside his. He rubbed his temples. "Copilot seems fine, in case you were wondering."

At the sound of his name, the large black Labrador lifted his boxy head and looked up expectantly.

"You see," Mr. Rathburn said, "he wants a present too."

Not knowing what to say, I said nothing.

"So where are you from, Miss Jane?" He spoke my name with a trace of mockery.

"Just outside of Philadelphia originally. I was in my freshman year at Sarah Lawrence until last month."

"Sarah Lawrence. And you dropped out to work for me?"

I recalled one of the interviews I'd read, in which he'd been asked about his own refusal to go to college. "I thought I didn't need college," he'd said. "Whatever I needed to know I could learn on the road. But it turned out I was wrong, so I've spent all these years reading books, trying to catch up."

"No," I said. "I came to work for you because I dropped out."

"Why did you leave school? You don't look like my idea of a dropout. You look studious."

I didn't say anything for a moment; he may have meant to be

49

insulting, but I knew it was true. With my thin lips and my hair pulled back, I must have looked like a caricature of a spinster librarian, minus the glasses. "You can't tell if I'm studious by looking at me," I said finally. "I didn't choose to drop out. And I plan to go back someday."

"You just got here, and you're already planning to leave?" he said. "We'll get used to you, and you'll take off?"

"Maddy's already used to me," I told him. "And I'm not planning on leaving anytime soon."

Just then, Maddy ran back into the room dressed in a sequined ballerina costume, a tutu rustling around her waist. "I'm a ballerina," she declared, whirling around in circles. A tiara hung at a precarious angle in her hair. She came to a stop at her father's knees. "I love it, Daddy."

He kissed her on the forehead. "I knew you would." She beamed.

"Did you say thank you?" I asked her.

"Thank you," Maddy said dutifully. "I'm going to go show Lucia." On tiptoes, she danced out of the room.

"Sequins," Mr. Rathburn said to me. "Can't go wrong with sequins and tiaras. There's nothing she loves more. Just like her mother." He lowered his voice to a whisper. "Do you think she'll ever outgrow it?"

"Most girls do."

He laughed again. "You haven't met the crowd I hang out with." Then his tone changed. "Maddy's a handful," he said. "Has she given you any trouble?"

"Hardly any. She just needs firmness and consistency."

"So you won't let her twist you around her little finger like she does me?"

I promised him I wouldn't and stood to go.

"Where are you going?" He sounded surprised.

"I'd better get Maddy out of Lucia's hair so that she can go home for the evening," I replied. "Excuse me, Mr. Rathburn."

His eyes widened. "Nobody calls me that. Call me Nico."

I complied but felt strange addressing him by his first name.

"You make me feel about a hundred years old," he told me. "How old are you, anyway? Seventeen and three quarters? Eighteen?"

"I'm nineteen."

"You were a kid when my first album came out," he said. "When I was your age, I was traveling the country, sleeping in a bus, playing dive bars, and getting into brawls. Shouldn't you be off having adventures?"

"I wouldn't know where to begin," I told him.

"Backpack through Europe? Sit at a sidewalk café in Rome? Go clubbing in Stockholm? Ski in the Alps?"

I had always wanted to travel and couldn't imagine being lucky enough to get the chance. "If I had the money to backpack across Europe, I wouldn't be here right now," I said. As soon as I said it, I realized how rude I must have sounded, but at least it was the truth.

His eyes held mine a second. "Huh.... Well, you're right. You'd better go get Maddy. Feels like it's almost bedtime."

As anxious as I'd been to get away from Mr. Rathburn, as I fixed Maddy's bath and laid out her pajamas, I found myself thinking back to our conversation. Though I was his paid help, he

51

had seemed truly interested in me for a moment, and that was rare in my life. When Maddy's fingertips wrinkled, I wrapped an enormous fluffy pink towel around her and a smaller one on her hair like a turban.

"Daddy's nice," she told me as I felt around under her bed for her slippers.

"He loves you," I assured her.

"I know," she said. "But his job takes him away a lot." For a moment, she sounded older than her years. "Daddy's famous."

"I know."

"Mommy is too, but Daddy's famouser."

"More famous," I corrected her.

"But Mommy wears shiny dresses and sings onstage. I'd rather wear shiny dresses than be more famous. I like to sing."

"I thought you were going to be a ballerina." I untied the towel on her head and used it to rub her hair dry.

"Ballerinas can wear shiny dresses," she said. Then, matter-of-factly, she added, "I can't see Mommy anymore. She lost custody. She sometimes would leave me alone in the hotel room, and I didn't like it there."

I bent to kiss her on the cheek. "You're a sweet girl."

I read her an extra story that night, in no great hurry to get back to my room. *Poor thing,* I thought. *Even a less-than-perfect mother would be better than none at all.* Before I'd finished reading, she fell asleep, mouth open, snoring gently. I set the book down and stretched out beside her for a moment. I must have fallen asleep. When I startled awake and slipped out into the hallway, the house seemed much quieter. I tiptoed downstairs, through the center of the house and past the living room, to get a glass of water. As I approached the kitchen, I caught sight of someone walking my way from the opposite direction. In the faint glow of a small Tiffany lamp, left on as a nightlight, I could make out the bulky figure of Brenda, whose strange mirthless laughter I had heard ringing out in the otherwise quiet house. Could this middle-aged woman, her iron-gray hair tied back tightly in a bun, really have let loose that wild, cackling laugh?

I paused in the shadows, waiting for her to pass before I continued on, but she looked right at me. In her arm, she held a glass bottle of something clear, probably alcohol. Our eyes locked, and a long moment passed before either of us moved. Just as I was about to say something, she swept past me. "Good night, miss," she said in a surprisingly deep voice as she disappeared around the corner and out of sight.

CHAPTER 5

The next day, I asked Lucia about Brenda. "If she's a housekeeper, why don't I ever see her vacuuming or making beds?" I explained that I had run into her the night before, though I didn't mention the bottle she had been carrying.

Lucia looked up from the sandwich she was making to bring back to her office. She'd worked the whole day without a break even for lunch, and I already missed the casual conversations we'd had before Mr. Rathburn had returned from his travels. "Brenda?" she asked absently.

"She knew who I was even though we'd never met."

Lucia shrugged and deftly cut the crusts from her cucumber sandwich. "Everybody knows who you are. There's only one nanny here."

"I've hardly seen her around the house until now. Has she worked for Mr. Rathburn long?"

Lucia gave me a look that clearly said Brenda was none of my business. Then she opened the refrigerator, rummaged through, and took out a Tupperware bowl of fruit salad. "The food's so much better now that the cook's back," she said. Then she sighed. "Brenda is no great mystery, Jane. She's worked for Mr. Rathburn for eight years, so, yes, she's been here almost as long as I have. She's a seamstress. She mends anything we tear, on top of the light housework she does. Does that answer your questions?" Her voice sounded sharper than usual. Then she put a hand on my arm. "Brenda may be a bit strange, but she's reliable, so Nico puts up with her eccentricities."

That was all I could get from her on the subject, but her refusal to say more made me suspect she was hiding something. And just thinking back to the loud, cackling laughter I'd heard coming from the third floor convinced me that something wasn't quite right with Brenda. In the days to come, Brenda and I would pass each other on the stairs or in the hallway, and she would give me a cold, steady look, as if warning me not to say a word. And once, in the evening, I could have sworn I smelled alcohol on her breath.

Now that Mr. Rathburn was here, the house seemed busier. Every time I turned a corner, I bumped into a new member of his entourage. His manager, a cherub-faced bald man named Mitch, came and went, spending hours holed up with Mr. Rathburn in his office or the music room. Jake, the crew-cut, overly tanned personal trainer, dropped in most mornings. Javier, Mr. Rathburn's personal assistant, spent most of each day running errands.

56

The housekeeping staff — besides Brenda, two women in their twenties — often gossiped about Mr. Rathburn. It's not that I meant to eavesdrop, but they would chat in the hallway outside my shut door as I read or sketched, waiting out Maddy's afternoon quiet time. A favorite topic was his new album and the international tour that was being planned.

"Do you think this whole comeback thing is going to work?" I heard one of them say — Amber, I believe, though their voices were similar. "Will anyone buy it? The CD, I mean."

"For our sake, I hope so," said the other one — Linda, who had worn her dirty blond hair pulled back in a tight ponytail until Mr. Rathburn returned to the estate but now wore it loose. "He won't be able to maintain a house like this if he doesn't have some kind of a hit, and soon."

Amber's voice was breezier. She was the more confident of the two, with an abundance of auburn curls that reminded me, a bit unpleasantly, of my sister. "I wouldn't worry. He gets tons of royalties from that song he wrote for the movies. You know the one." She sang a few bars. "He's set for life. Unless he does something crazy. Marries some bimbo without a prenup or starts gambling."

"When I was in high school, I was *so* in love with him," I heard Linda confide.

"You only tell me that every day."

"He's even hotter now than he was back then." Linda sounded wistful. "Especially when he's onstage."

"Get over it, girl." Amber's voice rang out — imprudently, I thought. "You should know by now, Nico doesn't sleep with the help."

"Stranger things have happened," Linda said. "Don't you sometimes think about what it would be like? You're alone with him in this enormous house one afternoon, and he's feeling kind of lonely…"

"Lonely? Don't you mean *horny*?"

I had reached the bottom of the page but didn't turn it for fear of alerting them to my presence. I doubted very much that they would like me to be overhearing their conversation. At least I took care of my own room, so I didn't have to worry that they would open the door and find me there listening.

"You never daydream about it?" Linda asked.

Amber snorted. "No thanks. I like men who work for a living."

"As if you wouldn't. If he asked you, I mean. Sleep with him. You know you would."

"I'd sleep with his money," Amber replied with a laugh. And then, as if they'd finally realized they might be overheard, their voices fell to a whisper as the laundry cart creaked forward.

Perhaps they felt free to speak indiscriminately because Mr. Rathburn's travels through the house were so circumscribed. Since his first night home, I'd only seen him on the first floor — never up on my wing. Still, I couldn't help but think Mr. Rathburn would be enraged if he had heard them just now. Despite the way Lucia had talked him up as a nice, ordinary guy, he didn't seem to have much of a sense of humor or much patience with his employees, or anyone else for that matter, from what I had seen. Since that first evening, he hadn't really spent time with Maddy, which seemed a bit strange to me; he seemed much too busy noodling around in his music room, working out, or going over strategy with Mitch.

Though he would kiss his daughter warmly whenever she ran into the room he was in, he would soon shoo her away to play with me, and I would lure her outside to her swings or the playroom full of her spectacular collection of toys — a playhouse full of cunning, child-sized appliances, a rocking horse and a teddy bear as big as I was.

Then one night — his fourth night home — he surprised me. Maddy was directing me to build a castle out of blocks for her collection of princess figurines, and an impossibly high tower had just come crashing down when Mr. Rathburn walked into the playroom.

"Daddy!" Maddy looked up from the line of princesses she had put in careful order. "Come see what Miss Jane and I are building."

"It looks to me as though Miss Jane is doing all of the building." Mr. Rathburn stood for a moment, then sank into the rocking chair — the room's one adult-sized piece of furniture — as though he had every intention of joining us for a while.

Was he there to spend time with Maddy? He didn't approach her but instead sat back, observing our interactions. Maybe he'd come to get a sense of how I was getting along with his daughter. I willed myself to ignore his gaze — which was fixed intensely on the two of us — and concentrated on the tower I was rebuilding.

"Sleeping Beauty's going to live in there," Maddy said, half to her father and half to herself. "That's where she's gonna prick her finger and fall down dead."

"She only falls asleep," I reminded her. "The prince wakes her up."

Maddy nodded solemnly. "Don't knock it down," she said.

"I'll do my best, but no promises. This is a *very* tall tower."

Though my hands were shaking a little, I completed the tower without incident. And though Maddy would boss me around if I allowed it, ordering me to make matching towers for each of her princess figurines, I let her know that she needed to sit beside me and do half the building herself. Mr. Rathburn watched us for a full hour before he stood and, without a word, left the room.

I heard nothing more from him until later that evening. I'd just kissed Maddy good night and was shutting her bedroom door quietly behind me when he approached me from the other end of the hall. In his jeans and rumpled T-shirt, he looked like many of the fathers for whom I'd babysat, except maybe for the tattoo on his forearm.

"Maddy's almost asleep," I told him. "But if you slip in and give her a good-night kiss, I don't think it would disturb her."

"I said good night to her already," he replied, somewhat gruffly. "It's you I'd like to talk to."

I followed him downstairs to the living room; he motioned for me to have a seat in the armchair opposite him. Though the night was warm and the air-conditioning on, someone had lit a fire. I sat.

For a while he sat in silence, feet up on an overstuffed hassock. I waited for him to begin the conversation, and when he didn't, considered what he might want me to do or say. Copilot stretched out in his usual spot before the fire and looked up at me with mournful liquid-brown eyes. A moment passed and he stood, walked over, and dropped his heavy head in my lap. I scratched him between the ears, glad to have something to do. Just as I was about to ask Mr. Rathburn if he had something particular in mind, he straightened in his chair. "I don't need to call you *Miss* Jane, do I? I'd rather just call you Jane, if you don't mind."

I tried not to smile. "You're the employer, Mr. Rathburn," I reminded him. "You can call me anything you want. Well, almost anything."

The sides of his mouth twitched. "Yes, well. There's something very formal about you." His eyes were dark and piercing as they searched my face. "You say you're from Philadelphia?"

"From the suburbs. The Main Line."

"Are your parents rich, then? Are you some kind of debutante?" I continued to meet his gaze, expecting his eyes to glance away at any moment, but they didn't. "I know that's a rude question. I don't believe in wasting time. I'm not good at small talk. Are you?"

"I've never liked small talk. And I'm not a debutante." It seemed such a strange question. "My father was a dentist, and my mother was a homemaker. We had enough money, but I don't think we were rich by your standards, Mr. Rathburn."

"Was?" He signaled for Copilot to lie down. "You say your father *was* a dentist. Is he retired?"

"My parents died in an accident." By now I could make this statement with an unbroken voice. "About six months ago."

His expression remained unchanged. "Don't you have any family?"

"A sister in Manhattan, but we're not close. And I have a brother, at least I used to, but he isn't very stable. He disappeared last winter, and I don't have any idea where to find him. I don't think he would want to be found."

61

"What about friends?"

"I had a close friend at Sarah Lawrence, but she moved back to Iowa."

He thought for a moment, then continued. "Why did you drop out?"

"I couldn't pay my tuition."

"Your parents didn't leave you any money?"

"The stocks my parents left me turned out not to be worth much. My sister did a little bit better; she inherited some money market accounts, I think. And my brother was named executor of the will. He sold the house and kept the money."

He leaned in a bit closer. "You don't seem bitter."

"Should I be?"

"Most people would be. In your shoes." He got to his feet. "I don't imagine you drink?"

I shook my head.

"Stay here." A minute later, he was back with two glasses of ice and a bottle of mineral water. "Bottoms up."

I took a sip. I had been thirsty without realizing it. He sat back down. "Do you mind my asking so many personal questions?"

I thought a moment. "No. I don't mind." I wasn't just being polite. It was a relief to speak plainly and not have to hide my situation, as though it were something to be ashamed of.

"Are you lonely?" he continued. "The most personal question yet."

"I used to be. But I've gotten used to spending time by myself. And I haven't felt alone since I've been here." As I uttered the words, I realized they were true.

"I guess you've bonded with Maddy," he said without a trace of sentimentality in his voice, at least none that I could detect. "I can tell she's become attached to you."

I nodded. It was nearly impossible to reconcile this serious man in front of me with the persona in his songs, music videos, and news clippings.

"I've been watching the two of you. You've done her some good. She listens to you, and that wasn't true of the nanny before you. Or the one before that."

"She's not the easiest or the most difficult child I've taken care of." Then it dawned on me that he had paid me a compliment. I allowed myself a small smile. "But thank you."

"For what?" He poured himself another glass. "More?"

I held my glass out. "Thank you for the praise. It's always nice to feel... I don't know... useful. Capable."

"Huh." Mr. Rathburn tossed the empty glass bottle across the room into a waste can. It rang without breaking. "I've never seen you smile before. I didn't know you could."

I could feel the smile fade from my lips.

"No, no. That wasn't meant as a criticism. I wasn't laughing at you. It was just... the truth. From what you tell me about your life, it hasn't been a pleasure cruise."

"I guess not."

"I've got one more question for you, Jane." He eased his slippered feet back up on the hassock. "I've noticed that when you bring Maddy to preschool, you stay out instead of coming back here. Where do you go?"

I hesitated.

"You don't have to tell me. You're free to go wherever you want. I'm just curious. You're not off walking on the main road, are you? The way you were when I almost squashed you flat?"

"Not usually," I said. "Most days I drive around looking for a subject. I do watercolors when I'm not looking after Maddy."

"Watercolors?" He sounded intrigued. "Can I see some of them?"

I was so startled by the request that my reply came out ruder than I intended. "But why would you want to?"

Mr. Rathburn raised an eyebrow in reply.

"They're not that good," I said. "I'm just a beginner."

"Bring them out anyway," he said. "You're too modest."

"I'm too *honest*," I corrected him, but I complied. Back in my room, I quickly rifled through my portfolio, looking for the best of the paintings I'd done at Thornfield Park. I brought them downstairs and spread them on the living room's wide coffee table while Mr. Rathburn looked on with appraising eyes.

"These are interesting," he said finally. "You've got a graceful line and a fresh approach to color. Don't look so surprised, Jane." Now he sounded annoyed. "You shouldn't underestimate me. I may not have gone to *Sarah Lawrence*" — he drew the name out mockingly — "but I've had a lot of time over the past few years to study the things that interest me. Art interests me."

"I'm sorry, Mr. Rathburn." I set out the last of my paintings. "I shouldn't have been surprised."

"Or at least you should have hidden it better. Every thought that passes through your mind is written in neon on that face of yours." Then he picked up my painting of a family picnicking on a yellow blanket near the Sound; I'd worked quickly, hoping to finish it before they noticed me but really hoping they wouldn't notice me at all. "You've captured that woman's gesture very nicely, the way she leans in toward the man but also keeps herself separate." He set the painting down and picked up another, of a lighthouse at twilight. "And this one — the colors are a little muddy, but the composition's really striking. Were you happy while you painted these?"

This seemed like a strange question. "Yes."

"Were you looking for something to paint the day you ran my car off the road?"

"You were speeding," I reminded him.

He picked up another watercolor and scanned it. "These are good," he said, "but they're not worth dying over. I know I said it's none of my business where you go on your time off, but I want you to do me a favor. For the time being, do your painting at Thornfield Park."

I must have looked startled.

"There are plenty of interesting things to paint around the estate. I bet you haven't seen nine-tenths of the grounds," he said.

"I don't know," I told him. "Probably not."

"Have you checked out the path behind the pool house? If you follow it into the woods and bear right, you'll come to a stable. I don't keep horses," he added, anticipating my next question. "It was there when I bought the place. The building's run-down, a little haunted-looking, and there are these wild twisted trees around it. Would you try painting there instead of wandering all over the county? Not forever, just for a while?"

"I'll go there tomorrow if it doesn't rain," I promised him.

And I did. I spread out my supplies on a low, flat boulder and painted three landscapes — one of the stable's warping boards and deep, shadowy interior, and the other two of the gnarled tree trunks that looked, when I squinted, like figures in black caught in a ghostly dance. I got so involved in painting that I forgot to check my watch and was almost late for Maddy's pickup time. I hurried to the house and raced in through the back door and up to my bedroom to drop off my paints. Just as I was about to turn the corner into the hallway, I heard voices — Amber and Linda — and could tell by their tone that they were gossiping again.

"Nico pays her well, right? Benjamin mentioned something about her being rich. Not that you'd ever know it to look at her," Amber said.

"A lot better than he pays us," Linda replied. "I'm not complaining. I know I make more than most housekeepers, but she makes five times as much. She told me once that she's saving up to buy her own bed-and-breakfast someday."

Amber said something I couldn't quite catch.

"I know, she looks almost sixty with that bun of hers, but she's much younger. Fortysomething, maybe. So she's a long way from retiring."

They were describing Brenda.

"Why do you suppose she's worth that much money to him? What makes her so special?"

I could hear the creak of the laundry cart. Any moment now they would turn the corner and find me there. And wouldn't I be embarrassed to be caught listening to their private conversation? I forced myself forward, around the corner.

"If she were younger and prettier, I'd wonder if Nico...," Linda was saying, but Amber gave her a nudge, then both of them looked my way. I saw Amber shake her head emphatically, and seconds later, they were gone. I fumbled for the key to my room and dropped my portfolio and my tackle box of art supplies on the bed. Then I sat down to catch my breath and to give the blood burning in my cheeks a moment to cool down.

What I'd heard did little to answer my questions about Brenda. All it did was confirm for me that there was something mysterious going on at Thornfield Park and that it somehow involved her.

CHAPTER 6

Mr. Rathburn was in the breakfast room at eight the next morning, earlier than I had ever seen him there. Before she left for school, Maddy popped in to the kitchen to kiss him good-bye; from the hallway, I could see he had been drinking coffee at the table, the business section of the *New York Times* spread open before him. When we returned at lunchtime, the door to the music room was shut; the sound of electric guitar seeped through the walls. As Maddy carried her plate to the dishwasher, she announced that she would be spending the afternoon with her father.

"He's working," I reminded her. "You'll see him later."

While she was napping, I stayed in my room. I hadn't yet figured out how visible I should be to Mr. Rathburn. I needed to stick close to Maddy, of course; I had to stay within the range of her voice when she spent time with her father. But while she was off at school or asleep, I imagined I should keep out from under-foot. I thought about asking Lucia what was appropriate, but when I saw her in the hall she was gesticulating wildly with one hand, the other pressing a cordless phone to her ear. "Not Friday! I could be dead by Friday. Tomorrow. We need delivery *tomorrow*."

I read while Maddy slept, bedspread pulled up to my chin. The scent of baking bread wafted upstairs from the kitchen. I was feel-ing around the bed for the bookmark I'd dropped, thinking about closing my eyes for a brief nap of my own, when the intercom crackled, and Mr. Rathburn's voice startled me. "Jane? Are you there?"

I jumped to my feet. "I'm here," I told the intercom.

"Could you come here a second? I'm in my dressing room."

It seemed an odd request. I considered it for a moment, won-dering if maybe it would be unwise to join him in such an isolated part of the house. But then I caught sight of myself in the full-length mirror on the back of the door and realized how silly I was being. I looked completely unlike the women he had dated. Maybe he wanted to discuss Maddy? "I'll be right there."

I had to think hard to remember the location of his dressing room, just off his bedroom in the wing opposite mine. I hurried first to Maddy's bedroom and peeked in. She was still asleep, clutching her pink pillow. When I reached the dressing room, I found him standing there, piles of clothes flung on various sur-faces. He was holding a shiny, black button-down in front of his T-shirted chest.

"You're the demographic I'm trying to impress," he said. "Or one of them, anyway. What do you think?"

70

This was an interesting turn of events. I thought for a second. "It depends. What's the occasion?"

"We're doing a photo shoot for the tour program this afternoon. Javier is home with a migraine; usually I would ask him. I don't want to be at the mercy of the photographer and Mitch. I want to go in there with a set idea, so I don't get sidetracked into some ridiculous, trendy…" He tossed the black shirt on the chair and reached for a plaid flannel one. "How about this?"

"It's not very flashy."

His eyebrows shot up. "Well, right," he said. "I'm not going for flashy. I haven't been flashy since my first album." I'd been standing in the doorway; he beckoned me closer.

"What *are* you going for?" There must have been ten piles of shirts, pants, and scarves strewn around the room.

"What *am* I going for?" he asked the ceiling. "What should I be going for?"

"What does your new album sound like?"

"More acoustic than the others." He reached for a candy-orange silk shirt. "More folky. Lyric intensive, if you know what I mean. Less dynamic, more reflective. Intimate. My fan base is going to hate it; it will remind them they're not teenagers anymore."

I thought for a moment. "I wouldn't dress too formally, but I wouldn't go too far in the other direction and wear a ripped T-shirt or a lumberjack shirt or anything like that." I looked around; a crisp burgundy-colored shirt slung over a chair in the corner caught my eye. "That one would be nice — with blue jeans."

"That one?" he asked. "Why that one?"

"I think that color will suit you," I said. He waited, as though

71

expecting a more persuasive rationale. "But maybe you should get somebody else's opinion," I added. "I'm no expert on clothes, as you can see" — I gestured to my denim skirt and oxford shirt — "and I don't know anything about rock music."

"You don't?" He sounded shocked. "What do you listen to?"

"Classical music, sometimes."

"Do you listen to *my* music?" he asked in a somewhat quieter voice.

"I've heard it. My brother played your third album all the time, so I know it very well. And I've listened through all the others."

"Listened through all the others?" He massaged his temples. "You mean only once?"

I nodded, and he looked at me oddly for a moment, as though I were a bird who had flown in through the window and he was trying to figure out how to get me back outside.

"I believe the agency picked me for that reason," I reminded him.

"Oh. That's right. I told them not to send me any more fans." He made a snorting sound, a laugh devoid of humor, and picked up the shirt I had chosen. "You wouldn't believe the kinds of trouble it causes." His tone was grudging. He held the shirt up in front of him. "But couldn't you humor me for a moment? Pretend you like my work. Imagine you could be won over by something as frivolous as a tour program or a poster. Would this shirt do the trick?"

I considered the question for a second. It would be a nice color on him; it made his gray eyes seem darker and moodier, and it brought out the color in his lips, softening his rough features just a bit. "I think it would."

"I'll put it on." He grabbed a pair of jeans from the pile. "Don't go anywhere."

A minute later, he was back, standing in front of his three-way mirror, striking a pose, holding an imaginary guitar. "So?" he asked me.

"I'd go with that one. It's flattering. And it's not too formal, but it looks grown-up."

"Grown-up. That's me. Earrings?"

"Yes. You don't want to look too much like a soccer dad."

"Soccer dad? Ouch."

"And maybe roll up your sleeves to show your tattoo." He rolled them up, revealing the serpent that coiled through the sparse hair of his left forearm.

"Motorcycle boots?" he asked me, and when I nodded, "Black or brown? Maybe you've just found yourself a new career — stylist." He ruffled his hair, making it stand up. "Don't go yet. You're not done here." And he disappeared again into the bedroom.

When he came back out, the transformation was complete; I could half imagine what the cover of the tour program might look like. "What do you think?" he asked.

"Perfect. I think that's the right balance."

"Should I shave? I'm thinking about growing a soul patch," he said. "You know, one of those little blobs of hair right here?" He pointed to the spot beneath his lower lip.

"I know even less about beards than I do about men's clothes."

"That's right," he said teasingly. "You're a girl."

73

"Maybe you should ask your barber."

"I don't want my barber's opinion. I'm asking *because* you're a girl. A woman, I mean."

I didn't really know what to say to that.

He surveyed himself in the mirror a moment, then turned back to me. "Do you think I can pull it off?" he asked. "Will I pass?"

I waited for him to explain further.

"As a sex symbol?"

"Oh," I said. "I didn't think men worried about things like that."

"They do when they're using their face to sell CDs." He exhaled sharply. "And when they have to shoot a fucking tour program." Then he softened a little. "Sorry. I can see you don't like swearing. I'll try to rein it in. So. Passing as a sex symbol. Can I?"

I weighed my words carefully. "You might not be movie-star handsome," I said finally, "but you're good-looking for a rock star."

Mr. Rathburn's eyes widened. "That's three times you've hurt my feelings in one conversation," he said a bit gruffly.

"Three times?" I really hadn't meant to be rude.

He counted on his fingers. "You don't like my music. I'm a soccer dad. And I'm good-looking...*for a rock star.*"

"A lot of women throw themselves at rock stars."

He surprised me by laughing, a belly laugh that went on for a while. When he laughed, his eyes crinkled, and I could see how his fans might consider him attractive, despite the scowl and his less-than-classically-handsome features. Then his laughter gave way to a sly smile. "What about you, Jane? Can you imagine throwing yourself at a rock star?"

I probably should have tried to come up with a more diplomatic answer, but instead I spoke without thinking. "No, Mr. Rathburn."

His jaw dropped. "You're something else. You know that? What planet are you from?"

I felt the blood rise to my cheeks. How did I manage to keep saying the wrong things? "I should have chosen my words more carefully. I should have said I can't imagine throwing myself at *anyone*." I thought a moment. "I should have said looks aren't important, especially not in a man."

"You're kidding, right? Looks aren't important?" He snorted again. "We both know that's not true. You're not a movie star either, are you, Jane?"

"That's right," I replied. "I'm not."

"And has your life taught you that looks don't matter?" He dropped to a chair to adjust one of his boots.

I considered the question. Was he trying to hurt my feelings? His expression was calm enough, without spite, as he fiddled with the buckle of his boot. I decided he wasn't trying to hurt me any more than I had been trying to hurt him. "No," I said. "I mean, I know from experience that looks do matter. Quite a bit."

"Well then." He patted the other boot. "Have you had many boyfriends?" He looked up at me quizzically.

"No. Not many. Not any, actually."

"Why not? Don't you like men?"

"Yes." I thought for a moment about the other question. "At Sarah Lawrence the girls outnumbered the boys by far. And I wasn't the kind of girl the boys noticed."

"And you were perfectly fine with that?"

"I wasn't fine with it," I replied. "But I've learned to accept the way things are."

"The way things are," he repeated absently. "You don't mind, do you? That I'm prying into your personal life?"

"No, Mr. Rathburn."

"I don't suppose I'll ever get you to call me by my first name, will I?" He stood, walked back over to the three-way mirror, and looked at his reflection for a long time. "So," he said finally. "Be your usual blunt self. Is there any hope for me?"

"For a comeback, you mean?"

He shook his head. "Is there any chance I'll turn from plastic back into flesh?"

The question was such a strange one that I had no idea what to say. I waited a moment to see whether he would explain himself.

"Never mind," he said. "Thanks for your honesty. You'd better go. Maddy will be wandering around soon if she isn't calling for you already."

I left him rifling through his dresser drawers and went down to the kitchen for a quick drink of water. Nico's manager already sat waiting in the living room. By his side sat an elegant-looking woman with olive skin, glossy black hair, and a gauzy amber scarf — the photographer, I supposed — and several young assistants. I hurried past them on my way back upstairs to Maddy's room.

Maddy kept me so busy that afternoon — playing dress-up and, with the permission of Walter the cook, baking sugar cookies — that I didn't have time to process my conversation with

Mr. Rathburn or to make sense of his last, cryptic question. Later, I drove Maddy to dance class and watched her practice pliés in a line of preschoolers, the stern teacher tapping time with her cane and admonishing them to pay attention. Once I had wanted to take ballet like Jenna did, but my mother pronounced me too clumsy and sent me to violin lessons instead. The memory still stung a little, and I spent most of Maddy's lesson pushing it out of my head. And it was true. I'd never had Jenna's long-limbed grace or her flair for the dramatic. I probably would have hated performing onstage at the year-end recital. Instead, I'd been able to blend into the orchestra, hiding amid the other second violins. I could have taken ballet in college if I'd really wanted to, but by then I'd been unable to imagine myself *en pointe*, gravity suspended for a moment as I leaped through the air in a *tour jeté*. By then I wasn't really the dancing type.

When Maddy and I returned home, Lucia had already left for the night. Walter, a moody, gray-haired, boyish man who sometimes spoke in monosyllables and other times gabbed enthusiastically, was vigorously chopping a pile of leeks for that night's dinner. Maddy's meal was already in the oven, and she and I ate together in the breakfast room as we usually did. Most nights so far, Mr. Rathburn had eaten late, often with the entourage of guests who came and went. Tonight, I could hear conversation and Mr. Rathburn's distinctive laugh in the living room, soon joined by others. It sounded as though the photographer would also be staying for dinner. Lucia had mentioned that she was a celebrity herself; her work had been featured in *Vogue* and on the cover of *Vanity Fair*, and it was a real coup to have booked her. *What are they laughing about?* I wondered as I scooped a spoonful of stewed apple onto Maddy's plate.

"Do I have to eat that?" she asked, though by now she knew perfectly well what my answer would be.

"You have to try it." She crossed her eyes and stuck out her tongue, but she took a bite. Yet another burst of laughter reached us.

"I want to go see Daddy," she said, hopefully. "Can I?"

"Your daddy is in a business meeting."

"It doesn't sound like business."

"But it is. Two more bites of apple." Usually well lit and cheery, the breakfast room felt dreary, though the sun was far from setting. Like Maddy, I wanted to be in front of the fireplace, where Mr. Rathburn and his company were drinking wine and having what sounded like a good time. Unlike Maddy, I had no reason to be there.

Getting Maddy to sleep that night took two books and four lulla-bies. When at last her breathing grew deep and regular, I pulled her favorite furry pink blanket up to her chin and slipped down to the kitchen for a glass of water. Amber was noisily loading the dishwasher, but the downstairs was otherwise quiet. I waved good night to her, planning to take a nice hot shower and read myself to sleep. When I passed the darkened living room, in which the fire-place still crackled, I was startled to hear my name called out from the shadows. I paused in the doorway.

"I thought that was you," Mr. Rathburn's voice said. A lamp switched on to reveal him in his usual chair. "Come sit with me."

I took a step into the room, my eyes adjusting to the relative darkness. I could see he was still in the clothes I'd helped him choose that morning. Copilot sat at attention by his knee. I slipped into the chair opposite his.

"Don't you want to know how the photo shoot went?" he asked.

"How did it go?"

He shrugged. "They posed me in the music room; they posed me out in the yard leaning against a tree. They got me staring moodily out a window. By the time they were done, I felt like an action figure."

I thought of his earlier question, about whether he could transform from plastic to flesh. "Did any of the poses feel natural to you?" I asked.

"Not one, but then there's nothing natural about the process. About image building. It's all about taking something complicated, a whole personality, and boiling it down to a single trait."

"What's your single trait?"

"It's changed over the years. I started out" — he snapped air quotes with his fingers — "'Wild.' Then it morphed into 'Tortured.' And now, I'm 'Repentant.' Don't look at me like that. You know what I have to be repentant about. I assume a smart girl like you did her research before moving into the infamous rock star's house."

"I did read up on you."

"So then you know about my bad-boy days — the mountains of coke I hoovered up my nose. The alcohol and the women. I'm surprised you were willing to come here."

"I'm not afraid of you, Mr. Rathburn," I told him. "Besides, cocaine and women — isn't that just what rock stars do?"

He scratched Copilot under the chin. "I like to think I took it to a whole new level. On top of the binges and blackouts, I crashed cars, trashed my marriage, and probably wrecked my own heart." He tapped his chest. "Literally and figuratively."

"Plenty of people behave badly without feeling guilty about it. Why shouldn't you?"

"Because…" He fell silent a moment. Then, without warning, he leaned toward me. I could smell the faintest trace of spicy aftershave and something else; it must have been the smell of his skin. "Bibi — my wife — was an innocent when I met her. She'd never tried coke or anything else. But she wanted to keep up with me…to share my interests." He spoke the last phrase mockingly. "At the time, my only real interest was seeing how far I could go before it killed me. And Bibi…well, she worshipped me. She'd try anything I'd try." His eyes shone darkly in the firelight. "What kind of man does that to his wife?"

"I don't know," I said.

"People kept telling me how great I was, and the coke made me believe them. I wanted her there with me, on top of the mountain. I wanted to share all my highs with Bibi. It felt like the most loving gesture I could think of." He leaned back into his chair. "Look at your face. I can see you disapprove. You're trying to hide it, but you're not doing a very good job. Your forehead gets these troubled little lines."

"I'm trying to imagine what it must have been like," I said. "To be you, I mean."

"Suddenly I was surrounded by people who yessed me to death. My face was on the cover of *Rolling Stone.* My album had just gone platinum. All that shit. I thought I could get away with anything. I was just about your age, but I acted like a total child. I could have used someone like you to babysit me. As young and innocent as you are, you have about ten times more strength and self-possession than I did then."

"But what about your ex-wife?" I asked. "Where is she now? Is she still an addict?"

"She's far away." His face darkened. "Out of my reach. I don't mean to sound melodramatic, but it's true. At least she's not using anymore." He shifted in his chair. "Why am I telling you all this? I feel like I'm in confession. Are you going to tell me to say twenty Hail Marys and then wipe my slate clean?"

"I'm not Catholic."

"You're a good listener," he continued. "You'd much rather listen to me drone on all night than reveal anything about yourself. Is that right?"

I didn't answer.

"You've learned it's safer to watch from the sidelines, not to call attention to yourself. No matter what I do or say, you sit there with your hands folded in your lap, with that serious expression on your face. I feel like I could tell you anything. I could tell you I strangled Bibi and chopped her up into little pieces, and you'd sit there perfectly calm, waiting for me to explain myself." He bit his lower lip. "Well then, I'll keep going. The universe paid me back, in the form of Maddy's mother. France's singing sensation Celine. You've heard of her?"

I nodded.

"All image, no talent. You've seen her picture, right? Six feet tall — all legs, flowing blond hair, red lipstick, designer dresses, and stiletto heels. You won't be surprised to hear that her head is a pretty soap bubble — shiny and clean, with nothing but air inside. Sometimes I worry Maddy takes after her."

"You have some influence over how Maddy turns out."

"You mean *you* do. I don't know the first thing about raising children," Mr. Rathburn said. "But I pay you, so I guess I do have *some* influence." He laughed. "Anyway, it's a long story. I can see how tired you are; you've got blue circles under your eyes. Go to bed, and tomorrow after you've dropped Maddy off, come back to the house, and I'll show you another good view to paint. Good night, Jane."

CHAPTER 7

The next morning, Mr. Rathburn led me to a part of the grounds I'd never seen before — a cool grove of pines at the back of the property, completely out of view of the house. I had been expecting him to draw me a map to the spot and send me on my way, then get back to his usual morning routine — his workout and a long session in the music room. Instead, he met me on the back porch in jeans and a pair of new-looking hiking boots — had I ever seen him wear those before? — holding a couple of bottles of mineral water, and it dawned on me that he was going to walk me there himself. I was startled, though not displeased.

"You're taking the morning off, Mr. Rathburn?" I asked him.

"Well, it's not like I haven't earned it," he said. "You have some kind of problem with that? You like time by yourself?"

"Not necessarily." I decided not to ask him why he had chosen to be my personal tour guide. After all, to me his ways were generally inscrutable; I was getting used to his unpredictability. I followed him down the steps and past the pool house.

"Lucia tells me you never take Maddy swimming," he said abruptly when I caught up with him. "Why is that?"

"She never asks to swim," I told him.

"She needs to ask? It's good exercise. She spends too much time indoors with those little figurines of hers. Kids need fresh air."

"She goes out every day in her play yard, weather permitting," I countered.

He stopped in the path, hands on his hips, and looked down at me. "Don't you want to work on your tan?"

"What tan, Mr. Rathburn?"

He surprised me by laughing. "The one you'd have if you ever took my daughter to the pool."

"I can't swim," I admitted. "I couldn't rescue her if she fell in the deep end."

"Nobody ever taught you to swim?" His eyes narrowed. "That's criminal. We'll have to hire somebody, get you lessons."

"The agency didn't ask me if I could swim. Otherwise I would have told them. It didn't occur to me, and..."

"Never mind that. Why don't you at least put on a bathing suit and hang out by the pool in your off-hours? You do realize that's most people's idea of a good time, don't you?"

"I'm not even sure I have a bathing suit," I told him, trying to think back to the last time I'd been to a swimming pool. The summer of eleventh grade, maybe.

84

"What?" He was frowning now. "No bathing suit? Are you sure you're not a nun?"

"Some nuns swim," I said.

We had reached a grove of pines. A thick carpet of needles spread out soft and springy underfoot. "If I bring you to the top of that hill over there" — he pointed — "will you spin around and start singing that the hills are alive with the sound of music?" He watched my reaction. "What are you smiling about?"

"You do remind me a little bit of Captain von Trapp," I admitted, and to my surprise, he chuckled.

Something like a path ran down the center of the pine forest, and we walked the length of it in what, to me at least, felt like companionable silence. Rays of sunlight filtered here and there through the boughs; just then Mr. Rathburn stepped into a shaft of light. "What about here?" He pointed to a tree trunk, a perfect place to sit and take out my watercolors. "Would this work?"

I spread out my jacket on the rough bark and took a seat. The grove before me was cool and peaceful, as though the needles beneath my feet were absorbing all the noises of the world beyond. I began unloading the contents of my backpack. "It's perfect," I told him. "Lovely, really."

"Yes, well." He stood off to the side a bit awkwardly, it seemed to me.

I opened my sketch pad and began to draw a scattering of pines several yards before us, a felled one providing an interesting diagonal amid all the stark black verticals. Within minutes, I had the beginnings of what could make a good watercolor, but as I worked, I could feel Mr. Rathburn's restless presence just behind me, looking over my shoulder, making it hard for me to concentrate.

"Would you like to sit down?" I gestured to the trunk beside me. "I've got some insect repellent in my backpack."

"Insect repellent." He made a sound that was half laugh, half snort. "I can see I would only get in your way. You have important work to do."

"I don't mind if you stay," I told him.

I'd meant to be polite, but he seemed to take it as an insult. "You don't *mind* if I stay?" he repeated.

I looked up from my drawing. "Thank you, I mean." I set down my pencil. "This is a beautiful spot, and I'm grateful that you took the time to show it to me. It was very thoughtful of you." But this didn't seem to pacify him. "Was there something you wanted to talk about?"

"We'll talk later," he said, thrusting his hands into the front pockets of his jeans and stalking away, back up the path toward the house. I watched until he was out of sight. Should I run after him? Offer an apology? What had I said to hurt his feelings?

No, I decided. This was my time off, and I would spend it as I pleased. I went back to my work, but knowing that I'd upset him, I had a hard time concentrating. My watercolors ran together, making muddy streaks. I kept looking at my watch to see if it was time to pick Maddy up from preschool, and soon enough it was.

That next morning I rummaged in my drawers and found my bathing suit from a few summers ago; I hadn't tossed it out after all. It was a plain navy blue one-piece, a bit faded from chlorine. If

Mr. Rathburn wanted me to take his daughter to the pool, I would learn to swim. I threw my baggiest sweatshirt on over the suit and stepped into a pair of shorts. After dropping Maddy off at school, I drove straight home and hurried to the pool house, hoping nobody would notice what I was up to. I'd never been terribly comfortable in water. My mother's attempts to teach me to swim had always ended badly; I would cling to her arms or around her neck, begging her not to let go. But that had been years ago when I was just a little girl. Surely now I'd be able to teach myself the basics.

I wandered outside, to one of the white Adirondack-style chaise lounges facing the pool. The day was going to be hot; already the sun reflecting off the water was blinding. I shed my sweatshirt and shorts and put on my sunglasses, a cheap pair I'd picked up for driving. Never one to just jump in, I worked my way slowly down the wide Mexican tile steps. The water felt refreshing. Encouraged, I waded in until I was up to my chin, wondering how to begin. I tried hopping to get both feet off the bottom, paddling my arms as fast as I could, but I sunk like a bag of cement. Next, I tried pumping my legs bicycle-style while my arms flailed at the surface. But it was no use.

What was I doing wrong? I gripped the edge of the pool, kicking my feet up to the surface and then pushing off with my hands, but the second I let go, down my body sank. Though I tried not to dwell on how ridiculous my efforts must look, I did allow myself a quick glance up the hill to make sure nobody was watching from the house. Just then, Mr. Rathburn came whistling across the lawn, wearing only black swim trunks and aviator sunglasses. Before he reached the pool, there was time for me to thank heaven that he wasn't wearing a Speedo and to notice how muscular he was. Not that that was surprising; didn't he spend hours each day lifting weights? If I were a billionaire, maybe I'd be in good shape too.

Before I could collect my facial expression into something more casual, he was standing at the edge of the pool, hands on his hips, grinning down at me. "So you do own a bathing suit after all."

I shrugged, trying to look nonchalant. "You said you wanted me to learn to swim. But it's hopeless. I'm like a bag of rocks."

"You're never going to learn that way, struggling to keep your head above water. You have to relax, learn to trust the water, let yourself feel what it's like to go all the way under. You need to do the dead man's float."

I didn't like the sound of that.

"You don't have to do it in the deep end. You can try it right here in the shallow part, where your feet can touch bottom if you get worried." He loomed above me on the pool deck, arms crossed resolutely on his chest, which I noticed was hairless but for a soft tangle of black fur on his breastbone. I glanced down quickly, noticed his legs were covered with that same soft-looking hair, and turned my gaze to a more neutral object: my own white, goose-pimpled arms.

"I'm not a very relaxed person." As I said the words I realized they probably sounded like the world's biggest understatement.

"I can teach you," he said. And before I could respond, he was in the water beside me, an arm's length away. Had he ever stood that close to me before? A sudden shiver made me hug myself for warmth. "I used to be a lifeguard, believe it or not. Back in Wichita. I won't let you drown."

I remembered my mother trying to get me to swim, her hands

88

supporting me under my stomach while she exhorted me to let go of her neck, to flail my arms and kick. Would Mr. Rathburn touch me? The very thought brought blood to my cheeks; I was grateful for the protective wall of my sunglasses. At any rate, he crossed his arms again and took a step back to give me room.

"Start by putting your face in the water. Your feet don't even need to leave the ground. You'll have to take those glasses off, though." I handed them over reluctantly, took a deep breath, and dipped my face in. So far so good. "Now open your eyes. It's okay; the water won't sting."

I forced my eyes open and saw bubbles, the bright red, gold, and blue of the tiled pool bottom, and Mr. Rathburn's long legs tinted a bluish white by the water. Was this what I'd been so scared of? I kept my face underwater as long as my breath held out.

"See? Not so bad, right?" Through the water that streamed into my eyes, I could see him looking at me with something like concern. I nodded. "Are you ready for the next step?"

"That depends on what it is."

"Put your face in the water again, but this time let yourself relax. Your arms and legs will get lighter, and before you know it, you'll be floating. You won't even have to try."

Let myself relax? I wasn't sure I could, especially with Mr. Rathburn watching. But I followed his instructions, and, just as he'd predicted, I was floating as though I were weightless, the water gently rippling over and around me. I liked it so much — that feeling of drifting along, buoyant and free — that I did it again and again, and Mr. Rathburn watched with more patience than I had ever seen in him.

"What's next?" I asked when I finally surfaced.

"Haven't you had enough for one day? You just learned to float. That's a huge leap forward. Everything else will be a piece of cake." He hoisted himself up on the side of the pool and climbed out, and I felt a pang of disappointment. But then he returned, dragging a couple of enormous lime-green inflatable rafts. "How would you feel about getting on one of these?"

It took several tries, but I was able to clamber onto the raft from the highest of the steps leading into the pool. I spread out on my stomach. A moment later, his raft was beside mine. "If this doesn't relax you, nothing will," he said. "Short of Xanax." I allowed myself a glance over at him and caught his eye. "I'll have Linda bring us cocktails," he said.

"It's ten in the morning," I told him. "I have to pick Maddy up in a few hours. Besides, I'm underage."

"Oh, right," he said with a smile. "I forgot." Then he lowered his head onto the pillowy end of his raft and shut his eyes. I decided to do the same. For a long while the only sound was the gentle lapping of water against the pool's concrete lip. When I opened my eyes again, our rafts had drifted together. His eyes were shut, and for once I could study his face unobserved. He had a strong nose, dark brows, a square jaw, and a full lower lip. I had been right the other day: he wasn't classically handsome, but his features were appealing, full of character. I could even see why Linda thought he was sexy. Without meaning to, I glanced at his broad shoulders and the smooth, bronze skin of his back. Just then he stirred, and I looked quickly away, not wanting to be caught. That's when I noticed that our rafts had drifted to the center of the pool. I propped myself up on my elbows.

Mr. Rathburn opened his eyes. "Are you worried?"

I thought a second. The rafts seemed safe enough, and the side of the pool wasn't all that far away. "You were really a lifeguard?" I asked.

"The only normal job I've ever had," he said. "I worked at a country club near my house. I never had to save any lives, though. My main job was to flirt with the middle-aged housewives with too much time on their hands." He let his head drop back to the inflatable pillow. "If we drift into the deep end, I'll rescue you."

I shut my eyes again. The water rocked my raft soothingly.

"So the other night you wanted to know about Maddy's mother," he said, out of the blue.

"I did?" I couldn't recall asking, exactly, but I was curious. "Only if you don't mind telling me."

"It's not like the whole thing isn't on the public record," he said. "Didn't you see the stories, when you were sleuthing around on the Internet? The tabloids loved us to pieces. 'American Rock Aristocracy Meets Rising French Musical Star in a Transcontinental Romance.'"

"It sounds romantic," I said. "Were you happy?"

"I thought I was." He shifted, turning to face me. Our bobbing rafts were just inches apart. "Everybody kept saying we were the perfect couple, and I believed them for a while. I rented her an apartment on the Champs-Élysées, paid for everything she asked for — a Ferrari, designer dresses, personal trainer. I'd sold a couple

91

of my songs to the movies, and my greatest hits album was doing very well, so I was recovering from economic ruin. You'd think I'd have learned to be more careful with my money." He grabbed on to the nearest corner of my raft and paddled a bit to keep us from drifting away from the shallow end. "Anyway, it wasn't my money she wanted as much as my influence. Celine was dead set on breaking into the international market. She wanted a contract with my record label, and I was happy I could make it happen."

"Oh," I said. "She must have been grateful."

"You'd think," he said. He fell silent for several minutes, and just when I thought he'd dozed off, he spoke again. "I was on tour, and there was the usual temptation — the groupies, the love-struck fans — but I was on my best behavior. By then I was clean, completely off drugs, thinking I could start fresh."

I could feel my back starting to burn, so I turned, carefully, face side up. "Did Celine go on tour with you?"

"For a while, but she got bored just watching the action. She wanted to sing backup, and I let her on a few songs, but it wasn't enough. It killed her not to be the main attraction." He flipped over onto his back and tucked his hands behind his neck. "Soon she begged out, said she couldn't get a decent night's sleep in a hotel. She missed Paris. She was such a homebody she just couldn't cope with the travel. And I believed her, like an idiot."

"What happened?"

"The *National Enquirer* happened. They broke the story — 'Glittering Chanteuse Hooks Up with Handsome Gallic Leading Man.' Maybe you saw the article — and the pictures?"

Suddenly I recalled a photograph that had been widely published at the time: a distant shot of a French pop star clad in a white bikini and curled in the arms of a young, tanned actor, the two celebrities believing themselves alone on the pearly sands of a private beach. Maybe I had seen it in one of my mother's magazines.

"If you consumed pop culture like the rest of us plebes, you couldn't have missed it," he continued. Though his voice remained level, I thought I could detect a touch of agitation in it. "Those pictures were everywhere. Even worse, in an interview she forgot her agent's advice and started bragging. She'd been seeing her boyfriend, Jean Paul LeFevre — Can you believe that name? It's like a parody of a Latin lover in a *Saturday Night Live* skit, for God's sake — since before she and I had gotten together. Nothing like a good public humiliation to keep a guy humble," he concluded. "Good thing the media has a serious case of ADHD."

"What did you do after that?" I asked.

"What could I do? I had a tour to finish. I threw myself into it. I'd stopped drugging and drinking myself stupid by then, but I wasn't above getting…well…*attention* from groupies. I messed around. A lot. Took a lot of stupid chances."

"Mr. Rathburn?" I interrupted.

He lifted up his sunglasses and looked at me.

"Have you been tested?" I really was concerned for him.

He looked startled. Then he burst out laughing. "I don't mean to laugh. It's very kind — very typical of you, I guess — to be worried about me." He reached a hand toward me; it hovered for a moment as though it might land on my shoulder, but then he appeared to think better of it. I felt a momentary chill of regret. I wouldn't have minded a quick pat on the shoulder between friends.

"No worries," he said. "I've got the best doctors money can buy, and through sheer dumb luck…Well, I'm still here, aren't I?"

"You were lucky."

"Yes, well, yes and no. A few months later, I got a call from Celine's lawyer, telling me that she was pregnant with my child. She wanted child support, of course, but she didn't even have the courage to tell me herself. I paid her off—a ridiculous amount—and in exchange she promised I would never have to see her or it."

"But that baby was Maddy, wasn't it?" It hurt me to hear him call her "it."

He nodded. "I wasn't at all convinced she was mine. She's a little carbon copy of her mother, without a single drop of me in her."

"Didn't you have a paternity test?"

He nodded. "I'm Maddy's father all right, but you'd never know it to look at her."

"But how did she come to live with you?"

"That was more red meat for the tabloids. You didn't read about it before you got here?"

"I ran out of time," I told him. "There was so much to go through."

"Celine was pretty much the kind of mother you'd expect. To her, Maddy was just a siphon for extracting cash from my wallet. There was an au pair for a while. Then Celine's career tanked, she blew all my support money, and she fired the au pair. But instead of watching the baby herself, she kept going out to parties at night and left Maddy alone in hotels."

94

"Maddy said something about that," I told him. "She remembers."

"Eventually the tabloids found out, and I was able to get full custody. I may not have cared anything about Celine's baby, but I wasn't going to let the little thing die of neglect."

"And you love her now?" I asked.

"I don't know shit — sorry — about children," he responded. "That's why I hired you. But I do love her. You can see that, right?"

I nodded. "And she loves you. All children love their parents, no matter how…"

"Self-absorbed, neglectful, absent?"

"When you do spend time with Maddy, you're good with her," I said. "She can tell you love her."

"I know how to be the nice daddy," he said. "The one with the presents. It's the other part of it — the discipline — I'm lousy at."

I trailed a hand in the water. "You can learn."

"With the right teacher, I could," he said. "I'm not as hopeless as I probably —" He stopped midsentence and pushed up onto his elbows. "You're getting a sunburn," he said. "Across your nose. And on your shoulders."

I sat up, the raft lurching beneath me. The sun was high in the sky. "Maddy!" I squinted in the direction of the pool house, hoping to find a clock on the wall, but there was none. "It must be noon, at least. I'm so sorry, Mr. Rathburn. I'll be late picking her up."

"I'm the one who lured you out here and distracted you with my story," he said. "Come on, let's get dry." He slipped from his raft into the water and began towing me toward shore. "I'll call and let

95

them know you're running a little late. They won't give you a hard time."

Back on the deck, I zipped up my sweatshirt and tugged on my shorts, which were instantly soaking wet.

"Dammit, I left my cell phone back at the house." Mr. Rathburn draped the towel over his shoulders. "Here's a thought. Why don't you throw on some dry clothes, and I'll drive you there myself?"

He did, in a silver Maserati convertible with the top down. Maddy looked thrilled when he strode into the classroom and scooped her up in his arms, and her teachers were all politeness and smiles. "No need to apologize," one of them assured him. "We know how busy you must be."

Mr. Rathburn turned and winked at me, then shook her hand. "Miss Matthews," he said to her. "Maddy just loves you to pieces, and I can see why." He held her hand a moment longer than was strictly necessary, and she turned scarlet. She even giggled.

Instead of driving back to the estate, Mr. Rathburn brought us to a little seafood restaurant in the next town; it overlooked a river that smelled of salt. Between the parking lot and the restaurant, he was stopped by a burly man in a baseball cap. The man strode over. "Nico?" he said, hesitating. "Nico Rathburn? I'm sorry to disturb you. I know you must get this all the time. But I just have to thank you. For how much your music has meant to me — since I was twenty-five, the year my mother died…"

I led Maddy to the lobby and distracted her with crayons and a color-by-number place mat while we waited for her father to catch up. It took a while. When he entered the lobby, I saw the pretty young hostess's jaw drop. Then she looked me up and down, from my cheap sneakers to my still-damp hair. I read something like disbelief in her eyes just before they took on a more professional, neutral expression.

Mr. Rathburn beckoned her to the side, and they spoke in hushed tones. When they returned, she led us to an empty dining room. "No one will disturb you here," she told him. "Your waitress will be in shortly."

"I...*love*...restaurants," Maddy was singing softly to a tune of her own invention. "I...*love*...restaurants. Why don't we eat out more, Daddy?"

He put a hand on her head. "I didn't know you liked to eat out so much."

"Read me the menu." Maddy thrust her place mat at me. "Please, Miss Jane."

"Since you said please," I told her.

To tell the truth, I wasn't all that used to eating in restaurants myself. The dining room had large plate-glass windows overlooking the sparkling river. Mr. Rathburn ordered a Shirley Temple with extra cherries for Maddy and a bottle of Pinot Grigio for the table.

"You'll have some too?" he asked me. "You're with me; they won't card you."

"Ice water, please," I told the politest waitress I had ever been served by. The items on the menu were expensive. I ordered a bowl of clam chowder.

"You can have anything you want," Mr. Rathburn told me. "Lobster? Clams on the half shell?"

"Chowder is fine," I told the waitress.

Lunch passed quickly, in a whirl of silverware and white linen. Maddy was so happy to have her father's full attention that she prattled on about the morning's activities and about a field trip to an aquarium that would be coming up in a few weeks. Mr. Rathburn listened patiently. Once his cell phone rang, and he silenced it. And when Maddy pleaded for a second dessert, he told her no. She looked surprised and continued to whine for a few moments more. But he held firm, and she was smiling and holding his hand by the time we left the restaurant. Though the car ride back to the estate was only twenty minutes, she fell into a deep sleep before we were halfway home.

"How did I do?" Mr. Rathburn asked me.

"So far, so good," I told him.

Rather than wake Maddy, he carried her inside. Lucia met us at the door and looked at us with some surprise. "I've been trying to reach you," she told him. "The proofs are here for you to look over. Mitch is waiting for you in your office."

"I'll be back in a minute," he told her, and he carried Maddy upstairs and laid her on the bed. I found an extra blanket in her drawer and spread it over her.

"Thank you," I whispered to him.

He shot me a crooked smile, then slipped off.

I sat awhile, watching Maddy as she slept. It was true — she didn't look like Mr. Rathburn in the slightest. *Poor little thing,* I thought. I dug out her favorite stuffed animals from the space between the bed and the wall and arranged them beside her pillow so they would be the first things she saw when she woke up. On some level, mustn't she miss her mother, even as neglectful as she was? And wasn't it likely she'd absorbed some of Mr. Rathburn's early ambivalence toward her or his anger toward her mother? I resolved to take even better care of her now that I knew her story.

Mr. Rathburn stayed out of sight for the rest of that afternoon and evening. He again had a slew of dinner guests. In the kitchen, the cook was stuffing something elaborate into a pastry crust. The meal smelled wonderful, and the laughter from the dining room was enviable. But I didn't mind sitting with Maddy in the playroom, off at the fringes of Thornfield Park. As I helped her cut out paper dolls — books of them, purchased by Lucia by mail order, had just arrived — I thought back fondly to that morning, and the memory made me smile. I had felt trusted, even important. And though I wasn't quite important enough to Mr. Rathburn to be a part of his dinner party, I knew I was serving him and Maddy in a more essential way. I was right at the center of their lives, and I'd never felt at the center of anyone's life before. These thoughts warmed me, making the rest of the evening pass quickly. After Maddy fell asleep, I retired to my room and, working from a picture in the liner notes of his second album, did a quick sketch of Mr. Rathburn. It came out pretty well, so I added color, careful to capture the exact pale pink of his lip, the peculiar smoke-gray color of his eyes. When the painting had dried — *Not bad!* I thought to myself — I borrowed some thumbtacks from Lucia, who was packing her briefcase to go home for the night, and pinned up the image above my desk. All along the wall, I hung the paintings I had done since coming to Thornfield Park. Lucia had told me I could decorate the room as I liked. Since I could be here for a while, I might as well make it my own.

That night, as I waited for sleep, the skin on my shoulders and back tingling with sunburn, I thought of Mr. Rathburn floating beside me in the pool, his hand moving toward my shoulder as though it might come to rest there. I even thought of things I could tell him when I saw him next — precocious things Maddy had said or done. I felt the warmth of my blanket traveling from the tips of my toes up through my legs, spreading through my torso until even the tips of my fingers tingled with it. Just as I was relaxing into a delicious slumber, I was struck by an unexpected thought. Mr. Rathburn would be leaving soon; he was planning a tour. Mitch had been booking dates for shows across America and Europe. The thought of the house returning to its prior state of quiet made me suddenly sad. I tried to think back to what Lucia had told me about the tour — would it really last from fall through next summer? That seemed like such a long time.

After that, I tossed and turned. I may have slept a bit, but my mind was churning. And then — it might have been minutes or hours later — I startled awake to the sound of a faint murmur coming from the room just above mine, which until then had been unoccupied and silent. It didn't seem like a conversation. It was a single voice, babbling. I couldn't make out any words. I sat up in bed and listened more intently, and the noise stopped abruptly.

I waited awhile longer, still listening, but the house was silent. There was nothing to do but sleep. I lay back on the pillow, but my heart beat anxiously. Far down the hall, the clock struck two. Just then, I heard a sound, a different one, this time much closer. It seemed as though my bedroom door had been touched, as if fingers had brushed it as someone groped down the hallway.

"Who is it?" I said into my dark room. Nobody answered. I froze in place, too frightened to even click on the light.

Then I realized the sound might have been Copilot. He almost always slept in Mr. Rathburn's room, but occasionally he nosed his way out and wandered the house, finding his way back to the rug in front of the living room fireplace. Of course, it must have been him, bumping against the door, trying to find a bed to sleep on. The thought calmed me a little.

Once again, the house was silent, and I felt myself drifting back to sleep. I had just started dreaming when another sound startled me awake. This time it was a laugh — low, suppressed, and deep — that seemed to be coming through the keyhole of my bedroom door. I bolted upright. The room was pitch-dark; the only light would have come in between the slats of the window blinds, but tonight there was no moon. I sat perfectly still, waiting for my eyes to adjust. Had I dreamed that laugh? Had my sleeping mind taken a distant sound — a loon's cry, maybe? — and distorted it?

"Is somebody there?" I whispered, and heard a floorboard creak just outside my door. Then I noticed something that made my heart pound even faster — a faint aroma of sulfur. I switched on the light, crept to the door, and yanked it open. On the carpet, at the top of the stairs, I saw a match smoldering. The air was thick with smoke, but the blue billows seemed to be coming from Mr. Rathburn's wing, on the opposite side of the house. Smoke alarms began screeching all over the house. Without thinking, I ran toward the source of the smoke. I felt my way to the last door on

Mr. Rathburn's wing and pounded on it. No answer. What if it was locked? But it wasn't. I pushed it open.

Tongues of flame licked the ceiling inside Mr. Rathburn's dressing room. Beyond that, not twenty feet away, practically in the middle of it all, he lay stretched out, asleep on his high four-post bed. Or maybe he was unconscious?

"Wake up! Wake up!" I screamed. He murmured and rolled over. I didn't have a moment to waste. The heat was intense, unbearable. Flames shot out viciously, coming dangerously close to the drapes that ran around the perimeter of the room. *All of Mr. Rathburn's expensive clothes must be ruined*, I thought, though that was the last thing I should have been worried about. I remembered how in grade school I'd learned to stop, drop to the floor, and crawl under the smoke, but who had time for that? I grabbed Mr. Rathburn's arm and tried to pull him up, but he was dead weight. I needed to wake him somehow. I took a glass of water from his bedside table and splashed the water on his face. While he sputtered, I noticed a bathroom just beyond the bed. I tore the towels off the rack and soaked them in water, then ran back to the dressing room's open door and tossed them into the heart of the flame. In a trunk at the foot of the bed, I found a heavy blanket that I used to pound out the rest of the fire. By then, Mr. Rathburn was wide-awake. Though the smoke obscured him, I could hear him swearing violently. "What the fuck?" he said once, twice.

"There's been a fire," I told him. "Come on. Get up." The smoke alarms were still shrieking all around us. I groped along the wall for a light switch and flipped it on.

"Jane? Is that you?" He didn't seem quite alert yet.

"Yes. You have to get up right now." My voice sounded strange, high-pitched with barely contained hysteria. "This fire wasn't an accident. The person who set it may still be in the house." I helped him to his feet. "But first — Maddy. I'll be right back."

Amber and Linda hesitated at the bottom of the stairs, waiting for word from Mr. Rathburn. I ran past, ignoring their questions, to Maddy's room. She was awake, screaming, scared out of her wits by the smoke alarms. I scooped her up and ran. "It's okay, everything's okay," I reassured her, then carried her downstairs and deposited her with an astonished-looking Linda. "Could you watch her?" I asked. "Don't leave her alone for a second. Take her to the living room and wait for me there." I had reservations about leaving Maddy with anyone; in my eyes they all were suspect. But I had a very strong instinct about who had started the fire, and I noticed that Brenda was nowhere to be seen. "I'll be right back."

Mr. Rathburn was on the phone when I reached him. He'd thrown open the windows of his room, and the smoke had begun to clear. "A false alarm," I heard him say. "You can call back the fire truck. No, no. We're all fine. Sorry to have bothered you." He put the phone back into its cradle.

"Don't you want the fire department to come and investigate?" I asked, astonished. "It was arson. I'm sure of it." I told him about the match.

Mr. Rathburn blinked at me, his face and hands smudged with soot. He seemed to be collecting his thoughts.

"That's all I would need," he said finally. "The papers would pick it up, and the local news. Maybe even the national news. I'm already this character to them." He rubbed his eyelids with the backs of his hands, spreading more soot across his face. "Is Maddy okay? Is everyone accounted for?"

"They're all downstairs," I told him. "Everyone except Brenda."

He thought a moment. "Go to Maddy. Tell everyone I'm okay. You can tell them I left a lit candle in my dressing room, and my shirts caught on fire. Tell them I was meditating or something like that. Do you think you can? Lie on my behalf, I mean. I wouldn't ask you to if it wasn't important. Can you make it convincing?"

I nodded.

"I have to check out the third floor. I want you to send everyone back to bed. Then take Maddy to her room; get her back to sleep. Stay in there with her. And don't leave until I come to get you."

He went. I switched off the bedroom light and ran to retrieve Maddy, detouring on my way only to pick up the match and conceal it in my palm. The staff readily accepted my explanation of the fire. I didn't have to try very hard to sell the story, and they seemed eager to get back to sleep. I was relieved; I'd never been a convincing liar.

Maddy, though, was full of questions. "Is Daddy okay? What's meditation? Is the house always going to smell? Can I go see him?" I answered her as noncommittally as I could and made her lie back down. In her little pink-and-blue tiled bathroom, I flushed the match out of sight and scrubbed the soot from my face and hands. On my knees beside Maddy's bathtub, I washed the acrid smoke out of my hair with her bubble-gum-scented shampoo. My night-gown was ruined, streaked with black smoke, but there was nothing I could do about that now. By the time I'd neatened myself up, she was snoring gently. I watched her from the white rocking chair beside her bed. A very long time passed.

Finally, there was a soft knock at Maddy's door. I inhaled sharply. What if it wasn't Mr. Rathburn? But then I heard his voice whispering urgently, "Jane? Jane?" I opened the door to find him looking pale and very unhappy. Then he beckoned me out into the hallway and shut the door behind me.

"Did you find out who set the fire?" I whispered.

He nodded. "It's all taken care of. There's nothing more to worry about." I waited for him to say more, but he was silent.

"Who would want to burn your clothes?" I asked him. "They must have been trying to kill you.... They almost did."

Instead of answering, he stood a minute with his arms folded, staring down at the rug. Then, he asked, in a whisper, "Did you see anything between your room and mine?"

"Just the match I told you about," I told him. "I got rid of it."

"Good. Did you hear anything?"

"A laugh. It seemed to come from the third floor. And then fingers brushing my door. The laugh sounded like Brenda." *Come to think of it, what had she been doing on my wing of the house?* I pushed the question out of my mind for now.

"Brenda," he repeated. "You guessed it. You've probably noticed that she's peculiar. But I've dealt with her, so everything should be fine from now on." He wiped some of the soot from his eyes. "Did the others believe our story? About the candle?"

"I think so," I said. "They seemed to."

"I'm glad it was you who came to help me. You won't talk about this with anyone, will you?"

I promised that I wouldn't. "But where will you sleep tonight?"

"I'm not so high and mighty that I can't spend the night on the living room couch," he told me. "What's left of the night, that is."

"Okay, then. Good night." I turned to go.

"Wait." He seemed surprised. "Are you really going to leave me so quickly?"

"I thought you wanted to get some sleep."

"But not without saying good night. Not without thanking you." He looked at me, urgency in his eyes. "Jane, you saved my life tonight."

"It was nothing," I told him.

"Nothing?" He brushed back his hair. "You can be a bit strange, you know that?"

I nodded. I did know.

"At least give me a hug, Jane." He opened up his arms, and I stepped into them. "A hug between friends." For a moment, I felt the warmth of his body and the strength of his arms clasped around me. When he released me I took a step back so I could see him better. "If anyone had to save my life, I'm glad it was you." His eyes were softer, darker, than I'd seen them before.

"I'm glad I could help."

"The minute I saw you, I knew you were different. That you'd do me good in some way. I knew…" — he paused — "I knew we'd be friends."

My heart skipped a beat. Unsure of what I should do or say, I took another step back. "Well. Good night, Mr. Rathburn."

"Even now, you won't call me Nico?" A flicker of an emotion I couldn't identify crossed his face, but then he surprised me by laughing. "Go get some sleep, Jane."

When I was back in bed, my thoughts kept racing. One moment I was swept aloft by a wave of happiness, the next grabbed by an undertow of foreboding. What new and strange events would the next day bring? I could barely shut my eyes for wondering.

CHAPTER 8

In the morning, I drove Maddy to a playdate across town, but even though I more or less had the day off, I returned straight home to Thornfield Park, unsure what to do next. I hoped to see Mr. Rathburn, but I didn't know what I should say to him or how I should act, especially after what had happened the night before. And I worried that Lucia and the others would ask me questions about my part in the postfire tumult. What would I say to them? I'd never had such a big secret to keep before. I decided that I would answer their questions — and Maddy's — simply, in as few words as possible. With Maddy, this tactic worked well. She seemed satisfied with the explanation I had given her, and more than anything else she was excited because she'd been up in the middle of the night.

As it turned out, I didn't run into Mr. Rathburn that morning. He had gotten up unusually early and had already gone out somewhere. Something unsettling happened with the others, though. I got back to the house, punched in the security code, hung the car key on its hook, and slipped into the kitchen for coffee and toast. There I bumped into Lucia, who looked a bit frazzled, her reading glasses pushed back absently on her head. "I hear you had some excitement here last night," she said.

"Yes. There was a fire."

She poured herself a mug of coffee, stirred in a packet of Sweet'n Low, and headed back to her office, saying over her shoulder, "I know. Who do you think has to order a whole new wardrobe for Nico and call in the carpet cleaners?"

Did I detect blame in her voice? But what sense would that have made?

As for Amber and Linda, neither said hello to me when I passed by the laundry room, where they were folding towels. They had been chatting, as usual, but when they saw me, they stopped talking. It was almost as though they suspected me of something. Most startling of all was the moment, midmorning, when I returned to the kitchen with my coffee cup and happened to see, as I walked by the laundry room, Brenda loading clothes into the washer.

Our eyes met. I had thought Mr. Rathburn fired her early that morning, but there she was: her eyes a bit puffy, her plain, broad face shiny as if it had been vigorously scrubbed, her dull hair pulled tightly back. She looked the way she always did, not the least bit guilty. "Good morning, Miss Jane," she said in her usual matter-of-fact way, and poured blue laundry detergent into a measuring cup.

This was almost more than I could take. "Good morning, Brenda," I said. "Last night was something else, wasn't it?"

"Last night?" Her tone was casual. "You mean the fire in Nico's dressing room?"

"Of course. I didn't see you downstairs. Didn't the smoke alarm wake you?" I looked her straight in the eye.

"I'm a very heavy sleeper." She didn't glance away. "Slept right through all the commotion." She wiped her hands on the towel slung over her arm.

But I wasn't about to be brushed off that easily. "I thought I heard a laugh last night just before I smelled smoke. Was that you?"

"A laugh?" She didn't look or sound surprised at the question. "Why would you think it was me?"

"It sounded like you."

"Maybe the little girl was watching television past her bed-time," she said.

"She was sound asleep. It was two in the morning."

Brenda shrugged. "You never know with children."

I decided to take another tack. "What caused the fire?" I asked. "Does anybody know?"

She reached for the fabric softener. "I heard Nico was meditating in his dressing room before bedtime. He must have forgotten about the candle and left it burning. He says he's taken up meditation lately, to relax."

It seemed very strange to hear her parroting the official story to me, but then it was no stranger than seeing her still here in the house, pouring fabric softener into the washing machine and shutting its door with a firm hand.

I said nothing. It dawned on me that if she knew I suspected her of starting the fire, she might try to hurt me next.

111

"When you heard someone laughing, didn't you open your door to see who it was?" Her question surprised me. Was she trying to catch me off guard?

"No," I said. "I checked my door to make sure it was locked."

"You mean you don't always lock it at night before you go to sleep?" She asked the question casually, but she seemed to watch me closely.

"From now on I will."

"That's a very good idea." Her voice was flat and emotionless. "Even with guards and an alarm system, I always say you can't be too careful." At that, she turned and walked away.

On my walk that morning, I revisited the pine grove where Mr. Rathburn and I had walked together two days before. What a long time ago it seemed. I couldn't sketch or paint; I was too preoccupied trying to understand last night's bizarre events and Brenda's continued presence at Thornfield Park. Mr. Rathburn could have had her arrested, or at the very least he could have sent her packing. Instead, he'd done neither. But why? Did she have something on him? Some kind of knowledge she could use to blackmail him? Was he worried she might tell his secrets to the press? If so, what sort of secrets did he have left to tell?

Or could he have some kind of attachment to Brenda? If she were young and attractive that might have made some sense. Still, some men like older women. I supposed it was possible that they had been involved once, though it was hard to imagine that drab, flat-footed Brenda had ever been even remotely pretty.

I'm not pretty, I reminded myself. *Still, Mr. Rathburn seems to like having me around.* I remembered the look in his eyes last night, the warmth of his voice, his enthusiastic hug, and noticed that my heart was racing. *Calm down*, I admonished myself. *Stop imagining things that can't possibly be true.* I turned back toward the house.

That afternoon, I couldn't concentrate enough to read or draw, and I couldn't stand the thought of hiding in my bedroom. Instead, I haunted the main wing, reading the inscriptions under the gold and platinum records in the hallway, picking up magazines and putting them back down again, poking my head into the refrigerator even though I was far too agitated to eat. As the day wore on, I grew increasingly eager to see Mr. Rathburn, if only to gauge his attitude toward me. Would he look at me the way he had last night? I was sitting in the breakfast room, staring out the window at the pond, when Lucia walked in.

"You look different," she said to me. "Flushed. Are you feeling okay? Are you still shaken up about last night?" She took the chair beside me and set down a cup of yogurt and a spoon.

"I'm fine," I said. "Just overtired."

"Huh" — she stirred her yogurt — "aren't we all? At least I can have lunch away from my desk today, since Nico's out of town."

"He is?"

"Didn't you know? He went back to New York to tape some more TV appearances. He'll be on *Letterman* this week."

"On the spur of the moment?"

"No, of course not. The Letterman thing has been booked for a while. Sorry I didn't mention it; it's just been floating out in the air. I thought you knew."

"How long will he be gone?"

"He didn't say. He's got some other business to take care of in the city, he said. And be on your guard. Whenever he does get back here, it'll be sheer chaos. He's not coming back alone. The rehearsal show has been scheduled for three weeks from today. The whole band's going to descend on us, some of them with their lady friends. I have to start getting the guesthouse in order."

"They'll all be staying here?" I was having trouble taking in so much news at once.

"Nico likes it that way. Before the tour, he likes to do what he calls 'a little intense male bonding.' Seems crazy to me. They'll be in each other's pockets the whole tour, but by now I guess he knows what he's doing." She sighed. "And even if he doesn't, we're in the sidecar."

I hardly knew how I felt about any of this.

"Oh, and when they do get here, you might want to sharpen up your image a little," Lucia continued. "Wear your best clothes. That photographer's coming with them. You know, Bianca Ingram? She's doing a spread on Nico for GQ, and she wants to capture the beast in his natural habitat. Those were her words."

I thought back to the photo shoot. Had it really been only three days ago? And I tried to remember Bianca Ingram. All I could recall was her elegance, her glossy dark hair, her diaphanous scarf, and her laughter floating into the breakfast room with Mr. Rathburn's.

"I don't have much in the way of nice clothes," I said. "Besides, I'm sure she won't want to take pictures of me."

Lucia rolled her eyes. "She'll be shooting all of us. I doubt you or I will wind up in any of the shots chosen for the article, but you never know. At the very least, Maddy should look her best. She'll wind up in the spread for sure."

"Bianca Ingram ... That name is familiar."

"Of course it is. She's photographed just about everyone on the A-list — politicians, musicians, movie stars, you name it — and some of their glitz must have rubbed off on her. Every other week her face is in *People* or *InStyle*. The media like to follow her around and speculate about her love life. She supposedly has a habit of sleeping with her subjects, so it could get interesting around here."

Why did this news distress me? I said nothing, and Lucia disappeared for a moment, then returned with a bottle of mineral water and two glasses. "Want some?"

The water tasted good; I hadn't realized how thirsty I was. "Had she photographed Nico before the other day?"

"No, and she's been after the chance for quite a while now. She was thrilled when he called her to do the tour program. She told Mitch she's had a crush on Nico since she was a teenager."

"And will she stay in the guesthouse with the band?"

"Lord, no," Lucia said. "It'll be a real boys' club in there. The guys aren't as wild as they used to be, but they still like to live it up from time to time. The last thing we'd need is a photographer documenting their every move. She'll stay in an empty room in Mr. Rathburn's wing."

"And how long will the photo shoot last?" I asked. "How long will she be here?"

"You ask so many questions. As long as it takes, I guess."

*   *   *

115

After I put Maddy to bed that night, I let myself into Lucia's office to use her computer. I'd made up my mind to research Bianca Ingram. I had a vague impression of her glamour, and I wanted to see how reality matched up with my recollections. As it turned out, my memory had sold her short. Online, I was able to locate more photographs *of* Bianca Ingram than photographs *by* her.

"But will they click? Celebrity photographer steps out with leading man" read the caption below a photograph of a laughing Bianca, her white teeth flawless, her long hair sailing behind her as she walked in steep heels down the red carpet, hand in hand with a blond man in a tuxedo. Her low-cut, violet gown emphasized her full breasts and narrow waist; a high slit revealed a long, bare leg. A choker of diamonds circled her throat.

"Despite It All, I'm Lonely" read the headline of an interview in which Bianca spoke of her wish to have a simple life in the country with a husband and some children. "It hasn't worked out for me yet," she was quoted as saying, "but I have faith that one day I'll find what I'm looking for." The story was accompanied by pictures of Bianca in jeans and a tight black T-shirt, an expensive-looking camera hanging from her neck. Her large dark eyes were fringed with thick lashes.

I searched for and read article after article about Bianca, until my eyes felt dry and gritty. Then I searched online for Mr. Rathburn and clicked on a snapshot of him playing an acoustic guitar — now I recognized it as one of his favorites; I often saw it leaning against his armchair — lips parted and eyes half-closed in what looked like deep pleasure. I studied the image awhile and made myself imagine Bianca Ingram and Mr. Rathburn out together in public, emerging from a limousine to walk the red carpet, two rich, famous, glamorous people who were made for each other — and who were a species apart from someone like me.

You idiot, I berated myself. What on earth had I been thinking? I'd been living in a fantasyland for the past few days. No, if I was completely honest with myself, I hadn't been my usual, sensible self since I'd met Mr. Rathburn and he had spoken to me with interest and kindness.

He's pleasant to his employees; he lets them call him by his first name, I reminded myself. *Just because he talks to you doesn't mean he thinks of you as an equal. He's being a good boss, nothing more.*

Back in my room, I took down the sketch I had done of Mr. Rathburn, crumpled it up, and threw it into my wastepaper basket. Then I made myself look unflinchingly into the mirror behind my door. *Not only is Bianca Ingram beautiful; she's worldly and successful. And you're a nobody,* I silently told myself. *No boy has ever shown the slightest bit of interest in you, and now, just because Mr. Rathburn is kind to you, you think he could have feelings for you? When he could have Bianca Ingram — or any other woman?*

I promised myself that from that moment on, whenever I yearned for Mr. Rathburn or thought of him with the slightest bit of hope, I would find the closest mirror and stare down my own reflection — dull brown hair, overlarge forehead, ordinary green eyes with sparse lashes, stubborn chin, flat chest, and narrow hips — until reason trumped fantasy.

CHAPTER 9

A week passed with no word from Mr. Rathburn. A pall settled over the estate, as though nothing interesting could possibly happen while he was gone. On the night of his second day away, I sat by myself in Maddy's playroom to watch him trading quips with David Letterman on late-night TV. On the third day, several cartons arrived special delivery. It was Mr. Rathburn's new CD. An exultant Lucia handed out copies to the staff. "These will be in stores by midnight tomorrow," she said. "Doesn't he look fantastic?" The cover featured Nico all in black, seated on a low stone wall, staring moodily into the distance, acoustic guitar in hand.

That day while Maddy took her after-lunch quiet time, I stretched out on my bed, headphones on, listening to the new CD for clues, for insight into the personality that had written the words and music. Mr. Rathburn's voice, which once had struck me as abrasive, now sounded expressive and full of character, and I realized with some surprise that I had grown to like his music. I went back and borrowed his earlier albums and noticed wit and wordplay I'd been deaf to before. A few listens later, I was hooked. His songs played in my head as I pushed Maddy on her swing, as I spread peanut butter on bread for her sandwich, as I tried to fall asleep at night. I hadn't meant to become a fan, but there it was.

Throughout the day and especially at bedtime, Maddy would ask when her father would be back, and of course I had no answer to give her. Then, when he had been gone eight days, Lucia received a call. "They'll be here in less than twenty-four hours," she complained to me. "You'd think Nico would have given me more notice. Walter is going to have conniptions. Is Lonnie still a vegan? These trendy people. Remind me to call his personal assistant this afternoon."

I wanted to ask all kinds of questions, to get a sense of the personalities that would soon descend on Thornfield Park, but Lucia didn't have a moment to spare as she pushed to get the guest-house ready for its occupants. First she made a long to-do list. "Am I forgetting anything?" she kept asking. "Jane, can you help me out? I need you to make some phone calls." That day I pitched in by booking a waitstaff for the next night's dinner and polishing silverware. I picked the garden's most splendid sunflowers and arranged them in an enormous vase in the entryway. I drove into town to pick up Mr. Rathburn's dry cleaning.

Lucia's nervous energy proved contagious. Unable to fall asleep that night, I restlessly reviewed the contents of my closet. Lucia had told me that I should dress my best, but what did that mean for an on-duty nanny? Other than my denim skirts and oxford blouses, I had a peach-colored sundress I'd worn to a wedding a couple of summers before, but surely it was too nice to wear while I chased Maddy from room to room and sat with her on the floor. And at the back of the closet, half-forgotten, hung the clothes I'd worn to my parents' funeral — a simple black skirt and a white, scoop-necked shirt. A wave of sadness washed over me when I pulled the hanger out into the light, but I told myself that they were just clothes. Unlike the rest of my wardrobe, they looked almost new. With my pearl earrings and black ballerina flats, they would have to do. Earlier I had laid out a designer ensemble for Maddy — a black pleated skirt and a red plaid blouse, one of the few nonpink outfits in her extensive wardrobe. I hoped she wouldn't balk at the color.

Just before I shut off the light, I made myself look once again in the mirror to face my flaws. Still, despite my efforts to keep my expectations realistic, I was happy that I would see Mr. Rathburn tomorrow, no matter the circumstances.

The next morning, Thornfield Park went into a frenzy. I had thought the entire house was already pristine and well arranged, but it seemed I had been wrong. Amber and Linda ran from room to room, dusting, polishing silver candlestick holders, laying out fresh linens, and arranging bouquets of gladiolas from the garden. Midmorning, the cook arrived in the kitchen with a jumble of shopping bags. I helped him put the groceries away. After that, I pacified Lucia by listening as she enumerated the many tasks she still had to complete by dinnertime. Throughout the day, I noticed that only one employee was not pitching in on the whirlwind effort: Brenda. I saw her when she came into the kitchen to fix a ham sandwich that she promptly carried back upstairs; otherwise, she kept to herself. Nobody but me seemed to notice or care.

That afternoon, Maddy was far too excited to nap, and I worried she would be overtired and cranky by the time her father arrived. I watched her practice her routine from dance class over and over again; she wanted to put on a show for her father's friends. I hoped he would give her a chance to perform, even though I would rather have stayed in the playroom, out of the way until the visitors left.

When Maddy tired of dancing, she and I played game after game of Chutes and Ladders. I could still hear cleaning noises all around us. I was trying to teach her checkers — a game I thought she might be too young for but one she immediately took to — when I heard Amber and Linda in the hallway. As usual, they were gossiping, too excited to care who could hear them.

"I tell you, they're engaged," I heard Amber say somewhat shrilly. "I saw it in *Tattletale*."

"*Tattletale!*" Linda sounded scornful. "I can't believe you even read that rag. Wouldn't we be the first to know if he'd gotten engaged? Besides, he's only known her a few weeks."

"That doesn't mean anything. People jump into marriage all the time."

"And regret it. I hope you're wrong. That's all I can say."

"That's just 'cause you're warm for his form," Amber said. "Don't tell me you're not. At the very least, they're an item. You saw the photo in *Celeb World*."

"I might have," Linda said. By the sound of it, they were standing right outside the playroom door. I wished I could cover Maddy's ears or distract her with a toy, but it was too late. I could see she was listening intently. Linda continued. "One photo doesn't prove anything."

"Come on," Amber said. "The two of them at a restaurant, feeding each other? They looked pretty damn intimate to me."

"I suppose." Linda's voice sounded fainter; soon the two of them would turn the corner and be out of earshot. "It's not like he hasn't dated before. I've lost count of the women."

"There's something different about her."

"You think so?" Linda sounded incredulous.

"For one thing, she's not an airhead. She's one smart cookie," Amber replied. "The article said she speaks three languages and has a master's degree in art."

"I hope he gets a good prenup." Linda sniffed, and with that, they were gone.

Maddy looked up at me, her eyes large. "What's a prenup?" And then, when I didn't answer, "Were they talking about Daddy?"

"Maybe, but I wouldn't worry about it. I think they're letting their imaginations run away with them. Those magazines report all sorts of crazy things that aren't true."

"Why doesn't somebody punish the magazines for lying?" she asked me. It struck me as a sensible question.

"Maybe somebody will." For Maddy's sake as much as mine, I hoped the gossip magazines were wrong. "Here, help me put the games away, and we'll go find your new crayons. The big box."

By dinnertime, a trio of waiters had arrived. The housekeeping staff had changed out of their usual jeans and T-shirts into crisp black slacks and white blouses. Though their work was mostly done for the day, Lucia wanted them to be ready in case a visitor needed extra towels or something else. Lucia had changed into a fresh silk blouse and earrings, and Maddy and I were wearing the outfits I'd picked out the night before. A current of anxiety and excitement crackled in the air and grew stronger as 7 p.m., the estimated time of arrival, came and went.

Lucia's cell phone rang at 8:15. "They just passed the gatehouse," she announced to the assembled staff. "Brace yourselves." Maddy's bedtime was 9 p.m., but there was no way she would sleep before she'd greeted her father. Until she was called for, she and I stayed out of sight in the playroom. From the window, we watched three SUVs roll up the drive and stop near the front entrance to unload their passengers. I saw the guests emerge from the first two cars and recognized Mr. Rathburn's bandmates from their photographs on his CDs. The third and final SUV carried the man I most wanted to see — Mr. Rathburn. He stepped out first, his shirt a brilliant shade of blue I had never seen him wear before. It suited him. He went around to the other side of the car and held out a hand to Bianca Ingram. Her legs emerged first, then the rest of her. Though dressed casually in high-heeled boots, jeans, and a tight white tank top, she radiated opulence and style, as she had in the red carpet photo. I stepped away from the window and let the curtain fall into place. "You'll see them soon enough," I told Maddy.

In the foyer, they were a noisy bunch, the men joking with each other, the women laughing. From the playroom, I could hear their muffled voices. And then there was Mr. Rathburn's familiar, deep voice. "Why don't we pull out your figurines?" I asked Maddy, willing myself to be calm.

"Do we have to?" Maddy usually loved nothing more than to play with her precious collection, but she was on edge too. I thought about bringing her down to make cinnamon toast, but that would have required that we pass the newcomers, not to mention the risk of a mishap in the kitchen. Out of ideas, I popped *Sleeping Beauty* into the DVD player, and the video held her attention for a while.

Dinner came and went without our being called for. I could hear the chink of silverware against china and voices wafting from the dining room. I wasn't surprised when we weren't asked to join the party, and anyway Maddy and I had shared one of Walter's macaroni-and-cheese casseroles earlier. Still, I wanted to put her to bed, and I was disappointed that Mr. Rathburn hadn't called for her after having been away so long, especially when the crowd was gathered in the living room after dinner. I was just about to give up hope when I heard a knock on the door.

"Ready to go?" Lucia bent down and addressed Maddy. "The grown-ups want to see you now."

To my complete surprise, Maddy looked shy. She grabbed my hand. "Can Miss Jane come too?" she asked.

"You'll be fine," I told her. "Miss Lucia will bring you in."

Lucia folded her arms and gave me a stern look. "Nico specifically asked for you to join Maddy." I began explaining why that wasn't a good idea, but she cut me off. "No use protesting." She got behind me and gave me a little shove between my shoulder blades. "It's showtime."

Maddy grabbed my hand. Together we entered the living

room, where a collective "Ahh" went up from the women at the sight of Maddy. I noticed, though, that Bianca Ingram, who sat beside Mr. Rathburn near the fireplace, remained silent. I slipped into a chair in the darkest corner, hoping to see and not be seen. So far, so good; nobody seemed to notice me.

The eight of them were scattered about the room, settled in as if they planned to be there for hours. Several open bottles of Merlot and whiskey stood on a side table. Two of the men were deep in conversation — something about reverb. From my days studying Mr. Rathburn's CDs and liner notes, I recognized them as Mike Krikorian, the keyboard player, and Tom Rhodes, the bassist. Tom was the youngest in the group, with boyish features and a blond crew cut. Mike had curly black hair and the leathery skin of someone who'd led a fairly rough life. Neither seemed to notice Maddy, but the rest of the party was instantly drawn to her.

"Munchkin!" A man as big as a linebacker swooped down to lift Maddy in his arms; she shrieked with joy. "The last time I saw you, you were a toddler. You couldn't even say my name. You called me Deh-Deh. Remember?" This must be Dennis Everson, the band's rhythm guitarist, whose pale face and thick, black-framed glasses seemed an ironic twist on what rock-and-roll guitarists generally look like.

Maddy shook her head vehemently and clung to his neck until he put her down. Then she ran for Mr. Rathburn and threw herself against his knees. He bent over to help her onto his lap and kissed her hair. "Where's my gift?" she demanded. Everyone laughed.

"The child has her priorities straight," Bianca Ingram quipped. Mr. Rathburn grinned as though she'd said something very funny.

Though Maddy had practiced her dance routine for hours with surprising concentration that afternoon, she had no desire to leave Mr. Rathburn's lap.

"She looks just like Celine," a man said in a British accent. It was Lonnie Branch, the drummer, a handsome, dark-skinned man with a shaved head. The flame-haired woman perched on the arm of his chair leaned over to whisper something in his ear, and then the two of them laughed. I glanced at Mr. Rathburn; he was frowning.

"What a beautiful little girl," a woman with high cheekbones and extremely short platinum hair said. She edged up closer to Mr. Rathburn and bent over to get a better look at Maddy, who buried her head in her father's chest. "Don't be shy, sweetheart. Don't you want to come out and say hello?"

Maddy clung even tighter to her father's shirt. "Okay, okay," I just barely heard him mutter to her. "I've got you, cupcake." From my seat in the corner, I could watch him as long as I wanted. To see his face — his strong features, his dark brows, and those storm-colored eyes — was to instantly give in to the emotions I'd been trying so hard to ignore.

And what of his friends, the attractive, accomplished people who surrounded him, who drank his wine and laughed at each other's jokes? The women were beautiful, and the men all had the healthy glow that, I realized, must belong to the very wealthy, who can travel to sunny climes all year long, who eat only the best food and work out daily with personal trainers. All of them looked perfectly self-assured, knowing that wherever they happened to be was the center of the universe.

"Nico, who's that in the shadows over there?" a voice called out, startling me. It was Dennis, pointing in my direction. His words had the unpleasant effect of causing everyone in the room to turn and look in my direction. "Is this the new nanny you were telling us about?"

Maddy found her voice. "That's Miss Jane."

"Jane, let me introduce you," Mr. Rathburn said.

I had no choice but to stand up and step out of the shadows. "Hello," I said, nodding to the group. What else was I supposed to do?

"Jane Moore, my nanny," Mr. Rathburn said.

Bianca laughed, not pleasantly. "You mean *Maddy's* nanny." She gave Mr. Rathburn a playful shove. "Unless Daddy's messing where he shouldn't." Though she might have expected the others to laugh at her remark, only Mr. Rathburn did.

I took a step back and returned to my seat.

"No! No! Don't hide," Lonnie called out to me. "We don't bite."

"Come sit by me, sweetheart," Dennis said — a bit drunkenly, I thought — patting the empty sofa cushion beside him. "I'll take good care of you."

"I've seen how you take care of girls her age," Mr. Rathburn chided. "Jane, you're better off steering clear of that one. Why don't you put Maddy to bed and come back and join us?"

Maddy started to protest.

"It's at least an hour past your bedtime," Mr. Rathburn said. "Go with Miss Jane now, and in the morning I'll give you something special."

Although reluctant, Maddy let me lead her back to her room,

prepare her for bed, and tuck her in. "I wish all those people would go away," she said.

I knew better than to agree with her aloud. "You'll see more of your daddy tomorrow." I kissed her on the cheek, hoping I had spoken the truth. Then I sat beside her bed for a while, waiting for her to drift off, which didn't take long. I lingered there well after she fell asleep.

"Jane?" The static crackle of the intercom startled me. It was Lucia. "Nico wants to know if you've forgotten you were invited to come back to the living room?"

Invited? It seemed more like an order to me.

"I'll be right there," I told the intercom. Then I checked Maddy one more time to make sure she was still asleep, smoothed my hair in the bathroom mirror, and walked, as slowly as I could, back to the living room. I tried to slip into the same chair in the shadows.

"Oh, no you don't," Mr. Rathburn said. "Come sit with the adults for once."

Why me? I couldn't help wondering. Lucia hadn't been forced to join the group, and she was my superior.

"At least have some wine," Dennis called, waving me over. "You *are* over twenty-one, aren't you?" He wiggled his eyebrows at me, Groucho Marx–style. "If you're under eighteen, don't tell me. I want to maintain…what do they call it?"

"Plausible deniability?" Mike chimed in.

"She doesn't look a day over seventeen," Tom observed.

"Leave her alone, already," the blonde woman said, sounding annoyed. "Can't you see she doesn't want anything to do with you?" She crossed the room a bit unsteadily to give Tom a playful swat.

"Spoilsport," Lonnie said. "We all like to watch Dennis at work."

Then the redhead sidled up to me. "I'm Yvonne, sugar." She grabbed my hands and pulled me up. "You can't just sit by yourself like that. It's unhealthy. It's not right." Hands on hips, she addressed the crowd. "Nannies are people too, you fucking losers." Then she giggled. "Listen to me. I'm a crusader for nanny rights. Nanny liberation. Power to the people." She waved a fist in the air.

"I'm so *lonely*," Dennis called. "Come, have pity on the *lonely* guitar player."

The rest hooted at him.

"Jane, you realize these clowns won't leave you alone until you come out of the corner," Mr. Rathburn said. "You'd better join us."

Yvonne pulled me over to the couch and pressed my shoulders down until I was sitting, against my will, beside Dennis. To tell the truth, he scared me a little. I hadn't yet worked out how seriously I should take his big-bad-wolf routine.

"There." Yvonne gestured toward me with a flourish. "Liberation accomplished." She patted me on the head and collapsed into a chair across from me. "Mike, pour her a glass of wine. If it's okay with the Man, that is."

Mr. Rathburn scowled and waved her off. "She's underage. And as for you" — he turned to Dennis — "hands off. I can't have you corrupting my nanny."

Dennis raised both hands in the air. "Hokay, boss," he said. Then he leaned closer to me and whispered, "It's a routine, sweetheart. Don't look so scared. I'd never cross Nico."

Had I looked scared? I'd been trying hard not to let my face

130

register any emotion at all. I didn't know what to say, so I thanked him, and he smiled at me — not unkindly, I thought. Then he started trying to draw me out, and I decided I liked him after all. He asked me questions: Where was I from? How long had I been a nanny? I replied as best I could. I'd never been much good at small talk. Besides, I couldn't give him my full attention. A few feet away, Mr. Rathburn was chatting quietly with Bianca Ingram. Snatches of their conversation reached me. She was saying something about boarding school, how good it would be for Maddy as soon as she was old enough. I heard her say that being sent away from home was the best thing that had ever happened to her. Something about confidence and independence. And then something about puberty and sexual experimentation.

"Of course most of us outgrew it," she admitted, and Mr. Rathburn laughed.

"I'm glad to hear it," he said.

"But seriously," she said, leaning in so close that what she said next was lost to me. I heard her say the word *nanny* once and then again. Then her voice got louder. "How can you stand having live-in staff? I know it's a status thing, but what is it like? They never go away! Don't you feel … I don't know … *watched*?"

I could feel my cheeks get warm.

"You're flushed," Dennis said. "It must be hot in here."

"Yes, it must be," I said.

Yvonne and the blonde woman with the short, spiky hair approached us. "Dennis, you bad boy. Leave this poor little creature alone," the blonde said. "Can't you see she's too smart to fall for your sensitive-guy crap? You want to get her fired?" She beckoned to me. "We're going to rescue you, honey. Come with us. You need an intervention."

I looked over at Mr. Rathburn to see if I should go with them or not, but he was deep in conversation with Bianca. The bright manicured nails of her slender hand rested intimately on his forearm.

"Oh, he won't care," Yvonne said lightly. "Come on. We're bored to tears. Mike, Lonnie, and Tom will talk shop for hours and not even notice we're gone. Go on," she commanded Dennis. "Talk about guitars. You know you want to."

Dennis rose with a wry smile in my direction. I stood and followed the two women.

"Where's your room?" Yvonne asked me.

"The bathroom's better," the blonde asserted. "I'm Kitty." She held out a hand for me to shake. "Mike's wife."

What do the two of them want with me? I wondered.

Yvonne locked the bathroom door behind us. It was a large room, with an enormous mirror and a long white bench. "This will do," she said.

Kitty rummaged in her yellow crocodile handbag. "Oh, good. I brought my Nars with me." She pulled out a black compact with silver writing across it. "For a brunette, you're pale," she observed. "My shades should work on you."

I exhaled with relief.

"What did you think? We were bringing you in here to do a line?" Yvonne giggled. "Nico would never allow that in his house. Not since Maddy."

"Not that he'd have to know," Kitty said. She dug into her bag and brought out another round compact and a lipstick. "Sweetie, don't you wear makeup? You could use a little color." She knelt down in front of me and started rubbing sweet-smelling beige foundation across my face. "How do you ever expect to bag a husband and get out of the nanny biz?"

Yvonne giggled again. "Not everyone's interested in marrying up."

"Everyone should be," Kitty said matter-of-factly. "When's Lonnie gonna make an honest woman out of *you*?"

Yvonne shrugged. "After wife number four, he's a little bit shy."

Kitty rubbed the foundation deeper into my face. "Shit, I forgot my blush," she said. "Got any, Vonnie?" Yvonne looked in her purse and handed over another compact.

"Lonnie and Vonnie sitting in a tree," Kitty sang as she tickled my cheeks with a brush dipped in pink powder. "Think how wonderful 'Lonnie and Vonnie' would look on monogrammed bath towels."

"She's a Winter," Yvonne said. Then, to me, "That means you should wear deep, rich colors."

"That whole season thing is so dated," Kitty said. She was painting my lips, so I didn't respond. Besides, what could I have said? That I had never really cared about makeup? That was obvious. I remembered my mother squatting in front of me just as Kitty was doing now, the first and only time she'd tried making me up. The sweet, slightly floral fragrance of foundation and lipstick brought that afternoon back vividly. I'd enjoyed having my mother stand so close to me, and I liked the attention. A hopeful feeling had risen within me: maybe her makeup would transform me, make me pretty. And if I were pretty, maybe she'd love me as much as she loved Jenna.

But when she finished, she stepped back for a look at her handiwork, and I saw the disappointment in her eyes. "You inherited your father's face," she said. It clearly wasn't a compliment. "Right down to his eyelashes. It's a crime." She snapped her makeup case shut. "Life's so much harder for a..." — her voice trailed off — "for a girl like you. It's a good thing you don't care about these things," she concluded.

I was at a sensitive age then. Had I been thirteen? Fourteen? She thought she knew so much about me, but she didn't know anything. I'd felt tears welling up in my eyes, but I didn't want her pity. So instead of crying, I let a righteous bubble of anger burst in my chest.

"Stop trying to make me into Jenna," I shouted. Until that day, I don't think I'd even so much as raised my voice to her — or my father — in my whole life. Instead, I'd tried to please them with good grades and obedience. And, yes, she and my father had praised me for those things, but never with the warmth and enthusiasm that Jenna received for her shiny auburn hair, wide, white smile, excellent posture, and ballerina grace. "I'll never be what you want me to be." My voice rose; I heard anger in it, and a newfound defiance. "I'll never be your little Barbie doll. Why can't you love me the way I am?"

My mother's face blanched. "How dare you talk to me that way," she said under her breath, in a firm voice that frightened me more than yelling would have. "Nobody speaks to me like that."

She glared at me a moment, her nostrils flaring. Then she snatched up her makeup kit, wheeled around, and was gone.

From that moment on, she lavished even more attention on Jenna — her face, hair, and clothes — reserving her approval for Jenna's small acting triumphs and Mark's athletic achievements. Every now and then, she'd look at me and complain, "If only you'd take a little care with your appearance." But then she'd bite her lip and turn away. I can't remember her showing the least bit of interest in my grades or art after that. Soon I stopped playing the violin; I'd only been doing it for her. But I continued to work hard in school. I enjoyed school, and studying and writing term papers came easily to me.

When my paintings won first place in a high school competition, my father came to the show and afterward slipped a fifty-dollar bill into my hand — his way of saying he approved. My mother had begged off, saying she had to drive Jenna to an audition, which, I suppose, was the truth. (Had I really heard her say to him, "She's all yours"?) When I graduated high school with honors, my parents sat through the ceremony, but the only congratulation I could recall was my father's gentle kiss on my cheek, and, this time, a hundred-dollar bill. When I'd gotten into Sarah Lawrence, my parents didn't take me out to celebrate the way they had when Mark got a lacrosse scholarship to Ohio State and Jenna got into NYU. If Dad hadn't been away on a business trip then, I suppose the job would have fallen to him. Until the accident, they had dutifully paid my tuition, but they never asked how I was doing or said much, if anything, about the class reports I mailed home to them from the first semester.

"Don't look so sad, sweetie," Yvonne said, giving my shoulder a squeeze. I looked into her concerned, blue-rimmed eyes and felt a wave of irrational love and gratitude for this woman I hardly knew. "You'll look beautiful when Kitty gets through with you."

"Don't blink." Kitty applied two strokes of mascara to each of my eyes. I did my best to comply, willing the tears back. A moment later, I was fully composed. "There. Am I a genius or what?"

"You're a genius. Come on over here, Jane."

I joined Yvonne in front of the mirror. She pulled my hair out of its ponytail and fluffed it up on both sides of my face. "Look how pretty you are," she said softly.

I looked. My face in all that makeup looked alien. Not bad. Better than usual, in fact. But still, alien. I knew I could never walk around in the world like that.

"Your eyes are such a pretty green," Kitty told me. "See how a little eyeliner makes them pop?"

"Give us a smile," Yvonne said, and I did. My gratitude was genuine. How could it not be after all their kindness? "You have dimples!" she exclaimed. "Lucky."

"You should smile more often," Kitty told me. Then a mischievous look crossed her face. "Let's take her out and show her to Nico."

"But of course."

"No." I could feel myself panicking. "No, I can't."

"Why not?" Kitty asked, in the middle of reapplying lipstick to her own pouty lips.

"Honey, he's just your boss," Yvonne told me. "He's not your daddy. What's he gonna do? Order you to go back to your room

136

and wash that trashy makeup off your face, you little slut? No, wait a minute." She scrunched her face up adorably. "That's *my* daddy."

I thought a moment about Mr. Rathburn. *What might he think if he saw me this way? Would he think I was trying to be attractive for his sake? Would he — could he — think I really* was *attractive?* I hesitated.

"What's the harm?" Kitty asked. "Let's go knock him back on his ass."

I couldn't answer. Suddenly I remembered — how could I have forgotten? — Bianca Ingram, sitting beside Mr. Rathburn, her hand perched intimately on his arm. Her sleek, shiny head of hair, her deep black eyes, her full lips. Her expensive clothes, her long legs, her curves. No. I could never compete with that. It would be foolish to try.

"Thank you so much for all you've done for me," I told the women waiting in front of me. "I really appreciate your kindness...more than I can say. But I have a splitting headache." I said the words, and suddenly they were true; a throbbing started behind both my eyes. "I'd better go to bed."

Yvonne dug in her purse. "I've got some ibuprofen." She dropped two pills into my hand, closed my fingers around them, and kissed me on the cheek. "Enough fun for one day," she said to Kitty.

"Back to the damn guitar talk," Kitty said with a sigh. A moment later, they were gone.

CHAPTER 10

The next morning, the main house was quiet. I tried to wake Maddy for preschool as usual, but she fell back asleep three times. Finally, I propped her up and tried to dress her like a rag doll. When she dozed off again while I was tugging her shirt on over her head, I gave up and decided to let her stay home for the morning. At 11 a.m., she finally got up. I was buttering her toast when Mr. Rathburn stepped into the kitchen. He looked past me into the breakfast room, where Maddy was clinking her spoon against a row of half-filled water glasses, improvising a little song. When his eyes fell on me again, he looked annoyed, and I thought he might upbraid me for keeping Maddy home without permission, but then he surprised me. "Why did you leave the party last night when I asked you to stay? Kitty said you had a headache, but I know you too well to believe that. You were just looking for an excuse."

"I did have a headache," I told him, "*and* I was looking for an excuse."

He raised an eyebrow. His hair was damp, and he wore an aftershave that made me think of wood smoke and cloves. "Is that right?" he said. "You know you blew a chance to be seen with the rich and famous. Most people would have given their right arm to come to that party."

I mixed some cinnamon and sugar in a small bowl. "Be seen by whom, Mr. Rathburn?"

"Ingrate." He opened a cupboard and rummaged around, finally finding a box of Shredded Wheat. Then he opened another cupboard. "Who moved the bowls?"

I found them and handed him one.

"Thank you." He opened the silverware drawer. "What? Are all the spoons dirty?"

I fished one out of the dishwasher for him. "Walter put on some coffee," I said.

"Yes. Well." He poured milk into his bowl. "I won't disturb your precious solitude if I eat breakfast with you and Maddy, will I?"

"My solitude isn't precious — and Maddy would like that very much."

Maddy squealed with delight when her father sat down next to her. He kissed her forehead and rumpled her matted hair. "You come over to the barn after you're dressed," he told her. "We'll be practicing. You like to listen, right?"

Maddy nodded emphatically. "Where's my present? You didn't forget, did you?"

"One-track mind." He gave me a small, grudging smile. "Finish your cinnamon toast. Then go look in the suitcase in my bedroom. But wash your fingers first." He turned back to me. "So, Jane. What do you think?"

Puzzled, I waited for him to say more.

"Of Bianca," he prompted me. "What do you think of her?"

What could I say in reply? I thought of several answers and chose the most diplomatic one. "She's very beautiful."

"Well, of course she is. I was counting on you for some insight. What do you think of *her?*"

I thought of the angry look she'd flashed at Maddy, of the bits of their conversation I'd heard the night before. "I've barely spoken to her," I said finally.

"Well, speak to her, then. I want to know whether you approve of her."

"But it isn't any of my business."

"I'm making it your business." Then his voice softened. "I trust your good sense."

"I don't think she particularly wants to speak to me."

"Are you saying she's a snob?"

"No." I chose my words carefully. "She seems more interested in talking to you, so your judgment on her character would be more informed than mine."

"Huh." He finished the last of his cereal in silence, got up to put his bowl in the sink, and poured himself some coffee. Maddy was just finishing her last bite. "And one more thing, daughter of mine," he called to her.

"Yes, Daddy?" She looked up, a ring of crumbs around her mouth.

"Bring Miss Jane with you to the rehearsal." He looked straight at me, though he addressed her. "Don't let her run off like a scared bunny rabbit." Then he was gone.

Not long after noon, music began wafting up from the barn into the relative quiet of the main house. Maddy had been transfixed by the pricey kaleidoscope her father had bought her, exclaiming over the colorful shifting patterns, but at the first guitar chord, she set the toy aside. "Let's go. Daddy said we could."

"Yes, we're going." I got to my feet and brushed some of Co-pilot's black hair from my skirt. No matter how often the house-keepers vacuumed, they were no match for his exuberant shedding.

Maddy grabbed my hand and tugged. "Let's go, let's go, let's go."

On our way down the hill toward the barn, I felt a by now familiar trepidation overcoming me. As nice as Kitty and Yvonne and even Dennis had been to me the night before, the chance to spend more time with them didn't lessen my dread of seeing Mr. Rathburn flirt with his new girlfriend. But it was clear that I had no choice. I followed Maddy through the swinging red door into the barn, a building that till then I'd only seen from a distance.

Inside, any resemblance to an ordinary barn disappeared. The rough wooden interior was outfitted with all manner of speakers and musical equipment. Rattan armchairs and love seats were scattered around the fringes. Mitch sat scribbling notes in what looked like the least comfortable chair of the bunch; Javier hovered nearby waiting for instruction. A handful of men in gray T-shirts — where had they come from? — adjusted the instruments, working deftly around the band members, who when I entered were joking and improvising. Mr. Rathburn strummed an electric guitar, listening intently.

"Cut it out!" he shouted. "I can't hear myself think." The roadies and the band fell silent, and Mr. Rathburn strummed again. "Out of tune," he said finally, and one of the T-shirted men rushed over to swap the guitar for a different one.

Where are Yvonne and Kitty? I wondered, then decided they must still be back at the guesthouse. And where was Bianca Ingram? I'd spied her earlier, pouring herself coffee in the kitchen, long hair swept up loosely so that a few dark strands fell fetchingly around her face, the casual look of her faded blue jeans accented with silver stiletto heels. *Honestly,* I wondered, *who could work in shoes like that?* But I had to admit that if anyone could, it was probably Bianca Ingram.

Maddy chose to sit in the love seat right in front of her father's microphone and patted the cushion next to her until I joined her. I made her put in the earplugs Lucia kept for occasions like this, then wished I had a pair for myself. I hadn't heard live music since my best friend in college had dragged me to a handful of clubs during our first semester. Even the noodling around I'd heard so far was just this side of head splitting; I braced myself for the tidal wave of sound that must be coming. Still, I relished the chance to watch Mr. Rathburn without being seen. Absorbed in business, he hadn't noticed me at all.

A moment later, Mr. Rathburn held up one hand, signaling to the others. "Let's work on 'Blue Moon Rising,' key of C. You ready?" Then he began to count. "A one, a two, a one, two, three, four," and the band launched into a song I hadn't heard before. It was an easy one to like, catchy and upbeat, although, as I'd noticed in listening to his albums, the music's tempo was at odds with the words. I strained to make out the lyrics, catching just a phrase here or there above the torrent of sound, only enough to get the general gist, something about being stranded on the barren face of the moon. The song was about loneliness, isolation. Was this about him? I wondered. Could Mr. Rathburn, with all his fans, friends, and employees, really be lonely? If so, was that why he so often wanted to speak to me?

And, I wondered, how had I not liked Mr. Rathburn's singing voice? Why had I been put off by its gravelly edges? Now, to my ear, its roughness was more genuine, more affecting, than a more mellifluous voice would have been. As he sang, I noticed how he leaned back, throwing his whole body into his vocals, his deft fingers playing the chords so easily, the guitar almost an afterthought. I saw how when he launched into a solo, his attention shifted from his voice to his fingers, and how quick his hands were. I wished I could simultaneously watch the expressions on his face and his fingers moving on the strings, and not have to tear my gaze from one to look at the other.

Then something primal awoke in me. With a deep breath, I found myself wondering how those fingertips would feel on my skin. But what was I doing, thinking about Mr. Rathburn that way? Besides torturing myself, that is. I forced myself to look away, off into the shadows behind the stage, and was startled to catch sight of Bianca Ingram, motionless as a hunter stalking a deer, her camera trained on me. A moment later, she lowered the camera and glared at me, her face expressing naked dislike. Then she was gone, and if I trusted myself less I might have believed I'd imagined the whole thing.

"No, no, no." Mr. Rathburn's voice rose above the music. The band ground to a halt. "Lonnie, try not to speed up on me. Keep it constant." Now Bianca was at the front of the stage, snapping picture after picture of Nico, though he hardly seemed to notice. "The rhythm's not working at all. Tommy, my man. Crisper. Cleaner."

Tom muttered something under his breath.

"If you won't do it, I'll find somebody else who will," Mr. Rathburn said gruffly. "One more time." And they started from the top.

For a while, Maddy listened to her father's music with more concentration than I would have imagined possible, her legs swinging, her eyes intent. After forty-five minutes or so, she slid off her seat and started dancing at the side of the stage, her ballet moves charmingly incongruous. I'm sure she wished her father would pay her some attention, but he was focused on his music. Between songs he exhorted the band. "Tighter, tighter. We sound unbelievably sloppy." To my untrained ear, they sounded perfectly professional. "Fuck it, Dennis, can't you put some soul into it?"

On the next run-through, Mr. Rathburn yelled at Dennis again. "Now you're lagging behind the bass. I need it soulful *and* up-tempo. Can't you manage both?" I'm sure I would have found Mr. Rathburn frightening if I didn't know how quickly his anger could give way to the gentler self that hid behind the scowl.

Just then, Bianca sidled up to where Maddy was pirouetting, taking shot after shot until the little girl looked up, noticed her audience, and began posing for her, smiling, even curtseying. Bianca frowned and moved off as quickly as she'd swooped in, apparently annoyed that her subject had ceased to be spontaneous and natural. Maddy looked to me, puzzled.

It was no use trying to speak to Maddy; I would have to shout to be heard. Instead, I beckoned to her, and she sat beside me, her head on my lap. Together we listened as the band finally made it all the way through the difficult song.

"Not bad," Mr. Rathburn pronounced. "But let's try it again. We can still get it tighter."

A few run-throughs later, the band took a break. While Mr. Rathburn conferred with Dennis, Bianca Ingram joined them onstage for some close-ups, one after another, first of the pair of them, then of Mr. Rathburn alone, his guitar still dangling at his hip.

"You get enough of those yet?" he asked her, teasing. "Isn't it time you found yourself another subject?"

"Not yet." She dropped her camera and made a little spinning motion with her hand. "Now turn around so I can get a picture of that famous ass of yours."

Mr. Rathburn laughed. "You'll have to catch me when my back's turned. And good luck with that; it's not like I can take my eyes off you."

Bianca moved in closer and said something I couldn't hear. Mr. Rathburn, his arm slung across her shoulder, whispered something back. They looked so natural together — two supremely confident beings, drawn together by the inexorable laws of celebrity.

Mr. Rathburn whispered something else in Bianca's ear, and she slipped from under his arm. "Not here," I heard her say with a laugh. "You naughty thing. Later. Tonight."

"Is that a promise?"

"I don't make promises. Catch up with me later and convince me all over again."

"Huh. There's nothing I like more than a challenge." His finger sought her neat little chin, tipping her face up toward his. For a moment, I held my breath, sure that he would kiss her. "But there's one thing you can do for me now. Right here — on the spot."

She leaned and whispered in his ear.

"What a dirty mind you have." His tone made it clear that he approved of whatever proposition she'd made. "Save that for later. Right now, though, you can let me do this." His hand found the butterfly clip that held up her hair. He removed it, and the black silk fell down her long back. "Wear it like this — the way I like it."

"I don't take orders from men. Not even men like you."

"No kidding." He genuflected. "You're the queen, and I'm just one of your subjects. So consider it my humble request. Let me drown in that black hair of yours." He straightened and drew closer to her, taking a deep breath, apparently inhaling the scent of her shampoo. Didn't they realize I was watching?

"You're insane." Bianca sounded pleased. Then he took her hand, turned it over in his, and kissed the delicate skin of her inner wrist.

I felt my heart pause, as though I had just realized the river I'd been wading in contained piranhas. Every word and gesture of their exchange bit into me, but nothing hurt more than the sight of that kiss. I couldn't stop myself; I looked on, helpless. And I wasn't alone. Maddy had sat up in her chair and was watching them with wide-eyed interest. I wanted to put my hands over her eyes.

Instead, I got to my feet. "It's your quiet time," I told her in the firmest voice I could muster at that moment. "Let's go."

She protested mildly, and I was able to get her to her room without too much of a struggle. After reading her a story, I sat on her bed for a moment, considering what I should do next. Mr. Rathburn had virtually ordered me to be present for the rehearsal, but the thought of returning for a front-row view of his intimacies with Bianca, of what I might overhear next...well, I just couldn't imagine it. I slipped quietly out of Maddy's room and prepared to hide under the covers of my own bed until the rest of the spectacle was over. Before I could get to my door, though, I noticed something bright and small on the plush hallway carpet — one of Maddy's pigtail holders. As I stooped to pick it up, I heard someone turn the corner. Rising hastily, I stood face-to-face with Mr. Rathburn.

"How are you?" he asked me. It seemed like an odd question. How should I be?

"Okay," I said. "Fine."

"Why didn't you come speak to me in the barn?" Another strange question. He'd been busy, and then he'd been deep in conversation with Bianca.

"I didn't want to interrupt."

"What have you been up to while I've been busy with my guests?"

"Nothing much. Watching Maddy, as usual."

"You look pale. I noticed it all the way from the stage. Are you coming down with something?"

"I'm just tired."

"And a little depressed," he said. "What about? Tell me."

"Nothing, Mr. Rathburn. I'm not depressed."

"But you look sad. I haven't seen you smile all morning, and right now it looks like you're holding back tears."

At this observation, the tears spilled; it was impossible to keep them back. Mr. Rathburn reached toward me as though he might wipe them from my face with his bare hands. Then he pulled back and felt in the pockets of his black jeans. "I don't have a handkerchief on me."

"That's okay. I'll just go and..."

"I have to get back to the barn," he said. "The guys are waiting. I'll let you go, Jane. For a little while. But after dinner tonight, I want you out on the deck with my other guests. Wherever we are, I want you to be there for the rest of their visit. Now go, get some rest." And then he reached toward me again, this time with both arms, as though he might wrap them around me to give me some comfort. But then he stopped, bit his lip, folded his arms, and strode away.

CHAPTER 11

That night after Maddy's bedtime, the music continued, though now it was loose and informal. On the back deck, overlooking the woods, Mr. Rathburn sat barefoot on a step, strumming one of his acoustic guitars, playing folk songs, a few of which I recognized. Beside him, Dennis played along. From an Adirondack chair behind him, Mike blew his harmonica. The rest of the group — Tom and Lonnie, Yvonne and Kitty, Bianca, her long hair still floating about her shoulders — nursed Heinekens and sang along. At the end of each song, the group hooted with joy; the singers called out requests.

I sat on a bench at the opposite end of the porch; if I had to be out on the back deck, I would be as far away from Mr. Rathburn and Bianca as I could get. After she'd had a few drinks, Yvonne came over to invite me to join the rest of them. I thanked her sincerely but told her I was comfortable where I was, and she returned to the group.

Mr. Rathburn seemed loose and happy. As the night progressed, he became more and more of a showman. "Bianca, you haven't made a request yet. Isn't there anything you want to hear?"

"I don't know." Bianca took a long swallow from her Heineken. "How about 'The Highwayman'?"

"Which version? There are three I know of, probably more."

"Any version. I love any variation on the Highwayman ballad. I'm a sucker for the bad boys."

"You hear that?" Mr. Rathburn asked the others. "Which of us fits that description?"

"Oh, please," Lonnie said. "Don't you read your own press?"

"You're the baddest of the bad," Mike added. "I read it in *People* magazine. It must be true."

Mr. Rathburn grinned. "Well then, this song is dedicated to the beautiful Bianca Ingram." He launched into the ballad, and the others listened. Once again I felt a stinging in my heart. Hearing him sing those lyrics, about an innkeeper's daughter who shoots herself to save the highwayman with whom she has fallen in love, brought me close to tears again. I was glad when the song was over — that is, I would have been glad if he hadn't turned around and called my name.

"What about you, Jane? Any requests? Have you been enjoying our little hootenanny?"

I struggled for a response.

"Leave the little girl alone," Bianca commanded in a mocking voice. "Can't you see she'd rather be inside watching *American Idol*?"

"Aren't you supposed to be taking pictures, Bianca?" Dennis's tone was perfectly calibrated to sound playful. "Instead of picking on the help?"

"Ooooh." Bianca took another long swig of beer. "Clever boy."

"You're missing an excellent photo op," Mr. Rathburn interjected, "but I guess even the queen of celebrity photographers needs to take a vacation every once in a while. Dennis, push over. Go sit by Mike. I'm not kidding." After Dennis moved, Bianca slipped into his place next to Mr. Rathburn. "If your voice is as stunning as the rest of you," he told her, "we'd better sing a duet — the first of many, I hope."

And they did, she taking one line and he the next, of a song I recognized, though I couldn't recall its name or who had popularized it. I was chagrined to note that Bianca Ingram had, if not a stunning voice, a pretty one that blended very well with Mr. Rathburn's idiosyncratic baritone. To tell the truth, though I stayed on the deck as ordered, I barely paid any attention to the rest of what was said or sung that night. All I could do was stew in the poisonous feelings roused by their voices harmonizing in the song's chorus. I was jealous, of course, but it was more than that. I felt that I was watching my best friend make a tragic mistake. Whatever Bianca Ingram was, I was fairly certain about what she wasn't: kind, loving, or even genuine. And I was disappointed that Mr. Rathburn hadn't noticed the sharp edges of her personality, or that — enamored by her silky hair and long legs — he'd decided to overlook them. I would have been willing to bet that this relationship would end as unhappily as his others, but there was little — nothing — I could do about it.

From my place in the shadows, I saw Bianca Ingram lean her sleek head on Mr. Rathburn's shoulder. I saw him draw closer to her, their two silhouettes merging. I tried to remember his less attractive qualities — his bad temper, his bossiness, his tendency to spoil his daughter one moment and to ignore her the next. Not to mention his strange insistence that I be present at moments like this, though there was no place for me in the circle of people sprawled around him. Once I had barely liked him. Now, with a shiver, I realized I'd gone well beyond liking him: I had fallen in love with him. Love had snuck up on me, and now I could hardly imagine a time when I hadn't treasured his wry smile, his smoky eyes, his broad shoulders, his voice and its distinct, sandpapery edge. If only I could regain my indifference, but I doubted I could ever get it back.

When the revelry finally ended, it was almost two in the morning. As soon as the party broke up, I hurried to my own quiet room. Unlike the others, I couldn't sleep in until noon. I would wake up feeling no more rested than I had the night before.

CHAPTER 12

A storm moved in early the next day and stalled over Thornfield Park. Rehearsals went on anyway, despite cold, torrential rain, and the moat of mud that had formed around the barn. At lunchtime, Amber and Linda carried an urn of coffee and a tray of sandwiches into the barn, their hair flattened by their short run from the house. I'd kept Maddy home again that day; she'd petitioned her father on the matter before breakfast, and he'd given her permission to hang out in the barn. After lunch, she set up her figurines in a corner and listened to the band as she began one of her protracted games of pretend. I wrapped my hands around my coffee mug, trying to get warm, and was listening to what seemed like the hundredth iteration of a single song when Yvonne sidled up next to me.

"You bored yet?" she asked me. "Why does he make you sit here hour after hour?"

"I don't pretend to understand his logic." Rehearsals seemed not to be going particularly well, and Mr. Rathburn had been too preoccupied that morning even to pay much attention to Bianca. She continued her stealthy photography, hovering wherever the action seemed to be, but I thought I detected a brusque, slightly miffed air to her.

"Well, whatever," Yvonne said. "When he's not looking, slip out. You need to put Maddy down for her nap anyway, right? Once you're out of the barn, come over to the guesthouse. I've got my tarot cards. I'll tell your fortune."

The opportunity to get away from rehearsals was a relief, even if I risked Mr. Rathburn's censure. Less than an hour later, I knocked on the guesthouse door. Even with my umbrella, I was pretty wet around the edges.

"Take those shoes off!" Kitty ordered. "Make yourself comfy."

I'd never had reason to be in the guesthouse before. Its living room was cheery — white and yellow, with a fire in the hearth. I settled onto the couch, and Kitty handed me a wooly red throw; I wrapped it around my shoulders. "Have you ever had a reading before?" she asked me. "Yvonne's amazing."

"The cards are amazing," Yvonne corrected her. "I just know how to interpret them. I used to pull cards for myself every day, but I stopped. They were so right, they scared me."

"So now we get to be scared," Kitty said with a small shiver.

"You *should* be scared after the reading I did this morning. We got Miss Thang to put her camera down and sneak over here for a while."

I recalled that there had been a brief stretch that morning

when Bianca hadn't been present. It also dawned on me that neither Kitty nor Yvonne particularly liked Bianca. And why should they? In her days at Thornfield Park, I'd never once seen her speak to either woman; all her attention had been focused on the band.

"You read Bianca's cards?" I asked. "What did they say?"

"Oh, she drew the Tower," Yvonne said offhandedly. "Let's just say her reading centered around a serious blow to her ego."

"I'm not sure I want my fortune told," I said. "If bad luck is lurking around the corner, I'd rather not know."

Yvonne cut and shuffled the deck. "Oh, the cards don't tell you the future, sweetie. They just tell you about yourself, give you hints on how to go about getting whatever it is you want. So you start by coming up with a question. What is it you want to know?"

I hesitated. It would have been foolish and unprofessional to share the subject that most preoccupied me. And what would I ask, anyway? Even if the cards could tell me the future, I knew mine didn't hold hope for the one thing I wanted most. There was no point in asking how to get Mr. Rathburn to love me; it was beyond my power. Besides, was I really silly enough to believe a card chosen from a deck could tell me anything useful? "I think you should know I'm a skeptic," I said.

Yvonne shrugged. "Doesn't matter. You might not believe in the cards, but they believe in you. There's got to be something you want."

I thought a moment. "Will I ever go back to college?"

"Boring!" Kitty sang out. "Is that the best you can do?"

"Ask about love," Yvonne urged me. "Do you have a boyfriend?"

"Oh, no."

"Is there someone you like?" she persisted. "Somebody you've got your eye on?"

"Look at her blush," Kitty said. "There's your answer, Vonnie. Who is it?"

"Nobody you know."

"It's Dennis!" Yvonne guessed.

"I've only known him three days," I said. "No, it's not Dennis. It's someone from my other life. Before I came here."

Was that disbelief I saw cross Yvonne's face? At any rate, she stopped pressing me for information. "Think about him while I shuffle the cards. What is it you want to know?"

I closed my eyes and thought of Mr. Rathburn's face, a little shocked at how easily and vividly I could conjure up the image of his smoke-colored eyes and crooked smile. "What do I want to know?" I tried to formulate the question as vaguely as I could. "Is there...I don't know. Is there hope?"

I opened my eyes and saw a fan of cards spread out a couple of inches in front of my face. "One of these cards is screaming your name," Yvonne said. "So pick it."

I made my choice and laid the card faceup on the table. It featured a colorful drawing of a nude woman kneeling on one knee beside a stream. Water poured from the pitchers she held in each hand. An enormous, eight-pointed star took up most of the night sky above her.

"It's the Star!" Yvonne exclaimed.

"Is that good?" Kitty asked.

"You bet," Yvonne said. "The Star is the card of hope and healing."

"Why is she naked?" I asked.

"She's stripped bare, completely vulnerable. And that water she's spilling symbolizes tears you've been holding back."

"Have you been? Holding back tears?" Kitty asked.

"Well, not exactly." That much was true; yesterday I'd been unable to hold them back. The memory of how I'd fallen apart in front of Mr. Rathburn still rankled.

"Well, cheer up," Yvonne said. "What you want is out there. You just have to go and meet it halfway. That's not me talking, honey. It's the card."

I shook my head. "I'm pretty sure that's not the case," I told them. "Nothing against your card-reading skills."

"You may not see it now," Yvonne said. "But you need to be on the lookout for opportunity."

I took the throw from my shoulders. "Thank you both. This was very nice of you. I should probably get back to the barn."

"What, are you worried about big, bad Nico?" Kitty said. "Let him wonder where you went. Hang out for a while. Vonnie's going to read my cards. I'll make some coffee; that'll warm us up. And if Nico says anything, just tell him we kidnapped you."

"He's a softy underneath all that bluster," Yvonne said. "But you know that, right?" And before I could answer, she turned to Kitty. "So what do *you* want to know?"

I lingered with them awhile longer before going back to the house to check on Maddy. She was already up and out of bed, and had probably run over to the barn herself, and I was most likely in hot water for slipping out of the rehearsal and not watching my charge properly. In fact, I *should* be in trouble. I was thinking grim thoughts when the intercom by the front door buzzed. I would have expected Lucia to answer it, but she must have gone out to run an errand. It buzzed a second time and then a third.

I ran down to the entryway and pressed the button to reply. "Yes?"

"It's Teddy in the guardhouse. There's an Ambrose Mason here to see Nico. He's not expected, but he says it's important, and Nico will know what it's about."

I offered to run over to the barn and relay the message, since I was headed there to find Maddy anyway. Sure enough, she was parked on the love seat right in front of her father's mike stand, watching him with still-sleepy eyes, a figurine clutched in each hand.

Mr. Rathburn was swapping one guitar for another when I climbed up onto the stage to get his attention. He looked up distractedly. "Jane?" He seemed surprised, even happy, to see me standing there. "What's up?"

I relayed the message. When I pronounced the visitor's name, the smile on his lips faded. "I'll be right back," he announced to the band. "Take five."

Bianca, who had been sitting just offstage reviewing pictures she had stored on her camera, got to her feet as if to go with him. "No, stay here," he ordered her. "Jane, come with me."

I had expected him to hurry down to the guardhouse or at least to the intercom. To my surprise, the moment we got out of the barn, he pulled me aside to a space between the trees. It was still drizzling; I could feel the dampness of my clothes against my skin. He grabbed my hand. "Ambrose Mason? Are you sure you got the name right?"

I assured him that there was no way I could have mistaken a name like that.

"Did you see him? Did he say anything to you?" His face was paler than I'd ever seen it before.

"He's down at the guardhouse. I haven't seen him. What's wrong? Are you okay?"

"Jane, you have no idea." He loosened his grip on my hand a bit. "This is a nightmare." We walked on, toward the pool house. He looked both ways, let himself in, and held the door open for me. Once inside, he dropped to the nearest chair. I sat beside him.

"Who is he?" I couldn't help but ask.

"He was a friend of mine" — his voice was grim — "a long time ago."

"Can't you just tell him to go away?" I asked. "Teddy will send him away if you don't want him here."

"No, Teddy can't help me with this."

"What about me, Mr. Rathburn? Can I help you?"

He reached over, took my hand in both of his, and rubbed it. "Your hand is cold," he said. "It's too bad the two of us can't just run away together somewhere. But tell me something," he asked in an urgent voice. "If all this disappeared tomorrow" — he let go of my hand and gestured to the house — "if the tabloids invented a scandal about me and turned my name into shit, and nobody bought my records, and the recording company let me go...if I had nothing and went back to being Nick Rathburn from Wichita, would you stick by me? Would you still be my friend?"

"Of course I would," I told him. "No question."

"You know what, Jane?" he said quietly. "I believe you."

161

"Let me help you. I'll do whatever you need."

"Nobody can help, not even you. Not with this. This I need to handle myself."

He told me to go back to the house and started down the long path to the front gate. Once inside, I sat in the living room and waited for what felt like hours, though it must have been only minutes. Just when I was wondering if I should have insisted on going down to the guardhouse with Mr. Rathburn, the front door opened. I hurried to the entryway to find him with a man of about thirty — handsome in a feminine way. He wore what looked like an expensive suit and carried a suitcase.

"Jane," Mr. Rathburn said in a low voice. "Do we have a spare bedroom?"

"I think there's still one empty in your wing. I don't know if it's ready for a guest."

"Could you dig up some towels and whatever else the room needs? Just leave them outside the door." He looked past me, into the hallway behind me. "Is anyone else in the house?"

"Some of the staff, maybe," I told him. "I passed Walter in the kitchen a while ago. I haven't seen anyone since. Lucia is out, and all of your guests are still in the barn and the guesthouse."

"Good, good." He sounded somber. "Once you've taken care of the towels, get out to the barn and check on Maddy. Tell everyone I'll be there soon. Keep them out of the house. And whatever you do, don't mention Mason to anyone." Then Mr. Rathburn left, with Ambrose Mason hurrying to keep up.

After I'd taken care of the towels and an extra blanket, I ran out to the barn and found Maddy right where I had left her. The

162

band was milling around a buffet table; they all looked up when I entered. Behind the stage, Bianca paced back and forth. The look she gave me was as cold as that of a Bengal tiger eyeing a human on the other side of its wall of bars.

"Where is he?" Tom asked. "What's taking him so long?"

"He said he'll be here any moment," I told them. "He had some urgent business to take care of."

"We're out of coffee," Lonnie said. "And we're low on sandwiches."

I assured them I would let the cook know and said again that Mr. Rathburn would be back shortly. This seemed to pacify the band members, if not their agitated photographer. Why she so obviously disliked me, I had no real idea, and there wasn't time to puzzle it out. I made sure Maddy was happily occupied, then ran off to the kitchen to find Walter. By the time I returned, Mr. Rathburn was back, and the rehearsal had started up again. The music lasted until sunset. For the rest of the day, throughout dinner, and at that evening's party in the living room, I saw no trace of Ambrose Mason. And though I watched him closely, Mr. Rathburn didn't look my way once.

CHAPTER 13

That night I fell asleep easily but woke abruptly a few hours later. The day's storm clouds had cleared, and my room seemed flooded with moonlight despite the drawn venetian blinds. I sat up in bed, lifted up one of the slats, and observed an enormous full moon, its light transforming the familiar view from my window into something beautiful and strange.

Just then, a scream pierced the quiet. Loud enough to wake the entire house, it seemed to come from above me.

I froze, and for a moment there was an ominous silence. But then I heard more startling sounds: some kind of struggle just above my head, a crash like a piece of furniture being toppled over, and then glass shattering. And then a man's raspy voice cried, "Help! Help! Help!" After a brief pause, he called out again. "Nico! Nico! Please...get up here."

I heard footsteps, someone running down the hallway. There was more stomping above my head. Something heavy fell, then silence. I raced to Maddy's room to check on her. Unbelievably, she slept on, so I returned to my room.

Had anyone else in the house heard? Maddy and I were the only ones with bedrooms on our wing. The wide playroom stood between us, and the walls of the house were thick and mostly soundproof. Even so, Linda and Amber, who slept on the floor below, must have heard the footsteps. I thought of Bianca on Mr. Rathburn's side of the house and everyone else in the guesthouse, and wondered if the scream had woken any of them. I sat on the edge of my bed wondering what to do next when I heard voices coming from the end of the hall. One of them was Bianca's; the other belonged to Mr. Rathburn. Apparently, Linda and Amber were there too.

"It's nothing. One of the housekeepers had a nightmare," he said. "You should go back to bed."

Brenda, I thought to myself. But I hadn't dreamed whatever had transpired on the floor above. My nerves vibrated, and my hands trembled.

"I couldn't possibly get back to sleep," Bianca said. "Whoever it was, I'd fire them if I were you."

"I'll take care of everything," Mr. Rathburn replied. "Linda, would you go out to the guesthouse? If they're awake over there, let them know it was nothing. Amber, you can go back to bed. Nothing more to see here." He laughed dryly. "Move along."

Bianca's voice rose again. I could hear her say something in protest, though I couldn't make out the words.

166

"You'll be fine," I heard Mr. Rathburn tell her. "I promise, there won't be any more excitement tonight."

Then all was quiet, both down the hall and on the third floor. Though everyone had heard the scream, apparently only Mr. Rathburn and I had heard the scuffling and the struggle. Something told me that Mr. Rathburn would need my help after all. I changed into jeans and a T-shirt, pulled on shoes, and sat waiting until the knock on my door came at last.

"Jane?" It was Mr. Rathburn. I opened the door. He slipped in and closed it behind him. "You remember how you said you'd help me if I needed it?"

I nodded.

"We have to be quiet," he said. "Do we have a first-aid kit?"

"There's one in the downstairs bathroom, off the kitchen."

"Can you go get it? And do we have any clean rags?" I nodded. "Good. Bring some to the third floor. Lots of them, as many as you can find. But be as quiet as you can."

"Won't I need a key?"

"Knock gently on the door at the top of the stairs. I'll be listening for you." I started toward the kitchen, but he called me back in an urgent whisper. "Jane! Are you afraid of blood?"

"I don't know. I don't think so." The question should have terrified me, but instead I felt strangely cool and competent — a feeling I'd had only one other time, when I got the call about my parents' accident. That calm had accompanied me on the train back to Philadelphia, to the hospital morgue where I'd had to identify their bodies. It had enabled me to plan the funeral while my sister lay sobbing in bed and my brother was absent, off with his friends for a two-day drinking binge. It had gotten me through the funeral and the reading of the will, and had only deserted me when I was back on campus, suddenly weak with sorrow and alone in a dorm full of people.

Acting quickly, I gathered up the supplies, careful to make as little sound as possible. When I couldn't find any clean rags, I raided my bureau for freshly washed cotton T-shirts. I climbed the creaky stairs as quietly as I could. As soon as I knocked on the low black door at the top of the steps, it opened, and I entered a room illuminated only by the moonlight that spilled in around the drawn shades.

"Wait here a moment," Mr. Rathburn said, and disappeared through the door on the far side of the room. I heard him say something in sharp tones; a low voice mumbled a few syllables in reply. Then I heard another door farther back open and close, and then a muffled laugh. It must have been Brenda.

"I'm in here." Mr. Rathburn called me into the inner room, where he stood beside a large sleigh bed. It was dark in this room too, except for an emergency flashlight set on a bedside table. Its beam fell on a figure stretched across the bed. I stepped closer. It was Ambrose Mason, his eyes wide with pain or fear, his full lips white and trembling. His pale shirt was soaked in blood on one side; it seeped into the bedspread under him.

"Give me the rags," Mr. Rathburn ordered. I complied, and he balled several of them up and pressed them to the bloodiest portion of Mason's chest.

Mason moaned and thrashed his head from side to side. His breath came in rapid bursts. "The doctor is on his way," Mr. Rathburn told him. "You'll be fine."

"Has he lost a lot of blood?" I asked Mr. Rathburn, whispering so as not to panic Mason any further.

"The wound looks worse than it is."

I touched Mason's cheek; his skin felt damp. "He might be going into shock." I'd taken a first-aid class to earn my babysitter's license, and some of what I'd learned came flooding back. "He'll need a blanket for warmth...and one to elevate his feet."

"Find some," Mr. Rathburn said. "There must be blankets in here." He stayed at Mason's side, pressing down on the rags with a look of deep concentration.

In a nearby dresser, I found several quilts, rolled one up, and put it under his feet, then draped the other across the bottom half of his body.

"Is there gauze in the first-aid kit?" Mr. Rathburn asked. "Or a bandage? And some tape?"

I pulled a roll of gauze out of the box. "It doesn't look like enough to wrap around his body," I said.

"Never mind then. I need you to take over for me. Come over here. Pick up a couple more rags. Don't peel off the ones that are already there; just put the fresh ones over them and press like I'm doing. As hard as you can." I complied, leaning into the task with all my weight. Mason groaned again.

"I've got to get downstairs and listen for the doctor," Mr. Rathburn told me. "I don't want him ringing the doorbell and waking up the whole house. Keep putting pressure on the wound."

I nodded.

"While I'm gone, Mason, don't you dare say a word. And Jane?"

"Yes?"

"You don't speak to him either. Don't ask any questions. And whatever you do, stay away from that door." He pointed to a heavy wooden door at the back of the room that was secured with a dead bolt. Though I'd been too concerned with Mason to notice, I now heard murmurings and sounds coming from behind the door.

"I'll stay away," I assured Mr. Rathburn. And he left, locking the door to the third floor behind him.

The minutes passed by agonizingly slowly. Mr. Mason seemed to grow sleepier and less agitated. Every so often, I would attempt a reassuring smile meant to convey that the doctor was on his way and that he'd be taken care of soon. Though I willed my hands to be steady, I could feel my composure beginning to desert me. Blood bloomed into the rags beneath my palms. What if Mason bled to death? What if I couldn't stop him from going into shock? Worse — just behind that wooden door was the woman who had done this to him. Those strange sounds coming from behind the door — grunts and an occasional low chuckle — told me that Brenda was waiting on the other side for a chance to break free and do more harm. What was she? It was hard to imagine how any human being could look so ordinary by day but turn so murderous by night.

A fresh rag lay on the bed. With one hand still on Mason's wound, I grabbed it and spread it over the others. As hard as I tried, I couldn't come up with a logical answer to the questions that gnawed at me. Why would Mr. Rathburn risk his own safety, not to mention Maddy's, to keep someone so dangerous locked away on the third floor? And what other secrets was he keeping?

170

It felt like hours before the doctor arrived, but it must have been more like thirty minutes. Copilot barked, and soon I heard a car creep up the driveway, then halt by the side of the house. Moments later, Mr. Rathburn arrived in the company of a short man with disheveled gray hair. I recognized him as the doctor who had come to the house once when Maddy had an earache and a fever. "Step aside," he told me. He bent over Mason and checked under the rags. "The bleeding's almost stopped," he said. Then he wrapped a blood pressure cuff around the patient's arm. We silently waited for the result. "He's at the low end of normal."

"Am I dying?" Mason asked. It was, I realized, the first time I'd heard his voice. He had an accent I couldn't quite pin down — Spanish, maybe.

"You should be fine with some antibiotics and stitches." The doctor looked up at Mr. Rathburn. "This is an ugly wound. You say she used a steak knife to do this?"

"She tried to," Mr. Rathburn said. "I got it away from her, but not before she'd done some damage. There's another cut on his shoulder, up near the neck."

The doctor shifted for a better view, pushing Mason's torn shirt aside. "This one wasn't done with a knife. These look like teeth marks." He sounded horrified.

"She bit me," Mason murmured. "Nico got the knife away from her, and she came after me with her teeth." He sounded agitated. "I didn't know how to stop her. I didn't want to hurt her. She caught me by surprise. When I came in, she looked so peaceful." The doctor worked, removing Mason's shirt, cleaning the wounds with an antiseptic solution, and wrapping gauze around Mason's chest.

171

"I warned you, didn't I?" Mr. Rathburn said. "You didn't have to go in alone; you could have waited until morning and brought me in with you."

"I couldn't sleep," Mason said. "All I could think of was her, up here — how lonely she must be."

"She's not lonely!" Mr. Rathburn snapped. "I see to it that she's not lonely. I take good care of her."

The doctor glared at him. "Don't get him excited," he said. "Just give me another minute or two, and I'll be able to drive him to the hospital. He's got a third wound here on his arm. Another bite, it looks like."

"She tried to suck my blood. She said she was going to dig out my heart and eat it."

"Enough!" Mr. Rathburn's face twisted. "Stop talking!" He glanced over at me, then back at Mason. "I warned you not to …"

"Promise me you'll take good care of her," Mason said in a choked voice.

Mr. Rathburn's tone softened. "I've always taken good care of her. You've seen she's all right. Now you can go home and leave everything to me." He turned my way for the first time since he'd reentered the room. "Jane, you'd better go downstairs and wash the blood off your hands. I'll be down in a minute. I'll knock on your door."

I complied, taking a quick, hot shower, glad to clean myself off. I dressed in fresh clothes and waited in the chair beside my bed. Before long, Mr. Rathburn knocked on the door. I let him in and closed the door behind us so our voices wouldn't carry. "How are you?" he asked me. "Besides exhausted?"

"I'm fine," I said, "but I was terrified up there when I was alone

172

with Mr. Mason. I thought Brenda might break down the door or pick the lock."

"It's a very thick door. Reinforced with steel. And the locks are state-of-the-art. Besides that dead bolt you could see, there are four other locks. I wouldn't have left you up there if I thought you were in even the tiniest bit of danger."

"Is she still going to live here?" I asked. "What if she found another way out? She could hurt you. Or Maddy."

"There are no other ways out. We're safe. And I'll make sure that nothing hurts you, ever. You believe me, right?"

I told him that I did, and he took my hand. "Your fingers are still ice-cold," he said. "How is that possible?" He pressed the palm of his other hand to my forehead. "Are you sick?"

"I don't think so."

There were so many questions I wanted to ask him about what had happened. Why was it that Mason cared so much about Brenda? And why had he shown up at Thornfield Park? But I could hardly concentrate. Mr. Rathburn's hand on my face was large and slightly, pleasantly rough. I could smell the faintest trace of his aftershave — familiar by now — with its hint of wood smoke. I shut my eyes. "Your forehead's hot. I think you have a fever."

"I'm sure I don't. I'm just…" I trailed off, not knowing how to end that sentence. When I opened my eyes, he was still looking at me. Dizzy and afraid of what I might say or do next, I took a step backward.

After a long moment, he looked at me quizzically, then broke into an absentminded smile. "So tell me, Jane. What do you think of my new girlfriend? Don't we look good together?"

I reached out for the corner of my dresser to brace myself until the dizziness passed. "Yes," I said after a moment. "You do." Why on earth was he asking me about Bianca now, after all that had just happened? How could he seem so caring one moment and so callous the next? I shook my head from side to side, trying to clear my thoughts.

"Isn't she everything I could want in a woman? Gorgeous, sophisticated, talented?"

"She's all of those things."

"Don't you think we'll be happy together?"

I couldn't think of a reply that was both truthful and polite, so I kept silent.

"I want your honest opinion. Should I ask her to marry me? I've been alone too long, don't you think?"

"I wouldn't know, Mr. Rathburn."

"Would you drink a toast to me at my wedding reception? Or you could say a word or two at the ceremony. Read a poem, maybe. Would you do that for me?"

"I'll do whatever you need me to." I shut my eyes a second. They felt so heavy; I barely had the energy to open them again.

"I'll let you sleep," Mr. Rathburn said. "The sun will be up soon, and I'll have a lot of explaining to do to our guests. Sweet dreams."

And he left me to dreams that were anything but sweet.

CHAPTER 14

Dawn came too soon. I had fallen asleep in my clothes and had slept only fitfully. Just before I threw last night's jeans into the laundry, I found my cell phone in the pocket. It had been turned off for days. I hadn't received a phone call on it in weeks, maybe even months. Still, I turned it on to check for messages, just in case, and to my surprise discovered that I had three. I played them back.

All were from my sister, Jenna, her voice pitched increasingly higher from one to the next.

"Jane? This is Jenna. Listen, call me back, okay. It's important." The second ran on awhile: "Jane, you've got to get back to me. Where are you, anyway? Mark called, and he's in New York City. He wants to stay with me. David's really pissed, and I don't know what to do." David was her investment-banker fiancé. "Mark keeps calling. He sounds terrible. He scares me. You've got to come." The third was brief again: "Jesus, Jane, are you dead or what? Don't you answer this thing?"

I waited until midmorning to call her back; Jenna had never been an early riser. She answered the phone on the first ring. At the sound of my voice, she groaned in frustration, then launched into a monologue. "Oh my God, where have you been? Never mind. I need you here right now. Mark's been sleeping on my couch, and David's about to throw him out onto the street. He's gotten wasted every night since he's been here, and he's been absolutely horrible to me, so unpleasant you wouldn't believe it."

Oh, wouldn't I? I thought.

"He has a girlfriend in Massachusetts — some suburb of Boston, I forget the name — that's where he's been all these months. Anyway, she kicked him to the curb, and he dragged himself down to my apartment, and I don't know what to do with him. I need you. I *need* you. He's your brother too."

I waited until she had run out of pleas. "I have a job, Jenna," I told her. "I can't just leave."

"Tell them you're sick. Tell them it's a family crisis. It *is* a family crisis. They'll have to understand."

I noticed she didn't ask me what sort of job I had taken or how I was doing. "I'll see what I can work out. I'll call you back."

I found Mr. Rathburn in the barn, taking a break from rehearsal and trading quips with Bianca as she danced around him with her camera. His back was to the door; she saw me first, lowered the camera to her chest, and glared at me as she might a mosquito. "What does she want now?" she demanded.

"I need to talk to you for a moment," I said to Mr. Rathburn. "In private, please."

Mr. Rathburn turned, made a strange grimace, and followed me out of the barn. "Well, Jane?" he said once we were out on the lawn.

"I need a leave of absence for a day...maybe a couple of days. Possibly longer."

"You do? What for?"

"My sister needs me. She says it's urgent."

"Your sister? Didn't you tell me once that the two of you weren't in contact? I think you said she hates you."

"I may have said that, but it's probably more accurate to say she doesn't care for me."

"And you're going to drop everything and run to her?"

"There's a family crisis. My brother's in trouble."

"Your brother has turned up?" Mr. Rathburn looked exasperated. "What other secrets are you keeping from me?"

"I wasn't keeping secrets. I just found out."

"And now you're going to leave me to fend for myself just now, when I... Dammit, Jane, I'm about to start a tour. What do you expect me to do with Maddy?"

"What did you do with her before I arrived?"

He stared at me, his mouth set in a hard line. "You're something else," he said. "I'll give you one day off."

"I'll need *at least* one day. I'm not sure how long this will take."

"Promise you'll be back before the rehearsal show," he said. The show was a bit more than a week away.

"If at all possible, I'll be back before the rehearsal show."

"Is that the best you can do? And how are you going to get there? Do you need to use one of my cars? Would you like a driver?"

"I'll get there just like I got here. I'll take the train. It would be nice if Benjamin could take me to the station, though."

"Well, of course." His voice was still gruff, but his features were less steely. "I'm not going to make you walk twenty miles to the train station, am I? And what about money?"

"I have some in the bank."

"You mean the money you were saving up to go back to school? You're not going to give any of it to your brother or sister, are you? You'd better not. You're too softhearted."

"I'm not. They've both got plenty of money."

"Well, you shouldn't waste any of your savings to get back and forth. I'll give you some cash." Waving off my protestations, he dug in his pockets and came up with nothing. "Bloody hell. I never carry money. I'll tell Lucia to give you something from petty cash."

"You will not. My family is my problem. I'll use my own money."

"You really are unbelievable, you know that?" he said with a grudging smile.

"Yes, you keep telling me that. And there's one more thing, Mr. Rathburn." I braced myself and continued. "You know how you told me you might be getting married?"

"What about it?" The crease between his brows reappeared.

"Is it true?"

"What if it is?"

"If you're getting married, I'll need to find another position. Your fiancée doesn't like me very much."

"And who would take care of Maddy? You've probably noticed that Bianca isn't the motherly type."

"Maybe Ms. Ingram would like to help choose the new nanny," I said. "That way you can hire someone she likes…or at least approves of."

"You have a point. But what would you do then?"

"I'd go back to the agency — if you'll give me a good reference."

"A good reference! Go back to the agency! I can see you've given this some thought. What if I refuse to give you a good reference? What if I tell them you're a little brat who left me high and dry when I needed you most?"

"You wouldn't do that," I told him. "It's not true."

"Screw the agency. I'll find you a new position myself. I have friends, you know. Someone always needs a good nanny. Promise me you won't go back to the agency."

I gave him my word.

"When are you leaving?" he asked.

"I was hoping to leave this afternoon. I know that doesn't give Lucia much notice."

"Lucia will bust a gasket, but she'll survive. Me, on the other hand…Well, I guess this is good-bye, then. I'm terrible at good-bye."

"Good-bye, but not for long," I said.

"It had better not be. Do I get a handshake?"

I shook his hand, but he stood there as if unsatisfied. "That's

179

not it," he said. "That feels so phony and formal. What about a hug?"

I stepped forward, and he threw his arms around me and held me there awhile. For a moment, I could feel his heart beating. I knew that if I was going to walk away, I'd better do it right then. The thought of leaving him with Bianca Ingram was getting more painful by the moment. "Mr. Rathburn?" My voice was muffled by his shirt.

"Yes?"

"I'd better go pack my suitcase and check the train schedule." He released me and without another word disappeared into the barn. For a moment, the landscape — with its flitting moths, acres of trees, songbirds, and cicadas — seemed empty and unbearably quiet.

CHAPTER 15

I had never been to Jenna's apartment before. She buzzed me in from the lobby, and as I rode the elevator up to the twenty-first floor, I wondered if she had changed, if she might seem at all happy to see me. Jenna met me at the door. Her auburn hair had been straightened and cut into a sleek bob, and she wore olive-green capri pants, a matching blouse with a snakeskin print, and a charm bracelet that jingled as she walked. She didn't smile, throw her arms around me, or offer to take my suitcase.

"Took you long enough." She swept back a lock of hair from her eyes. On her left hand, an enormous diamond caught my eye. "You can set your suitcase down in the back room for now. You do realize I can't put you up here, right? Mark's already taking up every spare inch of space we have, which as you can see isn't much."

To my eye, the apartment looked large by Manhattan standards; it was austerely modernist, done up in metal and more shades of white than I had dreamed existed. The white leather sofa looked singularly uninviting, barely meant for sitting, much less sleeping. I tucked my suitcase into a corner of the small back room beside what I took to be my brother's belongings — a large duffel bag, a pile of thick books, and a rolled-up sleeping bag. A smaller, less-expensive-looking couch took up a third of that room.

"Where's Mark?" I asked.

"I kicked him out for the afternoon," she said. "I told him to start looking for an apartment of his own. I can't stand to have him here all day, moping around, breathing up all my oxygen. Let's sit out in the living room; this place makes me claustrophobic."

When we were side by side on the couch, she held out her hand for inspection. "You haven't seen my ring yet. Isn't it beautiful?" The pear-shaped diamond on her finger sparkled in the light. "We're going to have a small, tasteful wedding, just David's family. And his colleagues. And a few of our friends."

"It's a gorgeous ring," I told her. "Are you happy?"

"I was thrilled, until Mark dropped on our doorstep. I can't even think about planning the wedding with him breathing down my neck, sneering at me. Calling me superficial and image obsessed. He's such an asshole. I don't even know how he could possibly be related to me." She caught my eye. "To us. He's nothing like either of us."

I had to agree. "Tell me again why he's here." Over the phone, her explanation hadn't done much to satisfy my curiosity. "What's he been doing all these months? Why did he disappear after Mom and Dad's funeral?"

Jenna wrinkled her nose. "He went on a bender, I imagine. He drinks too much, that's clear. Anyway, I think he just wanted to get as far away from us as possible and take Mom and Dad's money with him."

"You got some of Mom and Dad's money," I reminded her.

"Well, yeah. But I've been spending it responsibly. Look at this place."

"Isn't it David's?"

"But you should have seen it when I moved in. Very bachelor pad. He's got to make a good impression. Now we can see people socially and not be ashamed. This couch we're sitting on? It's Italian — from Milan. I hired Sheila Antoine; have you heard of her? She's one of the most sought-after interior decorators in Manhattan. What she cost, you wouldn't believe. But worth it, don't you think?"

"Anyway," I said. "Mark. Why is he here now?"

"Well, he landed in Massachusetts. I guess he met a girl. Someone he worked with at a software company where he's been geeking around since February."

"What sort of work is he doing?"

Jenna shrugged. "Something boring with computers. His girlfriend's name is Debbie. She's a braniac just like him, I guess. The two of them used Mom and Dad's money to put a down payment on a McMansion out in the suburbs. Can you just imagine how tacky it probably is?"

"What happened?"

"You know how Mark is. He says Debbie kicked him out because she's a selfish bitch who only wants his money. But I knew there had to be more to it than that, so when he was sleeping off a hangover in the back room, I went through his cell phone and got her number."

"You called her?"

Jenna broke into a naughty smile. "And she says she kicked him out because he drinks too much and gets really nasty. Calls her names, tells her she's ugly and stupid. And then he started knocking her around. Gave her a black eye. Can you believe it?"

I thought of how he had hit me when we were children and of how he threatened to hurt me if I told Mom or Dad. "Didn't he ever hit you when we were kids?"

"Not once," Jenna said. "He probably knew I could take his skinny ass if he tried."

"I don't have any trouble believing he beat up his girlfriend," I said. "He used to hit me when nobody was looking."

"Huh. Well, she got herself a restraining order, and he had to go sleep on a friend's couch. He started drinking even harder and lost his job. At least that's what I imagine happened. Mark, of course, says his boss was a total asshole and canned him for no reason."

"Why isn't he still staying with his friend?"

"Who knows. Mark's such a liar. I can't believe anything he tells me anyway, so I don't bother asking. He probably pissed off the friend too. And of course he put all his money into the McMansion, so while his lawyer thrashes it out with Debbie's lawyer, he's almost penniless. Stinking up my apartment with his beer breath." She rose. "I need a Bellini. You want one?"

"Could I have some ice water instead?" While she was gone, I looked around the room for signs that my sister actually lived in it. There were no photographs, no mementos, no pieces of furniture or knickknacks from our family home. She returned, handed me my glass, and sat down again, legs daintily crossed, holding her cocktail up toward the window to admire its peach color. Then she took a delicate sip. "I wait all day for this."

"What is it you need me to do?" I asked her.

"Can you take Mark to live with you? Wherever it is that you're living now?"

Maybe I should have expected that request, but it came as a total surprise. "No, Jenna. I can't," I replied when I had found my tongue. "I'm a nanny. I live in someone else's home."

"I don't suppose you have any money to loan him?"

I thought of my savings account in the First Bank of Old Lyme, a small but steadily growing sum. Then I thought of how I might soon need to leave Thornfield Park to take another job among strangers. "Isn't there some other way I can help?"

Jenna thought a moment. "You can talk to him. Convince him to go back to Debbie. Coach him. Tell him how to win her over."

"I won't do that," I said. "He hits Debbie. You just said so yourself. She's better off without him."

"What do you care about Debbie? She's just some stranger. And she was stupid enough to move in with Mark in the first place." She took a deep swig from her glass. "I'd almost forgotten how prissy you are," she said.

185

I hesitated, then spoke my mind. "Well, I haven't forgotten how self-absorbed and demanding you are." I'd never said anything as direct or honest to my sister before. Adrenaline flooded my body, and I waited for her to react — to look shocked or maybe hurt. But nothing happened. It was as though she hadn't even heard me.

A moment passed before she spoke. "If you can't do anything to help me, you're not much of a sister."

"Why don't you lend him some money to get him into a new place?"

"I need the money I've got left for the wedding," Jenna said in a pinched voice. "I know I said it was going to be small, but it's got to be perfect. David's got a reputation to maintain."

"Can't David lend him some money?"

"David *hates* him. Loathes him. He refuses to live here anymore until I get Mark out of here. Last night he checked into a hotel. The Envoy. It was featured in *Travel and Leisure* magazine a few months ago — maybe you've heard of it?" She gazed down at her ring. "I'm afraid he's going to call the wedding off if I can't figure out some way to unload Mark soon."

I had met David only once, at the funeral, not long after he and Jenna had first started dating. Trim and well dressed, he had driven Jenna, Mark, and me to the cemetery and had fussed over the heating controls of his car for half the drive and complained about the cold for the rest. Something told me he hadn't been all that pleased with the prospect of having me at his apartment either, even though I was there at Jenna's request.

"Why don't I talk to Mark?" I offered.

"And tell him to do what?"

"I'm still working on that part," I said. "When will he get back?"

"I have absolutely no control over when he comes and goes. Lately he's been rolling in here at three in the morning, waking me up. Why don't you go get yourself a hotel room? I'll call you when his sorry ass turns up."

The first reasonably affordable hotel room I could find was fifty blocks downtown. Once I'd settled in, I walked around town, window-shopping and people watching, waiting for Jenna to call me on my cell phone. At dinnertime, I had a pleasant, solitary meal — just me and a novel I'd brought along — at an Indian restaurant across from the hotel. The food was fragrant and delicious, and I could enjoy it as long as I managed not to think too hard about my dwindling savings account. I went to bed early, but the buzz of traffic from the street twenty stories below acted like caffeine on my nervous system. All I could think about was Mr. Rathburn at Thornfield Park with Bianca Ingram. I stayed up for hours, longer than I'd intended to, forehead pressed to the window, watching a string of tiny cars glide below me, headlights and taillights pretty as a string of beads. At 1 a.m., I went back to bed.

Jenna hadn't called me by ten the next morning, so I phoned her.

"I'm not sure when he got in." She sounded sleepy and crabby. "He's snoring now in the back room. I'm not going to wake him up and get my head bitten off. You come here and do it."

"No," I said. "When he wakes up, see if you can get him to go out to a coffee shop. Then call me with the address." I'd thought it over and realized I'd be better off meeting my brother in a neutral public place, where he couldn't get too angry or violent.

Jenna sighed and hung up. I didn't hear from her again until midafternoon. Once she'd given me the address, I hurried to the nearest subway stop. I found Mark hunched over his laptop computer at the Greek coffee shop up the street from Jenna's place. A cold half cup of coffee sat before him. The table was littered with crumpled sugar packets and emptied creamers. I slid into the seat opposite him, and he looked up, apparently surprised to see me. He was thinner than I remembered. His light brown hair had begun to recede.

"I'll take a coffee," I told the bored-looking waitress. "Hey," I said to Mark.

"Hey yourself." He typed for a few more minutes as if I wasn't there. His T-shirt was wrinkled, and it looked like he hadn't shaved for days. Finally he snapped the laptop shut. "I see Jenna called in the cavalry."

I poured cream into my coffee. "She's worried about you."

He snorted. "She's worried I'll never get off her sofa. You look the same. And that's not a compliment."

I decided not to take the bait.

"I assume she told you," he said, "about how my skanky bitch girlfriend locked me out of my own house."

"From the sound of it, she had a good reason to lock you out. You hit her, right?" I'll admit that it took some courage for me to speak my mind, but we weren't children anymore. Even if he lashed out, even if he got physical, I didn't have to sit back and take it.

His eyes narrowed. "I need a refill," he called across the room to the waitress who was taking someone else's order. "I hit her," he said, "but you don't know the whole story. Maybe she needed hitting."

"Nobody needs hitting. Jenna tells me you lost your job."

"Yeah, I'm a total loser. I beat my woman; I lost my job. I've stepped straight out of a country-and-western song." His tone was sarcastic. "That idiot manager doesn't have a clue what he's doing. I tried to make a suggestion or two about how to run the office. You know how people are — so protective of their pathetic little territories. I was right, he knew it, and he couldn't stand it. So he canned me."

"You weren't drinking?"

"Do you listen to everything Jenna tells you? You do realize she's a total airhead? You may not be much fun to have around, but at least you're not as stupid as she is. Did she tell you her snooty fiancé gave her an ultimatum? It's me or him. I figure I'm doing her a favor if he dumps her ass."

"That's not your decision to make."

"'That's not your decision to make,'" he mimicked. "So what are you doing these days? Still at Sarah Lawrence with the rest of the radical lesbians?"

"I had to drop out. I don't have any money. The stocks Mom and Dad left me turned out to be almost worthless."

He didn't reply.

"I'm living in Connecticut. I work as a nanny."

"A nanny?" He laughed. "I guess there's no point in hitting you up for cash, then."

"That's right, there isn't. But I can buy you dinner if you want."

"At the Russian Tea Room? The Four Seasons?"

"No. Here."

"How about buying me a drink next door instead?"

"Dinner here. That's it."

Mark hesitated a moment, then reached for one of the menus propped between the salt and pepper shakers and the wall. He looked it over in silence, then signaled for the waitress. "I'll take a western omelet, hash browns, whole wheat toast, some orange juice, and more coffee."

I ordered the same.

"I haven't eaten all day," he said. It wasn't *thank you*, but I knew it was probably as close to it as I could expect from my brother. "So you came all this way. That surprises me."

"You're my brother. I thought maybe you could use someone to talk to."

"Are we having an *Oprah* moment?" he said, but then his tone grew less malignant. "This isn't a very good time for me. As I'm sure you've guessed."

"What is it you'd want to do, if you could do anything?"

"Besides drink myself into an early grave?" The waitress set a glass of orange juice in front of each of us, and he downed his in two rapid gulps. "I want Debbie back. I want to live in my own fucking house."

"What would convince her to let you move back in?"

"Hell freezing over?"

"Besides that. Something you can control."

He looked miserable for a second. "I'm not going to stop drinking. Despite whatever Jenna told you, I'm not an alcoholic."

Not that I would have expected him to admit it if he was. "Anger-management counseling then?" The waitress set our plates down before us, and Mark tore into his.

"You're kidding, right?" Mark said, his mouth full.

"Why would I be kidding?" I pushed my hash browns around on the plate, suddenly aware that I couldn't eat a bite. "You hit your girlfriend, Mark. That's not okay in anybody's book." I thought a moment. "Okay. How about a plain old-fashioned psychologist?"

"How the fuck am I supposed to pay for that?" He kept his voice low, but I recognized the steely look in his eyes from childhood and had the sudden urge to run.

"I could help you find some kind of, I don't know, agency with a sliding scale. You're technically homeless. There are services for homeless people."

"Homeless!" Mark laughed. "You're such a freak. You always were. I may not have a home at the moment, but I'm not *homeless*." He lowered his voice. "Did it ever occur to you that maybe Debbie is the crazy one? That maybe I'm not the one with the problem?"

"No, it never occurred to me." I pushed my plate over to his side of the table. "You can have mine." I thought with longing of Mr. Rathburn and my quiet bedroom at Thornfield Park. Why had I believed I could help in any way? Mark was unreachable. Or maybe somebody else could reach him, but certainly not the sister he had never liked or respected.

"Why did you hit *me*?" I heard myself ask him. I hadn't intended to; the question just slipped out. "Why did you lock me in that attic crawl space and leave me there all night?" Maybe the answer would give me some kind of clue about what sort of help I could give him. Or maybe it would simply tell me something I needed to know for myself.

Mark had finished his eggs and moved on to mine. "When did I do that? Are you making stuff up now?"

"Can I get you anything else?" The waitress stood by our table, waiting for some kind of coherent answer — a yes or a no — but I couldn't remember my own name at that moment.

"I'd like some bacon," Mark told her. He looked at me appraisingly. Was he wondering if he'd pushed me past the limit? The waitress left to place the order.

"You hit me." I tried to keep my voice level. "You hit me often, and once you locked me in the attic and didn't tell anyone. I spent a whole night up there."

"I think you're blowing things out of proportion," he told me. "Siblings slap each other around all the time. A little rivalry's normal. As for the attic thing. . . . Is there any grape jelly?" He grabbed the bowl of jelly packets. "Was it really such a big deal? I didn't think it was, and I'm sorry you did."

"You're sorry I did?" Maybe I would have exploded with anger right there in the restaurant if I had been able to fully believe my ears. "That's not an apology."

"I don't have anything to apologize for," he said. "Not to you. Not to Debbie."

I waved a hand at the waitress. "Check, please," I said. Then I did what little — ridiculously little — I could do. "Then I can't help you. You're on your own. But you have to get out of Jenna's apartment. By tomorrow morning."

"You're taking her side?" He looked at me in disbelief. Maybe he'd expected me to keep trying to save him or, at the very least, to stay seated across from him, entangled in an argument I couldn't win, until he prevailed by sheer persistence.

"I'm not taking anyone's side. She wants you out, so you've got to get out. Wherever you decide to go next is up to you." I grabbed the check and paid at the cash register. Then I walked over to the waitress and handed her the tip, certain that if I left it on the table, Mark would pocket it himself. Without glancing over at him, I stepped out onto the busy street.

The sun hadn't yet set. I hurried back to Jenna's apartment building and punched the up button once, twice, three times, until the elevator arrived. In response to her questions, I delivered the news: I had told Mark he had to leave by tomorrow morning. If he didn't go, she should call the police and have him arrested for trespassing. That was the best I could do.

Jenna thanked me, or tried to, but I didn't want her thanks. I gave her a quick kiss on the cheek and headed off in the direction of the subway station. Though I would have expected rush hour to be over by then, the subway cars downtown were all crowded. I hung on to an overhead bar amid the exhausted and disgruntled-looking commuters. I would spend one more night in the hotel and catch the first train back to Connecticut in the morning.

I felt relief and sorrow and disappointment. The last emotion surprised me. What had I been hoping for? Against the rushing dark tunnel walls behind the subway window, I could see my reflection framed by the commuters to my left and my right. If my brother had apologized, if my sister had been truly happy to see me, if either of them had been interested in what I'd been doing with myself for the past six months, it would have made me happy. I might even have forgiven them. But they were just as I remembered them, and I understood, finally, that they would never change.

CHAPTER 16

The trip back to Old Lyme took what seemed like a hundred years. I read and reread the same paragraph of my book, but I couldn't lose myself in the words for fear of missing my stop. Benjamin was waiting patiently for me at the station, and at the sight of his craggy face I remembered the morning I had first arrived at Thornfield Park. I felt so glad that I had to ask myself what that gladness meant, and reminded myself that the home to which I was returning wouldn't be mine much longer. I knew Maddy would be happy to see me; Lucia would welcome my return. But I also knew very well that I was thinking of someone else, and that he wasn't thinking of me. Even so, I felt joy bubble up inside me and buoy me up like helium.

"How are the rehearsals going?" I asked Benjamin when we were on the highway. This time I had taken the seat beside him.

"They're over, I'm happy to say," he responded. "Nico sent the guys back to their homes. They need a few days to rest up before the rehearsal show. Once the tour starts, they won't get many days off. And we get a few days of peace too. About time."

"And what about Bianca Ingram? Is the photo shoot done?"

"She's gone too — at least for now."

I wanted to ask the question that had been nagging at me the whole ride home: had there been any big announcements in my absence? If Mr. Rathburn had gotten engaged, I supposed I would hear about it very soon.

When we turned into the driveway, I waved at the good-looking young guard. He waved back, looking almost as happy to see me as I was to see him. The sky was nearly cloudless that morning. Orange and yellow tiger lilies swayed in the front garden. Benjamin offered to bring my suitcase up to my room. I thanked him, jumped out, and started up the path to the house. Just then, I heard the soft strains of an acoustic guitar coming from behind the house. Instead of ringing the front doorbell, I hurried around the perimeter of the main building to the back deck, where Mr. Rathburn sat in an Adirondack chair, playing softly to himself.

I saw him before he noticed me, and my nerves vibrated like guitar strings. I thought about calling to him but couldn't find my voice. I stopped in my tracks and even took a step backward, hoping to slip quietly into the house before I made an absolute fool of myself. But then he saw me.

"Hello!" he called, setting his guitar down beside him. "There you are! Get on up here."

On trembling legs, I climbed the steps to the deck, hoping my

196

face hid my emotions. Mr. Rathburn pulled the nearest chair a bit closer to his and motioned for me to sit down. I complied.

"What took you so long?" His voice sounded more pleased than angry. "I gave you one day off, but you've been gone for three."

"I told you I didn't know how long it would take."

"I was worried about you off in the big city, with that family of yours. But now you're safely home." He patted my hand, then pulled back. "Did you solve the world's problems?"

"Not even close." I suppressed a smile, realizing that he had suggested Thornfield Park was my home too. If only it were.

"And did you worry how we'd survive here without you?"

"I was only gone three days, Mr. Rathburn. Benjamin tells me that rehearsals are over and the band is gone."

"And did you hear that Bianca Ingram has gone for the time being?"

The bubble in my chest popped abruptly. "I guess you must have been sorry to see her go."

"What man wouldn't be sorry to say good-bye to a woman like that?" He clasped his hands behind his head and leaned back luxuriously. "I only wish I were her equal in the looks department. What was it you said about me? That I'm a suburban dad? And I'm only rock-star handsome. While you're saving the world, can you whip up a little something to make me look like a movie star?"

"I'm not a magician," I said, and he laughed. Of course I couldn't say what I was thinking: to me, his face was more interesting, more attractive, than the clear-skinned perfection of any pretty-boy movie star. He seemed to read my thoughts and looked at me the

197

way he sometimes did when we were alone together, with a smile more genuine than his public one.

"Go," he said. "Get some rest. I'll look after Maddy today. You can just take it easy. You're back among friends now." He turned to his guitar and began picking out a complex run of notes.

I started into the house, but something stopped me. Before I could think better of it, the words spilled out. "Thank you, Nico." I'd never called him that before, and the name felt strange on my tongue. "You've been a true friend to me. I'm…I'm happier than you know to be back here. Thornfield Park feels like my home. My real home."

And before he could speak or stand, I slipped into the house, letting the door slam behind me. Cheeks burning, I ran up to my room without stopping to say hello to Lucia or Maddy. Without bothering to change or unpack, I lay down. My bed felt so much more welcoming than the one at the hotel had been. I burrowed under the covers and slept more soundly than I had in days.

CHAPTER 17

In the days between my return and the rehearsal show that would signal the start of Mr. Rathburn's tour, the name Bianca Ingram wasn't spoken. Maybe Mr. Rathburn was in communication with her, maybe the two of them had long telephone conversations when I wasn't around, but I didn't see any evidence that he missed her or looked forward to seeing her again. During those days, he spent more time with Maddy and me than usual. He even took us out to lunch again at the seafood restaurant beside the Connecticut River, the three of us lingering for hours in the otherwise empty dining room, Maddy so giddy with her father's attention that she bubbled over with jokes and stories.

In the evenings, he played guitar on the deck and called me out to join him, trying out song after song on me until he hit on one I knew the words to and could sing along with. My voice was only serviceable, but he seemed not to care. He even brought out a second guitar and taught me a few chords, my fingers struggling to reach the right frets on the guitar's thick neck. Though he still worked out in the mornings, he skipped his afternoon sessions in the music room to push Maddy on her swing or to have splash fights with her in the swimming pool. Whenever he spent time with Maddy, he invited me along. He even joined us in the breakfast room for dinner. I had never spent so much time in his company and — sadly enough — had never loved him so well.

The day before the rehearsal show, I tried to keep Maddy out of his hair, thinking he must have last-minute details to attend to. He spent much of that day wandering through the house, talking on his cell phone, and working through the logistics of the show and the tour that would follow it. I learned from Lucia that the band would be arriving en masse to meet him at the XL Center the next afternoon. I assumed Bianca Ingram would be there to bask in her boyfriend's big night, but I didn't want to ask. As long as I didn't know for sure, I could hang on to one last smidgen of happiness.

I tried to put Maddy to bed early that night, but she was in a tizzy. It was, after all, her father's first major concert in as long as she could remember, and she was full of questions. "How many people will be watching Daddy?" she wanted to know. "Will they be looking at me?" It took three stories to get her to sleep, but once she was out, I went for a walk on the grounds. As I passed by the window of Mr. Rathburn's office, I heard him on the phone, conferring with someone about the stage setup and the procedures for letting fans into the general admission pit. The thought of tomorrow night's show, and the likely presence of Bianca Ingram, made me sad. The prospect of the tour taking Mr. Rathburn far away made me even sadder. I didn't feel up to polite conversation, so I walked on.

The sun was just setting, the sky above the guesthouse streaked with fuchsia and orange. The air was redolent with new-cut grass and freshly laid mulch. I walked past the pool house, toward the line of arbor vitae that made a lush screen to hide behind. Nearby, butterfly bushes rippled in a row, their purple flowers giving off a delicious scent. I walked around the wall of slender trees, slipped off my shoes, and felt the cool evening grass on my feet. I was wishing I'd brought my paints and brushes — it had been a while since I'd found time to paint — when I heard a familiar voice calling my name. There, coming around the trees, was Mr. Rathburn. I was seized by an impulse to hide, standing still enough to be unnoticed until he had passed by. But, no, he had seen me and was heading my way.

"I thought I saw you slip out of the house," he called as he approached. "What are you doing back here?"

"Just going for a walk. I'm going to head back now."

"Back to the house?" Now he was standing just inches from me. "On a beautiful night like this? There's no reason to go in just yet. Why don't you walk with me?"

I tried to think of a believable excuse. Failing that, I was silent and walked beside him. We took the path that led down toward the pine grove. In the clearing stood an enormous horse chestnut tree with a wooden bench beneath it. Mr. Rathburn paused there. For several minutes neither of us spoke.

He broke the silence. "I sometimes forget how gorgeous it is back here. As much as I love touring, I'm going to hate to be away from all this. What about you, Jane? Do you like it here? At Thornfield Park, I mean."

"Of course I do." Hadn't he been listening the other day when I'd blurted out my confession that Thornfield Park felt like my only home?

"It's too bad you're thinking of leaving," he said. "Maddy and Lucia will miss you."

I looked at him in surprise.

"I'm thinking of that conversation we had a while ago," he said. "You said I should look for a new place for you, so that's what I've been doing."

The news hit me like a punch in the stomach, but I stayed on my feet. "Does that mean you're getting married, Mr. Rathburn?"

"I guess it does."

I had to look away from his face. I bent down as if to scoop up a couple of the horse chestnut burrs that littered the grass. I touched one, and it pricked my fingers. When I could trust myself to speak, I dared only a single word. "Soon?"

"Very soon." He thrust both hands in his pockets and rocked back and forth on his toes. "I might even propose before the tour begins. Bianca Ingram's not the kind of woman who waits around for a ring. If I don't tie her down soon, she's liable to find herself some crown prince or a movie mogul, don't you think?" He turned around. "Why won't you stand up straight and look at me? And quit playing with those seedpods when I'm trying to talk with you...especially about something so important." His tone was petulant, as if *I* were the one hurting *him*. "Remember, leaving was your idea. And you're right; sensible as always. Bianca wouldn't be very happy to have you around the place."

"Yes, Mr. Rathburn." I wanted to warn him about the hardness I'd observed in Bianca Ingram's character, but what good would it do? I was too late. Maybe he would have listened to me a few weeks ago. He'd even asked my opinion of her. Why hadn't I spoken up then?

"As I promised, I've been on the lookout for a new position for you. I remember you saying you wished you could travel..."

"I said that?"

"You said you wouldn't be here if you could afford to backpack across Europe, remember? I've been thinking that the least I can do is make that wish come true. Oh, don't look at me like that. I'm acting in your best interest, that's all. What would you say to Ireland?"

"Ireland?"

"I have a friend — you may have heard of him; he had a few hits around ten years ago — Duncan Webb. Does that ring a bell? He and his wife have a house outside Dublin, and they have five daughters. Can you imagine that? A lot of kids, but nothing you can't handle."

"It's so far away..."

"Well, that's the point, isn't it? You're not going to wimp out on me, are you, Jane? An independent young woman like you. You'll be fine on the plane, and Duncan will send someone to pick you up at the airport."

"It's not the traveling. It's the distance...all the way across the ocean."

"The distance from what, Jane?"

"From America, and from Thornfield Park. And…"

"Well?"

"From you, Mr. Rathburn."

I said this almost involuntarily, and as I spoke, the tears I'd been holding back trickled out. Even so, I did my best not to sob. "It's so far away," I repeated.

"We'll see each other again. When the band plays Dublin, I'll send you a ticket. I know you're not my biggest fan, but you'd like that, wouldn't you, Jane? The best seat in the house?"

"It's not the same."

"Not the same as what?"

I couldn't think of a reply.

"We've become real friends, haven't we, Jane? Not just boss and employee, I mean."

"Yes," I replied.

"Here, have a seat." He sat down on the bench underneath the tree's wide canopy and scooted over to make room. "After tonight, I'll be so busy getting ready. We've got so much to talk about — the tour, my wedding, your trip to Ireland." I sat beside him. He continued. "How do you feel about me, Jane?"

It struck me as a strange question. I said nothing, because what could I say?

"Because I've had a strange feeling about you, ever since I first saw you…"

"When you almost flattened me with your car," I supplied mechanically.

"Right. Even as I was giving you shit and you were standing up to me in that quiet, stubborn way you have, I had this feeling about you...that we were, you know..."

"No, I don't," I said. "I really, really don't."

"Kindred spirits," he said. "Maybe that sounds all New Agey and cheesy, but it's how I felt. How I feel. Like we were meant to take care of each other. That as different as we are, we're weirdly alike." He paused, then cleared his throat. "But I guess I was wrong."

"But what if...what if you were..." I wanted to ask him what if he was right, what if there was such a thing as kindred spirits, and we fit that description? But I couldn't get the question out. I broke down and began to cry, sobs racking my body. "I wish I'd never come to Thornfield Park."

Mr. Rathburn moved a bit closer on the bench but didn't touch me. "Because you have to leave?"

Emotion won out over reason. "Yes. Of course. I love Thornfield Park. It's the only place I've felt...valued. And that's because you're here, Mr. Rathburn. You could have treated me like an employee, but instead you've been a friend to me. No, *more* than a friend. And now I have to leave you."

Mr. Rathburn's voice softened. "Maybe you don't have to leave."

"But I do. I couldn't live here with you and your new wife, and watch myself become nothing to you...because that's what would happen, and I couldn't stand it. Do you think because I'm... ordinary...that I don't have feelings?" I could hear my voice rising, carrying across the field, but for once I didn't care what the world thought of me. "Because I do have feelings, and if I were beautiful and talented and famous, I'd make it as hard for you to leave me as it is for me to leave you."

"Of course I know you have feelings." And Mr. Rathburn stunned me into momentary silence by throwing his arms around me and pulling me to his chest. As I had the day he'd hugged me good-bye before sending me off to New York, I felt his heart pounding against mine. "Jane." And then, before I could speak again or even think, he pressed his lips to mine.

An electric shock passed through me. For a moment I let him kiss me, but then I pushed him away. I wasn't thinking clearly. If I had ever suspected that Mr. Rathburn had feelings for me, I'd long since convinced myself I'd been wrong, so why was he kissing me? "No," I said. "You're a married man."

He looked startled. "What do you mean?"

"Maybe not yet, but you will be…soon…and to Bianca Ingram — of all the women you could have chosen! She may be some kind of famous beauty, but if you can't see that she's not good enough for you, then you're not as smart as you pretend you are." I struggled to free myself from the circle of his arms. "Let me go." He released me, and I scrambled to my feet.

"I'll let you go if that's what you really want," he said. He looked up at me from the bench, his gray eyes bottomless and warm. "But I wish you would come back and rest your head right here." He patted his chest. "And let me love you the way you deserve."

"It's a little late for that, isn't it?" I took a step backward, then another. "You've already made your choice. I'm not going to come between you and your fiancée."

"No. Of course not." He fell silent for a moment. "Sit down next to me. Please. I won't touch you again if you don't want me to."

I remained standing. For a moment, neither of us said a word, a mockingbird's song the only sound. I still couldn't stop the tears from running down my face. I rummaged in my pockets and found a tissue.

Some time passed before he spoke. "What if I told you that I'm not engaged to Bianca, that I never had the least intention of proposing to her?"

"I wouldn't believe you," I said. "You're...you're sleeping with her, right?"

"No," he said. "Maybe the old Nico Rathburn would have." He thought a moment. "The old me *definitely* would have. But no, I'm not sleeping with her."

"But she wanted you. Anyone could see that. Why not?"

He rose and reached me in a single stride. "Because you're the one I want," he said, pulling me close again. "You're the *only* one I want. Don't you believe me?"

"Of course I don't."

"Don't you trust me, then?"

"Not one bit."

I shut my eyes and inhaled his familiar scent. It would be too easy to just give in and let him hold me, to let him do whatever he wanted to. And why shouldn't I? Except, of course, that the closer I let him get, the harder it would be to leave him, as I knew I soon would have to. I forced my eyes open.

"How do I make you believe me?" he said. "Bianca Ingram

207

didn't want me, not really. All she wanted was to butter me up and get me to lower my guard. She wanted to get the best, most intimate photo spread she could pull off, so she flirted with me. Maybe she would have slept with me if that was what it took. I've been with a lot of women, Jane. That doesn't come as any great shock, right?"

I shook my head.

"After a while, even a guy like me wants to be wanted for more than just his money and his power. Do you believe me now?"

I still wasn't sure I did. "Some of them probably want to sleep with you for your music," I told him.

"Maybe so. But that's still not the same as wanting me because they know and understand me and like me even though I'm a flaming asshole," he said. "Jane, you *get* me. And I think I get you. Now can you fucking well believe me?"

"But *me*?" I asked, for the first time allowing myself to entertain the possibility that he might, just might, mean some of what he was saying. "I'm not even pretty."

He bent and kissed my forehead. And then he pulled the ponytail holder from my hair, brushed back the strands that fell free, and kissed me on my neck. I felt my body turn to liquid beneath his lips. "Jane, Jane, Jane," he whispered. "Who made you believe you aren't pretty?" And then, more distinctly, "Can't you tell how much I want you?" I opened my mouth to speak and he pressed two fingers across my lips. "No matter what you do, you'd better not call me 'Mr. Rathburn,'" he warned. And he lifted his fingers to let me speak.

"Nico," I said. And he kissed me again, his hands in my hair, and then on my waist. His lips were gentle at first, then more insistent. Then he released me. I opened my eyes and looked up at him. When had it gotten so dark out? With one finger he traced my profile, from my forehead, down my nose, to my chin, then down my throat to the top button of my blouse. Looking me straight in the eyes, he undid the top button. Then, when I didn't object, he undid the next one.

"Come inside with me," he whispered, "and let me make love to you" — he undid another button — "all night long, and then all day tomorrow, and then the day after that..."

"You have a show to put on tomorrow night," I reminded him.

Mr. Rathburn — Nico — sighed deeply. He brushed my hair back again, tucking it behind my ears. "That's the spirit. You'll keep me honest, won't you?"

"I'll try." The wind had picked up. It sent the line of arbor vitae bowing back and forth, rustled the horse chestnut canopy above us, and blew my hair into my eyes so I could hardly see. I gave Nico my hand and let him lead me back to the house.

CHAPTER 18

That night, the dark of Nico's bedroom was slashed again and again by lightning; the storm buffeted the house for an hour. As he undressed me — so slowly I thought I might stop breathing — electricity flickered outside, almost as if caused by the heat in the air between us. In my plain cotton bra and panties — how I wished I'd had on something prettier — I stood and watched him unbutton his shirt while lightning crackled, first on one side of Thornfield Park and then on the other. Nico lifted me in his arms and set me down on the bed. He unclasped my bra, his eyes looking intently into mine, watching for my reaction. Then he eased the panties down over my hip bones. Just then, the clouds opened, and rain pounded against the windows. He kissed his way down my body. I shut my eyes tight and felt myself arc upward to meet his lips. Every nerve in my body sang out at once, till something inside me burst like a soap bubble.

"Darling, darling Jane." Now the face I loved so well was before me, kissing me again, his lips soft on mine. I ran my hands down the skin of his chest. It felt smooth and warm, with that tangle of coarse fur just at the breastbone.

"Nico." I savored the taste of his name on my tongue. *Could I really be kissing Nico Rathburn, the man I've grown to love so hopelessly?* The thought made me light-headed. I said his name again, loving the sound of it.

At the exact moment our bodies merged — and to be honest, it hurt, though I know he was trying to be gentle — a bolt of lightning struck so near that the house shook. Barely a second later, thunder rattled the windowpanes. We froze, stunned by the violence and, I think, a little surprised to see each other in the sudden, temporary brightness, to discover each other — so familiar and yet so strange — in this new way. Every so often, a lightning flash would reveal us to each other, and the expression on his face — so rapt, so helpless, so utterly mine — was the most beautiful thing I ever expected to see in my life.

The next morning I woke before Nico. It took me a while to realize I wasn't dreaming. Strewn across the floor were our clothes. Impulsively, I grabbed Nico's soft black T-shirt and pulled it on over my head. In the bathroom, I bent over the sink to splash my face with water, and when I straightened, what I saw in the mirror surprised me. It was the same face I'd known all my life — and yet it wasn't. Though not a particularly glamorous shade of brown, my hair shone in the morning light and fell below my shoulders. My eyes gleamed a brighter green than I'd ever seen them before, and my face was rosy, a dimple in each cheek. My parted lips revealed straight, neat teeth. I looked happy, even pretty.

"What are you smiling at?" Nico had slipped into the room behind me; he wrapped his arms around my waist. I didn't answer — how could I admit I'd been admiring myself in the mirror? — but he read my mind. "You're seeing what I've seen all along: a lovely, adorable woman." He nuzzled my neck.

I suddenly remembered my duties. "Maddy...she must be up by now."

"Lucia's got her," Nico said. "Today would have been your usual day off, right? No need to worry."

Those last four words were the same ones he'd used the night before when, after I'd inquired about being safe, he had reached into the drawer of the bedside table and drawn out a satin-lined mahogany box of condoms. "Standard rock-star equipment," he'd said with a sly smile. "There's a stash of these in every room." Now, blushing at the memory, I slipped from his grasp and began gathering up our clothes from the bedroom floor.

"You can leave that. Amber will take care of it." His hair rumpled and his eyelids heavy with sleep, he sat down on the bed and yawned. "We need coffee." He jabbed at the intercom button beside his bed. "Where the hell are Amber and Linda?" He jabbed again and again. "Lucia?"

"Lucia's busy," I said, pulling on my jeans. "You know, you could make your own coffee."

He looked momentarily puzzled.

"Or don't you know how?"

"My secret's out. When I'm not onstage or in the studio, I'm utterly useless."

"Oh, I can think of some other things you're good at." I reached for both his hands and tried to tug him to his feet. "But it's time you learned to make coffee. Come on. I'll show you how. It's not exactly hard."

"Okay, then. Civilize me."

"I'm a nanny, not a miracle worker."

Nico's first-ever pot of coffee wasn't bad. We carried our mugs onto the deck and sat side by side on the top step, looking out at the damp grass glistening in the morning sun.

Nico took a sip of coffee. "Hey, this is better than Walter's."

"I wouldn't go quite that far" — I rested my head on his shoulder — "but it's pretty good for your first try."

"You'll make me into a whole new man." He threw his arm around my shoulders and pulled me in a little closer. "And that's only one of the reasons I love you."

"I love you too, Nico."

"And you'll always love me? Imperfect as I am?"

"I'll always love you," I told him, and meant it with my whole heart.

Later that morning, as we ate pancakes together in the breakfast room, our hair still wet from the shower, I looked up and saw Lucia, clipboard in hand. She was alone. Maddy must have been off at preschool.

"Nico, I need to talk to you about..." She stared as though she'd seen something disturbing, and I suddenly saw the two of us

214

through her eyes and realized how perfectly clear it must be that we'd spent the night together. Lucia pursed her lips, looked away, and continued. "You know the horse chestnut tree? The one out in the field? It was struck by lightning last night. Split right in half. I thought I'd call in a tree service to haul it away."

"Don't do that," Nico said. "Leave it as it is. I want to see it for myself." He turned the page of the *Times*, apparently unconcerned by Lucia's cool tone.

"Okay then." She hurried out of the room.

"Wasn't that the tree we sat under last night?" I asked. "The one where…"

Nico looked up. "It must be," he said, the frown line appearing between his eyes.

"Lucia's upset with us," I told him. "Or maybe just with me."

"Upset? Because we're?" He pointed first at me and then at himself.

"I think so."

"Well, it's none of her business." He put the paper aside. "Try not to worry about what Lucia thinks. You've got more important things to think about. For instance: what shall we do today?"

"You have a concert to prepare for, don't you?"

"All I have to do is roll in for a sound check a few hours before the show. You and I have the whole day to spend together. Let's zip into New York City. There's someplace I want to take you. No questions. It's a surprise."

Benjamin let us out in front of a boutique on Fifth Avenue. A woman in head-to-toe black buzzed us into the intimidating, ultramodern interior — stark charcoal-gray walls and spare furnishings. We were the only customers. "Nice to see you again, Nico." She extended a slender hand. "And Ms. Moore, it's a pleasure to meet you." If she registered the comparative drabness of the clothes I was wearing, she didn't let it show. "I'm Michaela. Come, make yourself at home. Would you like a glass of Prosecco?" She looked at me a bit more closely. "Or maybe some sparkling water?"

When she had disappeared, I turned to Nico, who had settled onto a long white sofa. "What's this about?"

"You need something to wear tonight, right?" During the long ride into the city, he had refused to tell me where we were going, and I had been too happy to care. "This is the flagship store of one of the best designers in the business. Just follow my lead."

When Michaela returned, I accepted the glass of water and occupied myself by looking at the racks of clothing, while Nico explained our errand to her. "Miss Moore needs a complete new wardrobe." I swallowed hard, not at all sure how I felt about this particular surprise.

Behind curtains, I submitted to the tape measure, and Michaela's appraising eye. She brought me racks of clothes to try on — every type of garment from silken underthings to summer sheaths in a rainbow of colors to high-heeled pumps in leather soft as butter. With each combination of items I tried on, she asked me if I wanted to walk out into the atrium to ask Nico his opinion, and I balked and told her no. When I had tried everything on, I excused myself, got back into the oxford blouse, narrow skirt, and flats I'd worn into the store, and told her I needed to speak to Nico.

I found him where I'd left him, on the couch in the atrium, where he was growling something into his cell phone. When I entered the room, he snapped the phone shut and stood to meet me. "You're done already?" he asked. "Didn't you like anything here?"

"What's this all about?" I asked him. "I appreciate your generosity, I do, but this is just too much."

"Too much? You need clothes, don't you?"

"I have clothes," I told him.

"Yes, of course, but you're my girlfriend now. I want to show you off to the whole world, tonight and always. Once we go public, your picture will wind up in newspapers, in magazines, on TV. It will be a whole new life. After this, I thought I'd take you to a little spa I know on Madison Avenue, get you a manicure, a haircut, a facial, whatever you like."

"You're ashamed of me?" I asked. "You want to make me over into some other kind of woman? What's next? Breast implants?"

"No, no, no." He looked for a moment as though he might start fuming and shouting. Then he thought better of it and changed his tack, caressing my cheek with the back of his hand until I could feel my resolve starting to melt. "You're everything I could ever want, Jane. No matter what you think of yourself, you're beautiful, and I want the world to see that. I want to dress you up in silk and lace — maybe some emerald earrings to match those eyes of yours — so you can shine like the jewel you are."

"That's not me, Nico. I'd feel like I was wearing a Halloween costume."

He harrumphed. "What planet are you from, anyway? How

217

did I find the one woman in the world who isn't thrilled by the chance to spend my money?"

I looped my arm through his. "Nico?"

"Don't look at me like that. It isn't fair."

"Remember when you told me about Maddy's mother? How she was using you? You called her a gold digger."

"Because she was," he said. "This is totally different. *You're* totally different."

"Yes," I told him. "I'm different."

"No kidding."

Just then, Michaela rounded the corner, asking if she could refill our glasses and if she might show me anything else. My eyes met Nico's. Then I turned to her.

"I don't need an entire wardrobe," I said, "but I'll take a few things for special occasions."

"More sparkling water," Nico told Michaela. When she'd departed with our glasses, he turned back to me. "At least pick something sexy for tonight," he insisted. "Something low cut. With a tight skirt. Maybe some stiletto heels?"

"Is it me you want, Nico?" I asked him. "Because that's not how I dress. I don't know how to walk in stilettos. I like people to talk to my face, not my breasts." I refused the second glass of water and followed Michaela back into the dressing room, where I chose what I would need for that night and a few other outfits. She promised to have that night's ensemble delivered to Thornfield Park by five.

"What did you get?" Nico asked

"You'll see tonight," I told him. "But don't expect me to look like a sex goddess, or you'll be profoundly disappointed."

218

"She'll look lovely and tasteful," Michaela assured him. "Think Audrey Hepburn. You'll be very pleased."

Emboldened, Nico handed over his credit card and insisted that we go to a jewelry store a few blocks away.

"I'll wear my pearl earrings tonight," I told him. "They may not be avant-garde enough for your public, but they're mine, and they suit me."

"A haircut then? A pedicure? A belly button ring?" He seemed to be kidding about that last one. I patted his hand.

"Can we please just go home? I'd like to sit on the back deck and eat a sandwich and read a book and think about anything other than clothes for a couple of hours."

"You win," Nico said, then remained silent until we were gliding uptown in the back of his Range Rover. "You know, though" — he took my hand — "you need to get used to being pampered. I plan to take you everywhere I go from now on. Paris, Milan, Barcelona, Stockholm, Edinburgh. Everywhere. Wherever I play, I want you to be. It's a win-win situation. You'll get to see the world. And I'll get you — to keep me company everywhere I go."

"You'll be sick of me. And what will I do with myself while you're working?"

"You can watch me play," he said. "And you can sightsee wherever we are. You can sketch and paint, make your art all day long."

"But how will I earn my keep?"

"Earn your keep? You're a rock star's girlfriend, angel. You don't have to earn your keep."

"Of course I have to work," I told him. "I can't just tag along with no purpose."

"No purpose?" He checked to see if Benjamin was looking in the rearview mirror, then he kissed me softly on the lips. "Your purpose is to be my love slave." He smiled mischievously and slid his hand up my skirt to caress my inner thigh.

I gasped and pulled away from him. "I'm not going to be any kind of slave." I kept my voice level. "If that's what you have in mind, I think you'd better find someone else to pamper."

Nico was silent for a long time. "You can sell your paintings. I can hook you up with a gallery, get you a show," he said finally.

"You know I'm not good enough for that yet," I told him. "I don't want some gallery to show my work just because I'm Nico Rathburn's girlfriend. I need to go back to school. And don't think about offering to pay my tuition. I'm saving up my salary, and I'll put myself through school."

"Salary?" he said. "Have you forgotten *I* pay your salary?"

"Not for a minute."

"Are you trying to tell me you still plan to work for me? As my nanny?"

"As *Maddy*'s nanny," I corrected him. "It's not you I'll be driving back and forth to preschool and pushing on the swings. And I don't think you need me to keep you out of trouble."

"You could give me baths and tuck me into bed at night," Nico said playfully. "I'd like that." His hand crept up my leg again. I removed it. "You mean you want to stay at Thornfield Park watching Maddy while I'm on tour, all by myself?"

"You'll hardly be by yourself," I said. "You'll have the band, and all your fans, and, I imagine, plenty of groupies."

"You want to give me back to the groupies?" He sounded petulant.

"Maddy and I could come on tour with you."

He looked surprised — apparently the idea hadn't occurred to him. I kissed him on the cheek, and he put his arm around me and held me close. "I bet she'll like traveling even more than I will," I told him.

"We'll be a family." He sounded pleased with the idea. We rode on awhile in silence. When we were halfway across the Triborough Bridge, he turned to me and said, "Let's make it official."

At first I wasn't sure what he meant.

"Let's get married." He grabbed both my hands, then hesitated. "Dammit, I'd get down on one knee if there were room. Will you marry me, Jane?"

For a moment I forgot to breathe.

"Don't torture me," Nico demanded.

"Torture you?" I asked. "How can I do that? If you really mean it, how could I say no?"

"If I really mean it?" Now he looked totally exasperated. "Jane, say yes quickly. Say 'Yes, Nico; I will marry you.'"

"Yes, Nico," I repeated. "I will marry you." And I let him envelop me in his arms and kiss me again and again, not worrying about what Benjamin must be thinking as he watched us in the rearview mirror.

"I'll buy you an engagement ring," Nico said finally. He pressed my left hand to his lips. "Before you say another single word, I promise not to go overboard. It will be modest and flawless, just like you."

221

"I'm hardly flawless."

"You see?" he said with a grin. "Modest."

I shook my head but couldn't keep from smiling.

"There's something I've been wondering about," I told him. "Will you answer one question for me?"

"Depends on what it is," he said — a bit warily, I thought.

"Are you planning on keeping secrets from me? That's no way to begin a marriage."

"I promise I'll tell you anything worth knowing," he said. "You'll have to let me be the judge of what concerns you and what doesn't."

"That hardly seems fair. I'll only marry you if you consider me your equal."

"Of course I do."

"Then promise you'll be completely honest with me. That's not too much to ask."

He hesitated a moment, the furrow between his brows deepening. "I'll answer whatever question you ask," he said. "I promise."

"Well then, why did you pretend to be in love with Bianca Ingram?"

"Is that all? To make you jealous, of course. How else was I going to get you to fall in love with me?"

"Subterfuge was hardly necessary. I loved you almost from the moment I met you."

"You did not. I've never met a woman so hard to impress. So unwilling to flirt."

"Not unwilling. Just incompetent. Nobody ever taught me how. Besides, it wasn't a very nice thing to do to Bianca."

"Bianca?" He laughed. "By now she's set her sights on her next victim. I can guarantee she was playing the same game with me. Your sympathy is wasted on Bianca Ingram. Instead, feel sorry for me."

"For you? Why should I?"

He lowered his voice to a whisper. "Because I'm dying to get my hands on you right now. I don't think I can wait till we get back to the house."

But, of course, he did wait. When we got home to Thornfield Park, we found Lucia in the breakfast room, piles of paper spread around her, trying to make phone calls while keeping an eye on Maddy, who was at the table cutting paper snowflakes and chatting a mile a minute. At the sight of me, Maddy leaped up and threw her arms around me.

"You go," I prodded Nico. "Make yourself busy. I need to help Lucia."

He gave me a wounded look but left the room.

When Lucia had hung up the phone, I caught her eye. "I'll take over with Maddy now," I told her. "I can see how badly you need to do your own work."

She thanked me, looking sincerely grateful, and I thought of our encounter that morning. "Lucia, I feel like I need to explain."

She waved me off. "Nothing to explain. I can see for myself."

"But you looked so disappointed in me this morning."

"Not disappointed. Just, I don't know, surprised."

"Surprised that Nico could be interested in someone like me?" I tried not to sound as hurt as I felt. "Am I really that unlovable?"

"Sweetie" — Lucia jumped up and gave me a hug — "no, that's

not it. It's just that you seem so...so sensible. So self-contained. Of course, I could tell that you'd become a sort of pet of Nico's, but I didn't think much of it. He's always been very careful to distance himself from the women on his staff." She motioned me out into the hallway, away from Maddy. "Stacy — two nannies ago — had a huge thing for him, and when it began to get in the way of her work, he had me find her another position. Said he wanted to keep things professional. So, you see, I just didn't see this coming."

I thought about telling her that Nico and I were engaged but then decided to let him make the announcement himself, when he saw fit. He was her boss, and I was still her subordinate. "Well, it won't make as big a difference as you might think," I said. "I'll be looking after Maddy, as usual."

Lucia glanced around, checking to be sure that Nico wasn't nearby. "One thing, Jane. I wouldn't say this if I weren't fond of you. I just hope you'll be careful."

"Careful of what?"

"Men like Nico, when they take up with their employees — well, they don't usually, but if they do — it generally doesn't work out well for the woman."

I felt impatience take hold of me and don't know what I would have said if Maddy hadn't come out into the hallway and tugged my hand just then. "Are you taking me to the show tonight, Miss Jane?" she asked. "Lucia bought me a new dress. Come see."

I let her lead me off, and the two of us spent an afternoon so like the many others we'd shared together that I found myself forgetting the enormous changes of the past twenty-four hours for as long as half an hour at a time. Then I'd notice the warm glow of happiness in the pit of my stomach or the faint tingling on my face from Nico's stubble, and I'd remember — and feel a sudden lurch of vertigo, as if an elevator had shot me to the top of the Empire State Building and I was suddenly staring down at the hundred-story drop.

CHAPTER 19

The rehearsal show was everything Nico could have hoped for. The local newspapers raved, and a number of magazines picked up the story of Nico's comeback. "Rathburn's Back and Better than Ever" announced a headline in *Entertainment Weekly*. The day after the show, Mitch swung by the house with feedback from people he'd hired to monitor the Internet: Nico's fan base was wildly enthusiastic about the show. The general run of opinions was that the coming tour stood a good chance of being Nico's best ever. When tickets for the U.S. leg went on sale a couple of days later, most venues sold out in fifteen minutes.

From where I had stood — a roped-off area stage left — with Maddy, Kitty, Yvonne, and assorted family, friends, and acquaintances of the band, the show at the XL Center was absolutely thrilling. Not that I had much to compare it with. I had never been in an arena full of screaming fans before. I'm not sure what I'd been expecting. In the hour before the show, the crowd sat tamely in their seats, but as time passed and the anticipation grew, the tension in the cavernous room became something I could actually feel, like static electricity. Then the houselights flicked off, and the crowd sent up a dull roar, like the sound a retreating wave makes against a pebbly beach but multiplied and echoing. Next the band took the stage — first Tom and Lonnie, then Mike and Dennis, and finally, after a long pause, Nico, dressed all in black, with bracelets of thick silver chain around both wrists. The crowd went wild. The fans were louder than I had thought possible. Nico looked up solemnly to survey the crowd, then a smile stole across his face. It was the smile of someone who had thought he might never make it home again but who has, unaccountably and against all odds, arrived. My heart flipped in my chest. "Good evening, friends," he said into the microphone, then pulled his guitar strap over his head and counted off.

What followed was a revelation. How had I felt I'd known Nico without seeing his face bathed in the spotlight, his ability to command the entire audience's attention by lifting a hand, that compact but muscled frame I loved so well set in motion by the music he himself had composed? Watching Nico play his guitar, exhort the crowd to sing along, and whip the whole arena into a frenzy, made me long for him even more than I had before.

And how could I have imagined I understood him without hearing him sing the songs he'd written? His recorded voice was one thing; onstage it was more expressive, ranging from light and playful to the occasional howl that channeled a sadness I'd never known was there. Hearing that loneliness in his voice made me wonder what else I didn't know about the man I was about to marry. I felt a chill through my whole body, a feeling very close to fear, though if anyone asked about it I wouldn't have been able to say what I was afraid of.

How strange it was to hear sixteen thousand people singing the words Nico had written, to hear their thunderous applause, and to see thousands of arms moving like a tidal wave threatening to sweep him away. In a silent moment between songs, a woman's voice rose up drunkenly from the crowd. "I just want to touch you, Nico!" she screamed. Her cry made me notice what I hadn't before — the crowd packed tight and straining forward just in front of the stage, and three burly men in black standing with their backs to the band, keeping watch. But what could they do to protect him if the entire crowd surged forward at once?

And then, just as my nerves threatened to overtake my pride and pleasure, Nico strolled midsong to the side of the stage where I stood, my hands on Maddy's shoulders. He was singing "Down Romeo Street," a love song from his third album, and now he stood before me with a teasing smile, looking down at me. "Hey there, angel," he called between verses. "Don't you go anywhere, okay?" — the private message made public by the microphone in his hands. I could see the crowd turn in my direction, trying to get a glimpse of whomever Nico had been speaking to, though from where most of them sat, I was invisible, obstructed by the stage and hidden in shadow. How to put a name to the excruciating pangs I felt at that moment — love, embarrassment, pride, fear, joy, all mixed together in equal parts? I didn't even stop to think that the words he sang had been written long ago, for another woman he used to love.

The night of Nico's comeback concert was like a diamond necklace, a string of luminous events, each one dazzling in its own right, yet taken together, an excess of riches. There was the moment when Yvonne and Kitty took one look at me in the clothes I'd picked for that night — a simple black satin sheath with spaghetti straps and silver sandals — and gave each other a high five. "Looks like girlfriend took our advice," Yvonne said to Kitty. And the drive to the XL Center, Nico feeling Maddy out on the topic of our engagement. "How would you like Miss Jane to live with us forever? What if you and I went into the city together and picked out a very special ring for Miss Jane so we can ask her to marry us?" Maddy's wide-eyed look and squeals of happy surprise came as a tremendous relief. And there was the unforgettable moment right after the show when Nico gathered the band together backstage for an announcement. "I want you all to meet my fiancée," he said, and nudged me forward to stunned silence and then applause and congratulations that seemed genuine. Each member of the band came up to congratulate and hug me. "Thank God it's you and not that horrible Ingram bitch," Dennis confided after downing most of a bottle of champagne. The biggest hug of all came from Yvonne. "Now you'll be one of us," she said into my ear. "We'll have so much fun." Kitty's congratulations were more subdued. "Brace yourself," she whispered, just before she kissed me on the cheek. "It isn't always what you think it will be."

To tell the truth, I wasn't sure what Kitty's warning meant, though I imagined it had something to do with being in the public eye. Then, two days later, Mitch brought us a copy of that day's *New York Post*—the *New York Pest*, he called it—and handed it wordlessly to Nico. "Rock-and-Roll Prince Chooses Cinderella" the headline read below a blurry picture of Nico and me ducking into the Range Rover after our shopping spree. We had only been on the street for a few moments; who had taken our picture? The brief story accompanying the photo stunned me even more: "Looks like veteran rocker and ladies' man Nico Rathburn is tumbling into matrimony once again. Rathburn and his fiancée, Jane Moore, 19, nanny to his daughter by French pop phenom Celine, dropped by the Big Apple to do a little impromptu shopping just before kicking off a world tour."

Nico glowered. "Who leaked this?" he demanded of Mitch.

"Anyone with a cell-phone camera could have taken that picture," Mitch replied. "As for your engagement, you weren't exactly discreet the other night. It was bound to get out."

"You're trying to keep me a secret?" I asked lightly. As I read, Nico and Mitch watched me closely. I decided not to overreact. "If I were a cynic, I'd say you were marrying me for the publicity." Then I handed Mitch the paper and went back to pouring blueberry syrup on Maddy's waffles.

Once the story broke, it was everywhere, and much of the reaction was unpleasant. One magazine interviewed Nico's female fans about his impending wedding. "Give me a break," a thirty-year-old woman was quoted as saying. "I was buying Nico's records when she was in elementary school. Nico owes his longtime fans more than this." And the female president of the Nico Rathburn fan club quipped, "I'd like to wring her scrawny little neck. Just kidding."

The reactions of Nico's male fans weren't much better. One was quoted as saying, "Who cares? The guy should be able to marry whoever he wants to," but another said, "What a disappointment. He could have had any woman he wanted. That wife of his, the Brazilian model? Now she was seriously hot. What ever happened to her?"

"Welcome to my life," Nico said grimly, reading over my shoulder. "I have to know what the press is saying about me, Jane, but you don't." He plucked the magazine out of my hand and tossed it at a window, which it hit with a smack. "Promise me you won't read any more of that shit."

It was an easy promise to make and keep. However, my new notoriety found other ways of seeping into daily life. Now people stared at me when I walked through town or dropped into the grocery store, so I stopped going out, except to run Maddy to school and to playdates. I limited my wanderings to the grounds of Thornfield Park. On the plus side, the mothers picking up their children at the Waldorf School now smiled at me and said hello.

The wave of publicity had another unforeseen consequence. Jenna called my cell phone. "I saw your face in Us, little sister. You've been holding out on me. When were you planning to fill me in on the details?"

"There isn't much to tell," I said.

Jenna laughed. "You've got to be kidding me. You're marrying Nico Rathburn, and there isn't much to tell? When did you two start dating? I never would have pegged you as the type to sleep your way up the ladder, but I admire your style."

I thought of an angry reply but bit it back.

"So, are you and Nico coming to our wedding?" She said his name with theatrical emphasis. "I ask because I never received your RSVP."

"You never sent me an invitation."

Jenna laughed. "Of course I did. You're my sister. It must have gotten lost in the mail. I'll FedEx it to you this afternoon, and you just call me back and tell me if you and that seriously hot fiancé of yours want the salmon or the filet mignon."

Again, I said nothing.

"And just so you know, I'm available to be your bridesmaid if you need me," she added. "Matron of honor, even."

I told her I would give the matter some thought. Then I found Nico in his office, going through that day's mail. "Can we get married at town hall?" I asked him. "Just you, me, and Maddy?"

He pushed aside the mail and rolled toward me on his desk chair. "You. Here. Now." I sat on his lap, and he buried his face in my hair for a long moment. "You are a woman after my own heart," he said finally. "Just the three of us would be perfect. How about early next week?"

"Why not tomorrow?" I asked, jokingly. "Or, if we're being wildly impetuous, why not today?"

He brushed back the hair that had fallen into my eyes. "Two reasons: you need a wedding dress and a ring. And we're going to L.A. over the weekend."

"We are?" This was the first I'd heard of it.

"I have to meet with Dino Marcusi. You've heard of him, right? The director. He wants to shoot a documentary about the tour. Didn't I mention this?"

"Not even once."

"You'll get to see L.A. You've never been, right?"

"I've never been anywhere. But I can't go with you. Maddy's class is putting on a play on Friday, remember? And she's been invited to Pia's birthday party on Saturday, at Mystic Aquarium. I'm supposed to help chaperone the thousand kids invited along."

"Can't you get out of it? Isn't my documentary more important?"

"More important to you and me, but not to Maddy. She'll be heartbroken if she has to miss the party, and she *can't* miss the play. They don't have understudies for preschool plays, you know."

"Shouldn't they?" Nico kissed the hollow behind my ear. "How am I supposed to get along without you for three whole days?"

"The same way you always did," I said. "As for the dress, if it's only going to be the three of us, do I really need one?"

"You're going to have a wedding dress. Don't even start with me on this. It's not negotiable. I will not be denied the pleasure of seeing you in white lace, looking like a princess, on this one day at least. *Capisce?*" He kissed the spot where my neck meets my shoulder.

"Nico?"

"What is it, angel?"

A question had been nagging me ever since the magazines had brought it up. "What ever happened to your first wife? Where is she now?"

Nico pulled back with a start. "Why do you ask?"

"Are you angry?" I was surprised by the agitation in his voice. "It's not that strange a question, is it? I didn't mean to upset you."

He sighed deeply. "I'm not angry with you. It's just a sore subject. You can understand that, can't you?"

"Of course."

"Anyway, I don't know where she is or what she's doing. She wasn't well when our marriage broke up. You know that much from the news stories, right? I think she wanted out of the public eye, and that's all I know. I don't want to talk about her anymore. Can you live with that?"

I nestled my head into his shoulder, and he stroked my hair, gently, as though I were infinitely precious. How could I give him a moment's pain by bringing her up again? "Of course I can," I said.

Though the dress Nico bought me for our wedding was exquisite and far too expensive for my taste, it represented a compromise. He had wanted me to wear one that cost twice as much — an ornate, beaded affair with a train that was better suited to Saint Paul's Cathedral than town hall. The dress we settled on was simple white satin, modestly cut. To bargain him down from the Princess Diana gown, I let him pick out a poufy waist-length wedding veil, and though it wasn't the kind of thing I would have chosen for myself, I had to admit that I found my reflection in the boutique's three-way mirror secretly thrilling.

Was it bad luck for my fiancé not only to have seen the dress ahead of time but to have chosen it himself? Nico waved off the question. "Left to your own devices, you'd show up for the wedding in overalls," he said.

"But they'd be white ones." I let the subject drop. Back home, I hung the dress and veil next to my black concert dress, allowed myself one last look at them, and ran off to keep Nico company while he packed for his trip to L.A.

"Come with me," he urged one last time, and I repeated the many reasons I couldn't go with him. Before he left, he made love to me one more time, running his hands over my body again and again, as if trying to memorize it. Then he showered and kissed me good-bye.

When he was gone, the estate felt lonely and emptier than it ever had before. I couldn't help feeling restless, thinking of the delights that lay in store: a wedding and a honeymoon tour that would take us all over Europe and then across the United States. The night before Nico was scheduled to return — the eve of our wedding — after putting Maddy to bed, I found myself unable to read or relax. To expend some of my excess energy, I wandered the grounds and saw, for the first time, the wreck of the chestnut tree. It was black and split down the center. The two halves clung to each other, the firm base and strong roots keeping them upright. But the tree was clearly dead; one good storm would knock it over. For now, though, they formed one tree — a ruin, but an entire ruin.

I sat at a distance, hugged my knees to my chest, and watched the sun set behind the poor old tree. Something about the image moved me. I had brought pencils and a pad with me and made a hasty sketch, trying to capture the sight while the tree still stood; maybe I could paint it from memory later, when I was far from Thornfield Park. As I drew, I marveled that the two halves still managed to cling to each other. I continued drawing until it was too dark to see, then watched until fireflies dotted the field and the moon rose between the charred branches.

That night, despite my fears that I might get no rest at all, I must have slept deeply because I woke with a start. My room seemed unusually bright. I opened my eyes and saw that my door was opened a crack. Had I left it that way? That would have been very unlike me. Since the night of the fire, I always made sure I locked it at bedtime. I sat up in bed and noticed that the door to my closet was also open. I heard rustling deep inside. "Maddy?" I asked. "What are you doing in there?" No one answered, but a form emerged from the closet. Even in the half light, I could see right away that it was an adult, tall and broad shouldered. I gasped, realizing who it must be. Then the figure lurched toward me. The light from the hallway shone on the figure's face, and I could see that it wasn't Brenda, as I had feared. It was someone I'd never seen before in my life, a woman, with wild white hair partly obscuring her face. She wore a long, pale dress — a nightgown maybe. She moved again, and I got a better look. Her mouth was twisted into a grimace, and her frantic eyes were staring at me. I thought she might reach for me, maybe for my neck. As tall and strong as she looked, I doubted I'd be able to resist if she tried anything, and the haunted look on her face made violence seem possible, even probable. But no, her gaze left me and returned to the closet. She reached in and pulled out my wedding veil.

I thought about running for the door but was afraid to call any attention to myself. Instead, I stayed frozen in place and watched while she waved the veil in front of her like a long banner, then threw it over her head and turned to the mirror. *Am I dreaming?* I willed myself to wake up, but the scene kept playing out before me. The woman struck a pose, made a chuckling sound, then, without warning, ripped the veil from her head, tore it in half, tossed it to the floor, and stomped on it. A moment later, she startled, as though she'd heard some noise I couldn't hear, and bolted for the door. I heard her heavy footsteps disappearing as she made her way down the hall.

I leaped to my feet and ran for the door on shaky legs. I considered locking it but then thought of Maddy. After the fire, Nico had a lock installed on the inside of Maddy's door, one she could manage herself, and one only Nico, Lucia, and I had keys for. Still, that woman had somehow gotten into my room, and I was fairly certain my door had been locked. I had to do what I could to protect Maddy. I fumbled for my house keys, ran down the hall — the woman was by then out of sight — let myself into Maddy's room, locked the door behind me, and got in bed with her. In her sleep she squirmed closer until she was right up against me. I was glad to feel her warmth and to hear her soft, deep breath. I lay there for a long time, considering what I should do next. Should I call 911 and report an intruder? That seemed like the obvious choice, until I recalled all that had happened since my arrival at Thornfield Park: the mysterious laughter, the fire, Mason's wounds, and Nico's demand that I not speak to Mason and he not speak to me. I realized then that the intruder in my bedroom hadn't come from somewhere else; she had been living with us all along. And I also knew that Nico wouldn't want outsiders brought in to contend with that woman, whoever she was.

I had to talk to Nico, but Maddy's room had no phone, and I'd left my cell back in my room. I didn't dare risk going out into the hall and running into that woman again. By dawn, Nico would be flying home to us. There seemed to be nothing else to do but sit up until first light, keeping watch over Maddy, willing the hours to pass by without incident.

CHAPTER 20

When my wedding day finally dawned, I dressed Maddy and fed her breakfast, as usual, but I could barely speak, so preoccupied was I with the events of the night before. When Nico arrived mid-morning, he found me waiting for him near the driveway, Maddy in the grass at my feet blowing soap bubbles. He only had to take one look at me to know something was wrong. He raced out of the car and gathered me up in his arms. "What is it?" he asked. "Are you all right?"

"Yes, I'm fine, but we need to talk in private." I mouthed the last two words silently.

Nico bent to give Maddy a kiss on the cheek; she flung her arms around his neck, but he pried her loose. "Run off and find Lucia. Yes, I have a present for you. The faster you do what I say, the faster you'll get it."

As soon as we were alone, I told him the details of last night's visitation. Nico grew pale as he listened, and when I'd finished speaking, he pulled me close. "Thank God you weren't hurt." A moment later, though, his tone changed. "Maybe you were having a nightmare?"

"My veil was torn in half. It's still lying in pieces on the floor of my room. You know me better than to think I'd confuse a dream with reality, don't you?"

He rubbed his cheek against my forehead. "Of course. I guess I was hoping it couldn't really have happened."

"But you know who that woman was." My voice wasn't accusatory — at least I hoped it wasn't. I needed to know the truth. "Why won't you tell me?"

"Jane, Jane." He walked me away from the house, as though afraid we might be overheard. "It must have been Brenda."

"No. I saw her. She was tall and broad shouldered like Brenda, but she had long white hair and a very different face. It wasn't Brenda."

He thought a moment. "Long white hair," he repeated. "Could you have imagined that? Could you have been half-asleep?"

"I was wide-awake. I've never been so awake in my life."

"And the room was dark?"

"Except for the light from the hallway, but I got a good look at her."

"You say the woman was built like Brenda. Could Brenda have been wearing a wig? And makeup so that she looked completely different? A disguise?"

"Why would she do such a thing?" The idea seemed ludicrous.

"Why would she do any of the things she's done?" Nico asked. "Come into your bedroom, tear your wedding veil in half? Try to set fire to my room?" He put an arm around my shoulder. "She's not right in the head."

"But…" I tried to decide which of the thousand questions vying for space in my brain should be voiced first. "But…"

"Why would I keep someone like that on staff? Why would I let her live in the house?"

"Why would you?"

Nico inhaled and exhaled heavily. "It's a long, complicated story. She's a relative of mine. I keep her on here under my protection, because what else can I do? Send her to a mental institution?"

I tried to speak as gently as I could. "Maybe that would be safer. For her and for us. For Maddy."

"Do you know what those places are like?"

I had to admit that I didn't. We had reached the edge of the pine forest, far out of sight of the house.

"Jane, you're right. It hasn't been very safe to let her stay here. I've taken risks with your life and Maddy's, and I could never have forgiven myself if" — he seized my shoulders and drew me close again — "if anything had happened to you." He kissed me fiercely as if afraid that any second I might disappear in a puff of smoke. I felt my knees weaken. When he finally released me, he continued: "But today we're getting married, and in a few days you, Maddy, and I are out of here. We'll be out of the country and away from Thornfield Park — for months. I promise, I'll think of something in the meantime. Either I'll find another place for Brenda to stay

243

or…even better — why didn't I think of this before? — I'll build us a whole new house, any kind you like. A cottage? A log cabin? A castle with ramparts and a moat? You name it. We'll start fresh."

You're going to leave behind an entire estate just because you want to get away from Brenda? I thought to myself. The idea seemed absurd, crazy, wasteful. But Nico bent to kiss me again, then he ran his lips down my throat. He reached up under my blouse, and I felt myself melting like candle wax in his warm hands. Without knowing how I got there, before I could object or worry whether someone might come looking for us, I was lying in the soft fragrant bed of pine needles. We were kissing, and he was unbuttoning my blouse. Every question, every reservation I had, flew from my mind as I lay there — tingling all over, my hands tangled in the softness of his hair — and let him unmake me into a thousand glittering pieces.

We had scheduled the wedding for noon. Nico had made an appointment with a justice of the peace at the courthouse the next town over. I outfitted Maddy in a pink taffeta dress and white patent leather shoes; she was especially excited when she held the little basket of rose petals that she would soon scatter before me. I tied the last of six ribbons in her hair and handed her off to Linda with barely enough time left to get ready. Lucia helped me dress — a blessing, since my hands were shaking. That morning she had ordered a simple white veil from a local bridal shop to replace the torn one. All patience, she smoothed down my hair and pinned the veil in position; then she fastened the many tiny buttons that ran up my back. She even made me up — a little mascara, a touch of blush. As soon as she'd finished my lipstick, I hurried for the door.

"Stop!" she said. "At least look at yourself in the mirror. You haven't even taken a peek."

I complied. The dress fit perfectly, and the veil was understated but pretty. Still, it seemed that a stranger was looking back at me from the mirror.

"Jane!" Nico called me from the foot of the stairs. "What's taking so long?" He watched me make my way downstairs and kissed me lightly when I reached him. "You look amazing," he said. "Let's roll." And then, to my surprise, he turned abruptly and hurried toward the front door with a stride I could hardly match. Lucia stood in the hallway as we passed. I wanted to speak with her, but Nico hurried me along. Maddy was already in the car, clutching her white basket of rose petals. The twenty-minute ride to the courthouse was oddly quiet. I glanced over at Nico only once; the frown on his face was enough to keep me still, on my side of the backseat, eyes glued to the view out the window, Maddy between us. *What is the matter with him?* I wondered. It seemed like more than just a case of nerves. He said nothing for the duration of the ride except to command Benjamin to drive faster. When we pulled up to the courthouse, Nico was out the door before the Range Rover came to a complete stop. I helped Maddy out, the two of us struggling to keep up with her father.

Inside, Maddy played her part prettily, walking slowly and solemnly toward her father, scattering rose petals on the floor. I followed. It wasn't much of a walk: the office wasn't large, and my dress and the whole rose-petal idea seemed a little ridiculous.

Worse — much worse — when I reached Nico, I expected to see the usual warmth in his eyes, but instead I saw impatience. As tightly wound as my emotions were that day, I surprised myself by my reaction to Nico's hard look. Tears sprang into my eyes.

Regret crossed over Nico's face like a ray of light breaking between storm clouds. "I'm sorry, angel. I'm sorry," he said. "Don't cry. I'm not angry...just eager." And he turned to the justice of the peace, whose name was Donahue, and asked him to begin.

"Dearly beloved," Mr. Donahue intoned. "We are gathered here to join this man and this woman in holy matrimony..."

A door slammed, I could hear footsteps, running toward us from the hallway. Then shouts. For a moment I thought one of Nico's desperate fans had somehow learned of the wedding and was here to throw herself between the two of us. Someone pounded on the door. "Let me in." To my surprise, it was a man's voice, a slightly familiar one. "Stop this wedding!"

"Keep going," Nico told Mr. Donahue through gritted teeth, his gaze steady, as though he were completely unfazed by this turn of events. Maddy looked terrified. I grabbed her hand, as much for my own comfort as for hers.

"Let me in," the voice from the hall repeated, louder this time.

Mr. Donahue gave Nico a warning look and crossed the room. In through the open door came a man I recognized: Ambrose Mason. "What's this about?" Mr. Donahue asked.

Mason looked as pale as I remembered, as nervous as he had been the night Nico had saved his life. He hesitated a moment under Nico's steely glare, then said his piece. "Nico Rathburn already has a wife."

Nico didn't flinch. His face flushed a shade I'd never seen before. He continued to stare down Ambrose Mason as though trying to intimidate him into silence.

"Is this true?" Mr. Donahue turned to Nico.

"I have proof." Mason withdrew a piece of paper from his pocket. "A marriage license..." — he handed it over — "between Nico Rathburn and my stepsister, Bibi Oliviera."

"That piece of paper means nothing. It doesn't prove the woman I married is still alive."

"She was alive less than a month ago," Mason said.

Nico's fists were clenched. He made a move toward Mason as though to hit him. Mason flinched. "I should have left you to die," Nico said under his breath.

Mr. Donahue cast an admonishing glance at Nico. "I could have the police here in thirty seconds," he said. "I don't care *who* you are. You'd better watch yourself." Then, to Mason: "And you need to explain. Where is this alleged wife?"

"Bibi Oliviera Rathburn is living at Thornfield Park. I saw her three weeks ago."

"Didn't you divorce her years ago?" the justice asked Nico.

A grim smile contorted Nico's lips. He said nothing.

"He never divorced Bibi," Mason said. "He's trying to commit bigamy...with this girl." He pointed at me.

"Bigamy." Nico laughed bitterly. "That's an ugly word. Not untrue, but still, ugly." Then he grabbed my hand. "*This girl*, as you call her, is completely innocent. Leave her out of this." He dropped my hand unceremoniously. "Come on, all of you — you're in for a treat, an inside look at the freak show I call my life. Be sure to bring

247

your camera phones. I'll give you something you can sell to the tabloids for half a million dollars. An exclusive!"

Maddy looked stricken. Though she couldn't have understood half of what the grown-ups around her were saying, she knew something had gone terribly wrong. She was hurt and scared by this new defiant tone in her father's voice. I held her hand as we walked to the car, then wrapped her in my arms on the long, silent ride back to the house. For once, she didn't ask a single question. Nico didn't even look at me. Perhaps I would have fallen completely apart if it hadn't been for the need to comfort Maddy.

As Benjamin pulled into the drive, Lucia and the rest of the staff ran out onto the front steps to greet us, bags of rice in their hands. At the sight of the train of cars behind us, they fell silent. "Never mind," Nico told them. "There's nothing to celebrate."

He went into the house and strode toward the back staircase with Mason. I hurried behind with the police detective Mr. Donahue had sent in a patrol car to investigate. I'd left Maddy on the doorstep clinging to Lucia's legs. When we reached the landing of the second floor, Nico grabbed my hand and beckoned to the men who were lagging behind us. We proceeded to the third floor. The low black door, opened by Nico's key, admitted us to the dark room with its heavy sleigh bed on which I'd stanched Mason's wounds.

"You'll recognize this room, Mason," Nico said. "She bit and stabbed you here."

Brenda sat in the armchair in the corner of the room, heating something over a hot plate. She was startled to see our small procession and jumped to her feet.

"Good afternoon, Brenda," Nico said with overstated cheer. "How are you? And how is she doing today?"

"She's having a good day," Brenda said warily. "Cranky but not off the charts."

"You'll let us into the turret, Brenda?" Nico asked, though it wasn't really a question. She undid the heavy latch, fished in her pocket for her keys, and unlocked the door. The round room on the other side was dark but for the light that bled in through a small window. In a far corner of the room, in deep shadow, a figure rocked back and forth, muttering and grumbling. Brenda snapped on a switch, the light revealing a tall, broad-shouldered woman with wild white hair covering most of her face. Though it was midday, she wore the same long nightgown she'd had on the night before; it was stained and smelled musky. Her bare feet were long, the toes slightly gnarled. The skin of her arms was covered with scratches, but I could make out the familiar coiled snake tattoo. At the sight of us, she reared back a bit, startled, and uttered a choked cry. "Nico?" I heard her say. "Nico?"

"You'd better not stay," Brenda said. "You're going to upset her."

"Only a few moments," Nico said. Arms outstretched, he stood between us and the woman, Bibi Oliviera. I could now see a resemblance to her former self. Her long legs. Her dark eyes and full lips, half-hidden by thick, matted hair. She was heavier, her skin raw, and she looked nothing like a model anymore. Still, I could imagine the beautiful woman she had once been.

"Be careful," Brenda warned Nico. "I wouldn't get too close."

Bibi tipped her head to one side, studying Nico. Then her gaze traveled across the room to me. She turned back to him. "You cock-sucker," she said in a low voice. "Motherfucking piece of shit."

"No need to be afraid, Mason," Nico called out behind us, where Mason cowered in back of the burly police detective who was ready to draw his gun. "She doesn't have a knife this time. Right, Brenda?"

"You never know," Brenda replied. "She's gotten so good at hiding things in her clothes. I can never be a hundred percent sure she's not armed."

"We'd better leave her," Mason whispered.

"Go to hell," Nico replied.

Nico threw himself between me and the woman — his wife — as she sprang at him, grabbing for his throat. Brenda grabbed me by the shoulders and shoved me toward the door, out of the way. Bibi was taller than Nico and probably as heavy. The two of them struggled. He could have knocked her away with a well-planted punch, but he didn't. Instead, he grappled with her until he managed to grab her arms and twist them behind her back. She screamed — a horrible, chilling cry. "Cocksucker! Cock-sucker! I've seen that whore you're with. That one." And she gaped at me, her dark green eyes peering between the hanks of her wild white hair. She bared her teeth. "You. You know what you've done."

Behind me, I could hear Brenda rummaging through the chest of drawers beside the bed. She produced a hypodermic needle and, with incredible speed, plunged it into Bibi's arm. Bibi flailed a minute, still cursing.

"Shhhh," I heard Nico say. His voice startled me. It was gentle, even loving. "Calm." A moment later, Bibi's body relaxed in his arms.

She looked up at him with love in her eyes. "My Nico," she whispered.

Nico stroked her hair. "There, there, angel." After a few moments, she went slack, and her eyes closed. He dragged her backward to a bed pushed against the wall. "Don't just stand there," he called. Mason and the detective didn't move, so I went to him. But there wasn't much I could do but watch. With help from Brenda, he lifted Bibi's long, limp frame onto the bed. I stood beside Nico while he unfolded a thin blanket — sky blue, a hopeful color that made me suddenly sad — and covered her. Though she was out cold, he patted her hand and brushed back her tangled hair.

Then, over his shoulder, he addressed the men in the other room. "This is my wife," he said. "A schizophrenic. You've probably heard that schizophrenia is treatable with the right prescriptions, and it's true most of the time, as long as the patient takes her medication —"

"I do the best I can," Brenda interrupted, sounding defensive. "You wouldn't believe how wily she is. She must hide them under her tongue or between her teeth and her cheek. When I try to check, she bites me. I find stockpiles of pills under the rug, in the closet, in the toes of her slippers."

"Sometimes she takes her medication a few days in a row," Nico added in a choked voice. "Just enough so that I get a glimmer of her old self, so I get hopeful that she's coming back to me. She lets Brenda comb her hair. She stops hearing voices. She makes sense. But then she falls apart again." His eyes glistened with unshed tears. "I guess I deserve every bit of bad luck I've been given. So many times I've thought my wife was coming back to me, she was almost back, and then she was snatched away, replaced by a maniac who accuses me of terrible things and tries to kill me any way she can."

I thought of Bibi — of *her* misfortune — but said nothing. As if reading my mind, Nico turned to me, laying his hands on my shoulders. "I just wanted a normal life with this woman. She's amazing, isn't she? Calm and rational, even standing here at the gates of hell." He gave me a gentle push toward the door. "Go into the other room, Jane. I need to lock the door."

While Nico paused to confer with Brenda about Bibi's care, the police detective whispered in my ear. "Nobody blames you for any of this," he said. "Anyone can see you're the victim here."

The victim. Is that what I was? Numbness set in; I could barely make sense of anything that had just taken place. I started down the stairs to my room, leaving the men behind me. I had to get away from everyone. Not to weep or mourn: I was still too shocked for that. No, I had to change out of my heavy satin wedding gown, out of the stiff underwire bra poking into my flesh and the excruciating shoes. I had to get back into *my* clothes, the ones I'd brought with me to Thornfield Park.

In the shower, I ran the water so hot it scalded my skin, then scrubbed the makeup from my face. I dressed in my usual clothes and sat down on the edge of my bed. Weak and tired, I pulled back the covers and climbed under. At last I was alone and could think. But every thought brought pain. Nico owed me an explanation. I waited for the knock that I knew would eventually come.

But it didn't.

Hours passed. I considered leaving my room, looking for Nico. He hadn't come for me, so what good would it do to look for him? According to my alarm clock, it was 5 p.m. Night was coming. I knew I should make a plan, figure out what to do next. But how could I decide what to do before I understood why Nico had misled me? Six o'clock came and went, then seven. I hadn't eaten a thing all day. I hadn't heard a single voice in hours. Where was everyone?

By then, pride seemed beside the point. I unlocked my door and looked out into the hallway, and there, to my surprise, was Nico. He'd dragged a chair next to my door; he must have moved it very quietly. He had been waiting — possibly for hours — for me to leave my room.

"Finally," he said quietly. "I was beginning to think you might never come out. Why did you lock yourself up in there? Why didn't you come out and scream at me? Hit me, throw plates at my head? Anything but this." He stood and cradled my chin in his hand, tipping my face toward him to better study it. "No sign of tears," he observed. "You look exhausted and pale, though — and sad." He removed his hand. "Say something, would you? You're starting to scare me."

But I still didn't know what to say.

"I never meant to hurt you, Jane. You have to believe me. I've done a lot of damage in my life, most of it unintentionally, some of it deliberately. But I swear, you, of all people, I never meant to hurt. Will you ever forgive me?"

How could I not forgive him? He looked down at me, his gray eyes full of sadness and, yes, love. Still I said nothing.

"I'm an asshole, right?" His tone was wistful. "A man who would try to marry a sweet, innocent girl under false pretenses."

"Yes, Nico."

"Then tell me so. Call me an asshole."

"I can't. I'm tired, and I think I might be coming down with something." He heaved a sigh, scooped me up in his arms, and carried me downstairs. He set me down on one of the living room couches and brought me a glass of water and a plate of crackers.

"Start with these," he said. "You need to eat."

I did. Then, with my stomach full, I drifted to sleep. When I woke, the fireplace was lit, and Nico was sitting on the floor beside the couch, his dark head next to mine, keeping watch. When I opened my eyes, he smiled and leaned to kiss me, but I pulled away.

"Oh, Jane," he said sadly. "Don't tell me you hate me."

"I don't hate you."

"Then why won't you kiss me? Because I'm a married man?"

"Aren't you one?"

"You saw Bibi. Can you consider me married? My 'wife'" — he said the word with scorn — "is psychotic and spends half her time thinking I'm trying to kill her and the other half trying to plot ways to kill me. Is that what you'd call a marriage?"

"Then why didn't you get an annulment or a divorce?"

"I couldn't do that to Bibi. She's the way she is because of me."

"How is that possible? You didn't cause her mental illness."

"Schizophrenia runs in her family, and I didn't find out right away. We got married so quickly. We met, fell in love, spent one long weekend in a hotel in Rio, and got married on a whim. She

254

didn't think to tell me that when she was a little girl her mother was institutionalized or that her grandmother had killed herself decades ago. Bibi might have meant to hide her family history from me, or she might have thought nothing like that would happen to her. She wasn't one to worry about the future. She was brave and funny, and she didn't care how the world saw her."

I couldn't help noticing the tenderness in his voice as he spoke about his wife as she had been. I recalled with a sharp pang how he had called her "angel"— the same term of endearment he had given me.

"Remember that night I told you Bibi had never even tried drugs before she met me?" he asked. Then, more bitterly, "I'm a corrupter of young women."

I nodded.

"I've always felt responsible for…for this." He pointed up toward the third floor.

"Responsible?"

Nico reached out to smooth my hair. I pulled back. "Don't pull away from me like I disgust you. You'll break my heart."

"Why do you feel responsible?"

"Guess. You're smart. Figure it out."

"Do you think the drugs the two of you used caused her schizophrenia? Or brought it on prematurely?"

"I can't know for sure," Nico said, "but it's a strong possibility. Cocaine can do that — trigger schizophrenia if it's in someone's genetic makeup. And then there were all the other things we tried — acid, mushrooms, ecstasy, Jack Daniels — in all sorts of combinations. If I hadn't pressured her, surrounded her with wild parties and hangers-on, just looking to win us over…If I hadn't —" His voice broke. "She'd never tried anything before I met her, but she wanted to be a part of my world. I promised I'd watch out for her, I'd never let anyone harm a hair on her head."

I thought for a while. "She was a model, right? Aren't they exposed to a lot of drugs and parties too?"

"She wasn't a model when I met her," Nico said. "She was a waitress. I got her connections, started her down that path. The schizophrenia might have taken years, even decades, to kick in if it weren't for me. Maybe it wouldn't have happened at all." A long silence ensued. "Say something. Do you think I'm a monster?"

How could I sit so near him — his eyes burning with sadness, his shoulders slumped with the weight of his history — and not stroke his hair, not kiss his forehead, not hold him in my arms? Just sitting there, hands in my lap, not reaching out to him, was the hardest thing I'd ever done in my life. "No. I don't think you're a monster."

"Then let me hold you. Let me kiss you."

"I still have questions," I told him. "Why do you keep her here when you know she's dangerous?"

"What else would I do with her?" he asked. "Have you ever been inside a mental institution?" He clapped a hand to his forehead. "God forbid. Of course you haven't. You're the sanest person I've met in my life."

"Aren't there some nice ones?" I asked. "For rich people?"

"There are bad ones and worse ones. I couldn't stand to see her put away…to have her live out the rest of her life among strangers. And, well…since I'm owning up to every sleazy thing I've ever done in my life... I wasn't just thinking of Bibi. If I'd sent her away, the press would have gotten wind of it. 'Rock Star Hides Wife in Mental Institution.' I'd be the villain. Instead, I coasted for years on 'Rock Star Pulls Life Back Together.'"

"Won't the press find out the truth now?"

"No doubt," Nico said. "It doesn't take too much imagination to see what the headlines will look like. 'Famous Musician Locks Wife in Attic.' And, then there's the inevitable 'Bigamist Lies to Child Bride.'"

"Oh, Nico. How is that going to affect your tour? And your album?"

He laughed incredulously. "My tour? My album? How like you, Jane. You catch me lying to you and the entire world, and you're worried about my PR."

"Then why *did* you lie? I understand why you hid things from the press. I don't think it was the right thing to do, but I get why you did it. But why did you lie to *me*?"

For a long moment he said nothing. "Would you have married me if you knew?"

I didn't know how to reply.

"Would you have fallen in love with me?" he asked.

I hesitated. "I might have. Yes, I think I would have no matter what."

"But would you have ever let me touch you if you knew I had a wife? Or would you have run straight back to the agency and found yourself a new job?"

"I... I don't know."

"In the beginning, my romantic history was none of your

257

business, none of anyone's business. Then, suddenly, I was in love with you and wanted to make you love me. And then I knew you loved me back, and all I wanted in the world was to marry you. It seemed like such a simple thing. Everyone should be entitled to happiness, even me. Don't you think so, Jane?"

"Yes. No. I don't know. I need to go someplace quiet and think."

"Someplace quiet? You want to go to your room or out for one of your walks?"

I shook my head.

"What if I put you up in a hotel for a few days?" he asked. "You could rest there and order in room service. You could think everything through and then come back to Thornfield Park."

"I don't think so," I said.

"You can't be thinking of leaving me."

I didn't respond.

"Why would you even consider such a thing? We don't have to get married. We can live together, travel around the world. We could buy a house on the Mediterranean. You'd like that, wouldn't you? We could live anywhere, as far from Thornfield Park as you like." He studied my face. "This isn't about my being a married man, is it?"

"A little bit," I told him.

"I'll get an annulment tomorrow."

"All these years you chose to stay married to Bibi," I told him. "That tells me something."

"I had no reason to get an annulment. I never thought I'd want to get married again. How could I know I'd meet you?"

His words caused a spasm of grief at my core.

"You loved her enough to stay married to her," I said. "If she weren't schizophrenic, you would still love her...and it's not her fault."

"It's *my* fault." Nico's face contorted.

"It's not anyone's fault," I said. "And there's that whole 'in sickness and in health' part of the marriage vows."

"You can't know what it's like. It's complicated."

"I'm not judging you," I said. "But I could never be a home wrecker."

"In case you hadn't noticed, the home was wrecked a long time ago — long before you stumbled into it."

"The press would judge me too. I'd be the jailbait who stole Nico Rathburn from his sick wife."

"I'm not going to let those parasites decide how I live my life anymore. If I can say 'fuck the press,' you can too."

"You lied to me. More than once. You lied to me this morning. On our wedding day. How could I ever trust you?"

He didn't answer, because there *was* no satisfactory answer. "So you don't love me then?" he said finally.

All this time I'd been struggling to hold back my emotions because I knew he wouldn't want to see me weep. Now, though, I couldn't help myself. Tears gave way, and I spoke through sobs. "I do love you. More than ever, now that I know everything you've been through. But that's beside the point."

"Beside the point?" He rose to his feet and crossed the room. "Beside the point?" He faced the bow window, with its long view of the front yard, the pond, and its resident swans. "Anything I've

259

done since the moment I met you — the good and the bad — has been out of love. That includes the lies I told. I was wrong, I know. I shouldn't have done it. Maybe you'll have trouble trusting me for a while, until I prove to you I'm not what you think I am. I'm not a liar. Not really." He walked back to me. "Let me prove it to you." He fumbled in his pocket, brought out a handkerchief, and handed it to me. "Let me make it up to you."

I wiped my eyes and blew my nose, trying to think straight. Though Nico had lied to me, I knew he'd done it out of love. I believed him when he promised he'd never lie to me again. But something gnawed at me and kept me from giving in. It was the tenderness in his eyes and voice as he'd spoken to Bibi, the trusting way she'd looked at and spoken to him before she'd seen me. She wasn't the woman he'd married, and yet she was. If he could only get her to take her medication, she could be her old self again. And then what? Who would I be if I stayed with Nico, betting Bibi would remain unwell, hoping she'd continue to spit out her pills? As much as I wanted to reach out to Nico, I couldn't forget the loving look I'd seen pass between them. And then I thought of her hatred for me, her bared teeth, the way she called me *whore*, and the way, for a moment, I'd felt the label was deserved. I remembered how that morning Nico had distracted me with my desire for him, how he'd made me push my doubts aside. Given how much I wanted him, could I ever trust myself to make the right choices?

I waited a moment to see if the gnawing feeling would pass, but it didn't. I got to my feet. "I need you to promise me one thing."

"What is it? Anything."

"Promise me you'll take good care of Maddy. Treat her the way you have lately — like your daughter, not your ward."

He looked stricken and then furious. "You think you can just run away from me? Just like that?" He grabbed my wrist — not hard enough to hurt, just hard enough to show that he could hold me against my will and there was nothing I could do about it. "I could make you stay." His eyes glowed with rage.

For a moment, I was afraid, but the fear passed. "You mean you could lock me in a room and keep me there?"

His grip tightened. Then, suddenly, he released me.

"You're leaving me?"

"Yes."

"And you don't care how much you're hurting me?"

"I do care," I said, and stood on tiptoe to smooth his hair and kiss his cheek. Then I walked straight to my room and locked the door behind me.

CHAPTER 21

After a night of strange and vivid dreams, I woke just before dawn. I had packed before I went to bed: a few changes of clothes, my pearl earrings, the passbook to my savings account, my paints and brushes. I left behind the clothes Nico had bought me, the paintings I had done at Thornfield Park, and my small collection of books; these were luxuries I didn't have room for in the small suitcase I was taking with me. On my way out the door, I stopped in the kitchen, grabbed a bottle of water, and made myself a sandwich for the journey.

I slipped out of the house quietly. The lawn was wet with dew, and as I hurried downhill, I found myself immersed in morning fog. The grounds smelled like fresh air, newly mowed grass, and the first hint of autumn. At the bottom of the hill stood the guardhouse. I dreaded the thought of passing it; what if Nico had ordered the guard not to let me leave the grounds? The guard on duty was the same one who had smiled at me the day I first met Nico. He gave me a questioning look as I approached but pushed the button that opened the gate, saying only "Good morning, miss."

It was a very long walk into town, so I planned to call a cab once I'd gotten off the road that led to Thornfield Park. If Nico had wanted to find me, it wouldn't have been hard; he'd simply have to go in one direction and send someone else in the opposite. I didn't think he would hunt me down and drag me back. Still, I was troubled by the violent anger he'd shown me — if only for a moment — the night before. How strange it was to fear being forcibly returned to Thornfield Park, the place in the world I loved most. But I *was* afraid, as though my will were a very high, thin branch from which I was dangling, a branch that could snap at any moment.

My head down, I hurried toward town. Eventually I came to a cross street and turned off the main road, zigzagging into the heart of a housing development I'd never seen before. There I found a street corner — Hyacinth Avenue and Rising Sun Drive — and called information on my cell phone for a cab company. The dispatcher promised to send someone right over. The cash I had in my wallet — several twenty dollar bills — seemed like enough to cover the cab fare with a bit left over.

The morning was colder than I had expected. I dug a sweater out of my suitcase and jogged in place awhile to keep warm. It took almost half an hour for the cab to arrive, long enough for me to second-guess my decision to leave and to have qualms about heading out into a world where nobody, not one soul, cared about me. I thought of Nico, angry and sad and possibly desperate, and of how easy it would be to turn around and go to him. But then I thought of the sound of Bibi's voice when she had called his name, like someone happy to see a dear, old friend, and how gently Nico had covered her with the blanket when she'd succumbed to the hypodermic. Something in me froze at these recollections. Was I jealous? Maybe, but as I waited on Hyacinth Avenue in the morning chill, it felt like more than that, as though the higher part of my nature was telling me to walk away from something that could do me harm, something that could erode my soul and my sense of self. It felt like I was doing the right thing, and maybe I was.

When the cab pulled up, its driver was in no mood to speak. Once I'd told him to take me to New Haven, he turned up his talk-radio station, which was fine with me. My hastily conceived plan was to lose myself someplace anonymous and urban. I didn't know much about New Haven except that Yale was there and a good portion of the city was poor. Somewhere between the wealthy students and the poor townies, I hoped I could blend in and find work.

Beyond New Haven loomed New York City. If all else failed, I could take a Greyhound from the smaller city to the larger one. For the time being, though, Manhattan was out of my reach. Rent there was exorbitant, and I couldn't turn up on my sister's doorstep. Even if I convinced her to take me in, I could be tracked down there too easily, and I knew my sister couldn't be trusted to keep a secret from someone as rich and famous as Nico. Also, the obvious way to find a new job — Discriminating Nannies, Inc. — was out of the question. They would want a reference from my previous employer, for one thing. For another, their office was the only one on the planet through which Nico would be fairly certain to find me, if he wanted to. I had to start fresh somewhere. New Haven would be the place.

"What street?" the cabbie asked as we entered the city. The best answer I could come up with was Yale University, anywhere on campus. Fall semester had apparently begun; students swarmed across the road at every crosswalk. He pulled over on a tree-lined avenue and let me out. I stood for a long time, clutching the handle of my suitcase, while students my age walked past talking animatedly, backpacks slung over their shoulders, looking as if they had never in their lives experienced a moment of not knowing exactly where they were headed.

CHAPTER 22

I spent that afternoon trying to set up interviews for apartments I had found through Yale's off-campus housing service. It was discouraging work. For one thing, rents were higher than I expected. I left voice-mail messages at five of the six group houses that were more or less in my price range; an actual human being picked up the phone at the sixth house and told me tersely that the room had already been rented. I was beginning to see how naive I'd been to think I might have a place to sleep lined up by nightfall. Even if someone had wanted to speak with me, how attractive a house-mate would I be with no job and no money other than what was in my measly savings account?

By midafternoon it occurred to me that what I should have done first was line up a job. I found my way to a main drag near campus and began going door to door. The first HELP WANTED sign

I ran across was in the window of a pizza parlor. A bored-looking counter girl gave me an application to fill out. I stared at it a long time, realizing the obvious: I had no address to put down, no experience in food service, no references except for a couple of teachers back at college and the families I used to babysit for, and no way to account for the hole in my résumé where Nico Rathburn had been. I did have a phone number, but as I wrote it in, I realized I couldn't remember the last time I'd paid my phone bill, which probably meant the bill was on its way to me at Thornfield Park. Before long my payment would be past due and I wouldn't be able to use my cell phone.

By the time I handed in the application and the counter girl assured me the manager would call if he was interested, I could feel panic beginning to set in. As badly as I needed an apartment and a job, what I needed most of all was someplace to sleep that night. Back out on the street, I found a bench outside a grocery store and sat down to call information on my cell phone. I found a Motel 6 in the New Haven area, although its distance from where I was standing was a mystery I'd have to solve later. The cost of a one-night stay brought me up short. At that rate, it wouldn't take long for me to burn through most of my savings. Then where would I get the money for a deposit on a place to live?

I had eaten the sandwich I'd packed for the road long ago. It tasted like home, and as I swallowed the last few bites I had felt like crying. Walter's sourdough bread seemed like my last link to safety, comfort, dignity, and people who cared about me. As miserable as I was beginning to feel, I realized that worries about where

I would sleep and how I would earn money had so far that day driven out the pain of missing Nico. I was almost out of cash and would have to find an ATM soon — one that would probably have a huge withdrawal fee — but I resolved to use the last of the money I had with me to buy something to eat.

At a nearby deli I ordered the cheapest meal I could find — a bagel with cream cheese and a glass of ice water. The sweet-faced college-age waitress wore a crisp blue uniform and smiled as she took my order; I wanted to throw my arms around her as though she were a long-lost friend. Instead, I asked if the restaurant had a phone book I could look at. She brought it with my bagel. "Here you go. Take as long as you want."

I turned to the Yellow Pages and looked up *youth hostel*, finding not one entry. Next, I tried *boardinghouses*. There were five of those, but none in New Haven proper. I looked up *motels* and found pages of listings, but a few phone calls reinforced my earlier notion that the cost of a few nights in one of them would devour my whole bank account.

By then, I'd exhausted every idea I could think of except one. I looked up *homeless shelter* and came up with nothing but a low-income housing complex — maybe useful for the future but not much help for the quickly approaching night. So I tried *human service organizations*. If that failed me, the next best options on my shrinking list of possibilities would be sneaking into a campus library to sleep sitting up in a study carrel or maybe stretching out under some shrubbery. Or crawling back to Thornfield Park, returning to Nico out of need and desperation. No, it would have to be the library or the shrubbery, unless I could find one helpful agency in the long list of soup kitchens and Head Start programs. But the list yielded nothing that sounded remotely like a shelter.

As I sat in the booth clutching my phone, a new worry occurred to me. Could Nico use my cell phone to track my whereabouts? Since we'd been in each other's company almost the whole time that we'd been a couple, I'd never had a reason to give him my phone number, but my phone bill was on its way to Thornfield Park and might be in the mailbox there already. Even if Nico couldn't track me down, he could call me once the bill arrived and he had my number. Would I really have the strength not to go back to him if he called? Especially if I were sleeping among the homeless? No, I would have to ditch my phone somewhere. But then how would I ever get a job?

Another troubling thought slapped me across the face. If I tried to withdraw money from my savings account back in Old Lyme, Nico might be able to track me down. Maybe this was a paranoid notion; I had no way of knowing for sure. I could close my account at the First National Bank of Old Lyme, but wouldn't I have to go all the way back there to do it? Suddenly I felt exhausted by logistics. If I took another cab back toward Thornfield Park, I doubted I'd have the strength to leave again. I took out my wallet and thumbed through it. I had about twenty-seven dollars and change left, not enough for a night in even the cheapest hotel. And then I remembered my pearl earrings. My parents had given them to me on my sixteenth birthday. My father's eyes had lit up when I kissed him on the cheek and thanked him, though as usual he'd been hard-pressed for words.

But I couldn't think of that now. I looked up *pawn shops* in the Yellow Pages. There were hundreds, but I had no way of knowing which ones were within walking distance. I rifled through the pages, my eyes glazing over.

"Can I get you anything else?"

"Just the check, please," I told the sweet-faced waitress. "But maybe you could help me?" I pushed the phone book toward her. "Do you recognize any of these addresses? Are any of these shops near here?"

"I'll take this out back and ask the manager," she said. "He'll know."

A few minutes later she came back with a list jotted in pencil on the back of a piece of scrap paper. "He says this one's just a few blocks in that direction." She pointed. "And these two aren't much farther."

I thanked her profusely, paid the check, left a tip, and started down the road. The gray-faced old man behind the counter of the dimly lit pawn shop offered me just fifty dollars for my earrings.

"But they're worth much more than that," I protested.

He shrugged. What could I do? I took the money. According to the slip he gave me, I had three months to come back and retrieve them. But when I tried to imagine where I would be living and what I would be doing in three months, my mind began spinning. The thought of my future made my limbs feel heavy and my mind numb. All I wanted was a quiet place to lie down.

As darkness fell that night, I kept to the edges of campus, trying to come up with a plan. One thing seemed certain: I couldn't spend the cash in my wallet until I'd figured out a way to bring in more; I would need that money to eat. As streetlights switched on, I walked across a well-tended lawn past a small stampede of young men playing touch football; just before me on the path, a trio of carefully dressed young women seemed headed somewhere festive. High heels clattering against the sidewalk, they shrieked with laughter and talked loudly about somebody named Smedley. At one point, caught up in their conversation, they stopped completely, blocking my way. As I walked around them, I felt invisible. Then I wished I were a ghost, able to walk through walls and get into the library — a warm, quiet place to hide until dawn. Entering through the front door was out of the question; when I tried, a guard asked me for my ID card, and I had to apologize and retreat. Similar guards sat stationed at the entrance of each dormitory I passed. I stood a moment before each welcoming facade, looking up at the brightly lit rooms above. Some windows were cheerily decorated. One had been strung with tiny lights shaped like red chili peppers; a rainbow banner hung from another. Music seeped from the closed windows — reggae from one, death metal from another. I hesitated a long moment. If I were a better liar, I could probably bluff my way in, but I'd never been able to lie without blushing and stammering. And even if I did get in, I'd have to sit up in the lounge, pretending to belong there all night long. The very idea exhausted me.

I kept walking, hoping for some opportunity for rest to present itself. The full moon had risen. Hanging just above the skyline, it looked enormous and pumpkin orange. I noticed a few benches I could stretch out on, but I didn't want to be that obvious. Then

I passed a wall of shrubs with a person-sized space under the bottommost branches. Could I bring myself to sleep down there, and would darkness and those branches camouflage me from those who might want to do me harm or arrest me for vagrancy? I thought of the cobwebbed attic crawl space where my brother had forced me to spend that long and terrifying night. Though my shoes were chafing the backs of my heels, I kept slogging along, retracing my steps from earlier that day. I reached the edge of campus, crossed several streets, and wound up in front of the diner where I'd eaten earlier. This time, I noticed a small red neon sign that said OPEN 24 HOURS.

I went in and took a seat in a booth, the one nearest the kitchen. A few other patrons were scattered around the room, but the place was mostly empty. My waitress this time was an older, irritable-looking woman who smelled not so faintly of cigarette smoke. I ordered a glass of ice water and another bagel with cream cheese. I hadn't realized I was hungry, but when my order came, I ate it very quickly and still wanted more. I ordered a second, and took just a bite, determined to make this one last so that I could prolong my stay in the most comfortable place I'd been that whole day. I scooted over until I was up against the wall, crossed my arms on the table before me and, just for a moment, rested my head on them. I'm not sure how much time passed — ten minutes? twenty? — but an angry voice cut into my sleep. "Hey. You can't do that here." I sat bolt upright. "You'd better pay and get out."

"But I haven't finished my food," I protested.

"You'd better not go to sleep again. Hurry up and eat." She glared at me. Because I had committed the crime of nodding off in

273

a public place, in her eyes I had suddenly changed to a deadbeat. I was too tired to be outraged, too woozy with sleep to take another bite of my bagel. I sat there for a long while, trying to wake up all the way, to become alert enough to figure out what I should do when I'd finished the last crumb on my plate. Every so often, the waitress passed by again and eyed me with contempt.

"You gonna finish that?" she asked on her third trip past my table.

"Yes," I said, "in a moment."

"There's a time limit on these booths."

"There are plenty of empty tables," I pointed out. "Nobody's waiting for this one."

"I don't care. Eat, pay, and go."

My next bite was sodden, almost unchewable. I spit it into a napkin and tucked the mess under my plate. I couldn't help what happened next. Tears started slipping down my face, but I wouldn't let that horrible waitress see my distress. I pulled napkin after napkin out of the metal dispenser, trying to wipe away my storm of self-pity and frustration. A sudden bout of sobbing must have given me away.

"Hey. What's this about?" a familiar voice said. "Oh, it's you." It was my waitress from earlier, the only friendly person I had spoken to all day long. She plunked herself into the seat across from mine and put a finger to her lips. "Shhh. I can't let my boss see me sitting here. So tell me fast: what's wrong?" Her long, straight hair, tied back in a ponytail, was the color of honey; her name tag read DIANA.

"I don't have any place to sleep tonight," I told her, all pride and reticence gone. "I hardly have any money, and I don't know how I'll find a job if I don't even have an address to put on the application, and my cell phone…" But I couldn't trust myself to say another word.

Diana looked around, checking to see who was watching. Then she ducked her head and whispered, "Don't cry. I'll help you. Can you come on over to my station and sit there until my shift's over? I get off at midnight — about forty-five minutes."

"I can sit here all night and pretty much the rest of my life."

"Good. Do you like coffee? I'll bring you some." She looked around to make sure nobody was listening. "On the house."

After her shift, Diana swooped by my table to spirit me away. She still wore her blue uniform and smelled slightly of fried things. "C'mon," she said. "What are you waiting for?"

"The check?" I asked.

"No problem. It's taken care of." When I tried to object, she waved me off. "Listen, I live with my sister and brother. You can stay on our couch tonight. It's old and a little smelly, and we have a cat. Are you okay with that?"

Was I okay with that? It took all my restraint not to throw my arms around her neck and weep with relief. "You're saving my life."

"Well, it's not the Ritz. We live off campus…way off."

"It sounds perfect," I said.

I followed her out the door and up the street to a small blue Hyundai parked at an expired meter. "Look at that: no ticket. This must be my lucky day." She got in and leaned over to unlock my door. "What's your name? And what's your story?"

"Jane Martin." The made-up last name slipped off my tongue. "And I'd rather not tell my story."

"Oh, really?" She shrugged. "We'll get it out of you."

She drove out of the lush green area around the university, past streets of redbrick row houses, and before long we were in an area with fewer trees, the darkened storefronts shielded by metal grates. As she drove, Diana cheerfully filled me in on her own background, so there was no need for me to talk about myself. She had recently graduated from UConn and was living with her sister Maria, also a UConn graduate, and their brother River, a seminary student at Yale Divinity School. They had family back in Greenwich, but none of them particularly wanted to move back to the suburbs. "Too smug," Diana said. "Too safe. We wound up out here with River because he needs us. He's socially hopeless and can't cook or keep house to save his life — you'll see — but he's kind of an idiot savant, and we love him to pieces."

She pulled up in front of a white house that pitched slightly to one side. It wasn't much to look at, but it was one of the better-kept houses on the fairly bedraggled street. "We've got the second floor," she said. "Above the illegal aliens and below the junkies." I followed her up the dark, narrow staircase, and she unlatched three locks before opening the door. "Maria!" she shouted. "We've got a visitor."

From a lit-up room beyond the darkened kitchen in which we stood, a woman, clearly Diana's sister, swept in. "Well, turn the light on," Maria said, and flicked a switch to reveal a clean, old-fashioned kitchen, with harvest-gold appliances that must have predated both women who lived there. Maria was thinner and taller than her sister, but she had the same round, clear-skinned face and wide brown eyes. "Who's this?" She took my suitcase from me and stowed it in the hallway.

"Jane Martin," Diana said. "She needs a couch to crash on. You mind?"

"Why would I mind? Where are you from, Jane? Are you a student?"

"She's a woman of mystery," Diana answered for me. "Let's ply her with beer and get her secrets out of her." She opened the fridge. "We've got Rolling Rock. River doesn't want us to buy anything fancier. He's such a dweeb."

"But he's *our* dweeb," Maria said fondly. Then she turned to her sister. "He'll be late tonight. Of course."

"Of course. Here, Jane. Sit down and drink up." Diana set a sweating green bottle on the table in front of me.

"I shouldn't," I said. "I can't." I was conscious of an aching in my joints that hadn't been there a moment ago. "I don't feel right."

Diana's cool hand felt my forehead. "You've got a fever. Do we have a thermometer?"

"I dropped it," Maria said. "Glass everywhere."

"She's like an oven." Diana turned to her sister. "I'll set up the couch for her. You run interference with River when he gets here. Do we have any ibuprofen left?"

Before long, I was stretched out on a slightly lumpy couch in the darkened living room. My head felt like a balloon filled with damp sand. I slept awhile, then woke shivering in what must have been the middle of the night, unsure where I was for a long time. The apartment was silent. I could feel a weight on my feet. When I tried to move them, it shifted; the disgruntled cat jumped down from the couch and ran off. When my eyes adjusted, I saw that a glass of water had been set on the coffee table beside me; I took a

277

sip. The events of the past forty-eight hours came back to me slowly. Despite the sheet and blankets Diana had spread over me, I couldn't stop trembling with cold. I lay there a long time, utterly miserable, but then I must have fallen back asleep. The next thing I knew the room was filled with daylight; voices murmured from the kitchen. A bit later, Maria brought me more ibuprofen, a fresh glass of water, and a plate of toast I couldn't bring myself to touch.

"Go back to sleep," she said, spreading another blanket over me. "Sleep as long as you need to." So I did, for what must have been hours. When I finally woke again, I felt well enough to sit up, but when I did, the room swam around me. The sky beyond the small square living room window was darkening. I lay back down, trying not to think too hard. Wondering where I would go when I was well enough to leave the couch made me nauseous, so I pushed all those worries away and let sleep come again.

It must have been another twenty-four hours before I was well enough to get up, brush my teeth, take a shower, and change into fresh clothes. I ventured into the kitchen and found Maria and Diana there.

"Look who's up!" Diana exclaimed. "We were beginning to think we'd have to sling you over our shoulders and carry you off to the clinic. How do you feel?"

I assured them that I was starting to feel better. Maria offered to make me some tea, and I let her.

"You've been asleep for days," Diana told me. "Seriously, we were starting to worry about you."

"We're trying to figure out what's for dinner," Maria told me. "Do you think you could eat?"

"I'm not sure," I said. "I'd like to try."

Diana started pulling out produce from the crisper. "Carrots. Broccoli. Green pepper. What's this?"

"Ew. Throw that out," Maria directed. "We've got tofu. Chicken's all gone; I didn't make it to the food co-op today."

"Looks like stir-fry," Diana said. "Jane, put your feet up." She pulled out one of the three wooden chairs around the small kitchen table.

I took a sip of the orange zinger tea Maria had set before me. "Please let me help," I said. "I'm feeling well enough now."

"Tonight you just sit there." Diana pulled a chef's knife out of a drawer and went to work at a thick chopping block on the Formica counter. Though they wouldn't let me help, it felt good to sit near them while they bustled around, readying the garlic, broccoli, and scallions. It felt like a million years since I'd listened to easy, companionable conversation between friends. Maria put rice on to boil, and Diana manned the wok.

Just as the kitchen was starting to smell really good, a key rattled in the locks. A young man in a windbreaker came in carrying a bicycle. His blond hair was tousled, his cheeks flushed. He took instant note of me — the stranger at his kitchen table. "She's still here?" he asked.

"Manners, nimrod." Diana spoke without looking up from her stir-fry. "Put that bicycle away, and we'll talk."

He disappeared and soon returned. "We'll need an extra chair," he observed.

"Go get the one from your desk," Diana told him. Then, to me, she said, "Don't mind River. You'll see. He's worth the effort."

He returned and held out his hand for me to shake. "I'm River St. John," he said, a bit stiffly.

I introduced myself as Jane Martin.

"Diana likes to bring home strays," River said.

Diana gave him a playful punch on the arm. "That's not a very nice way to talk about our dinner guest," she said. "Jane's new in town, and she just needs a leg up."

"Are you a student?" River asked. "Do you have a job?"

"No and no," I told him, uncomfortable under his very direct blue gaze. River St. John was quite possibly the most handsome guy I'd ever seen in my life. His skin was perfectly clear, and with his chiseled features he resembled a marble statue of Apollo. When he took off his windbreaker, I could see he was thin but muscular. His faded T-shirt bore a photo of earth as seen from space.

"Do you have friends in the area?" he asked. "What brought you here?"

"I don't have any friends." I saw fit not to answer the second question.

"Where are you from? Don't you have any family?"

"I'm from Pennsylvania," I said, thinking that answer was vague enough and not untrue. "And no, my parents died almost a year ago."

"And you have no place to live?"

"Stop interrogating the poor thing," Diana said. "Can't you see she's still unwell?" She gave her brother a look that communicated something very directly, although I couldn't say what. The two of them slipped out together to another room.

Maria set the table with mismatched plates, silverware, and glasses. She put a steaming bowl of brown rice on the table and the wok full of stir-fried vegetables on a broken trivet. "Let me go see where they went."

I sat alone in the kitchen for what felt like a very long time. I knew the three of them must be talking about me and that River might be objecting to the presence of a strange person in his home. What if he wouldn't let me spend another night? But I didn't think Diana would let him toss me out on the street, especially now that it was getting dark. And they were locals; they could tell me where I might go to find a bed for tomorrow night.

When the three of them came back into the kitchen, they said nothing, but Diana had a small, satisfied smile on her face. River spread a paper napkin across his lap and folded his hands. Taking their cue from him, Maria and Diana did the same. A heartbeat later, so did I. "Bless this food to our use and us to Thy service," River said, and then dug in.

The food smelled good; I spooned some rice onto my plate and ate a little to steady my stomach. The chipped and mismatched dishware and the creaky chairs we sat on somehow made the room feel more, not less, comfortable. Diana and Maria joked and talked about their day. From what I could gather, Maria worked in the law library at Yale and was taking a night class in German literature with a professor she called Herr Bachmeier. Diana was looking for some kind of work that was better paying and more satisfying than her waitressing job, but she'd been a philosophy major and couldn't quite decide what direction her life should take. And River, who was studying to become a minister, put in long hours as a volunteer at a soup kitchen. I was cheered by this last bit of news; certainly he would be able to point me in the direction of a shelter and maybe even put in a good word for me there, if such a thing would help me get a bed. I waited until River had all but finished his beer and seemed to have loosened up a bit.

"Tell me more about the soup kitchen," I said. "Is it far from here? Can anyone eat there?"

"It's a couple of miles from here. We serve anyone who shows up."

"And do most of your clients have homes, or do they live in shelters?"

"There's a mix," River said in his serious way. "Some are the working poor who make barely enough to pay their rent, much less buy food. Others are homeless."

"And is the kitchen affiliated with a homeless shelter?"

"Not affiliated, no. But there's a shelter a few blocks over. A lot of people come to us from there." Then he started telling stories about his day — the men he'd served, the conversations he'd had with them. I noticed, though, that Diana was watching me as her brother spoke. When there was a break in the conversation, I dared another question.

"Can anyone stay in the shelter?"

River piled his plate with seconds. "If they get there early on any given day. They often have to turn people away."

"Can women stay there as well as men?"

"Yes," he replied. "But the men outnumber the women two to one."

"Can I change the subject for a moment?" Diana asked.

"As if we could stop you," River said, his tone a bit lighter than before.

Diana cleared her throat. "Well. Jane, the three of us were thinking—"

"We have this room," Maria cut in. "It's really more of a closet."

"We tried to rent it out," Diana said, "but nobody wanted it. It's too small, and it has only one very tiny window, and we didn't like any of the people who came to check it out anyway."

"So Diana was wondering," Maria said. "Well, actually, we were all wondering..."

"Would you like to live in it?" Diana said.

I sat there dumbfounded for a moment, filled with intense relief and the feeling that somewhere out there I must have a guardian angel or a fairy godmother. "How much?" I asked finally.

"It wouldn't have to be much," Maria said. "You should see the room. You might not even want it. River keeps his bicycle in there now."

"But...you know I don't even have a job yet," I said. "I'm looking for one, and I'm sure I'll get work soon, but I don't know...I can't promise..."

"We can't let you stay in a homeless shelter!" Diana exclaimed. "You seem too nice."

"Nice people stay in homeless shelters all the time," River said. "Jane, my sisters say you won't tell them anything about yourself—where you come from, what brings you to New Haven. That concerns me."

Could my silence be a deal breaker? "I have my reasons."

"Maria thinks you're running away from an abusive husband,"

Diana piped up cheerily. "Or maybe you're fleeing a cult. Or you're married to a mobster and want to escape."

"Nothing so glamorous," I said, and immediately realized the truth I was hiding was even stranger than the fictions that the sisters had invented for me. For a moment, I wished I could share my story, if only because I knew it would amuse them. "I can tell you I'm hardworking and honest, and I'd try to be a considerate roommate."

"Of course you would," Maria said. "We can tell."

"How would you feel about working at the soup kitchen with me?" River asked. "It would be volunteer work. Meaningful work."

The question took me by surprise. "Volunteer work? Don't you want me to be able to pay rent?"

"You answer first: how would you feel about working at a soup kitchen?"

It occurred to me that I was being tested. "I would like that," I said, which fortunately was the truth.

River seemed satisfied. "If you volunteer for a while, I might be able to help you find a paying job at one of the nonprofits where I've got connections. In the meantime, you can stay here rent free. We're not really using the room, and the soup kitchen always needs more volunteers — regular ones, that is. Not the kind that come and go on Thanksgiving."

I allowed myself a sigh of relief and thanked them profusely. "You're saving my life." I meant it literally. Now I would have work and a place to stay. I wouldn't be alone.

After dinner, Maria and Diana took me to look at the room, and I saw that they hadn't been exaggerating its size. It was barely a room at all; I might be able to fit a twin bed into it with some space left over, but I'd have to crawl into it over its footboard. The small high window overlooked an alley behind the house. I could see broken glass, tall weeds, an abandoned mattress. "It's the most beautiful room I've ever seen."

"We'll have to clean it out," Maria said. "And you'll have to get a bed somewhere."

"In the meantime, you can keep sleeping on the living room couch," Diana added. "Fergus seems to like sharing it with you." She indicated the fat tabby cat twining itself around my ankles. "River says to tell you you'll need to be ready to go by ten tomorrow morning. I'll give you a ride to the church — where the soup kitchen is. Unless you want to ride on River's bike handles."

"I'll take the ride. With you, that is," I said. "I don't even have an alarm clock."

"I'll wake you. And tomorrow I'll take you out to get the things you need. We could probably find you a bed at the Salvation Army."

"I do have some money. Not much, but some. I can pitch in, buy some groceries for the household. I don't want to be a burden."

"Aw, cut it out." Diana reached down to scoop Fergus up into her arms. The big cat purred and shut his eyes, looking blissful. "*Mi* couch *es su* couch."

The next morning, I followed Diana's directions to the nearest post office. It was a good half mile from the apartment, and the streets I walked through weren't particularly well kept or welcoming, but I had an important task to accomplish. At the counter in the back of the post office, I wrapped my cell phone in tissue paper, packed it in a cardboard box, and sealed it. Then I made up an address — 35 Oak Street, Sacramento, California — and wrote it on the box. I put down a made-up return address. This was my solution to the cell-phone problem, dreamed up late the night before when I had been too restless to sleep. I had considered carrying the phone to the far reaches of New Haven and leaving it in a garbage can, but even that seemed too risky. If, in fact, cell phones could be traced, I didn't want Nico to know what city I was in. There may or may not have been a 35 Oak Street in Sacramento, but I hoped the phone would wind up in a dead-letter file, unclaimed. I couldn't imagine Nico, even with his money and resources, tracking it down that far away. And perhaps he didn't want to find me anyway. I'd deserted him, after all.

I thought of my phone in its white tissue-paper shroud, the last link to my old life, and had a powerful urge to break open the box, dig it out, and put it right back into my pocket. It took all my willpower to give the box to the postal clerk, who punched in my invented address to find the ZIP code. But my good luck held; there really was a 35 Oak Street in Sacramento. I quickly handed over my money. I needed to head back to my new home as fast as my legs could carry me; Diana would be waiting to drive me over to the Ebeneezer Baptist Life Center, where I would begin my working life anew.

CHAPTER 23

At the soup kitchen, River put me to work cubing meat and peeling potatoes for beef stew to feed about 150 people. I joined an assembly line of cooks who greeted me warmly and chatted with each other in a meandering stream of conversation. River supervised; I noticed that though the other volunteers responded quickly to his commands, they seemed fond of him, half jokingly calling him "Captain." When River thanked a skinny blond man for organizing the pantry full of donated food, the man beamed as though he'd been given something rare and valuable.

At noon, the soup kitchen opened its doors, and a line of people began filing through to pick up trays and food. I ladled stew into their bowls and gave each comer a square of corn bread. I tried to talk to some of them as they came through, but the line had to move fast; there was barely time to say hello to the men and women who passed by my station. I couldn't help thinking how easily I could have been in their place, accepting food instead of dishing it out.

When the line had tapered off and the last of the stew was gone, out of the corner of my eye I noticed somebody hovering just behind me. It was River. "Now we need you out back to clean up," he said. I complied, scouring pots and soaking the front of my shirt in the process. I noticed that the other workers had started to clear out; the large, brightly lit kitchen was getting emptier.

"So, Jane" — it was River again; one minute he was nowhere to be seen and the next at my side — "satisfying work, right?"

I nodded. It certainly was simple work — useful and clear-cut. Less fortunate people needed something, and I had helped to give it to them.

"So do you think you're up to doing this on a daily basis?"

"I'm up to it," I said, and was on the verge of asking him how I could get back and forth without always relying on Diana to drive me, when a bright female voice cut in.

"Hey, River." It was the young woman who had dished out apple crisp at the other end of the serving table. She looked about my age. Tall and slender, with creamy brown skin and the longest eyelashes I had ever seen, she smiled engagingly at River, who blushed deeply.

"Hello, Rosalie." His gaze fell to the industrial green tile under his feet.

"How was your summer? Did you get away at all?"

"My summer was fine. I took classes and worked here at Ebeneezer." I waited for River to follow up with a question about the young woman's summer, but he was silent. Undeterred, she volunteered the information anyway.

"I had the most wonderful vacation. My family and I went up to our summer camp in Maine, and then we took a month on Naxos, you know, in Greece. But as gorgeous as it was, I missed this place and my friends here."

From the tone of her voice and the eager look on her face, I guessed that "my friends here" really meant River. As she spoke, she leaned in toward him and twirled one of her loose, glossy curls around an index finger. River stood stiffly, not knowing where to put his hands. First they landed in his pockets, then they dropped to his sides, then his fingers interlaced. As hard as she tried, he refused to meet her gaze.

"So I decided to do service work again this semester and asked to be assigned here. I'll have to take a summer course to catch up on all my requirements, but it's worth it to help people, don't you think?" She giggled. "Of course you do, or you wouldn't volunteer so many hours here yourself. I tell my friends you're the most selfless, committed person I've ever met."

"I doubt that's true."

"Well, it is. And now they all want to meet you. They've heard so much about you. So I was wondering, would you like to come over on Saturday night? My roommates and I are having a little party, very low-key."

"I don't go to parties. I need to stay focused on getting my course work done."

"And you *are* very focused. Anyone can see that. But it would only be a couple of hours, and everybody needs a little fun now and then."

"Thank you for the invitation. I'm sorry I can't make it." River's words were clipped, as though he were in a hurry to cut the conversation short.

Until that moment I would have sworn that Rosalie hadn't noticed my presence, but then she turned to me. "What do you think? Shouldn't River take a break and come to my party?"

"A night out every once in a while is probably good for everyone."

"You see? Your friend agrees with me." Rosalie extended a hand and introduced herself. "You're new here, right?"

"Yes. I'm Jane."

"You work on him for me, okay?" She pulled a piece of paper out of her purse and jotted down a phone number and an address. "The party starts at nine." She handed the information to me.

"I think my powers of persuasion are limited," I told her.

"Try anyway." She held out a hand for River to shake; he barely touched it. "See you next week, River." And she was gone.

Slowly, River's composure returned. We were the last to leave the soup kitchen. As he locked up, he offered to help me find my bus stop. We walked in silence. I wanted to ask about Rosalie — why he was so standoffish with her when their mutual attraction was so obvious. His response to her certainly wasn't indifferent; his stiff posture and bright blush gave that much away. Either he was painfully shy, or he held some kind of grudge against her. At any rate, I knew better than to mention it.

That night, though, when Diana got home from her shift and

Maria and River were still out of the house, I tried to feel her out on the topic. "Have you met a young woman named Rosalie who works at the soup kitchen?"

"Rosalie? Is that the one River complains about all the time?"

"Complains?"

"He says she's a rich party girl who only does volunteer work because it will look good on her résumé. Of course that's probably true for nine-tenths of the college students who work at the soup kitchen, or do any volunteer work, really. For some reason, she grates on his nerves. Last spring he complained about her all the time. What's she like?"

I was surprised at this report but decided not to give away too much of what I had observed. "She seemed very friendly. She tried to talk him into going to a party at her place Saturday night."

"River at a party?" Diana laughed. "Can you imagine?" And I had to admit I couldn't.

Living and working side by side with River, I soon got to know him better. Not that we made a lot of idle chitchat; he tended to focus like a laser beam on the things he found important — his studies, the soup kitchen, and his plans for the future. I found out a great deal about that last subject when one night over dinner I asked what he planned to do when he finished his studies.

"Haven't I told you already?" River's handsome face grew animated. "I'm surprised I didn't mention it. I'm moving to Haiti to help rebuild a school in one of the poorest communities you could imagine. The place was in rough shape before the earthquake, and now it's just devastated. You wouldn't believe the suffering, the lack of clean drinking water, the disease…" He soliloquized on the topic with a passion I'd never heard in his voice before.

"You big geek," Diana said fondly when she could get a word in. "Look at the sides of Jane's head. See anything missing?" And when he looked up, puzzled, clearly caught off guard, she said, "You've talked her ears off."

Still, it was clear that Diana and Maria doted on their big brother and were proud of his idealistic bent. The quieter and more serious of the two, Maria also admired him more openly. She once told me over coffee that she and her sister had always considered themselves ordinary compared to River. "Diana and I are average," she said, without rancor or jealousy. "But we've always known River would go on to do something important. Mom says he's destined for greatness."

And I had to admit that River's sense of purpose and intensity of focus were extraordinary, even if he had some difficulty relating to people in a regular, day-to-day way. I couldn't say whether he liked me, but as time went on, it became clear that he approved of me. After I'd put in a few months at the soup kitchen, he came home from class one night eager to talk. "There's a position opening up at Open Doors, the shelter up the street from Ebeneezer. They're looking for someone to run the office and write grant applications. I told the director about you, and she'd like to give you an interview. Would you be interested? It's a paying position."

"No!" Diana grabbed me by the hand. "River, what are you thinking? Once Jane gets a paying job she'll save up money and move out of her little hermit's room, and then what will we do?" Diana and I had become particularly close friends. When the time off from our jobs coincided, we spent it together, taking long walks in the park and drives into the country; mostly, though, we just hung around the house and talked. After I got to know her better, I asked for permission to paint her portrait. She was thrilled by my modest skill and insisted on hanging up the paintings I'd finished. You would have thought she'd done them herself.

"You mean I'll be able to pay rent as I should have been doing all along?" I said. "I happen to love my little hermit's room." And it was true; the room was cramped, but I was happy to be an honorary member of the St. John household.

And what of Nico Rathburn? I hadn't forgotten him or stopped worrying about him or missing him. Luckily though, in my daylight hours, I kept busy enough to keep regrets at bay.

Open Doors hired me as an administrative assistant to the director. The job was mainly secretarial. I kept the office organized and running smoothly, wrote articles for the little newsletter the office produced for donors, and learned to write grant applications. The pay was barely more than minimum wage, and Diana and Maria refused to let me pay more than two hundred dollars a month toward the rent.

"You need to save your money," Diana said. "You've got to go back to school."

"You can't let your talent go to waste," Maria agreed. "We won't let you."

So I really couldn't complain. I had plans, work, and caring friends. Certainly the work I'd been doing taught me that I had it better than many, even most. I was determined not to drown in sadness and self-pity.

Another blessing of my new life was how little it reminded me of my old life. None of my housemates listened to the radio; they didn't even own a television. I didn't have to hear Nico's music. My new friends didn't care for gossip magazines, so I never had to stumble across one on the coffee table or, in a moment of weakness, open it to learn of Nico's whereabouts. We did all our shopping at a local food co-op, so I never even had to glimpse a tabloid in the checkout aisle. We lived in an alternate universe, very different from the one in which Nico's every move was broadcast to a voracious public. I might not be able to forget him, but I could steer clear of all reminders and hope that someday I'd miss him a little bit less.

At night, though, I would drift into dreams so vivid I felt I was actually reliving moments Nico and I had shared — his hands on my back, his smell, his taste on my tongue, his voice calling my name, his weight beside me in the bed — and I would startle awake. For minutes afterward, I refused to believe it had only been a dream. And then I couldn't get back to sleep, my sadness so heavy and palpable I feared I might never sleep again. In those long, dark hours, Nico haunted me like a phantom limb.

One quiet day at work, when I was getting to the end of my filing, the phone rang. "Jane, is that you?" a voice asked. It was Rosalie. "I was wondering if you'd have dinner with me tonight." She named a little bistro not far from campus. Though we'd become casual friends, Rosalie and I had never socialized outside of work before. Curious about why she might want to see me, I agreed to meet her.

"My treat," she said as we pored over the very long menu. "It's the least I can do since I'm here to pick your brain."

This was an interesting start. "What about?" But before she could begin to tell me, I realized what she wanted. She would ask me about River.

Her opening question took me aback. "Are the two of you...involved?" She asked the question sweetly and shyly. That night she was wearing a soft butter-yellow sweater; her hair was loose around her face. Whenever she moved, the many charms on her gold bracelet tinkled, making gentle music.

I hurried to set her mind at ease. "Oh. No, not at all. We're just housemates. River is more like a brother to me than anything else."

Relief crossed her pretty face. She took a long sip of iced tea. "Can you explain him to me? Sometimes I think he likes me, but I can't get him to...I don't know...open up, relax, act normal."

I had my suspicions about why River tensed up and turned hostile in Rosalie's presence, but I wasn't sure enough about my theory to share it with her. So I couldn't offer an explanation, but I promised that I would try to feel him out on the subject.

As it turned out, River was home when I got in, reading the *New York Times*, in one of his expansive moods. "You don't speak French, do you?" he asked when I took the chair across from his in the paneled living room. Neither Diana nor Maria was home yet. Apart from the circle of lamplight in which he sat, the house was dark. I told him I'd been planning to minor in French back at Sarah Lawrence, though I was a bit rusty.

"I've been studying the language for years, but I think I've hit a

295

plateau. Would you practice speaking it with me? I've got to get fluent so I can make myself understood when I get to Haiti. Maybe we could speak French to each other whenever we're around the house."

"I'm not sure how much help I would be. I'd have to go back and study some more before I'd be able to put more than two words together at a time."

"Would you do that?" I hadn't really intended that as an offer, but I could see how important it was to him. "We could study together."

"I could try," I told him.

"You're very generous, Jane. I'm grateful for your help."

Satisfied, he turned back to the paper. I remembered my promise to Rosalie and told him I had a question for him.

He put down the paper, looking a little surprised. "About what?"

"I saw Rosalie tonight. She asked about you."

He sat up a little straighter in his chair. "What did she want to know?"

I decided the direct approach would be best. "Whether or not you like her."

"What is this? Eighth grade?" River's tone was gruff, but I thought I detected a fleeting smile.

"She wouldn't have to ask me if you didn't send her so many mixed signals. You go beet red whenever she gets near you, but you're standoffish and rude to her. I don't blame her for being confused."

"I'm not blind. I can see she likes me, but I'll never go out with her."

"But why not? You find her attractive, right? Unless I'm totally off base." It had occurred to me once or twice that River might be gay, and yet there were those blushes, that trembling. "Don't you think she's pretty?"

Even the question caused River's hands to shake a bit. "I can't imagine anyone who wouldn't think Rosalie is pretty."

"And sweet," I added.

"Yes, she's sweet. She always has a kind word for everyone at Ebeneezer. I see how nice she is with Marshall — you know, the man in the Red Sox cap who comes in every day?" I nodded. "I've seen her sit down beside him and help him put an Ace bandage on when he sprained his ankle." River's blue eyes were bright, and his voice lively.

"So?" I asked. "What's holding you back?"

He folded his newspaper neatly and set it down on the table beside him. "Don't you think it's strange that so many people base the most important decision of their lives, their choice of a life partner, on something as frivolous as physical attraction? Doesn't it seem like an obvious explanation for the divorce rate? When it comes right down to it, what does physical attraction have to do with compatibility, with shared purpose?"

"You don't have to marry her. Just get to know her."

"I don't have time to waste on someone who clearly won't be a good match for me," River said. "What if I got...attached to her? What would I do then? I'm leaving for Haiti in a few months."

"Bring her with you?"

"Do you know who Rosalie's father is? Herbert Davidson, of Davidson-Worth Pharmaceuticals. Her parents are obscenely wealthy, and she's their only child. She won't have to put in a day of work in her life if she doesn't want to. She only started coming to Ebeneezer to fulfill her service requirement."

"You said yourself she really seems to care for the people there. Who's to say she won't do volunteer work all her life? Maybe she'll pour all her money into good works."

"I'm not looking to get involved with a society woman who occasionally writes a check to charity or who puts in a few hours a week at a soup kitchen." He turned the full force of his gaze on me. "Since I was ten, maybe younger, I've felt that my life had a bigger purpose. I can't waste time — not when there are children contracting dysentery because there's no clean drinking water, or people dying of AIDS because drug companies like Davidson-Worth only care about profiting on the misfortunes of others. Can you imagine Rosalie building a shack in a developing country with her bare hands and living in it, not just for six weeks or a year, but for the rest of her life?"

I struggled for a way to phrase my answer. "If you gave Rosalie a chance, she might surprise you. I think people can change. Especially with kindness and love. She could influence her father, talk him into donating medicine to Haiti or opening some kind of free clinic."

"You've watched too many Hollywood movies. Or listened to too many love songs."

"That's not it," I said. "I've seen...I've felt..." But I couldn't say any more.

River looked at me questioningly for a moment, then turned back to his paper.

"Okay then. I'll tell Rosalie she's wasting her time." I got to my feet. "Good night."

"Isn't it a little early for bed? Wait here." He ran off in the direction of his bedroom and came back with several textbooks. "Here. You can study these. To brush up on your French."

I took them, a bit regretful that I'd agreed to help him. That night, as I lay in bed looking through the first of the two textbooks, trying to remember how to conjugate *être*, I kept myself awake by remembering the St. John family's many kindnesses to me. Diana and Maria were more like sisters than my own sister had ever been, and that made River a sort of brother. He needed my help, and I would do what I could to give it to him.

The night was the coldest so far that fall. I burrowed under my blankets, wishing I had a fluffy down comforter like the one on my bed at Thornfield Park. When I woke up the next morning, I found the textbook still open beside me in the bed.

CHAPTER 24

Several unremarkable months passed. I worked long hours at my new job and felt reasonably capable and useful. I put away a little money but despaired of ever having enough to go back to school. The leaves on the spindly trees along our street turned gold, then blew away. I got better at my job and, to tell the truth, a bit bored with it. I spent my spare time sketching and painting, hanging out with Diana and Maria, and helping River practice French as best I could. Our conversations in French became a nightly event; we often stayed up to speak our halting phrases to each other long after his sisters had gone to bed. When the St. Johns left to spend Christmas in Greenwich with their extended family, Diana invited me along, but I declined. I spent the holiday alone, reading novels, trying not to wonder if Nico was back at Thornfield Park sharing the holiday with Maddy. I was overjoyed when Diana, Maria, and

River returned with Tupperware containers of turkey and stuffing to share with me.

Then, on a dark late-afternoon in February, I arrived home from work and found River there, much earlier than usual. There was just a single light on in the living room. He sat in his usual chair, but he wasn't reading or doing homework. Instead, he appeared to be waiting. When I entered the room, he got to his feet. Though I couldn't have said why, I felt uneasy, as though I'd been caught doing something wrong.

"Jane," was all he said. Then he reached into his pocket and pulled out a piece of paper that he had folded into a tight little rectangle. He unfolded it and handed it to me. "Jane Moore."

It was a statement, not a question. I took the piece of paper, which had been ripped from a magazine. It was a photo of me I'd never seen before; I was in my wedding dress, holding hands with Nico. We were on the way up the steps of the courthouse. I had been caught unaware, looking right into the camera, my expression anxious. Nico was midstride, his dark hair windblown. He looked impatient, a vivid reminder of that day. At the sight of him, I was clutched by a feeling like that precarious moment just past the top of a roller coaster's highest hill when gravity takes hold and the car barrels downward.

What would River say now that he'd unearthed my secret? There was no denying the woman in the photograph was me. I said the first lame thing that popped into my head. "But you don't read magazines."

"I guess you've been banking on that." He took back the piece of paper as if it were a weapon with which I might harm myself.

"Why did you lie to us, Jane? Why didn't you tell us your real name?"

"When I first met you, I was afraid Nico might find me. I was paranoid that anyone I met might try to contact him or the press. And later when I knew you and your sisters better, my real name didn't matter. I'd broken off with my old life completely." I motioned toward the slip of paper. "Where did you get that?"

"One of the clients from the soup kitchen brought it to me," he said. "Darva recognized you. She knew all the details. I guess your story was all over the news for a while there. It's amazing you've managed to camouflage yourself so well until now." He looked at me quizzically. "I'd never have believed you were a rock star's girlfriend."

Even if those last words hurt, I didn't give myself time to register it. "All over the news?" Suddenly I was gripped by the desire to know where Nico was, how he was doing, if he was all right.

"He was looking for you. It was a big story. Prince Charming searching for his Cinderella." River took a closer look at my face. "Why look so panicked? You know how it all turned out. You evaded his clutches. By now, the story has died down, according to Darva."

But I was being swept by waves of emotion. The first was joy: Nico had looked for me? The second was fear: Had he stopped looking for me? Had he given up and found someone else to take my place? I didn't dare ask; the answer might split me in two. "How long ago was that picture published?"

"October, I think. Darva said she was going to throw out a pile of old magazines, and she happened to browse through one and there you were. She could hardly believe it."

"What if she says something? What if she turns me in?"

"Why would she do that? It's not like you've committed a crime. Darva's sixty-six years old with a history of mental illness. She can barely pay for her blood pressure medication. I don't think she's about to get on the phone with the *National Enquirer.*"

I felt less sanguine. Darva — who I couldn't recall at all from my soup kitchen days — might expect to get a little fame, even a little money of her own, from her part in my story. Why wouldn't she call the *Enquirer* or tell twenty of her best friends?

"Besides," River continued. "What's this Rathburn character going to do? Throw a net over your head and drag you back to his mansion? He doesn't own you. You left of your own free will."

He was right, of course. Still, a picture of Nico had turned me to Jell-O. What if he came to New Haven and tried to convince me to go back to him? Could I resist? And yet the thought of Nico climbing the stairs to the apartment I shared with Maria, Diana, and River was absurd. We might as well be living in completely different worlds.

River watched me carefully. Who knows what emotions he saw cross my face? There was a long silence. "You're still infatuated with him," he finally said. "I never would have believed it. Any of it. If I hadn't seen your picture, if I wasn't looking right at you..." There was something in his voice that I couldn't quite identify. He almost sounded hurt. But why would he be? "Don't you know that the ultrarich are the enemy of everything you've been working for these past few months?"

This was the last place I'd expected our conversation to go.

"That Rathburn guy got all his money — millions, possibly

billions, right?—by playing a guitar and singing. Doesn't that seem frivolous to you? He could live on a tenth of his income and give the rest away without even feeling it."

I didn't disagree with everything River was saying, but calling Nico frivolous struck me as absolutely off base. "His music gives a lot of people pleasure, or he wouldn't be so rich."

"Pleasure." River thrust his hand deep into his pockets. "Pleasure's all some people live for, but you're not just 'some people.' You're better than that. You know that, right? You're cut from a different cloth. You're not thinking about going back to him, are you?"

"I think it's a bit late for that," I said. "I've missed my chance." I was too focused on all that I'd just learned about Nico to wonder what River had meant about my being "better than that."

He changed tack. "What kind of man tries to trick a woman into marriage under false pretenses? And who keeps his first wife hidden in his attic like some kind of animal?"

"He was trying to keep her out of an institution," I said, but I could hear how weak the argument sounded. After all, it had been more complex than that, selfishness mixed in with selflessness.

"You're defending him? After what he did?"

"I'm just saying it was more complicated than you know."

Just then, much to my relief, the downstairs door creaked open, and we could hear footsteps on the stairs. It was Maria, coming home from her job, hugging an overstuffed bag of groceries. "Hey," she said. "What's going on?" She took a closer look at her brother. "Is something wrong?" Then she looked at me. "Oh." Clearly she thought we'd been arguing. She turned and went into

305

the kitchen, setting her bag on the table; River and I followed. "I'm making corn chowder for dinner. I got some of that bread from the little Italian bakery near campus. What time is Diana due home?"

"I don't know," River said. "But when she gets in, Jane has something to tell the two of you." He handed me the clipping and headed back to the living room. Quickly I slipped it into the pocket of my hoodie.

"You do?" Maria looked deeply concerned. "It isn't bad news, is it? Everything's okay, right?"

I nodded, unable to speak. Would Diana and Maria like me less when they knew I'd been lying to them? Wordlessly, I reached into the brown paper bag and pulled out some oranges; side by side, Maria and I put away the groceries. Though she said nothing, I could feel how badly she wanted to ask for an explanation. Such was her admiration for her big brother's intelligence and idealism that she didn't feel compelled to press me for more details. And I didn't want to have to tell my story twice, so I said nothing. As Maria and I peeled potatoes for that night's dinner, I considered why I was feeling so unsettled. I had enjoyed River's approval of me, and now I was upset to think that maybe he thought less of me, for withholding my true identity and for consorting with — what had he called them? — the "ultrarich"?

Diana came home just as we were setting the table for dinner. I drew the two sisters into the kitchen and made my confession. Diana and Maria let me tell my story without interruption, their brown eyes growing wider and wider as I spoke. I had expected it to be painful, reliving the story of falling in love with Nico and then learning the truth about him, but to my surprise it was a relief to share the secrets that had been weighing on me. When I was done, my friends sat in silence for a while. Then Diana finally spoke.

"Whoa," was all she said.

"Please don't hate me," I said. "I never should have lied to you, and I wasn't trying to deceive you, really. It's just…I mean…"

Diana threw her arms around me. "Of course we don't hate you," she said. "You poor thing. Going through all that."

Then Maria was hugging me too. "We always said you had some kind of wild secret in your past, but we never guessed how wild."

Relief flooded me, but then I remembered River's disapproval. "Your brother's disappointed in me," I said. "For lying. Also he seems to think I'm some kind of materialistic groupie."

"He does not!" Diana exclaimed. "River can be a little demanding of the people he's close to."

"He's so principled," Maria said. "He's even harder on himself than he is on everyone else."

"But he'll get over it," Diana concluded. "He's so strict with himself that sometimes he forgets the rest of us are *normal*."

I sighed. "I was afraid you were going to tell me to pack my bags — I mean, my bag."

Diana crinkled her nose at me. "We'd never let that happen. You're one of us now."

"Like it or not," Maria chimed in.

Then Diana laughed. "You almost married *Nico Rathburn?* Even I know who he is. Geesh, Janey. I can hardly believe it."

I pulled the picture out of my pocket and unfolded it. "Well, here's physical evidence."

Maria gasped. "That dress…"

"It's you, but it's not you," Diana said. "It's freaky to see you like that."

"It *was* a little freaky," I said. "The clothes, the paparazzi…"

"I know you must not want to tell us any more about him," Diana said. "Most girls would be dishing the gossip right and left."

"Is that why you changed your name?" Maria asked. "To put it all behind you?"

I nodded. "I couldn't talk about him. The only way I can get by is to build a wall between then and now. I have to keep the division clear. For my mental health."

"We understand," Maria said.

"But if you ever do want to talk…" Diana left the rest unsaid.

"If I ever talk to anyone, it will be you."

They were silent a moment. Then Diana giggled. "You slept with Nico Rathburn?"

I blushed.

"I'm sorry. I won't say another word." Diana squeezed my hand. "Let's go have some dinner. I'm starving."

Over dinner, River said little but watched me closely as I ate, talked, and laughed with his sisters, as though he was trying to figure me out all over again. He didn't look angry, exactly, just puzzled, and maybe wounded. His level blue gaze was unnerving; I could finish only half the soup in my bowl. After dinner, as Maria

308

and Diana cleared the table, and I pulled on rubber gloves and started the dishes, River appeared at my side and finally spoke.

"Can I help?" Usually his sisters and I did the cleaning up so he could return to his homework, so this offer seemed like a truce, maybe even an apology. Grateful, I handed him a dish towel.

CHAPTER 25

After that evening, I detected a slight change in the way River treated me. He was as polite as he had always been, and a casual observer wouldn't have noticed any difference between us; Maria and Diana certainly didn't seem to. But whenever we were in the same room, I got the feeling that he was watching me closely, paying careful attention to my words and actions. And sometimes in the evening when we sat together practicing French, I could have sworn there was a tension between us. At first, I thought maybe he was on guard because I wasn't quite the person he had thought I was. But over time, I began to rethink that impression. Though I would some-times look up from whatever I happened to be doing — writing a grocery list or drawing in my sketch pad — and catch him watch-ing me, his expression never struck me as suspicious. He seemed curious, as if I were a puzzle he was working to figure out.

Then one night, River surprised me. Maria and Diana had gone off to bed, and we'd been sitting up even later than usual. He'd been telling me of his preparations for moving to Haiti. As always, when he spoke about that country's brutal poverty, ravaging disease, and injustice, his French took on a fluency it lacked when he was simply making small talk. That night, though, he broke off in the middle of a sentence, rummaged around under the couch, and pulled out a package, clumsily wrapped in festive paper. With no explanation, he handed it to me.

"What's this?" I asked, disarmed back into English. River had never given me a present before, not even on my birthday, when Maria had baked a cake and Diana had surprised me with a big box of pastel crayons.

"Open it."

It was a book, an autobiography — *A Rude and Beautiful Awakening: One Woman's Fight for Social Justice in Haiti*. I looked questioningly at River.

"I wanted to thank you" — his steady gaze met mine — "for staying up late to practice French with me when I know you'd rather be sleeping. Or making your art. I hope this book will give you a sense of the important work you're contributing to."

I found my voice. "You didn't have to." From anyone else, the gift might have been a small gesture, but from River it seemed as premeditated and significant as everything he said and did. "But thank you." I was honestly touched that he'd thought of me.

"Diana tells me you're saving up to go back to school," he said. "She thinks I should let you have your evenings to yourself."

"Diana's better to me than I deserve," I told him. "And I appreciate her Mama Bear routine, but she worries too much on my behalf. I enjoy our practice sessions." I wasn't just being polite. Though I hadn't been particularly enthusiastic about our sessions at first, over time I'd come to look forward to them — the stillness of the house around us, the quiet companionship.

"You do?" River, usually so confident, sounded uncertain.

I nodded. I had thought he might hold my secret past against me; instead it seemed as though we'd broken through our polite formality to something like friendship.

"I'm glad, because I've come to count on them," he said. "To enjoy them."

Pleased and suddenly bashful, I opened the book and riffled through the pages. River drew a bit closer and looked over my shoulder. "You'll like this book, I think," he said. "I've heard the author speak, and she's very eloquent." Then he took the heavy volume from my lap, turned to a section of black-and-white photos at the center, and gave it back. He pointed to a snapshot of a slender little girl in a school uniform. "Look at the sadness in her face," he said. The girl had smiled for the camera, but he was right: her eyes were haunting. "We can only imagine the horrors she's seen."

"You'll help her," I told him. "Or maybe not her, but others like her. As much as any one person can."

River sighed. "I plan to try." This was as much uncertainty as I'd ever heard him voice about his life's calling. Then, abruptly, he changed the subject. "Sometimes I wonder, Jane…are you happy? Because living here must pale in comparison…to your life before us."

I thought a moment. "I feel like I've found a family here. That might not sound like a big deal, but if you knew what my actual family life was like..."

"You can tell me," River said. He had remained close to me on the couch, closer than we usually sat. I dared a glance over at him and found him looking back at me with that intense curiosity I had seen so often lately. "I know I must not seem terribly easy to talk to. Sometimes I wish I were a better conversationalist, that I knew how to make jokes and small talk like other people do."

Coming from River, with all his quiet certitude, this admission surprised me. I struggled for a reply. "Small talk is overrated" was the best I could do.

"I've always thought so." Then River smiled. Had I ever seen him smile before? He'd grinned wryly in my presence, but this was something different, warmer and shyer. "If you want to talk, I'll try to be a good listener." Then his bright blue gaze shifted from my eyes to my lips.

"Oh, I know you would listen," I said with a lightness I didn't feel, "if I wanted to talk." Suddenly dizzy, I longed to escape to the privacy of my room. I scrambled to my feet, thanked River again, and excused myself. I shut the bedroom door behind me and changed into my nightgown. Under the covers in my narrow bed, I replayed our conversation and found myself trembling. I brought my knees to my chest and hugged them to steady myself. Was I imagining things? Could River really have been about to kiss me? And had I wanted him to? Was such a thing possible when I still missed Nico so desperately?

Midnight came and went, the digital readout of my alarm clock casting a red glow across my blankets. I squeezed my eyes shut and wondered at my own irrationality. River was handsome, smart, and selfless. Why had I panicked and run away from him when he seemed so clearly interested in me? There was only one logical answer. Without even realizing it, I must have been waiting for Nico to track me down and beg me to come home. But what sense did that make, when I could so easily return to Thornfield Park and give myself to him? Something was keeping me in hiding. Maybe it was fear that I had wounded Nico's pride too grievously for him to ever forgive me. Had he resumed womanizing to spite me? Or — still worse — had someone else taken my place?

Of course, it was in my power to learn the answers to at least the last two questions. All I needed to do was go to the public library and look through celebrity magazines or browse the Internet. If the legendary Nico Rathburn had moved on to a new love interest, the celebrity gossip magazines would be bursting with the news. But did I really want to know if Nico had moved on? No, I decided, pulling the covers up over my head. I was better off with blinders on. I had to keep my gaze forward. I had to focus on the future. And if moving on meant finding someone else to be with, shouldn't it be someone more like me; serious, determined, straightforward? Shouldn't it be someone like River?

Over the next few days, I watched River carefully. After that first sleepless night spent mulling over the possibilities, I'd made up my mind. If River ever gave me another chance to kiss him, I wouldn't run away. I would meet his gaze and stay put on the couch beside him. I would allow it to happen. But then, to my disappointment, nothing *did* happen. Our meals and French sessions were friendly

315

enough, and over dinner I still sometimes caught him watching me, but beyond that things were as they always had been.

I had just about concluded that my mind had been playing tricks on me when the tables turned yet again. I was locking up the Open Doors office for the week. The director was out of town for a conference, and I had just spent a quiet day writing copy for the shelter's monthly newsletter. As I struggled with the dodgy lock, I glanced up, and there, striding toward me down the dark street, was River. He'd never stopped by the office for a visit before, and his purposeful step made me think he had something important to tell me. But after he reached me and said hello, he had surprisingly little to say. Door finally locked, I agreed to walk home with him instead of taking my usual bus. We were nearly home by the time he found his voice. "So, Jane. Do you like working at the shelter?"

"Yes, of course." I allowed myself to exhale audibly. If that was all River wanted to ask me, maybe I really *had* been imagining an interest that wasn't there.

"Because I've been thinking a lot lately. About you. Your future, I mean." Hands buried in the pockets of his sweatshirt, River looked not at me but at the street ahead of us. "I know art is your first love, but you have the right disposition for humanitarian work. You're calm and serious; you don't shy away from getting your hands dirty."

Now he was sounding more like a guidance counselor than a potential boyfriend. "Oh, thanks," I said. It was all I could think of at the time.

"No need for thanks. Your supervisor has been raving to me

about the work you've done at Open Doors. She's been impressed with your dedication and your meticulous nature." He spoke quickly, as though delivering a speech he'd memorized. We'd come to an intersection, and as we paused for the red light, River glanced at me to see how I was reacting to his praise.

I said nothing, wondering where this conversation was going. The light turned green.

"I would hate to see you waste those talents," River added.

"You mean by doing something as *frivolous* as painting?" The word had stuck like a burr since he'd used it to describe Nico.

"No, that's not it." He frowned. "I just think you might find humanitarian work even *more* meaningful."

"As opposed to work that would make me happy?"

"There's more than one kind of happiness," he said. "There's the kind that comes from getting what you want." *What do I want?* I wondered. I hardly knew anymore. I was simultaneously relieved and disappointed at the impersonal turn our conversation had taken. "And then there's the kind that comes from knowing you're doing something selfless."

"And you're lucky enough to have both kinds."

"Not yet," he said. "But I hope I might find both in Haiti."

"I hope so too, for your sake." We waited at another busy inter-section, and for a while, there was an uncomfortable silence. He watched me expectantly, and I found myself eager to speak. "I hope you don't come to feel that you've made too many sacrifices for the betterment of mankind."

"Too many sacrifices?" He looked truly puzzled. "You've been reading the book I gave you, right?"

I was. I'd stayed up late the night before, devouring a particularly moving chapter about Yvette, a young girl the author had met
on her first mission trip to Haiti. Having lost her parents to AIDS,
the girl would have faced a life of prostitution if it weren't for the
school the author had helped build in her village. There she learned
to read and write and showed such a flair for letters, in fact, that
she stayed on to teach in the school after she graduated. She'd
grown into an independent woman who could earn her own way,
beyond the clutches of those who would use her for their own gain.

"Yvette's story brought me to tears," I told River. "Not for her,
but for the other girls who aren't so lucky." He nodded, and it
occurred to me that he'd chosen the book carefully, picking one he
knew would move me.

"You have a good heart, Jane," he said. We were still standing
on the curb, though the light had changed more than once. His
bright blue gaze held me in place. "I wonder what you want from
your life," he continued. "I don't just mean your ambitions, wanting
to go back to school and all that. I mean, sometimes I wonder what
would make you really happy ... both kinds of happy."

A sudden, sharp longing for Nico took me by surprise. I fought
it off, struggling to give River my full attention.

"Because sometimes I think you want what I want. To help
people — the poor and the illiterate. To improve their lives," he
concluded.

The light turned green, and I resumed walking. "To tell the
truth, I don't know what I want," I said finally, when River caught
up with me. "I don't know what would make me happy anymore."

"You don't?" He seemed exhilarated, as though this was the

318

answer he had been hoping for. "Because I've thought of something that might be perfect for you. Something that might fulfill you beyond anything you've ever experienced."

"Really?" It was the only response I could manage. I had no idea what he meant.

"Can't you guess? Isn't it obvious? I'm asking you to come with me to Haiti, Jane. To help me in my work."

Now it was my turn to stop dead in my tracks. River saw my hesitation.

"For a long time now, I've seen something in you," he said. "A real genius for helping people. If you say yes, your every need will be taken care of — you'll have shelter, food, transportation. You'll even make a stipend you can save in case you still want to go back to school. Your life in Haiti won't be luxurious, but I promise, you'll feel needed in a way you never have before." He paused to gauge the effect those last words were having on me.

I have been needed, I thought, *and I miss that feeling.*

"I'll think about it," I replied, more confused than ever, wishing I dared ask if he saw me as more than just a potential coworker, wishing I were surer of my own feelings toward him. We had reached the front stoop of our apartment building. From the top step, River beamed down at me with that same warm smile I'd seen a few nights ago, as though I'd already told him yes. Then he fished the keys out of his pocket and struggled with the dead bolt. "Take all the time you need," he said, and swung the front door open.

From that night on, River seemed to watch my every gesture, as though he was seeking a window to my thoughts. Whenever we found ourselves in the same room, I could feel the unresolved questions between us crackle like static electricity. Before sleep each night, I read on in the book he had given me, imagining myself into the story of heroic relief workers struggling to build schools and hospitals, to give hope to the poorest of the poor. River's enthusiastic visions were proving contagious. Who wouldn't want to be needed by so many people? And who wouldn't be proud to stand beside someone so passionate about his work? In those rare moments when River wasn't watching me, as he studied his textbooks or read through the day's mail, I allowed myself to sneak long looks at him — his finely chiseled features, his lean build, his rumpled blond hair. Who wouldn't want to be wanted by someone like River?

The more I thought about his invitation, the fewer reasons I could think of for turning it down. Though pleasant enough, my mostly clerical job didn't satisfy my whole self; it wasn't something I could imagine doing forever, or even much longer. I loved living with Diana and Maria, but that didn't seem enough of a reason to turn down the chance to do more vital, necessary work. Here was an opportunity to travel, to have adventures. If something in my bones froze at the idea of voyaging so far away and staying indefinitely, I had to admit to myself that it was my stubborn, foolish attachment to Nico. Foolish because he hadn't come looking for me, or if he had, he hadn't looked hard enough. Doubly foolish because I had done everything I could to ensure he wouldn't find me. Hadn't I been right in doing so? Was I going to wait around forever for Nico to show that he still cared about me? That would be a slow death. Why not settle the question by disappearing to a place he'd never think to look?

One Sunday morning, while River and Maria were at church, Diana and I took a hike in a nature preserve a short drive from the house. It was a heart-piercingly beautiful day; a week of almost constant rain had made the landscape lush and verdant. Since spring had arrived, she and I took every opportunity to go for walks; she claimed she had five pounds of winter weight to walk off, though I couldn't see it. Ordinarily our talk was light and rambling. Today, though, was different. For most of the walk, she said little. My overtures at conversation led nowhere. Then, just as I'd given up, she stopped like a balky horse. "Aren't you going to tell me what's going on between you and River?" she asked.

So she had noticed. "Going on?"

"The two of you have been acting so strange these past few weeks. He's always staring at you like he's waiting for you to sprout wings and fly away, or something. And you seem so jumpy around him. Did he do something to hurt your feelings?"

"No, no, nothing like that, Diana."

She exhaled loudly. "Well, thank God." Then she looked at me more closely. "Is it something else, then? Do you two have some kind of secret? Maria has this theory that — well, I've been telling her she's crazy, but maybe she isn't after all."

"What kind of theory?" I trained my gaze off into the distance.

"That he's got some kind of crush on you. That he's thinking about putting the moves on you."

I forced a laugh. "Putting the moves on me?" If Diana thought the idea was crazy, maybe it really was.

"I know! Imagine River putting the moves on anyone! So that's not it? I mean, I didn't think it was, but Maria had me convinced you'd practically be our sister-in-law soon, and both of us kind of liked the idea."

"We're sisters already," I told her. "No need for the in-law part."

"But then what *is* going on between the two of you? Because I know it's something."

River hadn't sworn me to secrecy, though I suspected he wouldn't want me saying too much to his sisters about his invitation. Still, the idea of confiding in Diana, getting her opinion, was too attractive to resist. "Promise you won't tell him I told you."

"Hurry up and spill it already; the suspense is murder."

So I told her about River's plans for me, and how he was waiting for my answer. Diana's eyes got bigger and bigger.

"Get out," she said. "You're not seriously considering this, are you?"

I admitted that I was.

"Jane! No! We can't lose both River and you at the same time. Maria and I will fall apart all by ourselves. Plus, what about your plans to go back to school?"

I thought about confessing my recent confusion about River's motives; if there was anyone I could confide in it was Diana. But something kept me silent on that front. "It's not easy to say no to River."

"Oh, believe me, you don't have to tell me that. River's vision of saving the world is so grand and romantic. I can see the appeal. But you don't really want to go with him, do you? He's probably convinced you that it's your duty to mankind and all that, but in your heart you don't really want to…"

"I'm not sure. My life doesn't have a whole lot of meaning right now."

"Meaning?" she said. "You've got Maria and me. You've got a good job doing important work. You've got plans. I know you'll figure out a way to get back to school. How much meaning do you need?"

For a moment I almost confessed the truth about the enormous hole at the center of my life and how I'd been hoping River might distract me from my loneliness. "Something's missing," I said instead. "And I never expect to get it back."

She knew right away what I was referring to. "But you will," she said. "Just go about your normal life. Someday you'll get over him, and someone else will come along."

"I wish I could believe you," I said. "But I don't think so. I know this will sound completely melodramatic, but I think I've had the kind of love that spoils a person for anything else, like in a movie."

"Or a love song?" Diana smiled indulgently at me. "Believe that all you want, but don't let it chase you off to Haiti. Whatever you think, I know someone will love you the way you need to be loved. I'm completely certain of it. And you know I'm never wrong. How could I be? I'm River St. John's sister. We St. Johns have got the wisdom thing all sewn up."

I managed a smile.

"I'm not trying to boss you around," she said. "Despite how it sounds. I know you need to decide for yourself."

"Thank you." We had reached the end of the trail and stood at the edge of the Sound. The wind lifted our hair, and I recalled this was the same body of water I'd spent so many hours beside while

Maddy was at preschool, when I was waiting, without knowing it, to meet Nico Rathburn and fall in love with him. If I took off my shoes and stepped in the Sound right now, I might touch the very same water I'd skipped stones into back when I had my whole life ahead of me. I had an urge to dive in and ride the current east, back to Thornfield Park.

"I won't do anything rash," I told Diana, and believed I was speaking the truth.

CHAPTER 26

A week later, I made up my mind. I'd finished the autobiography River had given me, and every few mornings after I'd find a new book about Haiti on the kitchen table. He didn't say a word, but I knew he'd left them there for me. Each was more heartrending than the last. I would take my lunch break at my desk and, while eating my sandwich, would read about severely malnourished children dying of diarrhea and pneumonia. The more I learned, the sadder I became. So much needed fixing in the world, and there seemed so little one person could do to help.

At night, River and I continued on with our French sessions. Though some strange magnetism held us side by side on the couch late into the night, there hadn't been a repeat of that moment a few weeks before when I had thought he might try to kiss me. After we wished each other good night, I would go back to my room and read some more, unable to put the books down, sadness and restlessness gnawing at me. Instead of lessening with time, as I had hoped it might, the loneliness I carried around in the pit of my stomach seemed to grow. Every day the feeling got stronger: I had to do something, anything, to change my life.

So I waited one night until Diana and Maria had gone to bed, then told River I had an answer for him. The apartment dark and quiet around us, we sat in the lamplight, textbooks spread out on the coffee table.

"You've made a decision?" His tone was gentle, endlessly patient.

"I'll come with you," I told him. "I'm prepared to work beside you."

He reached for a book, picked it up, and set it down, his eyes not leaving my face. "You will? You're sure?"

I was sure, wasn't I? I inhaled deeply and forged onward. "I've given it a lot of thought. It's hard to say no when there are people out there who so desperately need my help."

"I need your help," River said, with an earnestness I'd never heard before. His arms closed around me, and I knew the tension between us hadn't been a figment of my imagination. We held each other for a long time, and tears sprang to my eyes when I realized how badly I'd missed being in a man's arms. I could have stayed like that forever, my head on his chest, his breath stirring my hair. But then he drew back, and I was startled by the intensity of his gaze. Before I could think what to say or do, his lips were on mine. His kiss was muscular, and I felt myself respond, melting into him.

We kissed awhile longer, then he pulled back, and we stared wordlessly at each other. He stroked my cheek with a steady hand,

and out of nowhere a distant memory popped into my mind: the way he had trembled and blushed when he looked at Rosalie, so undone by her. Now as he looked at me, his gaze was steady, his touch on my cheek sure and deliberate. Whatever he was feeling for me wasn't the same thing he had felt for Rosalie. So what was happening between us?

"Wait." I slipped away from him and said the first thing that popped into my mind. "I didn't agree to *this*." He looked hurt, and I instantly regretted my words. "I mean, I'm trying to understand. What is this? Between us. I've felt it too, but I'm just not sure what it is."

Though his look stung me, his voice remained calm, reasonable. "You said you wanted to come to Haiti with me."

I nodded.

"I thought that meant you wanted the same thing I want."

I struggled for the right words. "I can't tell what you want. From me, that is."

"Isn't it obvious?" River moved closer to me. "I want us to take care of each other. To keep each other company. We'll be so far from everyone we know. We'll need each other." Now his hands grasped my shoulders; he rested his forehead against mine. "Maybe you haven't noticed how lonely I've been. How badly I've been wanting to touch you."

Though his words should have thrilled me, I felt an unexpected reluctance. He leaned in to kiss me again. I felt myself getting warm. Everything was changing suddenly, irrevocably. Again, I pulled away. "But you don't love me," I said. "I don't love you." I felt certain that both statements were true.

He didn't contradict me. "That could change. In Haiti, we'll only have each other. We like and respect each other already, and I want so much to be close to you." He cupped my face in his hands. "In time, we'll come to love each other. Think what a team we could make. The two of us…we're so much alike." He bent to kiss me again, and I thought of Diana or Maria coming into the living room and finding us in each other's arms. I started to make a small noise of objection that River seemed to take as an expression of pleasure. His arms wrapped around me once more, tighter this time.

Was he right? Were the two of us really that much alike? I thought again of how I'd seen him resist Rosalie, turning away from the woman he really wanted, choosing to be governed by logic instead of desire.

"Jane," he whispered. "Jane."

Without meaning to, I stiffened and pulled back. His voice, saying my name that way, wasn't the right voice. "I can't," I said. "Not like this. I didn't intend this. I didn't mean…"

"You promised to come with me. Are you backing out?"

"No," I said. "I'll go with you, but I won't…I won't be with you."

"If you come to Haiti with me, this will always be there. We might as well just let it happen."

I slid out of his arms. "I need to think. I'm going out for a walk."

"You can't go out there now. Not by yourself. It's dangerous."

Was he worried about me because he cared about me? Or because he didn't want to lose his assistant, his support system, his comrade, his lover? I didn't know. "I'll be fine. I'll take a cab."

"To where?" he asked. "Where will you go this time of night?"

"I'm still working that out."

"You'll come back to me, won't you? Promise you will."

"I don't know," I said. "I'll tell you as soon as I've thought it through."

All I knew was that I had to get away from him right then, before he talked me into anything else. He followed me into the kitchen and watched as I called the cab company from the phone on the wall. I ran to my bedroom, grabbed my wallet and a jacket, and started down the stairs, out to the street, toward the corner where I'd told the dispatcher I'd be standing.

The cab took a while to arrive. A pair of men came laughing and talking loudly down the street, eyeing me curiously before passing by. The night was cold; the jacket I'd chosen wasn't warm enough. I stomped my feet and rubbed my hands together, trying to wrap my mind around the dilemma before me. I didn't love River, and he didn't love me, but maybe he was right. Maybe we could learn to have feelings for each other. Maybe the work in Haiti was something I truly wanted to do, but maybe I had only said yes to please River. In the past few weeks I'd gotten hopelessly confused about where my desires ended and his began. Then there was the most disturbing question of all: River was noble, smart, kind, and jaw-droppingly handsome, and he chose *me*. If I couldn't love him, what hope did I have of ever loving anyone again?

Finally, the cab arrived, driven by a young man with blond dreadlocks. The interior smelled faintly of marijuana. A button bearing the sad-eyed face of Bob Marley dangled from the rearview mirror. "Hey," he said, opening the door. "Where you going?"

I hadn't given the question much thought. "Take me to the Yale campus," I said.

"Anywhere in particular?"

"I'll let you know when we get close."

The cab's radio was tuned to a rock station and was so loud I could hardly think. I tried to imagine living with River, Diana, and Maria after I'd turned him away and backed out of our deal. Eating with him, living side by side with him, knowing how I'd let him down, would be excruciating. And when they learned what had transpired between us, maybe Diana and Maria would be disappointed in me as well. Wouldn't it be easier all around just to do as River wanted?

The cab took a sharp right, and I slid across the battered backseat. "Sorry about that," the cabbie said.

"It's okay." I watched the red numbers on the meter ratchet skyward and checked my wallet. Fortunately I had stopped at the bank and gotten cash yesterday. I put my wallet back into my pocket.

I could see we were nearing campus. What would I do then? And would I dare go home that night? If not, where would I sleep? There it was again, that question. Surely it would be simpler to drift on the current of River's will, let it carry me where it wanted. I thought of his hands on my shoulders, his eager lips. What on earth was the matter with me? And what was I holding out for? A memory, long gone, receding further and further with every day that passed...every day that would pass from here on out.

The cab slowed to a halt; we'd hit construction. The cabbie swore under his breath and turned the volume of the radio still louder. My head hurt from thinking so hard. *If only I didn't have to decide,* I thought. *If only the universe would send me some kind of clear, unmistakable sign.*

Whatever song the radio had been playing ended, and a new, slower one started. I sighed. It didn't look as though we'd be going anywhere soon. And then I heard Nico's voice. It was a song I'd never heard before. I struggled to make out the lyrics. "You were my hands," I heard him sing. "You were my eyes. There's nothing left to reach for now, nothing left to see." My heart pounded; I could hear the blood rushing in my ears. The song was about sadness, that much was sure. I caught something about a mistake, something about pain, something about someone being lost. As much as I was trying to concentrate, the words passed too quickly, slipping over and around me like water in a fast-moving stream. The very tone of Nico's voice tore me in half. I would have to hear this song again and again and memorize it to decode the subtleties of whatever message it was trying to send me. One thing seemed clear: the song had been written for me. Nico's voice sounded raw, haunted, disconsolate.

Then, too soon, the song was over. The DJ's voice came on. "That's the newest news from an old friend, Nico Rathburn. If you're a Rathburn fan, run out to the Film Forum and catch the new documentary about his life on tour — *Nothing Left to Reach For* — in a limited engagement. Catch it before it's gone."

I tapped on the Plexiglas window between me and the cab-driver so violently, I saw him jump. "Can you take me to the Film Forum?"

"That's the one just north of campus?"

331

"I don't know. I think so. Please just drive there, and we'll find out."

He half turned in his seat. "That film's supposed to be pretty good, isn't it? I'd go too if I didn't have to work. Shame what happened to Nico, isn't it? He used to be one of my favorites. Saw him in Boston on his first tour, and it changed my life, I swear…"

I froze and tuned out the rest of what he said. Had something horrible happened to Nico? A string of gruesome possibilities flashed before my eyes. If he'd been in some kind of accident, I'd have heard about it, even in the news blackout I'd been living in, wouldn't I? For a moment I forgot to breathe. Though I could barely speak, I couldn't help myself. I interrupted the driver with my blunt question: "Did he die?"

"What? No, of course not. You know what I mean, that business that was all over the news a while back…" We were moving by then, and as much as I wanted to hear the specifics, that one word, *No*, eclipsed everything else. Nico was alive. What else mattered? I could breathe again; I had a pulse. In my elation, I caught only stray phrases. "He had this wife…girl he wanted to marry…ran away. It was all over the news; how did you miss it?" He was retelling my own story, and I didn't need to hear it. Before the cabbie could come to the end of his tale — *my* tale — we had reached the theater, which, thank heaven, did turn out to be the Film Forum. I thanked him and gave him an exorbitant tip.

NOTHING LEFT 7:15, 9:30, MIDNIGHT, read the marquee. It was 11:25; the 9:30 show was just letting out. I bought my ticket and took a seat on the bench against the wall, watching the crowds emerge, hoping to catch bits of conversation. The minute the doors

332

opened for the midnight show, I slid into the theater and sat in the back row where I would be relatively hidden. I was frightened of what I might learn about Nico, but there was no turning back. I puzzled over the title. *Nothing Left to Reach For* sounded like a film about someone who had achieved his highest ambitions, but the abbreviated version on the marqee sounded ominous. What had the cabbie said? *Shame what happened to Nico.* Now I wished I had listened to the rest of the story. *Let Nico be all right,* I thought. *Even if it means he's forgotten me, let him be fine.* For a while it looked like I might be the only one there for the show, but just before midnight others started trickling in, filling the seats in front of me, chatting quietly. Again, I tried to listen to the conversations around me, to learn more about Nico's recent history. It seemed like a cruel joke: I who loved him — who might have been paying attention to his every move, watching him from a distance to make sure he was at least all right — knew nothing about him, while everyone else in the world possessed information that would have meant the world to me.

For a moment I considered moving forward to be nearer to the pair of young women three rows ahead of me; I could nonchalantly ask what they knew about Nico Rathburn. I doubted my ability to sound breezy, though. And apparently there had been pictures of me in newspapers and magazines. Would I be recognized? And, really, did it matter? I stayed in my seat, frozen with indecision. At midnight, the theater lights were lowered, and my heart quickened again, but of course there were coming attractions to sit through, a whole string of them. More people trickled into the theater, filling most of the seats.

The film began with a concert scene of Nico playing a blistering guitar solo. My heart twisted like a wrung-out rag; this looked like new footage that must have been taken after I had run away. The narrator confirmed this for me in a solemn voice-over: "September eighth, Emirates Stadium, London. Rock legend Nico Rathburn kicks off the European leg of his comeback tour. Rathburn and his band go on to sell out stadiums in twenty-five European cities. Reviewers in the rock-and-roll press rave." How good it was to see Nico's face. Apart from the picture River had handed me, I hadn't seen so much as a newspaper photo of him since I'd left Thornfield Park.

The concert footage ended abruptly. "Rock critic Gus Masterson, *Guitar Slave Magazine*," read a caption identifying a white-haired man with John Lennon glasses seated at an enormous desk. "A tour for the ages. That's what I called it, and I stand by that description. In these shows, Nico Rathburn surpassed not only his younger self but most if not all of his competition: the energy, the artistry, the sheer raw power of his singing and playing. He was on fire."

Then there were clips of interviews with a series of musicians I'd never heard of and a few I had.

"Nico Rathburn? He's the reason I picked up a guitar in the first place," an angular young man wearing dark eyeliner said. "I was twelve when I bought his first album, and I wanted to be just like him. I wanted the parties, the girls, but most of all the clubs, jamming with friends until dawn, the way he used to before he got his first record contract. The music, that was the main thing."

"He's a legend, man. One of the all-time greats. If there was a

Mount Rushmore of rock and roll, he'd be on it." This from a long-haired man in leopard skin, whose name I'd heard somewhere before. "Instead of playing it safe and becoming more derivative as he gets older, he just keeps taking risks." I was beginning to fidget in my seat, crossing and recrossing my legs, chewing on my knuckles. Enough, already.

But more glowing testimonials followed. When was the film going to tell me something I didn't already know? I didn't need anyone else to tell me how talented Nico was. I burned to see *him* — not his fans and protégés — and to hear him speak or at least sing. Eventually, there was more new footage, this time from Amsterdam Arena. "The critical acclaim for Nico's new album and tour was impressive," the narrator intoned. "Not bad for a musician whose wild lifestyle had once overshadowed his music."

"For a long time there, we weren't sure Nico was going to make it to thirty." It was keyboardist Mike Krikorian, dressed in a cool white gauze shirt, interviewed against a backdrop of trees. "He was a wild man. We all were back then, but Nico…" — he chuckled to himself — "let's just say he made the rest of us look like choirboys."

Then there was a clip of a younger Nico swaying onstage, slurring his lyrics, looking like a strong wind would topple him, and still more footage of him in front of an audience, berating the band for playing at the wrong tempo. It hurt to see him like that — his face so young and yet so miserable. The narrator ran down a litany of misadventures and drug-fueled exploits, then launched into the story of Nico's failed marriage to Bibi. There was a clip of him with Bibi on a beach in Brazil, both of them looking glamorous and

335

very high, holding hands, then kissing. My memory of how beautiful she once was had been eclipsed by my contact with her ruined self, but here she was again, stunning. Nico's wife. I cringed and slid down in my seat as if I were the one being revealed. Until that moment, I hadn't quite registered how awful it must be for Nico to have his past perpetually shadow him like this. Suddenly I understood the lengths to which he would go to keep his failings out of the press.

Next I sat through footage of Nico with Celine, followed by a discussion of his retreat from the public eye and his long hiatus. "Ironically, now that Rathburn had seemingly settled into maturity, his tumultuous personal life nearly derailed the Nico Rathburn express," the narrator said ominously. I was shocked to see my own face filling the movie screen; it was me, dressed head to toe in the clothes Nico had bought me for the rehearsal show, my hands on Maddy's shoulders, the two of us watching the stage wide-eyed. A moment later, there was Nico singing to me from the stage, his eyes shining. "Nico Rathburn fell in love again, not with a supermodel, a pop star, or an actress, but with Jane Moore, the nineteen-year-old nanny to his daughter, Madeline. After a whirlwind courtship, Nico proposed marriage." I stole a glance to my left, then to my right, but nobody was looking at me. I should have been relieved, but all I wanted was for someone to acknowledge me, to meet my eyes, to recognize me as the girl on the screen.

Then Dennis Everson spoke: "She brought life back to him. I've never seen him so happy. Or so miserable, after she disappeared. We thought he would cancel the tour. He just seemed so, I don't know…broken. He was crushed to pieces. We were really worried about him." Dennis! It was good to know he was looking out for Nico.

"On the eve of Nico Rathburn's triumphant return to the stage, personal tragedy struck," the narrator said. What followed was no surprise: the story of our nightmarish wedding, the revelation of Nico's secret, Bibi in the attic bedroom. Somehow the director had located photos of me in my wedding dress clutching a bouquet of lilies of the valley and of Nico looking anxious in his black suit. There was even a blurry snapshot of Bibi in her rumpled night-gown, her white hair wild, her face frozen in a grimace. Who had taken those photos? I couldn't begin to think clearly and could barely watch the screen. Someone directly in front of me loudly rustled a candy wrapper, and I fought the urge to shush him.

"A dramatic search ensued," the announcer continued. "Nico Rathburn filed a missing persons report with the police and hired a staff of private detectives, trying to track down his runaway bride. He offered a million-dollar reward to anyone with information about Jane Moore's whereabouts, but the mystery proved insolvable. The would-be Mrs. Rathburn vanished and left no trace."

And there, to my surprise, was Jenna, dressed in a low-cut black blouse, sitting demurely on her uncomfortable, spotless couch. "When I got Nico's phone call, I was shocked," she said, "and terrified for my sister. Jane was always so reliable, so practical — not at all the type to disappear without a word. I knew right away if she hadn't called me, she must be in trouble. If she were alive, she'd have phoned to let me know she was all right." One perfect, glitter-ing tear appeared in the corner of her eye and began its descent down her perfectly made-up cheek. "I'm afraid she's come to harm. Whenever the phone rings now I jump, expecting to hear bad news."

Then the director cut to grainy footage of Nico in his home office: "If anyone has information on the whereabouts of this woman" — the screen flashed a picture of me, apparently supplied by Jenna, from a family photo taken two Christmases ago — "please contact the number below. And, Jane, if you hear this message" — he looked beseechingly into the camera — "call me to let me know you're okay. I won't come looking for you if you don't want me to. I just want to know that you're alive."

I knew then what a cruel thing I'd done to Nico. What had I been thinking?

"But months passed, and there was no word of Rathburn's missing fiancée. Though her disappearance delayed the tour's start by a few weeks, Rathburn resolved to make up the missed dates and to perform the rest of the tour as scheduled."

"He was a mess," Dennis said. "I've never seen him like that. But he refused to stay home and feel sorry for himself. Instead, he channeled his despair into the music. It was something to see."

There was more footage then, a lot of it, from stadiums and arenas across Europe — Stadio San Siro in Milan, Parc des Princes in Paris, Amsterdam Arena, Esprit Arena in Düsseldorf — Nico playing with fire and emotion, "plying his trademark red Stratocaster like a man possessed," Gus Masterson said into the camera. "He took all that sorrow and frustration, all his regrets, and turned it into the most searing, redemptive music this critic has heard in a long, long time, as if by the sheer force of his playing, he could somehow right his wrongs."

The rest of the film played itself out in a three-song encore from Madison Square Garden, the last show of the tour. I braced myself for the closing credits as the film built to a crescendo of concert high points, relief spreading through me. Not only had Nico missed me and searched for me, his tour had been a success. But then, just as the film seemed to draw to a close, it took an abrupt detour.

Coda, a subtitle announced. A new figure appeared on-screen, an older man with severe glasses and wavy white hair. A subtitle identified him as Dino Marcusi, the film's director. He spoke solemnly into the camera. "As I was putting the finishing touches on this documentary, something shocking and unexpected happened. Into a life that has had more than its share of triumph and setbacks, fate struck again, adding a new and shocking chapter to Nico's story."

But what was this? The cabbie's words assaulted me again: *Shame what happened to Nico.*

Footage from a newscast flashed on the screen. "Old Lyme, Connecticut," a reporter said. "Tragedy strikes the secluded estate of musician Nico Rathburn, a longtime resident of Old Lyme, as his eleven-million-dollar home goes up in flames, in what the local fire department has termed suspected arson. The fire left death and injury in its wake…" And here my heart started pounding wildly. I'm not sure how I managed to even hear the rest. "Bibi Oliviera, Nico Rathburn's wife, jumped from a third-story balcony. Oliviera, a paranoid schizophrenic, died of internal injuries. The

339

rest of the house's occupants — Rathburn's young daughter and his staff — got out of the building unharmed, thanks to Rathburn's efforts, but the musician himself sustained serious injuries when part of the house collapsed." Nico was alive. But serious injuries? How serious? I forced myself to keep watching.

"Instead of running out of the building, he insisted on trying to save Bibi, to get her out of the house, but she refused." It was Linda speaking now. "He tried to coax her away from the balcony, to get her down the stairs and out the door" — Linda's face was frantic and tear streaked — "but she wouldn't go with him. I was out on the lawn watching, and she was laughing when she jumped." Linda covered her face with her hands and sobbed. "It was horrible."

The director returned to the screen. "In the interest of full disclosure, I should say that Nico Rathburn and I became close friends during the tour as I followed the band around the world making this documentary. So it is with no small degree of personal bias that I say that Nico's actions that night were truly brave — heroic, even."

The next newscast featured a blonde correspondent in front of a hospital, the words EMERGENCY ROOM spelled out in huge red letters behind her. "Guitarist and songwriter Nico Rathburn is recovering tonight from severe injuries sustained when he tried to rescue his wife, former model Bibi Oliviera, from a suspicious house fire at his Old Lyme mansion. The surgeon assigned to Rathburn's case has released a statement saying that his condition tonight is guarded. Meanwhile, fans are standing vigil outside Saint Joseph's Hospital, where the rock superstar is recovering." The camera cut

340

to a circle of people holding candles, softly singing one of Nico's songs, then back to the reporter, this time beside a weeping middle-aged woman. "I'm standing here with Andrea Bernard, a longtime fan of Nico Rathburn. Andrea, what are your feelings tonight?" Impatience overtook me again. What did I care about Andrea Bernard's feelings?

The woman spoke through tears. "I just want a chance to thank him. His music has meant so much to me for so long. My husband Jason and I played one of his songs at our wedding. And when Jason was diagnosed with terminal cancer, he asked me to have another of Nico's songs played at his funeral." Here she broke down completely.

The film cut to a horrific sight — Thornfield Park, its contours recognizable but charred and half-collapsed. I gasped to see it like that. And then an even more terrible photo — a woman's body, Bibi's body, limp and broken on the pavement. In contrast with such horrors, Marcusi's commentary seemed strangely calm. "Though Nico refused to leave the burning building until he had saved his wife, she ran from him and jumped to her death from a third-floor balcony. Arson investigators later learned that she had set fire to the bed that had once belonged to the nanny, Nico's missing fiancée. Though usually kept under close surveillance, Bibi Oliviera escaped when her caretaker fell asleep after a drinking binge. The caretaker, who fled to safety, admitted she had fallen asleep at her post and claimed that Bibi had taken a set of keys from her pocket to get out of the locked room. This wasn't the first time Nico's schizophrenic wife had escaped her constraints and tried to set the house on fire, but it was the deadliest and the last."

The camera returned to the director, who wore a trench coat while strolling through what remained of Thornfield Park. "In a few short months, Nico Rathburn had lost everything — his fiancée, his sick wife, his home, and his physical well-being. Still, he survived the accident and recovered, to a point. His left arm was crushed by a falling beam, crippling his hand. His many losses have battered him but haven't extinguished his creative spirit. Out of the hospital now, Nico lives in seclusion, several hours away from the wreckage of his once-palatial estate, Thornfield Park. Though he can no longer play guitar, he composed and recorded vocals for a song about his recent ordeal, the haunting 'Nothing Left to Reach For.'" And the song I had heard in the cab started playing.

I rose from my seat, though the film hadn't yet ended, and hurried from the darkness, through the painfully bright lobby. Out on the street, I hailed another cab. Nico was alive when he might have been dead. I didn't dare think about what his losses might have done to him, how depressed and discouraged he must be feeling now that he couldn't play his guitar. Nico was alive somewhere, and I had to find him.

Though it was the middle of the night when I returned to the apartment, River was sitting in the living room, waiting up for me. I was shocked to see him there, half-asleep in his favorite chair. The past two hours had all but erased him from my mind.

The sound of the apartment door opening had apparently jolted him awake, but his eyelids were still heavy. "You're back." He approached me with something like caution. "I've been worried.

Where have you been? It's after three in the morning." He took another step toward me, his arms outstretched. "But I'll stay up if you want me to. We can talk things over."

"River, no." I was in no mood to formulate a more diplomatic refusal. "I can't."

"You don't want to discuss it with me? That's fine. I can see that you're tired and upset. We can talk in the morning."

I knew he was trying to be kind. It took all the strength left in me to do the same. I put a hand on his arm. "I'm sorry, River. I can't go with you to Haiti. I know you'll do great work there, but you'll have to do it without me. There's somewhere else I have to go, somewhere I should have gone months ago."

He stepped in front of me as if to block the way to my bedroom. "Please don't go back to him, Jane. I know that's what you're thinking. It's written all over your face. He lied to you. I know how attractive that kind of life must be — who doesn't like money, comfort? — but you're so much better than that."

"It's not the money," I said. "I don't care about comfort. You don't know me as well as you think. Please, River. Let's not argue about this."

He stepped aside, but twenty minutes later when I emerged from my room with my hastily packed bag, he was still waiting, arms folded, face grim. "Don't go," he said again. "I need you. And think how hurt my sisters will be."

"Diana and Maria will understand," I told him. "I'll call and let them know how I am. Where I am." I reached out and put a hand on his arm. "I'm sorry, River. I didn't mean to hurt you."

There was no self-pity, no sadness in his eyes, just determination, as if he was confident that by casting around for just the right words he might change my mind. "It's three in the morning. Go back to bed for a few hours. Think it over a little bit longer. We'll talk more in the morning."

"I know you'll do great things in the world." Catching him off guard, I stood on tiptoe to kiss his cheek. "I'm sorry I'm not the woman you thought I was." When I turned to close the apartment door behind me, he was still standing in the middle of the living room, watching me with disappointed eyes.

From the phone of an all-night bodega, I called a cab to take me to the train station. Though the first train to Old Saybrook wouldn't depart until 6:18 a.m., I used my time in the well-lit, almost empty station to strategize. How could I find out Nico's whereabouts? Last night in the movie theater, I hadn't been quick enough to take down the phone number that had been advertised for anyone who knew my whereabouts, and besides, that public announcement had been made months ago. It was likely the number had been disconnected by now. I thought of Lucia; she lived somewhere in the area, but I wasn't sure where exactly. I searched the train station for a working pay phone, and when I finally found one, I dialed information with my last two quarters. Lucia Porth, Old Saybrook, was an unlisted number. As for Mitch, Nico's manager, I had no idea where he lived, and even if I knew, his phone number would likely be unlisted as well. The others who might know where Nico had gone — his former employees — either had dispersed to parts unknown or were living with him, wherever he was. Should I walk over to the Waldorf School where Maddy had been enrolled to see if she was still there? Her teachers would remember me, and maybe they would entrust me with any gossip they had. But it was now Saturday; I couldn't wait until Monday to find Nico. I got on the train to Old Saybrook with no idea where I would go when I arrived, but by the time the train pulled into the station I had devised a plan.

The police station was within walking distance; I remembered passing it in my daily travels. Pulling my suitcase behind me, I headed over there. When the woman at the desk asked if she could help me, I said, "I hope so. I have a lead on a missing person."

CHAPTER 27

Charles Pettigrew, the town's chief of police, insisted on personally driving me all the way to Nico's apartment in Manhattan. At first, nobody in the police department believed I was Nico's missing fiancée. I must have cut a bedraggled figure. I had dark circles under my eyes from lack of sleep and was hardly dressed to fit anyone's notion of Prince Charming's missing Cinderella. If I'd planned better, I would have showered before getting on the train, but my need to get to Nico had overridden common sense. So after I'd shown my ID to the officers on duty and they'd reveled over having "found" me, I sidled over to the policewoman at the front desk.

"Is there a place I could go to clean myself up?"

"Sure thing, if you promise not to climb out the window and go missing on us again."

With the bar of soap I'd brought along, I freshened myself up as best I could in the ladies' room sink and chose the least wrinkled blouse and skirt I could find in my suitcase. I brushed my hair and clipped it off my face, then changed my mind and took out the clip. Now as I rode in the passenger seat of the police cruiser, just a few hours away from Nico, I wondered if he still wanted me back. He might be angry with me. That was fine; I could handle his anger. If he were indifferent, though, it would kill me.

I worried also about how he might have changed after his accident. It wasn't that any changes in his appearance or personality would make me love him less; that could never happen. But I had to steel myself for the worst. If the Nico I'd loved was gone forever, I would mourn him, but I would love the new Nico no less — whether or not he was prepared to accept me back.

Chief Pettigrew was full of talk about the search, about the many dead ends the department had hit in their investigation of my disappearance, and how the absence of any leads had caused many of his colleagues to conclude that foul play was involved. "Where were you?" he finally asked. "How was it that nobody turned you in for the reward money?"

I told him about where I'd been living and working, and how one woman had recognized me but must not have known about the reward. "We did get a call from New Haven," he said. "An old woman claimed she'd seen you working at a soup kitchen, but we checked her out and dismissed her as unreliable. She had a history of mental illness." He scratched his ear. "Damn. And there you were the whole time. I imagine Nico will see to it that heads roll."

"Don't worry," I told him. "*I'll* see to it they don't." I may have sounded more confident than I was, but Chief Pettigrew looked relieved.

"Nico and I are old friends," he said. "I used to work on his security detail back in the day. If nobody's warned you yet, I probably should. He's changed. The whole ordeal — first losing you and then the accident — devastated him. Imagine Nico Rathburn not able to play the guitar. You should brace yourself."

I assured him I was ready, and he dropped me off in front of Nico's new place, handed me a business card, and said I should call him if I needed anything at all.

The Tribeca apartment house Nico was living in stood sleek and modern among the block's older, homier buildings. I stood out on the sidewalk awhile, squinting up at the facade — dark like a pair of mirrored sunglasses, and expensive-looking but blank and cold. It was about as different from Thornfield Park as anything I could have imagined. An imperious-looking man stood guard at the front door and frowned down at me when I told him I was there to see the gentleman in the penthouse. When I gave him my name, though, his expression changed.

"I'll ring right up," he said.

Moments later, I was in the elevator, whirring silently skyward. I expected I'd be greeted by Amber or Linda, but when the doors opened, I found myself face-to-face with someone I'd never seen before, a heavyset middle-aged woman wearing the pastel over-smock of a nurse. She took one look at me and stepped into the foyer, closing the door to the apartment behind her.

"I'll be damned," she said. "It really is you. He's got your picture up beside his bed."

I held out my hand for her to shake, but instead she threw her arms around me. "I'm Louisa — Nico's nurse. He's going to be so happy to see you. And I'm happy for anything that will cheer him up." She invited me in, and I followed her deep into the apartment. The gleaming hardwood floors were edged by exposed brick; a long bank of glass overlooked the West Side Highway and, beyond that, the sun-spangled Hudson. The rooms were sparsely furnished and looked barely lived in. If I hadn't known this was Nico's home, I never would have guessed he lived there.

Louisa told me Nico was upstairs in the media room. "I'll take you to him; I was just about to bring in his morning coffee. All he does is watch TV. He won't put any music on the stereo; it frustrates him. He sits there in his armchair hour after hour, refusing phone calls from his friends, so depressed it hurts to look at him."

I had never seen Nico so much as glance at a TV the whole time I'd known him, so Louisa's report alarmed me. "Will he regain the use of his hand?"

"I've seen cases like his before," she said. "If he would do his physical therapy like he's supposed to, he'd have a decent chance of getting some mobility back, maybe even most of it. But Mr. Stubborn in there won't have any of it. Maybe you can convince him."

I promised to try and asked if she would let me bring him his coffee, thinking a surprise might do him some good. She readily agreed, adding that she wished she could see the look on his face when he saw me.

In the kitchen, I fixed a mug of coffee the way he used to like it — black with two teaspoons of sugar — and climbed the spiral staircase, following Louisa's directions, to the media room. On the enormous flat-screen TV, cable news delivered the report of a hurricane bearing down on Cuba. I entered the room. The lights were turned down low, and the room appeared windowless and so gloomy it could have been midnight. Over an armchair plunked directly in front of the TV, I could see the back of Nico's head, a dark silhouette against the room's even darker shadows. The television's blue flicker played over his hair.

Copilot lay off to the side of the room, curled up as if he'd just been yelled at. He pricked up his ears when I came in, then he jumped up with a soft yelp and bounded for me, almost knocking the mug from my hands. Nico didn't even turn around to see what had excited his dog. "Go lie down," he said mechanically, then shifted in his chair and sighed. "Isn't the coffee ready yet, Louisa? What's taking so long?"

On the end table beside him was a remote control. Reaching around from behind, I set down the mug and grabbed the remote; he didn't so much as glance in my direction. I clicked the red button and heard Nico jump to his feet, probably working himself up to yell at Louisa for turning off his television. Instead, though, he was silent. Then he said, "Louisa? Is that you?" I took a step toward the wall, feeling around for a light switch. Where could it be? "You used a different soap this morning. It reminds me of…" Then his tone changed. "That *is* you, Louisa, isn't it?"

"Copilot recognizes me," I said. "I'm surprised you don't." My hand landed on a switch, and I flicked it. Light flooded the room.

Nico stood in front of me, but instead of joy what I saw on his face was something like horror.

"For fuck's sake! Am I losing my mind now, too?"

My voice came out much calmer than I actually felt. "You seem perfectly sane to —"

But before I could finish, he had run over and thrown his arms around me, hugging me so tightly I could barely breathe. "It's really you?" he asked, sounding more worried than happy. "I'm not hallucinating?"

"Who else could it be?" There was his scent again, the wood smoke and spice of his aftershave. I pulled back to get a better look at him, taking a moment to drink in the features I had missed so much: his dark eyes, his firm jaw, his full lower lip. Then I pressed myself into his chest. His cheek against mine felt warm and rough.

"Jane…Jane," was all he said.

"I've found you," I said. "I can hardly believe it."

"*You* found me? I'm not the one who was lost!" He kissed my face over and over again, my forehead, my cheeks. "This can't be real," he said into my hair. "This has to be an acid flashback."

I laughed, delighted to be in his arms. "I swear I'm not an acid flashback."

"That's just what I'd expect a figment of my imagination to say." He tightened his grip again. "Prove you're real, then. Kiss me."

I did. Then I brushed his hair back from his forehead and kissed that too. My lips found a scar that hadn't been there before, just over his left eyebrow, half-hidden by his hair.

To my surprise, Nico pulled back abruptly. "But where have

you been all this time?" he asked. "And why are you here?" As unpredictable as his moods had always been, I couldn't recall ever seeing a shift this abrupt.

"It's a long story." I wanted to reach out for him, to hold him again, but I was afraid he might rebuff me. "I'll tell you everything."

"I was sure you'd been hurt or even murdered. Or that you must have died of frostbite in an alley. I couldn't sleep for weeks, I was so worried."

"I'm fine," I said. "Better than fine. I found work, and I've been living cheaply and saving up, and I plan to apply for Pell Grants and loans and go back to college in the fall."

To my surprise, Nico smiled, albeit ruefully. "Pell Grants? I guess you really aren't a hallucination. My brain would never have made up that part about Pell Grants." Now his arm was back around me. I nestled under his chin. "You're okay," he said. "I can hardly believe it. You're really okay."

We held each other a long time. When he finally spoke, his tone had changed yet again. "Are you really going back to school, then?"

"That's the plan," I said. "I can apply to schools in Manhattan."

Again he released me, refusing to meet my eyes. "That's the only reason you're here in New York? To go back to college?"

"It's one of the reasons." I clasped my hands behind my back. "Would that be such a bad thing?"

"Not for you, I guess." He frowned. "You'll make new friends, and you won't have time for a has-been like me."

"Right. Because of course I'll be the most popular girl on campus." I tried to keep my tone light. "Don't you want me nearby?"

Nico retreated to his chair and sat silently for a while, opened his lips as if to speak, then closed them again. Suddenly I felt embarrassed. I had assumed he would be as thrilled to see me as I was to see him; I'd been so sure we would go back to being as close as we ever were. But his face grew somber, and I realized I might have gotten it wrong. Caught off guard, he'd been happy to see me, but once he'd recovered his equilibrium, he might hold my long absence against me. What I had done could be unforgivable: I had worried him and wounded his pride. Contrite, I approached his chair and sat down on the floor beside him, resting my head on his knee. He didn't pull away.

"I'm here because I want to be with you," I said. "That's the real reason."

"Yes, but why? Why would you want to?" The question startled me into momentary silence, so he answered it himself. "You feel sorry for me."

I bit my lip. "I'm sorry about Bibi…and about your arm."

He flinched. "So I'm right. You *do* feel sorry for me. And now I'll be your project, like Maddy was. Is that your plan? You'll visit me in your spare time?"

"If that's what you want from me, I'll visit in my spare time." I was hurt.

"Sure. Why not? Why shouldn't you go back to school and have a normal life like anyone else?" His tone was bitter. "Sooner or later you'll meet some art student. Someone with an actual future. You'll marry him and leave me again."

"I don't care about being married."

"You *should* care. If I were the man I used to be, I'd make you

354

care. But like this"—with his right hand he gestured to the one resting in his lap—"I can't play guitar anymore, and that's all I was ever good for."

He was silent again. If he'd been anyone else, I might have pitied him. Instead, I exhaled with relief. His last words gave me some insight into why he was holding back. They told me he didn't resent me for leaving him.

"It's about time you rejoined the living and started taking care of yourself." I got to my feet and ran my fingers through his shaggy hair. "Time for a trim. And what about this?" I slid a finger down his rough cheek. "Don't you have a razor in this place?"

"Am I repulsive, Jane?"

"Very, Nico." I kissed the top of his head. "But then you always were."

He chuckled, and I combed his hair as best I could with my fingers. Then I carefully touched his limp arm. "Louisa tells me you aren't doing your physical therapy. That's got to change."

"Aren't you disgusted by me?" He drew back his long bangs to reveal the raised flesh of his scar. It wasn't terrible-looking, but my stomach lurched to think of the pain he must have felt.

"Scars are sexy," I told him. "It makes you look dangerous." I took his face in my hands and kissed the tip of his nose. "Now, enough of this moping around. Let's go out in the fresh air. Do you have a terrace? A balcony? A nearby park?"

"There's a roof garden."

"Show me where it is."

At the top of another winding staircase, sliding doors led out to a terrace hidden to the world by a lush wall of potted trees. I gestured toward a pair of lounge chairs beneath a cheerful striped umbrella. "You wait here. I'm going to make you lunch."

"I never eat lunch anymore."

"But today you will. We'll eat together."

There wasn't much in the refrigerator, but I did find bread and cold cuts. I made a plateful of sandwiches and gave one to Louisa before taking the rest up to Nico. We stretched out side by side on the lounge chairs. I had so many questions for him. First and foremost, where was Maddy? She was living with her mother in Paris, this time with an au pair Nico had hired to keep her safe in case Celine proved as neglectful as she had before. The au pair called Nico every few days, putting Maddy on the phone. "I didn't want Maddy to see me this way," he said. "I didn't want to scare her." He seemed to think he had turned into some kind of monster. I took his broken hand in both of mine, brought it up to my lips and kissed it, hoping to dispel the despair that had passed across his face like a storm cloud.

I wanted to know what had become of Lucia and Benjamin and the rest of the staff. He'd given them all severance pay and had set them free to find new jobs. Lucia was only a town away from Thornfield Park, running an antique shop in Old Saybrook. "She comes into the city and visits me from time to time," he told me. "Says she'll come back to work for me if I say the word. She loves the antiques but can't stand the customers."

Sitting beside him, listening to him speak, it all came back to me: how comfortable we had always been together; how easy conversation between us was. Even so, I detected a sadness and anxiety in him that hadn't been there before. The whole time we talked, he held my hand, as though worried I might decide to run away again. When he fell silent, I asked what he was thinking.

"I won't be able to sleep tonight. What if you're not here when I wake up?"

"I'll be here, and I'll bring you coffee just like this morning. I won't always wait on you, though, so you'd better enjoy it while you can. Before long, you'll be taking care of yourself, or you'll have to hire some more servants to boss around. Like the old days."

When evening approached, I told Louisa she could have the night off and asked her for directions to the nearest market. She gave me keys to the apartment and drew me a map. The store she sent me to turned out to be a mind-blowingly expensive gourmet emporium. I wandered the aisles as though I were in some kind of museum, gaping at the forty-dollar jars of truffles and the hundred different kinds of imported cheese. I bought fresh figs, plump raspberries, and the most expensive block of Parmesan I'd ever seen in my life, along with the more prosaic stuff — vegetables, milk, cereal, pasta. My time with the St. Johns had given me a small repertoire of decent meals to make, and I would surprise Nico with a home-cooked dinner. He sat beside me at the white granite island in the airy kitchen while I chopped garlic, basil, tomatoes, and mushrooms.

"Where did you learn to cook?" he asked when I started sautéing the garlic and mushrooms. "Is that what you've been doing with your time since you left me?"

I added basil and a handful of chopped tomatoes to the pan. "It's one of the things I've been doing."

357

"And were you cooking just for yourself or for others?"

"Others." I paused for effect. "I shared an apartment with some people I happened to meet in New Haven."

"Some people. Could you be more specific?"

"Some very nice people," I said. "Smart, interesting, thoughtful people. They took me in when I was on the verge of being homeless."

"Yalies, I suppose. Overprivileged Ivy Leaguers." He wrinkled his nose.

I chose not to comment on the irony of a rock star calling others overprivileged. "Only one of them went to Yale, and they were far from rich. The apartment we lived in was pretty run-down."

Nico said nothing for a while. "Were they all women?"

I couldn't help myself; I laughed.

"Don't tease me, Jane. Answer my question." Now he was angry. His voice thundered the way it had on the day we'd met, when he'd almost run me over and had tried to blame me for walking beside the road.

"It's good to see your fiery side again," I said. "I'll keep right on teasing you if that's what it takes to bring the old Nico Rathburn back."

"Don't. Not on this subject. Anything else, but not this."

I tossed some oregano into the pan and poured him a glass of sparkling water. "Here. If you must know, one was a man."

And while the sauce simmered, I took a seat beside him at the table and launched into the tale of my travels, telling him how I had found myself in New Haven with hardly any cash and no job lined up. When I described my desperate search for a place to

358

sleep, Nico flinched as though he'd been hit. "Jane, what if you hadn't met those people? What if you'd had to sleep on a park bench in the middle of New Haven? You could have frozen or been kidnapped by some psycho." He grabbed my hand. "Imagine how I felt when I knew you were out in the world with no money. I couldn't stop wondering where you would go or what you would do. After a while, I was sure you must be dead. You know I'm not religious, not even remotely, but I prayed every night that you were safe."

I slipped from his grasp to stir the sauce. "Who knows? Maybe your prayers helped." I recounted how the St. John family had given me a place to stay and how River had helped me find work.

"I'm grateful to this River person for taking such good care of you when I couldn't." Nico pulled a bar stool over to the counter beside me. "But tell me...did you like him?"

"We became friends. He's a very good man. Noble, even. I know that's an old-fashioned word, but it's the best one I can think of. He cares more about people in need than about himself."

"Sounds like a riot. Is he smart?"

"Very," I said. "One of the smartest people I've ever met. Certainly the most driven. He's studying to be a minister."

"A minister? One of those Bible thumpers who think it's their mission to convert everybody else?"

"I never saw him try to convert anyone."

Nico fumed a moment or two. "Is he good-looking?"

"He's about six feet tall with wavy blond hair, blue eyes, and chiseled features. Like a painting of Apollo. So yes, I'd say he's good-looking."

Nico looked down at his hands. "Did you really like this Mr. Perfect?"

I suppressed a smile. "You already asked me that."

"After living with a noble Ivy League Greek god, what could you possibly want with self-centered, narcissistic me?" There was that note of self-pity in his voice again. "I'm such an idiot. Until this moment, I believed you still loved me even though you left me. And all this time you were living with somebody else. Why don't you go back to him if he's all you say?"

"You want me to leave?" I set the lid on the saucepan with more force than I'd intended. It clanged emphatically. "You really want me to go away?"

"Go find your boyfriend." His voice was quiet, defeated, and I was suddenly sorry for teasing him.

"He's not my boyfriend. I could never love him. I could never love anyone who isn't you."

"Is that the truth? You're not just saying that to make me feel better?"

"Have I ever told you anything but the truth? You have nothing to be jealous about. I wanted to rile you up a little, to see that spark I've missed so much." I nestled into him. "I thought I could shake you out of feeling sorry for yourself." His dark hair fell into his eyes, and I brushed it back, my fingers caressing the scar on his forehead. On impulse, I kissed it, but he turned away, and I saw now that the sadness of the past months had taken its toll. My heart swelled.

"You're right," he said. "I've lost my spark. I'm not sure I can ever get it back. It's as if I don't know who I am anymore. I'm just some guy who used to be Nico Rathburn."

"You're wrong." I took his good hand in both of mine. "You're still the guy who wrote all those wonderful songs so many people want to hear."

Nico was quiet a long while. Then his mouth twitched. It was small and tentative, but it was a smile, and a mischievous one at that. "So…you do like my music after all?"

"I love your music. Your music is who you are."

"Who I used to be." Sadness crossed his face again. What could I do to lift his spirits and keep them that way for more than a few seconds at a time?

I thought a moment, and then it came to me. "You know, your fans are waiting for you to come out of hiding."

"They're going to be disappointed."

"Louisa says if you'd only do your physical therapy you might get some of your mobility back. Maybe even most of it."

"Most of it? What good is a guitarist with most of his mobility?"

"You can still sing, right? Then you can perform. And you can still write songs. You can bring someone else into the band to play lead guitar."

"What band? They've all got their own projects." As contrary as he was being, there was fresh energy in his voice and expression. "They've moved on."

"They didn't want to." I was only guessing, but as I spoke the words I knew they had to be true. "The Rathburn Band was the highlight of their lives. I'm sure they miss recording with you. And touring with you."

"Dennis's solo career hasn't taken off like he hoped it would," Nico conceded. "He might want to take over lead guitar."

"He would do it if you asked him to," I said. "I know they'd all come back. They're your friends, Nico. I bet they're just waiting for you to ask."

"I see you've been thinking about this." There it was — the sparkle in his eyes. "So tell me, Jane. What else do you have planned for me?"

He was right; I had been giving some thought to his future. I gestured toward the glass wall with its skyline view. "This apartment's very glamorous and all. But don't you miss Thornfield Park? Wouldn't you like to rebuild it?"

"Why would I want to do that?"

"Because you need a place where the band can gather to rehearse. A real home with plenty of bedrooms, where we can entertain our family and friends on holidays."

"*Our* family?" Nico looked bemused. "I thought you didn't have any family."

"The band," I said. "Yvonne and Kitty. Lucia. And Diana and Maria, the women I lived with in New Haven. They're the closest thing I've ever had to real family. Besides you and Maddy, that is."

"Maddy." I heard regret in his voice. "She keeps asking when she can come home to live with me."

"Exactly." I gave this latest idea a moment to sink in and took a deep breath to summon my courage. "And there's one more thing I've been thinking." I looked off at the distant, sparkling water, unable to meet his eyes. "Don't you think it's about time you got married?"

"I don't know. I'm not sure I'm the marrying kind."

He *was* teasing me, wasn't he? Well, I deserved it after the hard time I'd given him about River. I dared a glance at him. There was that sly look I hadn't seen in so long.

"I think you're *exactly* the marrying kind…provided you choose the right bride."

Now he was grinning. "I could marry Bianca Ingram. Or if she won't have me, maybe a supermodel."

I made my voice casual. "I think you'd be much better off marrying *me*."

"Miss Moore, are you proposing to me?" He affected a shocked tone.

"Yes, Mr. Rathburn, and you'd better answer fast or I'll rescind my offer."

"Don't do that." His grip on my hand tightened. "Yes, Jane. My answer is yes."

Then he was in my arms, kissing me, his hand in my hair, the length of his body warm against mine, the sauce forgotten on the stove.

After a minute or two, he pulled away from me. "One last question. What finally brought you back to me? No, let me guess. You heard about the accident. Or you heard about Bibi's death and realized I was free. Or you heard the song I wrote for you, and it did what I hoped it would do — lure you back."

"All of those," I said, "and more. Something just snapped. I realized what an idiot I'd been, running away from the one person

I value more than anyone else in the whole world." I kissed him again. "That would be you…Mr. Rathburn."

"Miss Moore," he said fondly.

I tugged his hand, leading him to the staircase, then back up to the roof garden, where we sat out long after dinner, making plans. Side by side in our lounge chairs, we allowed our imaginations to run free, musing about the albums he would record, the tours he would take me on, the galleries I would show my art in, the fundraisers he would play for the soup kitchens and shelters of New Haven, the little brother or sister we would someday give Maddy. Below us, streetlights flickered, and I thought of the strange turns my life had taken. How shy Jane Moore from the Philly suburbs never would have imagined herself atop a Tribeca penthouse, holding the hand of her rock-star fiancé, preparing to walk with him into the blinding flashbulbs of a curious world. The very idea would have terrified me once, but now I felt ready.

"You're quiet." Nico squeezed my hand.

"Just catching my breath," I said. "I can't believe how far I've come."

"How far we've come. This has been a wild trip for me too." He got to his feet and pulled me up with him. "Come on. There's something I want to show you." I followed him over to the edge of the roof garden, where only a waist-high wall stood between us and a fifteen-story drop. "I love this view. I can't tell you how many times I've wished you were with me so I could show it to you."

I leaned out over the wall to see what he was pointing to, but a wave of vertigo stole my breath. "I can't look down," I told him, pulling back.

He gathered me to his chest. "Here. Hang on. I promise you won't fall."

Clutching Nico's shoulders for support, I let myself enjoy the view: the sharp blue of twilight, the velvety river, the pulsing red and white lights of cars headed uptown — and the intoxicating feeling that together we were poised on the brink of something immense. When Nico bent to kiss me, I shut my eyes, absorbing all that was familiar about him — his taste, the softness of his lips, his arms holding me steady — and I could tell he was doing the same, drinking me in, committing my kiss to memory, as we found our way home to each other in the gathering dark.

AUTHOR'S NOTE

When one of the recent updated versions of *Pride and Prejudice* was published, I found myself musing with my husband about why *Jane Eyre*, such a great story of love and self-discovery, didn't seem to be getting the *Pride and Prejudice* treatment. I love *Pride and Prejudice* and its spin-offs as much as the next person, but if I had to choose between Jane Austen and Charlotte Brontë, I'd be on Team Charlotte. I first read *Jane Eyre* in high school, with the sense that I was encountering a kindred spirit. I loved that Jane is such a freethinker and she never takes the easy way out. As deeply as she loves Mr. Rochester, she refuses to cave in to him when he's being unrealistic or selfish. And it doesn't hurt that Mr. Rochester is, for my money, the sexiest guy in literature. Now that I'm an English professor, I teach *Jane Eyre* whenever I can and am always thrilled when I encounter students who take to Jane the way I did.

Given how appealing *Jane Eyre* is, my theory about the lack of sequels and updates was that some elements of Jane's story seemed hard to bring into twenty-first-century America. These days, a young woman as bright and enterprising as Jane would have many careers to choose from. The sad fate of Mr. Rochester's first wife is tricky to envision in our age of medical miracles. But with some thought I knew I could probably figure out a way around those roadblocks. Hardest of all would be re-creating the insurmountable class difference that has to exist between Jane and Mr. Rochester for the story to make sense.

Then it dawned on me: Mr. Rochester could be a rock star.

Right away, I knew I had to write that book. My other life's passion (after writing and reading) is rock-and-roll music. I've always loved seeing live shows, and my recent obsession has been going to way too many Bruce Springsteen concerts, sometimes even traveling states away when there's a show I just have to see. Making the Mr. Rochester character a rock legend meant dreaming up the details of how such a person might live his daily life. And the idea of putting a shy, self-contained, and serious young woman together with a notorious bad-boy rocker was just irresistible.

After that, it was a matter of puzzling out how to update the rest of the details, finding answers to questions like: What causes a nice girl like Jane to take a job as a rock star's nanny? And, what sorts of dark secrets might a celebrity like Nico Rathburn be hiding from his public?

All in all, when I set to work on *Jane*, I felt I'd stumbled into the project I'd been born for. Once I worked out answers to the plot's many logistical challenges, the book practically wrote itself. Whenever I got stuck, I would open up *Jane Eyre* for inspiration and ideas. I had more fun working on it than on anything else I've ever written. I hope some of that fun has made its way onto these pages. And if *Jane* sends a few readers back to *Jane Eyre* to see what all the fuss is about, so much the better.

ACKNOWLEDGMENTS

First and foremost, thanks to my agent, Amy Williams, who performed magic on my behalf, and to my editor, Julie Scheina, and the rest of the Poppy team, whose enthusiasm and expertise have been nothing short of amazing. Thanks for believing in *Jane* and in me.

I'm more grateful than I can say for the help of friends who read this story in earlier versions and provided crucial feedback. Big thanks to Tenaya Darlington, whose careful reading of an early draft helped shape the story, and whose generosity helped *Jane* find a home. Rich Fusco's thorough and expert reading was invaluable, and his support over the years has been a real blessing. Thanks to Jo Alyson Parker, for her insight at a critical juncture. Also thanks to Melissa Goldthwaite, who provided much-needed encouragement at an early stage of the writing process, and who has always been a thoughtful and trusted reader.

Jane was eased into being by the calm support and selflessness of my husband, Andre St. Amant, who helped me come up with the idea in the first place, who sent me off to countless coffee shops and rock concerts, and who never made me feel like the crazy overgrown teenybopper that I am. Much love and gratitude to my sons, Eli St. Amant (leader of the hot new RaveRap band SplitGenetics) and Noah St. Amant, who knows how to hold his own in a mosh pit. Thanks to Chris Bamberger and Dorothee Heisenberg, for steadfast friendship, and to Eric Drogin, whose expertise in several fields has enriched these pages.

A shout-out to my friends at Greasy Lake, especially those with whom I've shared "the power, the glory, and the ministry of rock and roll." There are more of you than I can name here, but special thanks to Sharon Concannon, Mike Fink, Eric Coulson, George Skladany, Sherry Clements, Mark Boufford, Magnus Lauglo, Marty Rynearson, Dawn Ehlinger, Jim Patricelli, and Killer Joe and Brenda O'Donald, and to Christian Weissner, in memorium. Thanks also to Linda Morkan, who took *Jane* on vacation and sent back much-needed encouragement. Extraspecial thanks to my road buddy and first-ever pit partner, Dan Medina, and to Diane Wilkes, Louise to my Louise (since neither of us is Thelma), and my mentor in all things tarot and rock and roll.

Finally, while Nico Rathburn is a figment of my imagination, I couldn't let this moment go by without thanking the real-life rocker who has given me so much inspiration, solace, and joy, and

ACKNOWLEDGMENTS

First and foremost, thanks to my agent, Amy Williams, who performed magic on my behalf, and to my editor, Julie Scheina, and the rest of the Poppy team, whose enthusiasm and expertise have been nothing short of amazing. Thanks for believing in *Jane* and in me.

I'm more grateful than I can say for the help of friends who read this story in earlier versions and provided crucial feedback. Big thanks to Tenaya Darlington, whose careful reading of an early draft helped shape the story, and whose generosity helped *Jane* find a home. Rich Fusco's thorough and expert reading was invaluable, and his support over the years has been a real blessing. Thanks to Jo Alyson Parker, for her insight at a critical juncture. Also thanks to Melissa Goldthwaite, who provided much-needed encouragement at an early stage of the writing process, and who has always been a thoughtful and trusted reader.

Jane was eased into being by the calm support and selflessness of my husband, Andre St. Amant, who helped me come up with the idea in the first place, who sent me off to countless coffee shops and rock concerts, and who never made me feel like the crazy overgrown teenybopper that I am. Much love and gratitude to my sons, Eli St. Amant (leader of the hot new RaveRap band SplitGenetics) and Noah St. Amant, who knows how to hold his own in a mosh pit. Thanks to Chris Bamberger and Dorothee Heisenberg, for steadfast friendship, and to Eric Drogin, whose expertise in several fields has enriched these pages.

A shout-out to my friends at Greasy Lake, especially those with whom I've shared "the power, the glory, and the ministry of rock and roll." There are more of you than I can name here, but special thanks to Sharon Concannon, Mike Fink, Eric Coulson, George Skladany, Sherry Clements, Mark Boufford, Magnus Lauglo, Marty Rynearson, Dawn Ehlinger, Jim Patricelli, and Killer Joe and Brenda O'Donald, and to Christian Weissner, in memorium. Thanks also to Linda Morkan, who took *Jane* on vacation and sent back much-needed encouragement. Extraspecial thanks to my road buddy and first-ever pit partner, Dan Medina, and to Diane Wilkes, Louise to my Louise (since neither of us is Thelma), and my mentor in all things tarot and rock and roll.

Finally, while Nico Rathburn is a figment of my imagination, I couldn't let this moment go by without thanking the real-life rocker who has given me so much inspiration, solace, and joy, and who has served as a model of how an artist giving his all can truly work magic in the night. Without the soul-transporting music and electrifying stage presence of Bruce Springsteen and the legendary E Street Band, this book would not have been written. It's that simple.